Mine

by

Brenda Huber

Mine

Cover Art by *Rae Monet*

The Wild Rose Press
PO Box 706
Adams Basin, NY 14410-0706
Visit us at www.thewildrosepress.com

Publishing History
First Black Rose Edition, 2010
Print ISBN 1-60154-691-2

Published in the United States of America

Dedication

For Michelle~
My best friend by choice, my sister by chance.
You are always there—and I am the lucky one.

For Audra~
Thank you for all the romance novels and horror movies.
I haven't forgotten...

Acknowledgements

Deepest heartfelt thanks
to my editor, Joelle Walker.
You have been a bright glimmer
of hope and a supportive compass for my craft.

Special artistic gratitude to
H.I.M. and Velvet Revolver—
my musical inspiration.

Prologue

He slithered through the shadows and pulsing lights. Dark bass, driving drums, and screeching electric guitar pulsed all around him, vibrating the sticky floor beneath his boots. Bodies writhed and gyrated with the tempo, brushing against him, bumping into him. Alcohol flowed with slick bartender smiles—rivers of multi-hued liquid courage bearing imaginative names like Cosmopolitan, Hurricane, Strip and Go Naked, and Sex on the Beach—lowering inhibitions, making already easy targets pitifully effortless.

Stupid Humans.

They didn't have a clue. Death walked among them, and they danced. A reaper stalked them, and they drank. They celebrated. They partied. And, if he had his way, they would all bleed. They were food, and he was the ultimate predator—perhaps the most dangerous on the planet—because he could walk among them without detection. He could mingle with them, talk to them...lure them...and they were none the wiser.

Until it was too late.

Ignorant cattle.

Ah, there was his little pigeon now. She fluttered through the writhing mass, a butterfly among moths. Beautiful as she was, he would not drink from her. She was unworthy, nothing more than a means to an end, his emissary...a vessel for communication. Her blood the same to him as a fax or an email...a text message. He smirked at that analogy. Humans may be ignorant when it came to

1

his kind, but they were clever morsels when it came to technology. The advances they'd made in the last fifty years alone were impressive. Impressive...but irrelevant.

He sidled close. Moving with the music. Swaying with the tangle of warm bodies. Closer. His gaze locked on her neck, homing in on the pulse hammering at the base of her throat. Closer. Edging a shoulder between two dancers, he slipped into the gap with practiced finesse. One corner of his lips edged upward.

So easy.

His pigeon glanced up, smiling delayed recognition, her eyes offering shy invitation.

A wide grin spread across his face. Would she be so flirtatious if she caught a glimpse of the monster lurking behind his smile? He held out a hand to her, nodding toward the edge of the dance floor. She hesitated, pushing her long blonde hair over her shoulder, then placed her hand in his, allowing him to lead her away. Would she be so eager if she knew what waited for her in the darkness on the other side of those doors?

How many messengers would it take before the rest of his kind finally understood?

Chapter 1

Darth Vader's sinister, driven theme song echoed through the shadows of the spacious bedroom, pulling Alex up from the fuzzy world of slumber. Rolling over, she irritably pushed at the down comforter covering her head and ground a palm into her eye in a vain attempt to clear away the blurry edges of sleep. Blinking at the over-sized, lime-green numbers on the digital clock, she groaned. Seven thirty-four glowed back, unrepentant. Cheerful sunlight flirted around the edges of her closed vertical blinds, wringing another miserable groan from her lips. She didn't need the distinctive ring tone to know who was calling. Only one person had the audacity at this ungodly hour on a Saturday.

Dropping her head onto the thick feather pillow, she let out a long, resigned sigh. Why could she never remember to set that damned phone to silent? The spear of pain between her brows throbbed in tempo with her phone, dragging forth a strangled oath that would have made a sailor beam with pride. She'd stayed up too late last night...way too late...working on the Marston article, but then, such was her life.

She'd almost convinced her arm to reach for the phone, when the cursed device went silent. Praise the powers that be. Alex pushed the silken tangle of her long, golden hair away from her face, rolled back over with a dreamy smile, and snuggled into the warm, down-filled cocoon of her bed, intent on stealing a few more hours of sleep. The day would roll by soon enough, and she'd have to start getting ready for the charity gala at the yacht club tonight, but for now—blissful languid sleep was the cure for her raging sleep-deprived headache. Well, that, and maybe a couple Excedrin the size of man hole covers.

The world had just begun to slip away on the gentle wings of exhaustion...when good old Vader returned. Groaning, eyes closed, Alex stretched for her phone, knocking her book off the nightstand and tipping her water glass over.

Scrabbling to rescue her new addiction, a Kay Hooper paranormal suspense, from a soggy demise, she tangled in the sheets and fell to the floor, smacking her head against the soaked nightstand on the way down. Oh, yeah...*that* was gonna leave a mark.

With the heel of her palm pressed tight against her forehead, she scooped the book up, dangling it by the jacket as the sodden pages dripped all over her lap. Her bookmark fluttered to the floor. Terrific...just goddamned terrific. Not only had Tweetie joined the stars circling in her throbbing brain, but now her sheets were wet, and she'd lost her damned page, too.

And the phone went silent.

Of course.

With a disgusted snarl, she hoisted her awkward sheet-tangled body back onto the bed. Determined come hell or high water she *would* go back to sleep, she pounded a fist into her pillow, then jammed it beneath her head with enough force to dislodge a snowy feather. Giving the pillow one last smack for good measure, Alex drew in one long, slow breath through her nose, releasing it through parted lips with measured restraint, then closed her eyes, picturing serene gentle waves against a white sandy beach.

Cue Vader.

In the twitch of an eyelid, her serene beach morphed into a nice shiny, extra-value sized Glock with a whole case full of cell phone demolishing ammo. Cursing the fates that be, she buried her head beneath the oversized pillow, contemplating the merits of smothering herself. Glutton for punishment that she was, Alex fired one shrill scream into the Egyptian-cotton covered feathers, then flipped the cell phone open.

With sticky sweetness, she offered, "Good morning, Mother."

"Don't sass me, Alexandra." Lily Sinclair's icy voice cut straight to the chase. "Turn your television on."

Alex couldn't decide whether to rub her eyes again, or to roll them heavenward and plead for divine intervention. What heinous wrong had she committed in some distant past life to deserve Lily? It must have been a whopper. "What? Mother, it's seven in the morning—"

"Turn on your television, Alexandra. Channel 13," Lily interrupted, her snobbish, Fifth Avenue tone slipping just this side of frosty.

Yielding to the urge to roll her eyes—knowing the only way to placate the beast would be to comply—Alex leaned across the bed for the remote, yawning with gusto. "Mother, I was up late last night working. This better be..."

Alex's voice trailed away as the large plasma screen glowed to life with grievous insult. The background on the screen was a bit too familiar. That darkened nook was nestled in the back corner of *her* favorite, swank little restaurant. In that nook, a drop-dead gorgeous man and a knockout redhead came to vibrant Technicolor life beneath the camera crew's judicious lighting. The amorous couple writhed in a torrid embrace, every small, sordid detail captured in lurid HD clarity.

The man's hands were all over his companion, sliding up her curvy thigh, tangling in her long, salon-tinted hair...groping beneath her designer blouse. His tongue had to be halfway down red's throat, while her hand blatantly massaged his crotch. Without warning, the man lifted his head, batting at the camera in scowling outrage. The picture went to still frame, immortalizing his chiseled face, smeared with cherry-bomb lipstick, plummeting Alex's heart straight to her knees.

A raging river of blood crashed in her ears droning out Lily's catty remarks. Trapped in a nightmare she couldn't wake up from, Alex snapped her phone closed, her eyes riveted to the face on her television. She pushed herself farther up in the bed, hugging her knees to her chest. The frozen image of the man's face shrank and slid to the upper right corner of the screen, making way for the polished, smug countenance of a celebrity news reporter.

Fumbling with the remote, her eyes riveted to the TV, Alex groped for the volume button.

"...last night where NewsFlash stumbled across Griffin Myles, rising star of the up and coming primetime phenomenon, *Fairfax General*," the reporter's voice crooned saccharine sweet.

Then another picture flashed in the upper left corner, a candid shot of a petite blonde in a sleek, black slip dress and three-inch, spiked heels. The blonde stood, frozen in the doorway of a prominent jeweler's boutique downtown on Fifth, on the arm of the very same Griffin Myles. With a radiant, ignorant smile, the blonde beamed up at her Casanova. An enormous princess-cut diamond twinkled with dramatic flair in a setting of platinum and sapphires on her third finger, charming the flash of the camera.

The smug reporter grinned at Alex with malicious glee. "I wonder what Griffin's fiancée thinks about his choice of dessert. Apparently blondes *aren't* always more fun."

Then, adding insult to injury, the steamy clip from the restaurant looped, again and again, driving the point of her humiliation a little deeper with each thrust. Alex stared in morbid fascination at the TV, watching as her happily-ever-after slipped away in the vivid shade of cherry-bomb red lipstick.

Alex's hands shifted on her lap, her dry eyes glued to the flat screen. She wrenched the sparkling, platinum band from her ring finger, numb to the thin line of scarlet one of the prongs drew across her skin. Without giving the deceitful ring so much as one last glance of longing, she hurled it across the room. The glittering band hit the wall and bounced behind an antique armoire.

****

"Alex," chirped the intercom on the corner of her desk. "Stephan reported he sent the package this morning by messenger. Sam wants an overview for the article you're working on for next week's column, and you have a call on line two."

Heaving a reluctant sigh, Alex left her perch by the window and crossed her small, corner office to press the button on the intercom. Her voice was flat, as emotionless as her heart. "Tell Sam I'll email everything she needs this afternoon and call Maxwell Marston, set up lunch later in the week." She paused, gritting her teeth, and then pushed on with icy determination. "Did Stephen make sure the messenger understands the package is to be signed for?"

Her assistant's voice dropped to hushed tones, underscored with unspoken sympathy. "He has firm orders Griffin, and *only* Griffin, is allowed to sign for it."

Rubbing at the ache in her temple, Alex forced a swallow. It had been a long, rough weekend. Packing

Griffin's "left-behinds" and his precious ring—his sparkling little band of lies—had been difficult enough. Facing the yacht club socialites with head held high and a serene smile pasted on her lips had taken every ounce of panache she possessed. Squaring off against the bevy of reporters waiting for her at the front door of her office building, this morning had damned near finished her off.

Work, she reminded herself. Focus on work. "Do we have a name for line two?"

Her assistant's voice returned, all business. "The only name he'd give me was Cole. It's his fourth call today. I explained you're very busy, but he insists it's of the utmost urgency." Then Rita's voice dropped to conspiratorial tones. "His voice is positively *divine*."

Alex bit back a reluctant, albeit exasperated smile. "Thank you, Rita."

"Sure thing, boss lady."

Pinching the bridge of her nose, Alex settled into the high-backed leather chair behind an elegant glass-topped desk. She shifted her laptop to the side and reached for the phone.

Beneath the desk, her shoes slipped off, and her toes dug into the plush carpet. "Alex Sinclair, may I help you?"

There was a slight pause, then a velvety-rich voice slipped through the phone lines. "By the gods, I hope so."

That greeting both pricked her curiosity and sent a puzzled frown skittering across her brow. "Excuse me?"

"Ms. Sinclair, I'm Cole Gunnarrson." The deep voice paused, as though waiting for recognition to sink in. Good Lord, Rita hadn't exaggerated, although Alex wasn't certain "positively *divine*" was even in the same ballpark with this sexy timbre. Just the sound of it would have sent a nun racing for the nearest confessional.

When Alex failed to respond, appropriately or otherwise, the celestial, seductive voice assumed a more subdued tone. "I'm the lead singer for the band Stolen Innocence?"

"Okay..." Alex drew the last syllable out, her tone clearly unimpressed. She'd learned long ago, if you sound impressed, you lost your edge. That didn't stop the warm shiver from wriggling down her spine. "I'm sorry—Mr. Gunnarrson—was it? I don't do PR. My column's relationship based. However, I'd be happy to refer you to our—"

"I don't need PR," the voice cut in, diamond-sharp and yet still midnight sinful. Just the mildest hint of an accent tinged his clipped words, an accent she couldn't identify. "I *am* familiar with your work—as well as your column—and I believe we could be of mutual benefit to each other."

She frowned at the cool abstract painting on the opposite wall, toying with her pen. What was he talking about? Her column *was* her work, or it had been for the last three years. An icy knot settled in the pit of her stomach. He couldn't be calling because he thought...

Her tone was aloof enough to make even Lily proud. "Perhaps you could be a bit more specific, Mr. Gunnarrson. I don't mean to be rude, but I've had a very hectic day, and it's not over yet."

A very long, very measured breath answered her. Patience did not come to this man without a major amount of effort. "My band needs a new lyricist. We—"

"Mr. Gunnarrson—" she interrupted before he could disclose any more, her tone cold enough to bring on the next ice age.

"Cole," he broke in, authority ringing in his command. "Call me Cole."

Alex ignored the resonating power in his voice, plowing on as if he hadn't spoken at all. "*Mr.*

Gunnarrson, if you're familiar with my work, as you say, then you'd know I haven't written music in years."

"Three, to be precise..." A muffled, foreign-sounding word—uttered in a none too congenial tone—lifted the fine hairs on the back of her neck. Before she could take control of the conversation again, he pushed on. "I'm well aware you've turned your sights elsewhere, but I'm also aware when you *were* writing, every one of your tracks consistently slotted at the top of the charts."

Alex remained silent for a moment as bittersweet memories assailed her. She had been good. It had all been good...the music, the emotional high of hearing her music, her words, pumping from the radio at unexpected moments. She'd been better than good.

Until the whole thing had fallen apart.

He took her silence as an opening. "I'd like to meet with you to discuss—"

"Thank you for thinking of me," she interjected the cool dismissal, cutting him off. "But I'm afraid I'm just not the right person for the job. I hope you find what you're looking for—with someone else. Now, if you'll excuse me, Mr. Gunnarrson, as I explained, I have a lot of work waiting for me. Have a nice day."

With careful precision, Alex replaced the receiver on the cradle. She leaned back in her chair and drew a deep, cleansing breath, more shaken than she cared to admit. Grimacing, she reached for the bottle of antacid beside her computer and shook two tablets out onto her palm. Then she glanced at the phone, and shook out a third. Chewing the chalky tablets, she retrieved a chilled can of soda from the small refrigerator behind her desk. She popped the top, chasing the antacid down with three extra-strength Excedrin that were way too small—

and not nearly potent enough—for the pisser of a headache knocking on her door. Alex set the can on a coaster at the edge of her desk and turned her resolute focus to the stack of papers in front of her. Every now and again, however, her eyes drifted to her phone.

It *had* been years, she chided herself. She probably couldn't even remember how to...

But the notes were there, inside of her. The music she'd kept diligently contained for years. Measure upon measure of sound strained to pour out, provoked by Gunnarrson's unexpected, unwelcome phone call. Shaking her head, telling herself it was for the best, she ruthlessly shoved the notes back down. Turning her computer on, Alex called up the Marston file.

Yet even as one slim hand began tapping on the computer keyboard, the other reached for her intercom.

With a hesitant frown, she depressed the button, cursing herself for being ten kinds of fool. "Rita, pull everything you can find on the band, Stolen Innocence—and on their lead singer, Cole Gunnarrson."

Rita buzzed back, "Sure thing. Gina's on line... Did you say *Stolen Innocence*?"

"And Cole Gunnarrson," Alex confirmed.

Rita's voice shot up three octaves, from efficient professionalism straight to giddy awe. "Cole... Holy Mother of God!"

Chapter 2

Cole threw his cell phone on the desk, a dark feral growl of displeasure rumbled deep in his chest. With a flick of the wrist, he flipped open the latest edition of the *LA Globe*. His eyes glittered in the darkened room, unholy, icy blue beacons sizzling with irritation.

Express yourself, he read with narrowed eyes. *Don't let your creativity suffer because you've been burned. When faced with resistance, persist—don't quit. You owe it to yourself to let the music flow. Fight for it.*

Evidently, Ms. Sinclair didn't believe in taking her own advice. Shuffling through the stack of sheet music at his elbow, Cole's keen gaze zeroed in with unerring precision on the small, feminine print penciled at the corner of each page with meticulous care, the lack of light no problem for his preternatural vision. *Lyricist...Alexandra Sinclair.* Her talent leaped up to bite at him from every page, a cruel jab for all that she'd refused him.

A snarl ripped from his lips. Defeat was not an option, not for him.

The female who'd written this music had poured her heart out in every single word, and every last note. Only that kind of devotion to the music—only that kind of honesty and understanding of Human emotion—could give his band the edge they needed to stay on top of the charts. Cole's fierce, competitive nature wouldn't settle for anything less. His cover wouldn't allow for it. He'd never been one to settle for anything less than the best.

In this particular case, the best meant Alexandra Sinclair.

She hadn't even hesitated when he told her who he was, had shown no sign of recognition whatsoever. He'd worked too damned hard to warrant such a tepid response. Akin to tossing a gauntlet before him, her reaction only served to firm his resolve. This particular gauntlet was such that he held no compunction about snatching it up. Gritting his teeth with determination, Cole retrieved his phone. He thumbed in a number in his speed dial, then pounded his fingers on the desk as he waited for the call to connect.

His agent's voice cracked enthusiasm through the line. "Cole, my man, what can I do for ya?"

"The female said no, Tommy." Cole's succinct dark growl was a dangerous warning to the Vampyre on the other end of the line. He would not accept failure. "Make it happen."

Not waiting for a reply, Cole flipped the phone closed and tossed it back onto the desk. He should have just bloody well gone down to her office. By the gods, it would have been less frustrating than dealing with her watchdog assistant over the phone. He experienced a fleeting stab of guilt at having to resort to mind control in order to get past the assistant, but he consoled himself with the fact that he'd given her three previous opportunities to cooperate. It still didn't sit well. Free will was something Cole rarely, if ever impinged on. And then only when there was no other recourse. In those rare cases, he was vigilant to remain minimally intrusive.

Ms. Sinclair had been so quick to brush him off—and so frustratingly unaffected by his name— that he hadn't even had the time to consider, let alone attempt to control her response to his offer. Now, after their brief conversation, he had the unsettling impression his powers of persuasion would have held little sway with her, at least over the phone. Perhaps, face to face, he'd have had the advantage. Oh, hell, why worry about it. Tommy would take care of it.

Pushing the matter from his mind for the moment, he raked a hand through his hair and shrugged the tension from his shoulders. Drawing a deep breath, his gaze skated over the room—his own private domain—in all likelihood the only place on his entire estate that wasn't crawling with groupies and hangers-on.

He longed to go for a swim...a quiet, relaxing swim. Fat chance of that happening with a dozen or more perfectly tanned, surgically sculpted, Human females writhing around—and in—the pool. If the clinging females weren't deterrent enough, the cheerful, sizzling-hot UV rays bathing the estate grounds sure as hell were. Why had he never gotten around to having an indoor pool built? He'd have to remedy that situation, soon.

Along with the preternatural vision, he could also boast damned impressive hearing as well. He lifted glowing, narrowed eyes to the door. Whoever was ambling down that hallway better keep right on ambling, he was in no mood for company just now. His scowl deepened when the door opened without a knock.

Peering down the throat of danger with flagrant disregard, Styx stuck his head through the opening. "You decent, *amigo*?"

He glared a warning from behind the desk, but Styx sailed right in, sans invitation, and dropped to the sofa with negligent ease. "Guess not. I take it the female was less than cooperative."

Cole lifted a sardonic brow at the Spaniard. "You could say that."

Styx shrugged, unconcerned, and Cole could almost hear his thoughts aloud. The reluctant lyricist's employment was as good as a done deal. Five centuries of friendship had more than demonstrated that Cole *always* got his way. That same friendship also gave Styx a little more leeway than most could claim in the face of Cole's thorny temper.

"Take a night off from the hunt and come out for a bite," he offered with a disgustingly cheerful grin. "It'll improve your disposition."

Dispassionate and grim, Cole held up an empty tumbler, swirling the crimson dregs. "Already had a bite, thanks."

"No wonder you're so damned pissy." Styx wrinkled his nose with patent distaste. "Man, how can you stand to drink that swill? What you need is a nice warm vein, maybe a little piece of ass when you're done. Nothing cheers me up more than a sultry little brunette. Unless it's a blonde. You can't go wrong with a blonde. Their veins are always so tender." Styx chuckled diabolically, then tossed out with self-amused introspection, "Then again, I haven't been known to turn my nose up at a feisty redhead either." Shrewd, velvety eyes considered Cole for a long moment, and Styx sobered. "Was a day not so long ago you wouldn't have turned your nose either, *mi hermano*."

Just as Cole opened his mouth to shred Styx with a scathing retort, the dull roar of bass and drums blaring from the backyard cranked up to decibels capable of shattering eardrums. A seductive, intense masculine voice throbbed from an expertly hidden, hideously expensive stereo system. H.I.M.'s darkly sensual "Vampire Heart" filtered through the house.

Cole's rueful smile was blade sharp. "I take it Zack was in charge of our musical selections this afternoon."

Chuckling, shaking his head with mock

disapproval, Styx kicked his feet up on the coffee table. "I don't give a shit what anybody says, that Werewolf's got one warped sense of humor."

Cole paced across the room, and closed the door with a firm hand. Precious little sound filtered in. More important, with the door closed, only band members dare enter...and then only when it was critical. His privacy—specifically while he was inside his private domain—was the one and only cardinal rule of the house. A rule he guarded with jealous fury.

On his way back to his desk, he paused before a prominent display case. His gaze caressed the treasured weapons of war nestled therein. Sword and shield, helmet and battle ax. Once seamless extensions of his body. Remnants of simpler lifetime. One in which the enemy was a known variable met face to face on a battlefield of warriors, where blood was spilled with honor. Not like now, where the battlefields were posh, upscale nightclubs, and a faceless Rogue victimized helpless Human females.

Flexing his fists at his sides, Cole continued on to his desk, sinking into the leather seat. Filled with cold determination, he reached for a thick file.

Styx followed Cole's movements, resignation laced his voice. "Why bother, we've been through that file a thousand times. *No vale la pena intentarlo.* I don't know what you're expecting to find."

Ignoring him, Cole opened the file, spilling the contents onto his desk in front of him. Somewhere, buried in this slush pile of information, there had to be a clue. Some overlooked bit of evidence that might give him a hint of the Party Crasher's identity, or some indication of his next mark.

Perching on the edge of the desk, Styx reached for a photo that fluttered loose. Together they reread the reports, shuffled the photos, arranging them chronologically, until one crime scene began to blur with the next. The nagging suspicion they were missing something obvious crawled up the back of Cole's neck. Heaving a disgusted sigh, he tossed the stack of photos on his desk where they fanned out in a wide arc.

Pushing himself back from the desk, he depressed a concealed button on the underside of one of the shelves, and an oak panel slid sideways with a slight hiss. He reached inside the chilled compartment, snagging a crystal decanter filled with dark red liquid before he closed the door.

Cole refilled his tumbler. Then he lifted questioning eyes to Styx. The look the drummer shot his way clearly questioned Cole's sanity. Sighing, Cole tipped the tumbler to his lips, and grimaced. Styx was right. This blood bank stuff was nasty. May as well have gone out to some back alley and found some disease infested rodent to suck on.

Staring at the reports, Styx grumbled, "I don't know what the hell they expect us to do. They've been chasing this asshole for eight months now. If they can't catch him, what makes 'em think we can?"

Styx must have caught Cole's gaze drifting to the glass display case once more. His tone was sharp, albeit disgruntled. "You're not a goddamned warrior anymore, and neither am I. We gave all that up a long time ago, man."

No, they weren't warriors anymore. But that apparently inconsequential fact hadn't stopped *them* from asking. And it hadn't stopped him from saying yes. Now here they were...involved up to their fangs in the hunt for a cold-blooded murderer, an Immortal serial killer preying on unsuspecting Mortals. War was war, he supposed. The faces and reasons may change through time, but it was still war. He knew war.

And war knew him.

When the TFRA, short for the Task Force for Rogue Apprehension—otherwise known as the *Enforcers*, a Vampyre equivalent of the Humans' FBI—approached him, *asking* for his assistance, he should have told them to take a long walk on the beach at dawn.

If he hadn't been so damned bored, he almost certainly would have. Now he was having second thoughts—a lot of them—but it was too damned late to do anything about it. The only Vampyre that had better track records than Cole at getting what they wanted were the TFRA. Those that refused to cooperate had a way of disappearing. Even a Vampyre as old and experienced as Cole thought twice about defying the TFRA.

Granted, an Immortal serial killer stalking the Human entertainment business posed a threat to both races, Human and Vampyre alike. The gods only knew how the Werewolves would respond if this bastard wasn't caught soon. Frankly, the whole thing had begun to make him edgy.

Reluctant recruit that he was, Cole sifted through the files, having gone over them so many times now he'd memorized every damned detail. He'd given his word to find the killer, and, by the gods, that's what he intended to do.

"We're missing something, Styx. Eight victims in eight months. All Human females between the ages of twenty-two and thirty-three. Random numbers carved on the sides of each of their necks, just over the carotid...and obvious Vamp puncture marks." He recited the information aloud despite the fact that Styx knew this stuff every bit as well as he did. Maybe talking it out might shed light on some overlooked crevice. "Cause of death for each female, however, is a broken neck. According to the M.E. reports, the Crasher didn't drain any one of them. There has to be a key...somewhere..."

Moving across the darkened room with the ease of a nocturnal predator, Cole dropped onto the over-sized suede sofa. Straight across from him, his Louis XV Steinway mocked him, reminding him that he had yet another loose end to deal with. Alexandra Sinclair's cultured voice snuck up on him, toying with his concentration. That voice, heavy with underlying currents of smooth seduction that ran toward smoky and sensual, intrigued him. Would her face and body live up to the promise?

He shook his head, shoving such thoughts from his mind with ruthless resolve. When she came onboard—and there was no doubt in his mind that she would, Tommy was very good at what he did or Cole wouldn't have kept him around as long as he had—Alexandra Sinclair would be there for one reason, and one reason only. To write music. He'd learned a lot of lessons throughout the centuries, and one of them...perhaps the most valuable of all...had been to keep any and all entanglements with females—*Mortal* females—completely shallow and utterly meaningless.

With her proven track record, he wouldn't have to worry about the band's reputation slipping. He could focus on finding and dispatching the Party Crasher before the psychopath claimed another innocent life and increased the chances of exposure for Cole and others like him.

He hadn't existed since the mid-ninth century without having learned how to be cautious. He'd guarded his secret well, would continue to do so. Oh, sure, every so often one needed a thrill—a bit of excitement—or things tended to get dull. But his kind also had to know where to draw the line.

He'd seen firsthand what could happen when Vampyre got bored. It wasn't pretty. Villages were wiped from existence. The Anasazi. Roanoke... He shuddered when he recalled what Werewolves were capable of. Entire Human civilizations tended to topple when one of the races became restless. The balance between Humans and Immortals—most especially the Vampyre Nation—was tenuous at best.

On the other side of the room, Styx lifted a morgue snapshot, his gaze riveted to the sheet in his hand. "Cole, it's in the numbers...it has to be."

Lifting two of the crime scene photos, he compared them side by side. He set one down and picked up a third. And then a fourth. At last, he gathered up all the photos and carried them to Cole, depositing them on his lap without ceremony. "In every photo, the number is the only defining element I can find."

Cole leaned forward, balancing his elbows on his knees as he spread the pictures on the coffee table before him. Styx was right. The numbers were always present, and in the exact same location. Excitement coursed through him. They might be on to something. These weren't just random numbers. And they didn't denote succession of murders.

Was it code? Could it be that simple?

Shuffling the stack into sequence, he directed Styx, "Grab me a pen and a sheet of paper." A few seconds later, pen and paper in hand, he began making notations. "The first victim's number was two. The second's was five." He shot a glance up at the drummer. "The alphabet, you think? Two...B. Five...E. The third victim was the number three. C."

Eight victims. Eight months. Eight letters. He followed the trail until he'd spelled out "Because I..." Leaning back, he stared at the paper before him through grim eyes, then at the gruesome pictures. Numbers. Frowning, going on a hunch, Cole checked the dates. Each murder fell on the eleventh day of each month.

His eyes lingered on the photo of the last

murder. The outside shot displayed the alley entrance to a nightclub. Cole's frown intensified. He rose and went back to the desk, shuffling through the reports until he found the one he was looking for. The address for this particular nightclub was 1111 South Brooke Street. Eleven-eleven... It was just too damned much of a coincidence.

Too irritated to wait until he found the proper page, he snapped, "Where was the first body found?"

"Ah..." Styx stroked his goatee, his eyes distant as he searched his memory. "One Eleven Holly Lane, I think." Then, assessing Cole's ah-ha expression, Styx exclaimed, "You're on to something."

"Go with me on this," Cole urged. He shifted the papers, double-checking his theory. "Each victim was...Odin's teeth...each victim wasn't just between twenty-two and thirty-three...they were *either* twenty-two, or thirty-three. Multiples of eleven. The murders all happened on the eleventh day of the month. The slayings began in November...the eleventh month of the year."

Excitement glowing in his eyes, Styx drawled, "Yeah..."

"I need to check, but I'm pretty sure the locations all had variants of the number eleven in the address... By Thor, the guy's obsessed with numbers, eleven to be exact," he mumbled to himself as he picked up his phone and thumbed in the number to the TFRA agent assigned to the case. "Agent Crispin...this is Cole Gunnarrson. We found something you might want to take a look at."

Interest perked the agent's voice up to the equivalent of a teenager reading a dictionary. "I can meet you down at the warehouse on Baltimore Street tonight. Ten-thirty work for you?"

"We'll see you then." Cole clicked his phone closed with a slow smile of satisfaction. They were getting closer. The killer had a pattern. Knowing this important point, they should be able to zero in on his target zone.

Styx's voice cut his one shining moment of triumph today short.

"Cole...isn't today the eleventh?"

Chapter 3

He pushed the clutter of empty glasses to the side of the table with a wide easy grin. The Party Crasher laid his hand, palm up, on the tabletop between them and angled his body closer, leaning toward her as a lover would...a predator crouching toward its prey. Coiling a brunette curl around one finger, she leaned closer, placing her free hand in his palm.

"You have the most...unusual eyes," she remarked. Her ruby lips, full and glossed to a high sheen, curved up in a skillful summons. "Like...liquid gold." She tilted her head to the side, letting the lustrous strand of hair fall to accentuate her pronounced cleavage with cunning grace. "They almost...glow. They're so beautiful...and...eerie."

Smirking, he crooned, "Babe, you have no idea..." He knew her name. He just didn't care enough to use it. "So, angel, what say you and I slip outside for some fresh air?"

Her eyes flickered to the door and she hesitated. Reading her unease, he murmured, "It's awful hard to get better acquainted when I can barely hear you. We can stay right in the parking lot if you'd prefer."

"No farther than the parking lot?" she verified.

"Scout's promise," he vowed, shooting her an innocuous smile.

Her lips curled again. She picked up her purse and stood. He led her through the crowded dance floor and outside. Once they cleared the gaggle of clubbers on the sidewalk, he angled to the left, tugging her into the shadows at the corner of the

Brenda Huber

building. She immediately resisted, but her efforts were futile. Clamping his hand over her mouth, he wrapped an arm around her waist, jerking her off her feet. In the blink of a Mortal eye, he dragged her around the back of the building and into the dingy alley.

He swept a quick glance from one end of the alley to the other. One last check. All clear. Spinning her in his arm, he kept his hand fastened over her mouth. Her wet fearful eyes beseeched him. She whimpered against his palm.

Pitiful.

He shot an idle glance at his wristwatch while she strained, shoving at his chest. Almost time. He released her waist and sank his fingers into her hair, fisting them. Yanking her head back, he lowered his lips to her taut skin. She sobbed as he ran the tip of his tongue along the bulging vein. Her pulse rushed beneath his tongue, and his eyes burned as they changed. His fangs shot longer, the skin on his face stretched tight. Power surged inside him. The animalistic insatiable need to feed was almost undeniable. But he fought it.

He. Would. Not. Drink.

Thirty seconds. He lifted his head, leering down into wide, horrified eyes. Her jaw worked beneath his palm. Shrieks of terror filled her throat, trapped. She writhed against him, arms flailing. Fingers curled as she clawed at his chest. Tiny bursts of pain erupted all along his shin. Ten seconds. He opened his mouth...wide...fangs stretched, saliva pooled in his mouth. His nostrils flared. Four. Three. He swallowed the saliva. There would be no healing for her. And no pleasure in his embrace. This was not a *Kiss.*

His fangs sank into her throat, a hot knife through butter. Blood seeped onto his tongue, and his gut clenched tight at the alluring flavor. It would

24

be so easy to drain her.

No, no. She was meant for something else. He could stop off for a bite later. Now he had to focus. Her body stilled against him, her struggles faltered. Turning his head ever so slightly, fangs still buried deep in her vein, he sliced through the delicate tissue, severing the vein. Withdrawing his fangs took a monumental effort. Lifting his head, he grinned down into her dulling eyes, his lips damp as blood gushed from the puncture.

Without a word of warning, he snapped her neck, then he dropped her onto the filthy pavement. Like a used candy wrapper. Drawing a tissue from his pocket, he blotted at his mouth, and he shoved the tissue back into his pocket. He checked his watch one last time. Eleven o'clock on the dot. Perfect.

Bending down, he positioned her head, just so...so that one side of her neck, milky white beside delicious crimson, gleamed up at him. Swabbing a finger in the blood pooling beneath her, he stroked the number across her flesh. Straightening, he licked the blood from his finger with relish. Yeah, he'd have to stop off for something on his way home...a redhead would taste good right about now.

Humming the opening bars to H.I.M.'s "Bleed Well," he thrust his hands deep into his pockets and strolled away.

****

Cole's phone vibrated in his pocket as he eased his car from the garage. Glancing sideways at Styx, he dug the phone free. Flipping it to his ear, he offered a terse, "Gunnarrson..."

He listened for a few moments in silence, and snarled a nasty expletive. He flicked the phone closed, tossed it on the dash, and smashed his palm against the steering wheel.

"Another one?"

Cole nodded, his eyes killing the gravel lane

ahead of them.

"Where?"

"Eleven hundred Lusitania Road." As soon as they cleared the security gates, Cole hit the accelerator, pushing Styx back in his seat. "Change of plans."

Having set a new land speed record, Cole down shifted the Corvette and entered the parking lot connected to *Fangs*. A steady crowd milled beneath the blood-red neon sign. Pulsing music shook the windowless building and bumped against Cole's car. Cole slipped from behind the wheel, pocketing his keys while he strode across the lot.

As they pushed their way through the heaving mass of bodies, Styx eyed a buxom brunette near the door. She eyed him back, and he nudged Cole with his elbow. "How'd we miss *this* place?"

"Keep your zipper up...and your mouth shut. We're workin' tonight."

With a wistful glance at the invitation in the brunette's eyes, Styx grumbled, "You're too uptight. I'm telling ya, man, you need to find a female and get—"

"Save it," Cole barked, cutting him off.

A pair of broad-shouldered bouncers met them at the door. Heaving a sigh, Cole whipped his baseball cap off and drew his sunglasses down, treating the nearest bouncer to a full view of his face. Instant, startled recognition lit the bouncer's eyes. He all but fell over himself as he scrambled to open the door for Cole.

Styx snorted as they stepped into the flashing, swirling strobe lights. "You like doing that, don't you."

"Hell, yeah," he chuckled. An arrogant smirk curled the edges of his lips. "Stop bitchin', if it weren't for this face, you'd still be out there with them, *junior*." He tossed a thumb over his shoulder at the crowd behind them.

Sympathetic, Styx patted Cole on the shoulder. "You keep right on telling yourself that, *old man.*"

A little of the tension eased from Cole's shoulders as he ribbed Styx. Grinning, Cole paced across the dance floor beside his friend. Scantily clad women writhed and gyrated against them until even Cole struggled to remain indifferent. Cole's footsteps faltered as a particularly tasty morsel wound her arms around his waist. Hunger flared as his stare locked on the thumping pulse at the base of her throat. Heavy breasts brushed at his chest. Invitation danced in her eyes.

It would take nothing at all to convince her to step out into the night with him. By Valhalla, in all probability, he didn't need to do anything more than he'd done with the bouncers. Give her a flash of his face. As soon as recognition dawned, she'd be the one dragging him from the club. Then again, if he flashed his face in a place like this, he was liable to start a riot.

He heaved a reluctant sigh. Down boy... Smiling, he shook his head with true regret as he unwound her arms from his neck. But she was an octopus. As soon as he released her wrists, her arms slithered around him again. She clung to him like Velcro. Cole's reluctance turned to irritation in the blink of an eye. He tilted his head down, sliding his shades to the tip of his nose so she could see his eyes. His gaze bore into hers with burning intensity.

Go away...

She gave him a sassy little pout, released him, and twirled away. Cole's gaze followed her for a moment, lingering on the swing and shake of her hips, but his thoughts were of another woman. If only Ms. Sinclair were so easy to control...

When he turned back to the rear exit, his friend's smirk soured his mood.

Scowling, Cole pushed for the rear door. Another burly male stepped into his path, a polite but firm smile hovered at the edge of his thick lips. "Sorry, man, this exit's unavailable."

Cole's nostrils flared. Vampyre... Shooting a swift glance side to side, Cole smiled, giving the muscle at the door a quick flash of vicious fangs.

The brute's eyes widened, then narrowed with suspicion.

Cole leaned a little closer. "I believe Agent Crispin is expecting us."

Impassive, the brute nodded and moved aside, allowing them to pass. They stepped into the night, and the door closed behind them, muffling the throbbing music and the scent of sweating, lusting Humans. Warm air, sharp with ever-present smog, pressed against him once more, making him realize just how hot it had been inside the club. A hint of rain clung to the air, and just beneath that, the scent of death.

Vampyre swarmed the dank, shadow-filled alley. Two stood side-by-side, one tall and thin, one short and stocky, comparing notes in hushed tones while a third crouched near the victim snapping photos from various angles. Off to the side, two more waited beside a gurney, silent and still as statues. A short distance away, another Vampyre paced the scene, stopping now and again to lift a piece of rubbish with a gloved hand, sniffing like a bloodhound hot on the trail.

His long overcoat flapped at his calves as he skulked from one item of interest to the next. He wore his long hair skimmed back in a tight ponytail at the base of his skull. When he turned back toward the victim, the dim light above the door cast an eerie pall on the agent's meticulous, expensive suit.

Cole cleared his throat. The pacing Vampyre retrieved another piece of trash, inspected it, then placed the crumbled piece of paper back in the exact spot he'd picked it up. He eyed the paper for a second, shifting it a fraction of an inch before moving to join Cole and Styx.

His gait was slow and easy, conspicuously unperturbed considering the corpse on the ground only a few short feet away. Despite his impeccable stature, the agent's eyes reminded Cole of a basset hound. Big, brown, and sad. As he reached them, he held out a gloved hand. "Cole, sorry to have to do this here…"

Cole glanced at the rubber glove, then up to the absentminded agent.

Frowning, Crispin peered down at the glove on his hand, as if forgetting how it had gotten there. "Right, right," he murmured as he withdrew his hand, nodding a distracted greeting to Styx.

"Close call with this one," Crispin mumbled in bland tones. "We've been staking out every night club inside city limits for the last several weeks. It's stretching us a little thin. Happened to have an agent close by when the call came in. Young Human male found the body about an hour ago. The agent *convinced* him she'd only passed out and sent him on his way."

The tall, thin Vampyre approached them. "We're all done here, Agent Crispin."

Crispin nodded dismissal, and the two with the gurney moved in.

Cole stepped forward, interrupting their work. "Mind if we take a look at things first?"

Crispin gave an indifferent shrug, waving the gurney back. Cole and Styx began their own search. Styx wandered around the alley with deceptive nonchalance. His body was relaxed, but Cole knew his eyes and nose were on high alert. Cole sauntered to the body. Crouching beside it much the same as the TFRA's forensic photographer, his eyes drank in every detail.

Blonde, five-five…maybe five-six, one-ten dripping wet. His nostrils flared, pulling in the scents of the alleyway, but too many Vampyre had tramped through to isolate a specific scent. He could smell the blood congealing in her hardening veins, and he was willing to bet his last Grammy the cause of death was a broken neck. With the back of his knuckle, he turned her head to the side. Puncture wounds.

And the number three.

He added the letter 'c' to his list. 'Because I c…' The killer was sending them a message all right. He looked up to Crispin, requesting, "Age? Occupation?"

"Twenty-two…" Crispin glanced to Cole, his stare vague, then his gaze dropped back to the notebook in his hand. He flipped through several pages before muttering, "The female was a receptionist at Phoenix Records."

Cole's eyes slid to Styx, a grim frown settled between his brows as another piece of the puzzle clicked into place. Another common tie. In one way or another, every victim had a connection to the music business. A studio manager, a DJ, and a studio intern. An assistant events producer, two back-up vocalists, a publicity assistant, a road crewmember, and now a receptionist.

Crispin meandered over to stand beside the victim, giving the body one last dispassionate visual search. He glanced to Cole, his gaze bland. "On the phone you said you had something for me?"

Cole blinked at the agent, unaccountably unsettled. Had the man seen so many murder victims that he could dismiss a body…a slain female of any race…with such casual disregard? Was it professional detachment on his face…or something more?

Distracted, Crispin patted at his pockets, then

found his pen tucked behind his ear. Lowering basset-hound eyes to Cole, he waited to list the latest findings at Cole's leisure.

Stifling the urge to snort, Cole pushed to his feet. Vampyre or not, this guy was about as threatening as a paper cut. "As a matter of fact, I think we do."

Styx joined him, and together they outlined their theory about the numbers. Nodding, his face remarkably impassive, Agent Crispin took notes without uttering a word of interruption. When they finished, he promised to take their information under advisement. Stepping back out of the way, he cleared them to continue searching the crime scene, then gave the M.E.'s assistants permission to remove the body.

****

Smug, the Party Crasher's confident gaze followed Cole as he prowled through the alley. He hadn't figured it would take quite this long to get his message across. The fact that Cole had been the one to figure it out was vaguely insulting, and yet satisfying too. Even if the TFRA had provided him little entertainment, Gunnarrson was proving to be a worthy adversary.

Now, not only did he get the prestige of showing the TFRA for the fools they were, but he also got the added bonus of going head to head with an ancient warrior whose reputation among the Vampyre Nation had reached near godlike status.

He'd show them all.

Like the ancient relics Cole surrounded himself with on his precious estate, Cole himself was outdated, obsolete.

That's right, Gunnarrson, you think you're so smart. Keep looking for those clues. You won't find any. I'm too good for that.

Cole stopped in his tracks, peering into the

shadows. Did he sense the malicious eyes upon him?

Do you know how close I am? How close I've always been?

So close I could rip your throat out...

Chapter 4

Odin's teeth! That damned female was stubborn!

Slamming his foot onto the accelerator, throwing his phone on the seat beside him, Cole sped down the interstate. He'd spent the better part of two weeks on the phone with his agent, pacing and railing, threatening and bargaining. He hadn't had to work this hard since he'd escaped the French Revolution, and that time he'd damned near lost his head...literally.

Talking Alexandra Sinclair around had been an exhilarating, frustrating endeavor, and he wasn't through. After weeks of pursuit, she'd grudgingly agreed to come to the estate to give it a trial run. She'd consented to three weeks—*three paltry weeks*—to get a feel for things. To see if writing again was even viable for her.

However, when the three trial weeks were up— then and only then—would she even consider discussing a contract. And he'd be back to square one. He'd only had that one, brief conversation with her on the phone, all other communication had been through Tommy, and yet he looked forward to haggling with her over the terms of her contract with an odd sense of giddy anticipation. He refused to even let it cross his mind that in three weeks she might just walk away without so much as a backward glance.

By the gods, he should have just gone to her office and *made* her agree. He should have looked deep in her eyes and told her she wanted nothing more than to work with him. But he wouldn't have

33

been able to live with the guilt. This unnatural conscience of his was a real drag sometimes. Of course, *convincing* her like that would have taken all the fun out of the chase. His lips curved, dangerous and cunning. When you were a cold-blooded predator, it was all about the chase.

Where in the hell had he put that damned address anyway? Steering with one hand, at speeds that would have made a NASCAR driver twitchy, he reached over and riffled through his glove box. Papers fluttered this way and that until he couldn't tell which one he'd already looked at, and which one he hadn't. Pointing his car toward the off ramp, he eased up on the accelerator.

So what if he'd retained a sliver of his conscience—that small bit of humanity—through the centuries, something few others of his breed could boast...or curse. He rarely let his conscience interfere with his day-to-day activities anyway, and, in all fairness, he sure as hell couldn't complain about what he'd gained from the transformation all those centuries ago.

Superhuman strength and speed, finely tuned preternatural senses, and the ability to heal in mere minutes from wounds that would be fatal for a Human were nothing to scoff about, and, contrary to popular belief, he could tolerate brief stints in sunlight. Granted, creature of the night that he was, prolonged exposure to direct UV rays caused seriously painful burns, debilitating weakness, and, ultimately, an excruciating, sizzling death. All of which he understandably went well out of his way to avoid.

Of course, now that he was considering the pros and cons of being what he was, the ability to fly wouldn't have been half-bad. And shapeshifting would have been cool. Those were two marks myth has missed by a long shot. Too bad, that. He could have saved himself the trouble of getting a pilot's license, and the cost of a Lear.

Cursing himself for being such a stubborn, hardheaded cuss, Cole riffled through the papers once more as the needle on the speedometer jumped well past eighty. His call with Tommy nagged at the edges of his mind. It irritated a bit that he'd had to rely on the agent to close the deal with Alex Sinclair. Loki take it, what was done was done. She was on board now, that should be all that mattered. He should have learned his lesson by now. His obsessive tenacity had gotten him into more than one boiling pot of trouble. Nevertheless, he'd managed to convince himself the band needed Alexandra Sinclair. She was a brilliant lyricist, after all, and he...they...they wouldn't settle for anything less.

As a result, he'd put himself in a tenuous position. He was probably lucky Tommy had been the one to deal with her. She could have asked for the moon and stars, and he'd have plucked them from the night sky for her in a New York minute. Provided she met his expectations, of course. Then again, if she proved to be even half as alluring as her voice promised, he was completely screwed.

Ah-hah. Pulling a crumpled note from of the clutter, Cole scanned the wild scrawl then tucked the paper in his pocket. With steady determination, he turned off on one side road after another until he came to his destination, a new nightclub on the south end of the city. Easing from the car, he slipped through the crowd, angling not for the door, but for the shadows around the corner of the brick, two story building. Smiling with grim resolve, he swaggered toward the darkened alley, armed to the fangs for hunting. Then again, when a Vampyre went hunting, that alone was all he needed...his fangs.

It didn't take long to search the musty, smog

and grime stained pavement. The small puddles of murky water, lingering reminders of a late afternoon shower, were a nuisance, but his worn combat boots didn't mind. There were no vagrants to question, and the rats scurrying beneath the dumpster, scrabbling inside it, offered little in the way of information. The darkened interior of the thriving nightclub was minimally more informative, but not by much. As soon as he entered the rear door, Cole scented Vampyre, in outrageous numbers. However, by the faded scent trail, it didn't take Cole long to determine that none of his kind had been on the premises in at least two days, if not a little longer.

Frustration was mounting, and time was running out. The case had gone on far too long as it was. Wallowing in pride, the TFRA had dragged their collective feet before bringing Cole and Styx on board. Now the waters were too muddy for any solid clues to float to the surface, yet they expected Cole and his band to be the hook and the bait. It didn't take a genius to figure out that when the killer struck again—when, not if—Stolen Innocence would be the ones left holding the empty net. Bastards.

A feral snarl of aggravation slipped past his lips as he ducked back out the door and prowled around the side of the building. Then his nostrils flared. Female. Human. Separated from the pack. Predatory instincts engaged.

Hunger sat up and took immediate, rabid notice. He'd been without a hot meal for a long time now, having instead chosen to forego a fresh vein for the cold, bagged variety. That pesky conscience thing again, free will and all that. Warm blood wasn't the only thing he'd been living without. Somehow, after centuries of willing, nameless women, he'd found the entire process...stagnant. He'd wanted—needed— something more. The problem was he just couldn't quite put his fang on the pulse of the problem, couldn't figure out exactly what it was he craved.

The female wasn't a raving beauty by anyone's standards. Her clothing blended with those of the crowd near the door, yet she held back as if hesitant to enter the club. Her hair hung limp, a dull, dishwater blonde. Her features were unremarkable, though her eyes listed toward a mite too small for her long, oval face. She wore too much make-up. But she smelled clean, and she had a certain naïve hopefulness about her.

Cole tensed, prepared to leave without a backward glance. The wind shifted, carrying her scent to him once more. His eyes drifted to her, slow and considering. His nostrils flared again, his chin lifted, and his lungs dragged her in. His mouth watered.

It wouldn't be that difficult. He wouldn't take more than he needed. He wouldn't hurt her, and in exchange for her...donation...he would give her a *Kiss*—the thrilling, heady pleasure without the memory of that initial, unavoidable sting. He'd probably be far safer than anything else she might pick up inside a place like that. A simple suggestion sent on the winds. *Come to the shadows.* Then the ball would be in her court. If she walked away, so be it. If she was too weak minded to resist, was it his fault?

He knew it was the hunger talking, the primal beast inside taunting him with an easy excuse. He hadn't let the beast rule him in five centuries. But that beast was getting harder and harder to resist, prodding at him with startling regularity lately.

It really had been so very long. Almost half a century. One meal from her, that's all. One meal, and no attachment, just the way he liked it. He never drank from the same woman twice. That was another rule on his dismally short list of regulations. Somehow, on some level, drinking from the same

Human more than once equated to a personal intimacy. One he would never risk. She would remain faceless, nameless. A one night drink, so to speak, no risk of attachment.

No danger whatsoever.

Cole gave a resigned shrug. Everyone fell off the wagon once in a while.

He held to the shadows, a shade in the night. She couldn't see him from where she stood, not that she was looking, but he had an unobstructed view of her. He sent out a mental feeler, and smiled with hungry anticipation when she followed his suggestion to take the restraining clip from her hair.

Licking his lips, he sent another suggestion, though he was careful to temper the force of his will, his conscience poking at him to give the female one last chance to refuse. As if in a daze, she wandered to the side of the building, slipping into the shadows and straight into Cole's waiting arms. His burning eyes probed hers, staring with determined intensity, swirling her mind into a realm of blissful pleasure and oblivion. Then he lowered his head, fangs sharply extended, and pierced her vein. The female stiffened for half a second, then sagged against him, her body limp, yet vibrating with the rapture of a Vampyre's *Kiss*.

****

Alex pulled up outside the iron gates surrounding Cole Gunnarrson's estate, and, for the hundredth time, she doubted her sanity. With relentless determination, Gunnarrson's agent had hounded her until she'd finally caved. Somehow, despite her adamant refusal and serious reservations—and she was still trying to figure out just how he'd done it—he'd convinced her to give Stolen Innocence a chance. Now here she was, kicking herself for her stupidity.

Her gaze ran over the intricate wrought iron

scrollwork adorning the top of the gate. Security cameras peered back at her from dual vantage points.

She cringed.

Did she really want to plunge back into *that* world? She groaned aloud and shook her head. What had she been thinking? She'd sworn never to set foot in the music industry again. Although, thanks to the self-defense classes she'd taken, she'd made certain no one would ever be able to take physical advantage of her again, at least not without sustaining serious personal injury himself. Emotional scars were more difficult to overcome.

Why hadn't she been smart enough to walk away this time? She was a fool, plain and simple. Panic rose up to clog her throat. She shouldn't be here. She should turn her car around and head back to the city. No, better still— she would go straight to the airport. She could fly somewhere nice, like the Bahamas...or Italy. She'd always wanted to see Rome. Anywhere was fine, just as long as it was far, *far* away from here. She should've hung up on that damned agent, and not gone anywhere near this whopping mistake-in-the-making. Was she doomed to forever make the same mistakes, over and over?

Her grip tightened on the steering wheel, one hand reaching for the stick shift when a scratchy voice crackled through a speaker beside the security camera. "Can I help you?"

Cursing herself for not escaping while she'd had the chance...hating the long ingrained need to stand by her word...Alex leaned toward the window. "I'm Alex Sinclair. Mr. Gunnarrson is expecting me."

"One moment please."

Alex leaned back against the seat with a resigned groan. Glancing into the rearview mirror, she lifted a hand to her hair and could have screamed her frustration. Instead, she cursed beneath her breath.

She'd left the windows open so she could enjoy the sunshine and fresh air, and she hadn't given her hair a second thought. The tight, practical knot she habitually wore to the office had come undone. Her long honey-blonde locks now floated about her in wild, wanton disarray. Alex pushed her fingers through the tangles, then dug through her glove box in search of a hair tie. No such luck.

Drilling her fingers against her temple, grimacing at the vicious little spikes of pain, she let out a long-suffering sigh and rummaged through her handbag for her new best friend...the economy-sized bottle of extra-strength Excedrin. Too bad they didn't make industrial-strength. The way she'd been popping those little green and white suckers lately, it would have been more efficient to keep them in her pocket in a Pez dispenser. She drew out the tidy white bottle, giving it a hollow, rattle-free shake. Empty...

Of course.

The gate swung open, and the scratchy voice returned. "Have a nice day, Ms. Sinclair."

"Thank you." She smiled at the camera through gritted teeth and squared her shoulders.

Shifting gears, she let the powerful muscle car devour the long lane from the gate to the house. Pulling into the circular drive, she parked among a long line of vehicles that easily out-priced her Shelby, and one beat up old truck. Trying not to let herself think about what waited for her on the other side of those wide double doors, she withdrew her keys from the ignition and deposited them inside her sleek black purse. Alex ran a hand through her hair once more, trying to tame some of the wildness. She stole one last, fleeting glimpse in the rearview mirror, and then closed her eyes.

Cowboy up, Alex, it's show time...

She slid from the car and tread across the loose pebbles with extreme caution, wishing she'd worn more sensible shoes. Gravel and spiked heels did not mix. She ascended the steps, and, with a slight tremor, lifted her hand to ring the doorbell. Then Alex waited, nerves strung tight as watch springs.

And she waited.

Frowning, Alex rang the bell once more, nerves relegated to the back burner. And still no response. Music drifted from somewhere near the back of the house. Gunnarrson had enough cars in the drive to start his own dealership. His agent had assured her he'd be expecting her today. *Somebody* could at least answer the damned door. She jabbed a finger at the doorbell one last time, scowling now.

Evidently she'd set the old expectation bar a little too high in assuming he'd at least strive to make a good impression, given that his agent had stalked her with such diligence.

Grinding her teeth together, she let annoyance get the better of her. Backing off the front steps, she looked first to one side of the house, then to the other. Stiffening her spine, she set off around the north corner, and skidded to a stop, grimacing.

He *would* have to live in a house the size of a bloody football stadium. Squaring her shoulders, bracing herself for an unpleasant afternoon, she began the trek to the back of the house, aiming for the heavy blast of music.

As she tramped across the lawn, her eyes trailed over the scrupulously groomed grounds, skimming down the classical lines of the house itself with grudging appreciation. Roses and jasmine, lavender and lilies adorned the many flower gardens sprawling throughout the estate. A gardener knelt in one such paradise near a monster of a garage, tending the thriving foliage with gentle hands. Gunnarrson possessed some sense of taste, at least.

But then, out of sheer spite, she decided to reserve judgment until she had the chance to view the inside of this mausoleum, convinced it was nothing more than party-central...a puffed up, moneyed version of a frat house, swimming in empty alcohol bottles and half-naked women.

Alex smoothed her hand over the hip of her trim, black skirt, suddenly wishing she'd worn a pair of slacks instead, or a skirt with more of a conservative hemline. She'd just always liked this skirt, with its feminine lines and daring slash up the front right thigh, and she'd wanted to feel at the top of her game when she faced the determined stranger who'd uprooted her nice, tidy, content life.

Groaning aloud, she screwed up her courage. She was being a coward. She was overreacting, finding fault with anything and everything, just looking to find any excuse why this wouldn't work. There was nothing wrong with her clothing. She'd worn this outfit half a dozen times to the office— granted, she often wore a jacket to cover the sleek, red silk blouse, but it was just too hot today. There'd been nothing wrong with the security gate, a perfectly reasonable security measure for someone of Gunnarrson's position. And there was nothing wrong with Gunnarrson's house. It wasn't *overly* flamboyant or sexist, nor was it creepy, although the fact that all the windows were securely covered did give her pause.

Why then did a chill skate down her spine, as if an icy hand had feathered a warning over her back?

Run, while you still can...

No, she'd made this commitment—at least for the next three weeks—and she would damned well see it through. Determination lifted her chin. She'd be damned if she'd let them see how much the mere idea of this project had shaken her up. That legendary Sinclair steel stiffened her spine. Her grandfather would have been proud...even if Lily wasn't. Alex drew a deep breath, and took the last few steps around the back corner of the house.

She froze, appalled.

There were women *everywhere.* In the pool, lounging beside it, dancing on the patio, draped across the bar. They were...*everywhere.* Not a one of them wore enough to allow a Barbie the slimmest illusion of modesty.

To think, she'd been concerned *she* was underdressed. It took her a moment to find the men in the bevy of buxom beauties. There weren't many.

A tall, sleek man with long, scruffy black hair leaned casually against the bar with a busty blonde tucked beneath each arm. Another man sporting a blond crew cut and boyishly charming good looks lounged on a chaise by the pool, cuddling a little brunette on his lap while he nuzzled his face against the swell of her over-ripe breasts. She writhed in his arms in a poor imitation of a lap dance.

Alex shot the couple a look of disgust. *Hope he asks for his money back...*

Across the way, two men sat inside a gazebo, absorbed with a massive flat screen TV. They cheered as players streaked across the display, groaning intercepted plays and cursing fumbled balls. The women didn't seem interested in interrupting the male bonding session. Alex couldn't say as she blamed them. She'd rather have teeth pulled—minus the anesthetic—than get anywhere near that gazebo.

Chewing the edge of her lower lip, she searched for someone who looked even remotely responsible. She came up sadly empty-handed.

Drawing herself up, she sucking in a deep, grim breath. *Bar-guy it is.*

Then, as she took a bleak step forward, another man pushed through the ornate French doors. All but jogging across the patio, he vigilantly shielded his face from the sunlight with his forearm. He was slightly shorter than the others...but extremely muscular. Silky hair the color of fine rich sable flowed to his shoulders, unbound. His skin glistened a dusky olive. An expertly trimmed goatee gave him an iniquitous air, alluring and faintly sinister. He looked like a matador minus the props of cape and bull.

Zeroing in on the likely, unclaimed target, Alex made a beeline for the newcomer. "Excuse me..."

The crash of drums and roar of guitar from hidden speakers were too loud. He gave no indication he'd noticed her. Forced to repeat herself at a near yell, she instantly gained the attention of every person in the back yard—with the exception of the two sports enthusiasts, of course, who continued to whoop and heckle. Forcing a swallow, pasting on a cool smile, Alex stepped in front of the dark, attractive man.

A wide grin spread over the sensual curve of his lips. Eyes the color of smoky amber swept down the length of her with blatant interest.

Tall, dark, and dangerous purred, "Hel-*lo*, Slim."

Alex bit the inside of her lip. Oh, God, *please* don't let this be Gunnarrson, please, please, please. Not with *that* attitude. She thrust her hand forward, stiff with formality. "I'm Alex Sinclair. I'm looking for Mr. Gunnarrson."

Intrigued curiosity spiked through his amber stare. Offering her a rueful smile, he enveloped her hand in his. "That bastard always gets the best ones."

Alex's eyes flared. She shook her head, impatient to clear the air. "No, you don't understand. I'm here because I'm—"

"I know who you are." He refused to relinquish her hand; instead, he tucked it gallantly in the crook of his arm, shooting her a mysterious, wicked grin. Just the slightest hint of a Spanish accent colored his speech as he steered her inside the house. "I'm Styx, by the way. Like the river, not the wood."

"It's a—a pleasure to meet you, Mr. Styx." Alex granted him a tight, guarded smile.

"No mister, just Styx." Speculative, Styx tilted his head and eyed her. Then he ducked his head, grimacing as he shielded his face with his forearm again. "Come on, hotter than hellfire out here."

She couldn't argue there. He led her into the shade, down a long, cool hallway and around a corner. Alex extracted her hand from his arm with a polite, no-nonsense smile. She followed close on his heels and gave up counting the doors they walked by, already hopelessly lost. Her heels clicked on the chilled marble beneath her feet, her eyes widening with every priceless artifact and painting they passed. She'd been way off base, thinking this place a frat house. It wasn't the Waldorf, but it was damned close. Then again, the friggin' Louvre might have been more on point.

Styx's voice trailed behind him conversationally as he swaggered, unaffected, past a gorgeous Renoir. "So, you're the new lyricist, huh?"

"Possibly," she allowed, distracted by the glory surrounding her. A priceless Monet floated by, and she stumbled, fighting the urge to stop and gawk.

"Hear you gave up the music biz for the exciting world of journalism." He tossed the leading statement over his shoulder, and let silence hang.

Fully acquainted with the attitudes of critical musicians who believed she'd betrayed her talents, Alex's gaze swerved away from the paintings, determined to offer cool composure.

"Yes," she hedged, unwilling to take the bait.

Undeterred, Styx shot her an assessing look over his shoulder. "Cole filled us in on the arrangement. Boy, you sure made him sweat it out, waiting for your answer."

She mumbled a noncommittal, "Hmm."

Styx halted in the middle of the hall, so abruptly in fact, that she bounced off his broad back. Turning to face her, he raised an eyebrow. "You might be tiny, Slim, but I sure hope you've got more words in you than that, or we won't even be able to cut a single."

Alex blinked up at him in surprise, understanding at last that he'd only been teasing her. In spite of herself, she couldn't help but like this man who called himself Styx. *Like the river, not the wood.* She offered him an apologetic smile.

"I'm sorry if I was a little cool." Heat suffused her cheeks as she motioned toward the back of the house—or what she thought was the back at least. "I haven't had to deal with that scene for a long time. I guess it caught me off guard."

Accepting her apology with a dismissive wave of his hand, he grinned down at her. "Yeah, it can be a little much sometimes. No big deal, Slim."

Then, as they stood in the hallway smiling at each other, Styx did a quick, almost imperceptible double take. He stared hard at her face for a split second, then spun away. He was fast—and discreet—she'd allow him that, but she hadn't missed the light of recognition in his golden stare.

Styx led Alex into a quiet room on the far side of the house. He stepped just inside the door, flipping on a light switch. She caught her breath as her awed gaze locked on the Steinway. She stood transfixed for several long moments. The hand carved, walnut case was exquisite. Her fingers tingled, longing to reach out and stroke. Begging to pluck a few heavenly notes from that gorgeous instrument.

She stepped farther inside the room, her heels whisper silent now on the soft, thick carpet. She reluctantly lifted her gaze from the piano and scanned the rest of the room. Rich, dark paneling covered the walls. A massive, mahogany desk, buried beneath a haphazard muddle of papers, occupied the far end of the room. Floor to ceiling bookshelves lined the wall behind the desk. A tall, glass display case, filled with ancient weaponry, took up most of one corner.

A comfortable seating arrangement in subtle micro-suede occupied a majority of the middle of the room. The coffee table groaned beneath a messy pile of magazines and newspapers. A large fireplace loomed behind the Steinway, just to her left. A gigantic flat screen rivaling the one in the gazebo for size hung on the wall above the mantel. The clean, spicy scent of male cologne tickled her nose, and her curiosity. What kind of rocker had a room like this? Distinctly masculine...and yet very comfortable. Mature. Sophisticated.

"This is Cole's lair." Something in Styx's tone drew her gaze, but he pushed on before she could comment on his odd choice of words. A strange smile lit his eyes. "I don't think he was expecting you quite this early today. Why don't you hang out here, and I'll go find him."

Nodding, Alex thanked Styx and wandered to the sofa. She reached for a magazine as Styx slipped back out into the hall, closing the door behind him. Alex leafed through the pages. Her eyes skimmed the glossy photos without registering what she was looking at. Bored, she tossed it aside after only a few moments, and picked up another. It didn't hold her interest for long, either. Restless, she stood and shuffled the papers and magazines into neat, tidy stacks. Then she wandered the room.

Drawn inexorably to the display case, she ogled the ancient pieces within. Daggers, several swords, a lethal-looking battle-ax, a scarred shield, and a tarnished Viking helmet rested on pillows of luxuriant velvet. Protected and honored. She blinked, perplexed, leaning closer to the display. Then, eyes narrowed, she leaned back and tilted her head, bewildered. Each piece bore identical, distinctive markings of possession—the *Odhroerir*, the Triple Horn of Odin.

Having been a fascinated student of mythology, Alex knew the three, interlocking drinking horns at first glance, as well as the symbol's meaning. According to Norse mythology, the *Odhroerir* symbolized the magical mead brewed from the blood of the wise god Kvasir. The old Viking tales often varied, but traditionally it was said that on the god's quest, Odin used his wits and his magic to procure the coveted brew over the course of three days. The three horns reflected the three draughts of the magical mead.

The symbol of possession earmarking each piece in the case was, ironically, all too familiar to Alex. Her hand flew to the small of her back, and she frowned. Disconcerted, she moved away to drink in the eclectic artwork hanging on the walls. Again, to her surprise, good taste prevailed.

At length, she wandered to the bookshelves, marveling at the titles therein. Homer, Shakespeare, Poe. She took one down to examine it more closely. Her hands bobbled the aged leather bound tome. It was old. *Really old.* Appalled, she very gingerly replaced the book on the shelf and took a cautious, awed step back. As she turned away, she happened to glance at the papers strewn over the top of the desk. She didn't mean to snoop, she truly didn't, but she couldn't help notice her own name, time and time again. Careful not to disturb anything, she leaned over the desk and scanned the writing.

Sheet music—original copies of *her* sheet music—lay scattered over one end of the desk. A stack of newspapers covered the rest of the desk; each and every one folded back to reveal her articles. A clipping of an old magazine write up from when she'd first burst onto the music scene, a brilliant star on an upward climb, peeped at her from amid the loose score sheets.

She had to give the man points for doing his homework. The very idea that he'd expended such effort researching her past was flattering, and more than a little daunting.

Frowning, she moved away from the desk and wandered through the room until she stood in front of a long row of windows overlooking the manicured south lawns. Cocking her head to the side, she studied the windows with baffled interest. The glass didn't give off much, if any light. Peering directly at the pane of glass, she noted the window's heavy layers of tint.

Well, that was certainly...odd. She gave a slight shrug at Gunnarrson's eccentricities.

Well over half an hour passed, and she hadn't heard a peep from the now MIA Styx, or the elusive Mr. Gunnarrson. She'd quite obviously been stuffed somewhere and forgotten about. Irritation chewed at the susceptible spot between her brows. Nonetheless, that Steinway was calling to her, making her forget all about her irritation over a man who'd hounded her for two weeks, and then couldn't be bothered to come meet her.

Alex hadn't touched her fingertips to ivory in three long years. Would playing be like riding a bike...once you learned, you never forgot. Shooting a guilty glance at the closed door, Alex ran her fingers experimentally over the keys.

Rich notes flooded the room, the pitch perfect and true. She shivered with appreciation. Drawing a steadying breath, she slid onto the bench, shot another guilty peek at the door, and positioned her fingers over the keys, half expecting bells and alarms to go off the second her fingers connected with those precious ivories.

She spent a moment running scales, reacquainting herself with the instrument before she lost herself in the music. Alex closed her eyes and let the music flow. As always, the classics came first, Mozart and Rachmaninoff and Debussy, and her favorite—Bach. As the triumphant strains of *Fugue in G Minor* trailed away, she drew another breath, and her fingers stilled.

Then, hesitant notes poured forth. Notes *she'd* written filled her, flowing out through her fingertips. She found herself humming, words she'd penned in another lifetime. But the memories became too bitter, and the music fell away on a discordant note.

Only then did Alex become aware she was no longer alone. She whirled around, and her surprised gaze connected with the most compelling, sultry eyes she'd ever seen...eyes a startling, vivid shade of intense, furious blue. The face that went with those eyes was every bit as heart stopping.

Before she could utter a sound, the tall golden-haired stuff of erotic dreams stomped into the room, fury rolling from him in hot inescapable waves. His voice rang through the silence, compelling and dangerous.

"No one is allowed in here, and *no one* touches the piano."

Chapter 5

Alex gazed at him slack-jawed, totally at a loss. The man acted as if she'd been caught elbow deep in a safe or something. Her wide-eyed, involuntary stare skated downward, over his ripped frame, and she couldn't speak. Good Lord in heaven, he was gorgeous.

True, at present, he had a very strange, very concentrated look on his face, as if he were stripping away layers of her conscience, peering at her soul, but every ounce of him made her mouth water with greedy, astonishing hunger. His long, tawny hair stuck out in wild disarray beneath a frayed and stained baseball cap. He wore a snug, oil-splattered muscle shirt that outlined sculpted muscles all the way down the length of his long, lean torso. His arms shifted, muscles bunched as he planted fists to hips, proudly displaying an impressive, intricate tribal tattoo that covered his right shoulder and stretched to his elbow.

Smears of motor oil stained ragged, faded jeans...jeans that hung enticingly low on his narrow waist. A pair of wrenches stuck out of his front pocket beside a greasy rag. The line of his strong jaw was bristled in golden stubble, and it, too, sported dark smudges. Alex's heart stuttered and tripped inside her chest. She'd seen many, *many* attractive men in her life, but she'd never come across one who had the power to make her absolutely speechless just by *being*.

A fleeting image of this man brazenly wielding a lethal sword, boldly riding the raging waves of a frigid sea on the decks of a Viking long ship came to mind. Something stark and savage lurked in his eyes...something that warranted extreme caution. The inexplicable sensation to run away washed through her again, stronger this time, even as her pulses hammered with excitement. From somewhere deep inside, she dredged up the resolve to stay put. After a moment, the man stopped staring at her with such unsettling intensity. He rocked back on his heels, tilting his head with a bemused frown.

Hating to be at a disadvantage in any situation, irritation shook her temper loose. Rising to her full five foot eight inches—with the help of her spiked heels, of course—Alex leveled a deceptively calm smile at him. She was sure the smile didn't quite reach her eyes.

"Tell me, just where exactly *should* I be?"

When she stood, his gaze fell to her scarlet blouse. Then lower to the gentle curve of feminine hips, and the bold slit in the material over her thigh. His eyes paused there on her skirt, then lowered to her toned calves and her racy shoes with unmistakable sexual interest. By the time his gaze lifted to hers again, she was the one fuming. He, on the other hand, now appeared...fascinated.

With a much more inviting smile, he tipped his head to the side and regarded her with blatant, animal hunger, a long dormant conqueror rising up and roaring with an undeniable challenge in those beautiful, glittering eyes.

"Well, now," he drawled, prowling forward. "I could think of a few places, like in my bed...for starters."

He towered over her, his grin hungry. Alex's eyes narrowed dangerously, and her hands fisted at her sides until she made a conscious effort to sheath her claws. Perturbed, she ignored the swarm of butterflies his provocative comment—and the warm glow in his eyes—had turned loose in her stomach.

The chilly disdain in her eyes dropped the temperature in the room to a near sub-arctic freeze, her tone covered six shades of pure ice. "I have a much better idea..."

His eyebrow lifted to a sexy angle, and he edged forward, as if in anticipation of her suggestion. Muttering beneath her breath, she opened her purse and turned away, drawing out a small notepad and a slim, gold pen. She took a moment to pen a brief, angry note to the absent Mr. Gunnarrson, before spinning on her heel to face his mechanic.

From the angle of his head, it wasn't difficult to guess what he'd been checking out. Even now, he had difficulty lifting his gaze from her cleavage. Stifling a snort of disgusted disapproval, Alex stepped forward, her hand extended to him, a folded square of paper tucked between her slim fingers.

"Do me a favor and give this to your boss. I'm sorry, but I'm afraid you're just gonna have to settle for one of the ah—the *ladies* out back. I've seen all I need to see, and I'm leaving."

Disappointment shadowed in his confused stare. Though she mumbled beneath her breath as she headed for the door, he couldn't have missed a word. "I should have *known* better than to come here in the first place. I sit in here for damned near an hour, *completely* ignored, and the only person in this entire *mausoleum* that finally gets around to worrying about me is the mechanic. The bloody *mechanic*. And *he* propositions me! What the *hell* was I thinking?"

****

Dumbfounded, Cole stared at the door of the study as it closed with a resounding thud. He'd never experienced such a swift, all-consuming kick of attraction—attraction hell, it was pure, unadulterated lust—for a female before, and it left

53

him off balance. *Way* off balance. The scent of her still lingered in the room, wrapping around his senses.

His knees had gone weak, his breathing hitched awkwardly in his chest. Odin's teeth, he was damned near drooling with need. He dragged a hand across the back of his neck, doing his level best to reassemble his scattered wits. For Loki's sake, drooling? Drooling! He wasn't some damned Werewolf, thank the gods.

It took him a full minute for her words to sink in, and a moment longer to remember the note in his hand. Whoever she was, she possessed the face of an angel, the body of a goddess, and one hell of a short fuse. His brow wrinkled. She hadn't even batted an eyelash when he'd hit her with the full force of his powers of suggestion. By Valhalla, who did she think she was?

With a growing sense of unease, Cole flipped the note open and scanned the missive. He dropped his head back on his shoulders. The string of Norse profanities that burst from his lips would have made a berserker blush.

Yanking the door to the study open, Cole glanced to both ends of the hallway. Tipping his head back, his nostrils flaring, he sucked in a deep draw of air, searching for her. It wasn't hard to find her. The scent of wild honey beckoned him. Following her scent trail down the hallway, he ignored the sound of music blaring from the back yard.

Moving with phenomenal speed, Cole swore beneath his breath as he skidded down first one hallway and then another, mentally kicking himself. How had she'd gotten so far ahead of him on those ice-pick heels? For the first time in he couldn't remember how long, he'd stopped thinking with his head and let another part of his anatomy take over his cognitive abilities—and he *wasn't* talking about his fangs. In the process, he'd gone and royally pissed off the one woman he'd meant to impress...or reassure, at the very least.

By Thor, how could he have mistaken her for some damned groupie?

In all fairness, he hadn't been expecting her for at least another hour or so, but still, he didn't have any excuse for what just happened. In the past, he'd *never* allowed his attraction for a female to rule him, body or mind, and now he was beginning to understand exactly why.

He caught up with her just as she jerked the front door open. Cole skidded to a halt, biting back a hiss as brutal sunlight poured in through the doorway, pooling on the cool marble a few short inches from the toes of his boots. She shot a scathing look over her shoulder and stepped blissfully where any sane Vampyre feared to tread. Straight into a sizzling, direct UV caress.

He'd screwed up, big time. He wouldn't get another chance with her. He had to fix this. What the hell was he supposed to say to her?

"Alexandra..." Gritting his teeth against the ferocious sting of sunlight on his sensitive Vampyre flesh, he rushed after her.

She paused again, just long enough to sniff down her nose at him and roll her eyes in unmistakable disbelief. Undeterred, she dug in her purse as she made her way down the steps. Navigating the gravel drive must prove tricky in heels like that, but she did an admirable job of maintaining her dignity as she darted for her vehicle.

The beauty snapped over her shoulder, "Get a clue, buddy, I'm not interested."

"Alexandra," Cole growled insistently, shielding his eyes with one hand as he reached out with the other to snag her elbow. Gods, what he wouldn't give right now to be able to control her thoughts. The first thing he'd do was to convince her to go back inside, out of this sizzling sunlight. His gaze slid down the tantalizing curves of her body. Then maybe he'd convince her that those clothes were too uncomfortable. That the only thing she should be wearing...was him.

She glowered at him, yanking her arm from his carefully restrained grip. "Just give your boss the note. Do yourself a favor and find someone else. In case you didn't hear me, the answer is no—not interested—not even tempted."

The interest in her eyes was plain to see. The temptation crackled between the two of them like a bolt of lightning shot straight from Thor's hand. Like hell, she wasn't tempted. Cole narrowly managed to bite back the angry retort, but it still echoed inside his head.

His fangs stretched, an occurrence that only happened in an extremely heightened emotional state, or when he fed. Fiercely battling his body's involuntary reaction to her, he drew a deep breath and held the transformation at bay by sheer dint of will. Chasing her scent down the hall sure as hell hadn't helped him keep the predator within leashed, either. Even now, her essence tormented him, made the darker side of his nature howl for a taste. Only the bite of the sun held him in check.

Taking a firm grip on her arm, Cole tugged her around to face him. Her eyes glittered like brilliant aquamarines trapping the sun, lit from within.

"Alexandra, please," he argued, doing his best to maintain a level, reassuring tone. "Just come back inside for one minute and let me—"

She gave her arm another furious yank again, cutting his words short. Only this time, rather than gaining her freedom, her footwear betrayed her. She slipped on the loose gravel, wrenching her ankle. Crystalline eyes went wide with pain, and she tumbled headlong into his arms.

Cole moved with lightning quick reflexes. His arms shot around her, instinctively dragging her against him, supporting the majority of her meager weight. She clutched at his shoulders to maintain any semblance of balance. She lifted her shocked gaze, her lips mere inches from his...no distance at all. Her breath snagged in her throat and her heart lurched in her chest, the sounds were sweet music to his ears.

"Let go of me," she whispered, swallowing hard.

He ignored her soft entreaty, did his best to ignore the tight press of her body against his. By Thor, she fit so well...as if she'd been designed specifically for him. For him and him alone.

"Are you all right? Did you hurt yourself?"

"I'm fine," she claimed. She was a poor liar.

Cole forced the breath in and out of his lungs and told his arms to let go of her. Unfortunately, his arms—along with every other part of his anatomy—had taken on a mind of its own today.

Just then, a thick cloud covered the sun, giving his flaming skin a much-needed break. At this point, his control could ill afford the reprieve. The scent of her perfume writhed around his brain, effectively paralyzing his ability to control his thoughts. The feel of her lithe curves, pressing every intimate detail against his body, started a chain reaction his system couldn't seem to handle. One he had little to no hope of stopping. The blood in his brain rushed to his loins making coherent speech next thing to impossible. His fangs throbbed.

His mesmerizing gaze fell to her lips. He *needed* to taste her. Her delectable lips first, and then her sweet, tempting vein. Just one tiny, little taste... One small, harmless sip... The kiss she would remember, the sip she would not.

Bare seconds before their lips connected, she shifted in his arms, unwittingly placing her weight on her injured ankle. Gasping, she sagged against him. The spell they'd both fallen headlong into shattered.

Cole pulled back, blinking. His hands tightened on her in concern. "You *are* hurt!"

The sun broke through the cloud-cover, and Cole sucked in a sharp breath, squinting against the brutal rays. With an impatient oath, without permission, he swept her off her feet, cradling her high against his chest and carried her back inside the house.

"What are you doing?" Alex demanded, breathless, thumping his chest with a small fist. Her voice rose, strengthened, her eyes widened incredulously. "You're going the wrong way, my car is over there. Put me down."

Though she squirmed in his arms like a she-cat, pummeling at his chest with a fury, he didn't flinch. He pushed the door open, then stalked back down the blessedly cool hallways he'd just raced through moments before.

"Damn it...put me down..." Her voice trailed off, then exploded with alarming vengeance. "Good God, who the hell do you think you are?"

Without breaking stride, Cole tipped his face to hers and offered her a charming, if misplaced grin that barely concealed the lethal tips of his fangs. "Allow me to introduce myself, Ms. Sinclair." She stilled in his arms, obviously waiting for the other shoe to fall. It dropped with a resounding thud. "I'm Cole Gunnarrson. It's a pleasure to meet you."

The fight went right out of her.

"Oh, hell..." She gaped at him in astonishment, and fell silent. So much for her cool composure.

Amused but wise enough not to let it show, Cole

tucked away his wry smirk as he carried her back inside his den and kicked the door closed behind him. He lowered her to the sofa, and then strode over to the desk, bending down to remove two cans of Danny's beer from the mini bar. He hurried back to her side, dropping onto the coffee table directly in front of her.

Cole set the cans on the table beside him and turned his attention to her ankle. With infinite care, he skimmed his fingers down the silky skin of her calf, lifting it as he went, until he held her foot cradled in his lap. She was helpless but to stare. When he loosened the ankle strap on her shoe and slipped it from her foot, she finally reacted.

She blinked at him, pushing in vain at his hands. "Please, don't do that, just let me—"

"Can you move it?" His fingers trailed over her delicate skin, his eyes probing for any abnormal swelling. *Damn, she has nice ankles. And trim calves. And sexy knees. And a gorgeous...*

By the gods, he was starting to sound like the proverbial big bad wolf. Zack would be *so* proud. Cole stifled a snort of self-disgust.

She flexed her foot, shifting her ankle this way and that, testing her range of motion. "I think it's just a mild sprain. You can let me go now. I should go—"

Her words ended on a sharp hiss as Cole laid the icy cold cans against the sides of her ankle. She gritted her teeth, but she wasn't able to stand it for more than a moment or two, however, and made no bones about telling him so.

"The cans are too hard, that hurts worse than the sprain. I'll be fine, I swear," she insisted. "Just let me..."

The cans weren't the only thing that was too hard. He'd be willing to bet that right now his pain was just as sharp as hers was. He cut her off with a mere look. Removing the cans from her ankle, he popped the top on one, and thrust the can into her hands before she could protest.

"Here," he offered with a supercilious smile. "You look like you could use it."

He set the other can down and shifted her foot to the table beside the unopened beer. "Sit tight."

He went back to the mini bar and pulled a small tray of ice from the machine. Cole glanced about the room for a moment, searching for something to pour the ice in. Giving a slight shrug, he grasped the hem of his shirt and whipped it over his head. Her sharply indrawn breath pricked his ears, snaring his attention. From beneath lowered lashes, he considered her with no small amount of male satisfaction. Her eyes, locked on his body, rounded owlishly, and her mouth had fallen open. The sound of her breath shuddering in and out, and the stuttering of her heartbeat, kicked his already raging desire back into high gear.

Not interested, my ass, he could have crowed aloud.

Grinning like a cock in the henhouse, he laid his shirt flat on the desk and twisted the ice tray above it, pouring the ice into a neat little pile. Tossing the tray aside, he gathered the edges of his shirt up, forming a small pouch.

Cole ran his tongue over his teeth and, once assured his fangs had receded...for the most part, at least...he turned a wide grin in her direction. His reward was the sharp snap of her teeth and a fierce scowl. The challenge was irresistible. Working relationship or not, Mortal or not, he'd developed a craving...for her. One, it seemed, that was determined to grow ravenously until it was fed.

This time, rather than sitting on the table, he dropped to the sofa at her side. Cole took her by surprise when he scooped both her legs up and drew them across his lap, leaving her no choice but to turn sideways on the sofa to face him—or risk her skirt riding farther up her thighs. His wicked grin hinted that might have been his plan all along.

Leaning close, deliberately crowding her, Cole stuffed a throw pillow behind her back and nudged her back to relax against it. He held the makeshift ice pack on her injured ankle while his free hand ran over the top of her uninjured foot. His deft fingers released the strap and removed that shoe as well.

Protest bubbled in her eyes, but she remained silent, easing back against the cushion, eyeing him with wary resignation. Everything about him screamed dangerous predator, and yet she wasn't afraid of him. Wary, yes...but not afraid. He marveled at that.

Long, callused fingertips feathered over her legs, lowered to massage her injured ankle gently. A shiver ran through her veins, one he'd have felt even if he hadn't been Vampyre. How would those sexy legs feel wrapped around him while he buried himself deep inside of her?

Chagrined at his own wayward lack of mental control, he forced himself to look away from her legs. However, the alternative didn't seem to be any safer to his equilibrium. Her trim waist and delicious breasts called him to look...and touch...and taste.

Cole dragged his gaze upward, until his eyes locked on her face. But even her face held inherent perils. Sensuous lips, mesmerizing eyes, and an enticing splash of color filled her cheeks. The warm surge of blood pulsing beneath her satiny skin made his fangs throb again. Tousled hair invited his fingers to tangle.

The hand tucking a stray wisp of hair behind her ear was every bit as unsteady as her breathing. "So, what now?"

"Now..." His long, long fingers eased up the

length of her leg, languid and full of purpose, from ankle to calf to knee. And higher. His voice dipped, low and seductive, as the very tips of his fingers edged beneath the hem of her skirt. "I have you completely at my mercy..."

Chapter 6

His hands were nothing short of divine on her skin. His smoldering stare was strangely compelling. Swallowing convulsively, Alex trembled. Her eyes went wide, incredulous, at his suggestive innuendo. Laughter, deep as the night and rich as velvet rumbled up in Cole's chest. Before she could scramble away, Cole tightened his grip, pulling her more securely onto his lap. He leveled amused eyes on her then.

"Now you *have* to talk to me." His grinned turned wolfish. IIis hand caressed its way down her leg, allowing her a much needed breath. It didn't take long for that hand to make its way back to her knee, or for her lungs to freeze again. "That is, unless you have something else in mind?"

As Cole's fingers began toying with the hem of her skirt once more, Alex's lungs screamed for air. She was an attractive, financially secure, modern woman who knew her own worth. She'd fended off far worse than the brazen, single-minded purpose of the man beside her. But the way he kept shooting those intense, concentrated stares her way, sent shiver after shiver down her spine. *Never* had she been so tempted in all her life.

Not even Griffin had been able to...

Griffin!

The enchanted haze evaporated in the blink of an eye. She seized his wrist and pushed it away with an icy hand. "Let's talk."

Disappointment flickered in his hypnotic eyes, but he gave a slight shrug, settling his hands on her calf with a defiant grin.

"Hey, Slim..." Styx voice broke over them as he pushed the door open and strolled inside. "I looked all over, but I can't..."

His voice trailed off when his gaze landed on the couple nestled with such intimate familiarity on the sofa. His grin widened, a devilish glint darkened his golden eyes as he thrust his hands deep in his back pockets and cocked an eyebrow. "I rest my case."

Her companion shot the drummer an irritated glance. "What are you yammering about?"

Styx pointedly eyed Cole's hands where they rested on Alex's legs—legs draped across Cole's lap—and he grinned, smug. "I told her you always get the best ones."

Sputtering, Alex struggled to sit upright. Cole took hold of her shoulder, gentle but firm, and pushed her back against the cushions, his other hand clamped on her knee allowing her no escape.

She shot Cole a frustrated glare, before turning alarmed eyes to Styx. "This isn't—"

"A good time," Cole broke in with smooth finesse. "Come back later...much later. And close the door behind you."

"Styx!" Alex pleaded, her voice laced with equal parts exasperation and desperation. But it was too late, he'd had already deserted her, ducking out with a sly wink, closing the door behind him. Abandoning her to her fate.

Alex turned an indignant glare to Cole. "Why did you do that? Now he's going to think..." She couldn't even finish her statement. Embarrassed heat burned her cheeks.

Cole shrugged. "Styx knows when to keep his mouth shut."

"There's nothing to keep his mouth shut about," she protested.

The look he gave her declared otherwise, and he

argued, "Then why are you getting so upset?"

Alex scowled, subsiding back against the cushion with a harrumph. What was wrong with her? She was stronger than this. She did *not* want to crawl across this couch and taste those tempting lips. She was cool and professional. Detached. Aloof. Unfortunately, it was next thing to impossible to remain any of the aforementioned when such a blatantly sexual male caressed her bare legs with such masterful, enticing strokes.

Her resolve softened with each gentle caress. He must have been able to read the vacillation in her eyes, because his hands moved with more purpose now. His fingers feathered over her skin. One taunting corner of his sensual lips curved up. He brushed the arch of her foot, and her leg jerked. An intrigued brow lifted and icy blue eyes narrowed on her, speculative and assessing. Without any further warning, he repeated the motion. A giggle slipped free before she could stop it.

A sinful grin lit his face and he accused, "You're ticklish."

"I am not," she denied.

He arched a brow and skimmed his fingers over her arch again. She gasped and jerked once more.

"Okay, maybe a little," she conceded with ill grace.

Cole assessed her with shrewd eyes and then, without warning, his fingertips skimmed the inner curve of her knee. Alex's eyes flared. She gasped and squirmed, wiggling farther onto his lap without meaning to. Her hand grasped his wrist, but when he refused to let her draw his hand away, she frantically pressed his palm against her thigh, just above the inside of her knee.

Granting him a grudging, reluctant smile, she pleaded, "Stop!"

She needn't have spoken. The minute she

pressed his hand flat against her inner thigh, he froze. His eyes were riveted to the place where their hands rested—right at the edge of the widened slit in her skirt. His smoldering gaze lifted to her eyes, half veiled by the thick sweep of his dark lashes, pinning her to the spot with heat and intent. A delicious little chill slipped through her, sparking a shockwave of violent fluttering deep in the pit of her stomach.

Drawing a ragged breath, Alex tore her eyes away from his. The piano loomed before her, a cold reminder of her purpose here. Though her movements were sluggish and reluctant, she released his hand. Cole's palm remained firm on her thigh. His thumb began tracing lazy circles on her sensitive skin, and the swarm of butterflies inside her stomach took flight once more. Dropping her gaze to his hand, she cleared her throat. The sound came out more as a nervous gesture, rather than the firm rebuke she'd meant it to be.

Doing her best to ignore his provocative touch, she cleared her throat again, reminding him, "I thought you wanted to *talk*."

****

Cole was utterly lost. Warm wild honey tickled his nose. Her skin was exquisite beneath his fingers, pure ambrosia. Try as he might he just couldn't stop touching her. Her skin, baby soft and quivering beneath his fingertips, had become an addiction on which he was suddenly and irrationally eager to over-dose. The myriad expressions flickering across her face captivated him, the unease and the temper, the laughter and the desire, made him want to push to see what else he could wring from her.

Her hair tumbled around her shoulders, wanton and wild, driving him crazy. Her blouse—the way the blood-red silk molded to her curves—was nearly his undoing. She had the look of a woman who'd just been well and thoroughly loved...a woman who needed more loving still. Innocent. Erotic. Those delectable lips of hers were moving, but the lust pounding through his veins overpowered the sound.

He blinked, forcing words around a mouthful of painfully extended fangs. "What?"

"I said, I thought you wanted to talk."

"Talk..." he echoed blankly, fighting to regain a slippery grip on his control. Talking was the farthest thing from his mind, but he relented. "Yeah, we need to talk."

"I'm listening." She leaned back and folded her arms across her chest.

Well, he hadn't expected her to go easy on him. "First of all, I owe you an apology."

Surprise flared in her eyes, but she offered nothing more than a slight inclination of her head, the only acknowledgement for words that never came easy for a man like him.

He gritted his teeth and forged on. "I'm sorry for assuming you were... I didn't realize who you were, or I would never have... That is to say, I don't generally..."

Finish a sentence, you sound like a bloody idiot! He ground his teeth, irritated at this sudden inability to express himself. Cole opened his mouth to try again, but nothing came out. The beguiling smile spreading across her delicious lips went straight to his head.

She laid a gentle hand on his forearm, burning him to the bone. "I'm sorry for assuming you were the mechanic."

Glancing down at his stained clothes, he returned her grin, careful to keep his fangs concealed. "I could see how you might make that assumption."

"I'm sorry I touched your piano," she offered, her tone sheepish.

"No, that apology should be mine," he corrected. He caught her confused frown and explained, "I thought you were one of *them*, and *they* aren't allowed in this room for any reason." Then he found himself offering an invitation he'd never extended to anyone. "You're welcome to come here whenever you want, and you can use the piano anytime."

She frowned, confusion etched in her eyes. "Why aren't *they* allowed here?"

"This is the only place I can get any peace and quiet. Well, here and the garage..." The corner of his mouth curled ruefully as he shot his stained jeans a meaningful glance.

Obviously anxious to steer the discussion back to safer, more impersonal waters, she demanded, "Tell me what you have in mind."

His mind betrayed him, filling with so many erotic, sensual images that he shifted uncomfortably in his seat. However, the efficient, coldly professional frown on her face forced him to redirect his rebellious thoughts.

"You're still willing to give us the three weeks?" He cringed at his own question, kicking himself for giving her the opening to walk out the door again.

Her response was terse, her eyes reluctant but resolved. "I gave my word, Mr. Gunnarrson. You have three weeks."

"Cole," he corrected automatically. Relief swelled in his chest. He hadn't been eager to discuss the angry note of resignation she'd thrust at him before storming from the house, determined she wouldn't slip away so easily. "We obviously don't keep normal business hours," he began, focusing his gaze across the room, fighting to cool his blood. "That's going to make it difficult if we have to wait for you to drive up every time we get an unscheduled urge to work."

His gaze slid to hers to gauge her reaction. "I'd

like you to stay at the estate for the duration."

Impassive, Alex stared at him for a moment. "What if I have other obligations?"

His hands stilled on her legs, and a flash of alarm speared his chest. An unfamiliar, vicious, green-eyed monster had him by the throat, and he couldn't shake free. The unexpected stab of irrational jealousy blindsided him.

"I didn't think... I mean you're not... Are you involved..."

He'd kill the son of a bitch. Tear him limb from bloody limb and bathe in his entrails.

Preoccupied, she replied, "No, I have the next three weeks off from the paper, but my replacement will have to check in once in a while."

That didn't quite answer his question. "Is there someone waiting at home for you?"

Odin's teeth, please say no, woman, please...

Alex's wary gaze shot to his, and she stared hard at him for a long, long moment. "No, there isn't," she replied, succinct. Then in a calmer tone, she changed the subject. "If I'm going to stay here I have a few requirements."

A heavy weight eased from his chest. Up until that point, it hadn't even occurred to him she might be involved with someone. The knowledge she was available hit him like a potent aphrodisiac, and once again, he had to work to focus on her words.

"I need privacy," she warned, unwilling to bend on that issue. "I won't expect you to curb your lifestyle, but I will need someplace that I won't be constantly barraged by all those women." She thumbed toward the back of the house and grimaced in distaste.

"You're guaranteed privacy in this room—except from me, of course." His smile fairly glowed with iniquitous thoughts. "I'll set you up with the quietest room I can find."

"I have my cell, but I'll need an internet connection and a place to park my car," she haggled.

"Done," he agreed without batting an eye.

"I understand the creative muse. For the duration, you can consider me on call, day or night. However, I require one full day a week to myself."

Fighting to squelch the arousing thought of her within easy reach, Cole's jaw clenched, and he fought to keep a lid on the lust boiling through his veins. His voice was gruff, oddly strangled. "Deal. If there is anything else that you need, just let me know. I'll make sure you're taken care of."

Somehow, though he hadn't meant to make the words sound so suggestive—and he chided himself for tossing his rule of not letting a Mortal affect him right out the window—he didn't regret the provocative, sexual note in his voice. As if to punctuate his remark, he sent a transparent, seductive smile her way and caressed her silken thigh once more.

"None of that," she warned, poking him in the chest with her manicured finger.

He flared his eyes in a poor imitation of innocence. "What?"

"You know exactly what I'm talking about. This is a working relationship," she warned. "If you can't keep that in mind then..."

"No, no." He massaged the abused spot on his chest. "Point taken...literally. I'll behave myself, if I have to." He shot her a heated sidelong look, adding, "So long as I'm not provoked."

Alex shook her head at him, visibly torn between the urge to laugh and the need to scold. Rolling her eyes, she pushed herself upright, and made to swing her legs off his lap.

Loathing the mere thought of relinquishing skin that made his fingers tingle with need, his hands held her in place. "Where do you think you're going?"

"I have to go home." She nudged his hands off her legs. "If I'm going to stay here, I need to pack a few things."

He reluctantly released her, and an unsettling sense of loss overwhelmed him. As he pulled her to her feet, his hands found their way to her slender waist and lingered, cautiously supporting her weight. "Can you put any weight on your ankle?"

Alex's small hands gripped his biceps as she tested her injury. She chewed on her lower lip and stared straight ahead, her nose inches from the middle of his naked chest, as she transferred the majority of her weight to that foot. Her breath tickled his skin. She must have found the pain manageable. Not that he wanted her hurting...but dependant was appealing.

Tipping her head back, she smiled up at him with radiant relief. "You definitely earned your Boy Scout badge for First Aid, Cole."

There was nothing *Boy Scout* about the thoughts racing circles in his mind. As if able to read his intentions clear in his eyes, she cleared her throat, and stepped back. His hands fell to his sides, flexing and empty. She reached for her purse, and Cole gathered her shoes, hooking his fingers through the thin straps.

"Where's your cell phone?"

She stopped and dug in her purse. A moment later, she drew the slim device out and handed it to Cole with a curious look. He flipped it open and began thumbing in a sequence of numbers.

"I'm giving you my personal number." He flipped it closed and handed it back before pulling his own phone out of his back pocket, depressing keys as she gave him hers. "Call me as soon as you leave the city. I'll be here this time to meet you when you get back."

She smiled, nodded her agreement, and he led

her to the front door like an invalid.

Cole opened the door with care, then let out a slow, thankful breath. The sun had dipped below the tree line, and, although heat still rolled off the land in dizzy waves, for the time being, he didn't need to worry about frying. They reached the front step, and Alex glanced down at her bare toes, frowned at the gravel.

She groaned aloud. "You better give me my shoes back."

Incredulous, Cole stared at her, waving the spike-heeled shoes just out of her reach. "You can't put these things back on. You'll break your neck."

"I don't have a choice," she replied, making an impatient, useless grab at her shoes. "I have to get to my car."

Before she could blink, he swept her off her feet once more, cradling her effortlessly in his strong arms. She gasped, wrapping her arms around his neck. The thin barrier of silk between her soft flesh and his naked chest teased him. Ropes of steel flexed and bunched beneath golden, smooth skin as he shifted her in his arms. She gripped him tighter, and he grinned shamelessly at her, enjoying her hands on him.

"Is this one of your little quirks? Do you make a habit of sweeping women off their feet and carrying them around?" Alex eyed him, a suspicious, dark scowl crinkling her brow.

Her question gave him pause. He tilted his head to the side and stared at her for a moment, giving her question serious consideration. "Actually, I've found just tossing them over my shoulder much more effective. In fact, I don't remember the last time I did it this way."

"Oh," she murmured, dropping her gaze to the steady thump of his pulse at the base of his throat.

"Which one's yours?"

"Huh?"

His lips curled in conceited satisfaction. His brow arched. "Which one is your car?"

"The red one with racing stripes," she mumbled. Color climbed up her neck and blossomed in her cheeks.

Cole glanced over at the drive, and his gaze shot back to hers, widening with interest. His footsteps faltered. "The Shelby?"

Alex nodded, and Cole grinned, feeling like a child on Christmas morning. He covered the distance to her car in a few, long legged strides. After settling her behind the wheel, he popped the carbon composite hood featuring the classic Shelby KR design open before she could do little more than gasp in surprise.

In a blink, Cole's head ducked beneath the hood, scanning the motor in abject fascination. A 5.4-liter supercharged V-8 producing an estimated 540-horsepower and 510 ft.-lbs. of torque gleamed back at him. The racing power upgrade package featuring a revised calibration and cold air intake system nearly sent him into fits of excitement. Cars fascinated him, and this one, like its owner, was a beauty. Long minutes—and several pints of drool—later, he dropped the hood with a low whistle of admiration. Stepping around the side of the car, Cole leaned close and braced his forearms on the door.

"You know, I should probably drive you into town," he suggested, admiring the six-speed manual transmission. "I'd hate to see you injure your ankle any worse, and all that shifting..."

Shaking her head with a patronizing smile, she inserted the key in the ignition, and the engine roared to life. Patting his arm, she crooned, "You're concern is touching, but I'll be just fine."

Heaving a disappointed sigh, he straightened and stepped back. "I'll be expecting you back tonight.

Don't forget to call."

He stepped back, whistling again as Alex eased the muscle car down the long drive. Miss Sinclair was proving to be one fascinating surprise after another. How in the name of Valhalla he was going to sleep with her under the same roof—and not sleep *with* her. Then again, maybe the question should be, *after* he slept with her, would he be able to remain emotionally removed. Her shoes dangled from his fingers as he trekked back inside the house and down one long hallway after another, floating on her lingering scent every step of the way.

Chapter 7

Alex arrived at home to find a stack of mail waiting for her. After flipping through it and finding nothing of importance, she got down to the business of packing. She phoned Cole on the drive back to his estate and security had opened the gate the moment her car approached without even stopping her for a crackled hello.

Cole greeted her at the front door this time around. He'd showered and changed into a clean, black tee and sexy, black leather pants, though he'd kept the sturdy combat boots. His hair was still wet and hung in long strands the color of raw honey past his broad shoulders and down his back. Once again, the impression of a conquering Viking warrior, brazen and fearless, came to mind. He was, beyond the shadow of a doubt, a serious threat to a girl's moral resolve. He looked good enough to nibble on—nibble until she'd glutted herself—but she'd forced her eyes away and reminded herself that nibbling was not on the agenda. *He* was not on the menu, regardless of how scrumptious he looked—and smelled.

He'd given her a brief tour of his home. As Rita would concisely put it...Holy Mother of God! Then he'd shown her to her rooms where he left her to settle in alone. A silver tray piled with fresh fruit, hors d'oeuvres, and an icy pitcher of sweet tea rested on the coffee table. The thoughtful gesture eased the knot of tension balling between her shoulders. A few hours later, Alex scowled at the flashing cursor on the glowing screen for a moment, rubbing her temples over the number of emails waiting in her inbox. Shaking her head in a rare fit of irresponsibility, she ignored her inbox altogether and fired off a brief memo to Rita before she closed her laptop. She yawned and stretched, flexing her stiff ankle, and stood to wander around her room.

True to his word, Cole had indeed found her a quiet room, tucked away in a little used wing of the museum he called home. Room, hah, she thought with a delighted giggle. It was more like a suite. Very large. *Very* luxuriant. She had her own comfortable living room and her own private bath. Her bed was big enough to lose the entire defensive line for the Denver Broncos in, and her Italian-marble, gilt-handled shower had not one, not two, but three—count them—three shower heads. And if that weren't bliss enough, the bathtub was large enough to sink the Queen Mary in.

She'd rushed to unpack, then headed straight for the bathroom, torn between the pull of the tub and the tug of the shower. She'd ended up spending close to half an hour letting the showerheads pulse and pound the lingering stress from her flesh. When she'd emerged at last, she'd never been more relaxed. There was no doubt about it, she'd died and gone straight to Heaven, courtesy of Cole Gunnarrson. Alex let out a delighted little sigh as she sank down onto the plush sofa in front of a large plasma TV. All in all, things had taken a much needed turn for the better.

Now that she thought about it, aside from the unsettling attraction that smacked her right between the eyes every time Cole was around, this could be a positive experience. A working vacation of sorts. It didn't appear that Cole would demand too much of her time, which would allow her the opportunity to relax, something she hadn't allowed herself to do in a long, long time. And the pool out back was positively screaming her name...provided she could find a moment when she wouldn't have to vie for swim space with a bunch of Malibu Barbie wannabes.

Snuggling beneath a chenille throw, she shot a guilty glance at her laptop, and settled back, flipping on the TV. It wasn't long before her eyes grew heavy and sleep tugged her into a dreamscape of warrior Vikings with sexy smiles, tempting tattoos, and sultry, glowing eyes.

A knock on the door startled Alex awake. Snow filled the TV screen. She reached over and clicked the remote off. Yawning, blinking, she sat up and shoved her hair back out of her face, scrubbed her hand over her eyes, and pushed herself to her feet. Her head groggy, Alex glanced at the clock as she stumbled past the desk. Two a.m. barely registered as she staggered to the door.

****

Cole stood in the hall outside her door, staring at her in slack-jawed shock. He'd been expecting the cool, sophisticated woman in the sexy, scarlet blouse and the flirtatious skirt. He'd been expecting the gorgeous businesswoman who did her level best to keep him at arm's length. He sure as hell had *not* expected to be thoroughly seduced at the first glimpse of this stunning, enthralling creature before him.

Alexandra Sinclair blinked sleepily up at him from her doorway, unadorned by makeup and jewelry, wearing nothing more than a well-worn, abbreviated tank top and a thin pair of men's boxers. Her hair trailed down her back and over her shoulders in wild, damp tangles. Her nipples, puckered from the cool evening air against her damp shirt, pushed at the soft material, giving him the very solid realization that not only did she have nothing on beneath the skimpy shirt, but that she also had very, *very* nice breasts.

She was perfect, right down to her perfect pedicure, and he was certain—beyond the shadow of a doubt—that he'd never wanted a woman more than he wanted Alexandra Sinclair.

And, most likely, never would again.

That realization should have sent him reeling in the opposite direction. A warning flashed somewhere in the back of his mind, vibrant as a neon sign. Warning! *Mortal female*! Danger!

It didn't seem to matter.

Maybe it had been too long since he'd taken a woman to his bed. Maybe it was the way she looked right now—had looked earlier—two very different sides to the same coin. Maybe it was the simple fact that she was here, not to ride on his celebrity, but because she was immensely talented in her own right and could contribute to what he'd built for himself. Whatever it was, he was just too far gone to care.

He'd come to her room to deliver the iPod and to ask if there was anything else she needed. The time hadn't occurred to him, at least not until she opened the door looking as though she'd just tumbled out of bed, drowsy and sexy as hell. If he were honest, maybe he'd come to do a little more flirting, a little more seducing. He was as hot-blooded as the next male, after all. Only the tables had been turned on him, with resounding success. He, who in his long, long life had knelt before no one, was seriously contemplating dropping to his knees before this female and begging her for just one taste.

Yet somehow, instinctively, he knew...one taste of her would never be enough.

Alex's eyelids were heavy with sleep as she blinked up at Cole. It took her a moment to focus, but once she did, Alex offered him a serene smile that went straight to his head...and his loins. "Do you need me already?"

Cole's throat closed. His mouth went dry as a tinderbox, odd considering it had been salivating from the second she'd opened the door.

She offered him a sleepy smile and drew back into the room, leaving the door wide open for him to follow. "I didn't realize you'd want to start tonight."

Cole stepped into the room. His gaze darted to her bedroom door, then settled on the sofa with careful consideration. It *was* closer after all.

Closing the door behind him with a soft click, he stalked her across the room, the iPod dangled in his fingers, forgotten. The scent of her was everywhere, undeniable and intoxicating, and the closer he got to her, the stronger it became. He paused less than a foot behind her, drawing her scent in...deep. Shampoo, soap, and female. Yet that particular essence that was purely Alex was there too. Undeniable and all too alluring. Like a fresh breeze rolling in off the ocean, with the subtle hint of wild honey. Irresistible.

His pulses quickened, his fangs stretched, his pupils dilated. Hunger swelled in him, ravenous and insatiable. The hell with the sofa...right now, the floor looked damned good. Then he eyed the table she leaned across. His eyebrow lifted in speculation. It, too, had definite potential.

Alex stretched for a stray piece of sheet music, her back to him, and began shuffling papers together. A dark shadow at the base of her spine drew Cole's eyes. Every time she stretched forward, he got a delicious peek between her boxers and the hem of her tank top. The edge of his lips edged upward. Prim Miss Sinclair had herself a tattoo. She stretched again, a little farther, and he frowned. Those very distinctive upper lines of the symbol were suspiciously familiar.

His fingers itched to slip into the waistband of

her boxers and tug them down to reveal the rest of her tat and confirm his suspicions. But then his mind wandered away from him. If he slid his hands beneath her tank, would the rest of her skin be as soft as her legs. If he could just slip her clothing aside, would she let him sink into her... Hell, who was he kidding, he mocked himself. He wanted to tear them clean off and bury himself deep inside her.

"Let me just grab this stuff and my laptop," she called over her shoulder. "I started messing with a few lines earlier in the shower, and I think I might be on to something, provided the lyrics fit the mood you're looking for."

Vivid images of Alex, wet and soapy, water cascading down over her lithe body, slithered through his mind, tormenting him. "Are we going straight to the studio? If you give me just a moment, I'll change clothes."

Her assumption hit him like a bucket of ice water in the face, a harsh reminder that she was there with one purpose in mind. Work.

"No," Cole croaked as she turned to face him with a curious frown. He gritted his teeth and cleared his throat, trying one more time. "I didn't come here to take you to the studio."

"Oh? I just assumed..."

He was sure his eyes must be glowing in the darkened room, paler than she knew them to be, his pupils overly large and unnaturally elongated. She paused, blinking up at him, then glanced suspiciously at the moonlight pouring into her window before she turned back to him. But he'd turned away by then, giving her his back. The feather soft touch of her fingers brushing his back sent a violent wave of need rolling through him. He sucked in a sharp breath and took several steps away to put a little distance between them. He held the iPod up as he turned back to face her.

His voice was deeper, edgy and gruff. "I thought you'd want to hear what you'll be working with."

"Oh..." She stepped closer to him and took the iPod from his hand, her eyes averted, as she worried her lower lip. Their fingers brushed, and a tremor passed between them. Stepping back, she murmured, "That was very thoughtful. Thank you, Cole."

He nodded, liking the way his name rolled off her lips a little too much. He remained silent, however, and her curious gaze lifted to his. His face felt tense, muscles strained, and his throat burned. Disappointment cut him off at the knees.

"Cole?" She tilted her head. A slight frown wrinkled her brow.

He opened his mouth, only to snap it shut again. He let out a low, frustrated growl that reverberated through the room. Shaking his head, as one would after taking a vicious right hook to the jaw, Cole pivoted on his heel and stalked from the room, leaving behind a trail of whispered, furious expletives.

****

He sat back on his heel, braced his forearm on his knee, and lowered the camera. His steady gaze followed the petite redhead as she entered the apartment building across the street. The metal door closed behind her with a heavy thud, blocking her from his view. The sound echoed in the night, teasing a small grin from his lips. Humans were so predictable. They ate at the same restaurants, followed the same routes to and from work, kept the same hours. And they all thought hiding behind metal doors, and deadbolts, and programmed security systems would keep them safe from the things that went bump in the night.

Monsters like him.

Silly sheep.

Running his tongue over his fangs, he lifted the camera again, aiming the extended lens at the second floor, third window on the left. And he waited.

Three, two, one... The light blinked on, then the next one over. Any moment now, she'd pick the watering can up to give the thirsty plants on her windowsills a drink.

Plants watered. Check. Cue the music. Michael Buble poured from her open windows. Apparently, she was feeling a bit mellow tonight. Human females were laughable. A well placed compliment here, a small token of affection there, and they were putty in your hands.

Stowing the camera, he eased back into the shadows. He'd have to stop off and develop the pictures on his way back tonight. The memory stick was full now, thanks to Cole's little blonde acquisition. She was a tiny morsel all right, hardly more than an hors d'oeuvres. But, in his experience, the little ones were often the sweetest. Ms. Sinclair was an interesting development. One he'd be following with close interest.

Chapter 8

Late the next morning, Cole's mood was already ten degrees south of dangerous by the time he arrived at the studio, exhausted and late. He'd spent a long night tormented by visions of Alex in that sexy, abbreviated tank and boxers, with freshly washed, sleep-tousled hair and not an ounce of woman's war paint on her beautiful face. A pint of bland, chilled blood and an hour in an icy shower hadn't helped to put his lust to bed.

His agent had called in the wee hours of the morning, informing him there'd been a marked drop in sales. There'd also been some woman in Denver making accusations about several members of Stolen Innocence holding her captive in her basement and assaulting her—never mind the fact that at the time of the supposed crime the entire band had been on tour in Brisbane, an entire hemisphere away. Tommy had also reminded him they were long overdue to iron out the plans for their next tour, including going through the list of projected dates and cities.

Then security had phoned the main house reporting an attempted break in. It was the third in the last two weeks, and, once again, the intruder had managed to elude them. That call had been followed, nip and tuck, by one from the TFRA agent—a chillingly calm TFRA agent—informing him that the Rogue had mailed the agent a detailed stack of photos, boasting his handiwork and rubbing their collective noses in his continued freedom.

As if his day hadn't been bad enough, the cherry

on top was walking in to the studio to find Alex, the very female he'd spent a sleepless night obsessing over, sandwiched between Zack and Danny without enough air between them to breath. Styx occupied a chair in the corner, taking the scene in with a mischievous, self-indulgent grin, letting her flounder her way through.

The beast inside him roared to vicious, protective life, snapping at his control, snarling rabidly. *My female.* If looks could kill, the entire room would have dropped on the spot. Cole tensed, poised to attack. A deadly, savage growl ripped from his chest when Danny gave her cheek a brazen squeeze—and not the cheek on her face—but then he halted in his tracks as Alex beat him to the punch, literally. She responded to Danny's advances by planting a sharp elbow in his midsection, hard.

One would have thought—given the fact Danny had fallen back several steps holding his middle and gasping for air—that Zack would have taken the hint she didn't appreciate their attentions. He must have convinced himself he was a much better lover. That or he simply had a death wish, because as soon as the other man moved away, he swooped down to plant a kiss on her lips. Once more Cole tensed, fangs lengthened, claws curled. He could already feel Zack's blood dripping from his fangs.

Shocked silence filled the room when she brought the tall, fair-haired lothario to his knees in nothing remotely in the ballpark of sexual gratification.

Cole froze, biting back a howl of laughter. His little female had used not one, but two pressure points to bring Zack to his knees. It never occurred to him that he had no right to think of her in those terms—as *his* anything.

Her patience, her businesslike composure had abandoned her. Absolutely. Ferocious vengeance writhed in her eyes, dangerous enough to give a trio of Furies pause.

"If you don't mind," Cole drawled from the doorway, deceptively calm despite the riotous emotions swelling in his chest. "I'd appreciate it if you'd wait till *after* the session to give the guys their little lesson in polite manners." Then he caught sight of the snickering Styx. "On second thought, you want to take a couple pot shots at Styx first, by all means, be my guest."

With a snort of disgust, she released Zack and stepped back, glowering as he gained his feet and carefully backed away from her, an odd mixture of insulted pride and grudging respect shining in his bottle green eyes. She rounded on Danny and shot him a warning glare, just for good measure. Then she turned lethal eyes to Cole.

"Thank you so much for gracing us with your presence," she hissed icy sarcasm. "Perhaps now *you* can explain I'm not here for their entertainment."

Cole shot a dry glance at the disgruntled men, and the laughing Styx, and settled his eyes on her once more. Damn she looked hot. What was it about a woman with her temper on that made a male's mind turn to matters best left behind closed doors? Then, when he noticed the fire in her eyes aimed solely at him now, he cleared his throat and forced his attention back to the here and now.

He had to work to keep his lips from twitching. Judging from the way his band eyed her and hung back, hugging the walls, it was a safe bet none of them planned to get within arm's reach of her. Ever again. "I'd say, by the looks of 'em, they figured that out for themselves. Well, all of them except maybe Styx…"

Brushing them off in her fury, she advanced on Cole with driving purpose, mayhem dancing in her eyes. A manicured finger shot out and thumped him painfully in the chest. "I will *not* put up with being groped every time I walk in the damned room."

Her mask of cool professionalism had vanished. Hellfire couldn't have been hotter at that moment in time than she was...in more ways than one. How would she react if *he* wrapped his arms around her and attempted to kiss her senseless?

Before he could find out, she gouged at him again, warning flashed in her fierce glower. "Fix it, or I'm finished here!"

Alex sailed from the room, an offended, regal queen, leaving a stunned hush of unworthy peons in her wake. Cole stared after her, then turned burning eyes back to skewer the gawking men. Aiming an unholy flash of his icy blue glare at the laughing drummer, Cole bared gleaming fangs, and snarled. Styx's laughter choked off and his eyes widened as he sat straighter in his chair.

Cole stalked from the studio. He went to her room first, spent almost ten fruitless minutes cajoling and pleading with her door before he stopped to think. Tipping his head back, he drew a deep breath, realizing by the faded scent trail she wasn't on the other side. Raking a frustrated hand through his hair, cursing his band to Helheim, he stomped down the hall toward his study.

She'd better be there, because the only other place he could think to check was the garage. And if she'd gone there... Well, he wasn't all together certain he wouldn't drag her back, willing or not. He'd deal with the band later.

Wild honey beckoned him as soon as he rounded the corner, just past the Monet. Her scent enveloped him in a warm cloud of longing. Soaring music poured out of his study, drifting down the hallway on the tender, passionate strokes of a haunting melody—one he didn't recognize. It grew and grew. Anger began building in the notes, and the music hit a staggering crescendo. Then the notes fell away and the melody faltered, insecure and heavy with heart-breaking uncertainty.

Cole paused in the doorway of his study. The poignant notes tugged at him until his arms ached with the need to offer her solace and protection. He didn't move, didn't speak, staring at her with his heart on his sleeve.

Her head tilted back, her eyes closed, the arch of her neck a pale column in the shadowed room. Those notes flowing from her fingers through the piano had never seen paper. He was as sure of that as he was of the fact that strolling on the Santa Monica Pier at dawn would be detrimental to his health. This music was instinctual, pure, straight from the heart. She was composing it as she played. Floored, he took a step forward, drawn by the emotion swelling in the room.

The music died on an abrupt, discordant note, and Cole reached a hand toward her. The sudden loss of her music a stake in his heart. Painful. Lethal. She didn't look at him though. Instead, she sat with her fingers poised above the keys and her eyes closed, as if finishing the piece in her mind. Once she'd regained her composure, she swiveled on the bench and stared at him. Her hands folded serenely in her lap.

Cole stared back, lost. He couldn't read her, and it was killing him. What was she thinking? There was so much more to this woman than he'd ever imagined. Until he'd met her yesterday, she'd only been a talented Human female, albeit a sexy one, he hadn't been able to shake from the fringes of his mind. Then he'd seen her in her room last night, sleepy and wantonly tumbled, and he'd begun obsessing over her.

Truly obsessing.

Until last night, he hadn't known the meaning

of the word.

When he'd walked in the studio and seen her with Danny and Zack, jealous rage had burn through him, raw and unmistakable. Jealous rage—him! He'd never been jealous of a female in his entire existence. And a Human female—a *Mortal* female—by Odin, it was unthinkable. Jealous, possessive instincts of that magnitude in a Vampyre could only mean he'd found his...

No!

He ruthlessly shoved that thought away faster than a Leprechaun could hide his gold, cringing from the possibility as he would a prolonged shot of direct UV. That kind of thought was nothing short of emotional suicide. Taking a walk under the full moon with a pack of Werewolves would have been less painful. He didn't understand this primal pull between them, but that didn't mean he had to give in to it, that he wasn't able to control himself. It sure as hell didn't mean she was...

No! He had the hots for her. No big deal. He'd take her, drink her, and get her the hell out of his system. Simple enough. One shot and then it would be over.

But the music...

He wasn't aware she could play like *that*. Then again, a tiny little thing like her shouldn't have been capable of fending Danny off and bringing Zack to his knees either, but she'd proven herself on both accounts. True, Danny was only Human. But Zack was Werewolf, regardless of the fact he was self-admittedly more lover than fighter. Moreover, they were both damned near twice her size. Either one of them could have easily overpowered her in the blink of an eye. Yet she'd fended them both off without breaking a nail. He knew that for a fact. He rubbed at his chest with a rueful half-smile.

Her haunting melody hinted that the incident in

the studio was merely a reaction to something far more troublesome. It bothered him that she suffered.

Helheim, the fact that it bothered him that she suffered...bothered him.

"I'm sorry." The words tumbled out and, for the life of him, he wasn't sure where they'd come from. Since when did he apologize to anyone?

She remained silent. Detached. Empty. Her eyes followed him as Cole crossed the study and lowered himself to the sofa. "I got detained this morning. I should have been there to smooth the way for you."

She remained silent for long moments, and despite his inherent self-confidence, Cole wanted to squirm, something he hadn't wanted to do since...well, since he was Human. When she spoke at last, her voice was cool. Her eyes were downright frosty. "You could have explained things to them before this. Didn't you tell them I was here?"

"Well, I..." He paused, thinking back on his exact words. He grinned sheepishly at her. "I told them we'd be working with a new lyricist. But I think the only one I actually mentioned your name to was Styx."

Her teeth grated in the ensuing silence and a long breath seethe out of her. In no way did he feel let off the hook.

For a man used to getting his way in all things, pleading did not come easily. "Give this another shot...please."

She rose without a word, crossing the short distance to stare through the tinted window. Holding herself rigid, she folded her arms over her middle. The defensive gesture sat like a rock in his gut. The despair on her face, the utter dejection in her stance made him want to call the words back. God, he sucked at damage control. What now?

****

The past weighed heavily upon her slender

shoulders. Her all too brief engagement, and the very public break-up stung her pride. The memory of Lily's incessant, disparaging remarks grated on her nerves. She'd bravely faced down the smug smiles, the sympathetic frowns, the pitying glances. And the cameras... She shuddered. The press had been dogging her heels ever since the story broke, pushing for an interview, pleading for a comment.

But that was just the surface stuff. Griffin had been her Band-Aid, her way to prove to herself that she would survive after Angel's Fury. She'd figured that out when the initial anger and humiliation of a very public betrayal had worn off. She'd cared about him. But she hadn't really loved him. The loss of him was like the sting of a Band-Aid removed...shocking, but bearable. It wasn't the devastating, crippling wound she imagined the loss of a soul mate might inflict. Not that she thought overly much about soul mates, of course. No, Griffin didn't really factor anymore, except for being one more tally on her long list of people she'd made the mistake of trusting. Her wounds went much deeper. Wounds that, no matter what she did to ignore them, festered and continued to wear on her.

Maybe she'd been too vulnerable when she'd agreed to this whole situation with Cole and his band. Maybe she'd still been in shock, she mused. That surely had to be the only reason she would agree to something so insane. Something she'd sworn to never, *ever* do again. She'd walked away from this life three years ago with her fingers burned, and her heart bruised. She'd worked so hard to reestablish herself, steering well away from the music business as if it were the plague.

Alex shook her head as her gaze lifted to consider the cloudless sky above through the thick tinting. She should've taken one look at the whole "rocker scene" in the back yard yesterday, and gotten back in her car. Forgotten the name Cole Gunnarrson even existed. She should've remembered how stereotypical some band members could be before she'd even walked into that studio. How could she have forgotten what men like that were capable of?

A chill skittered down her spine as another studio and other faces swam before her eyes. She shuddered, pushing those memories away. She was past that now. She was a different woman, she told herself. She could protect herself. She'd made sure of that with three years of self-defense classes and grueling Aikido sessions.

Unaware she was speaking aloud, she murmured to herself, "Coming here...agreeing to this...this was all a lapse in good judgment...another one. I should have known better after last time..."

Cole's hands settled on her shoulders without warning, and she jumped. Lost in thought, her reaction was instinctive. Alex whirled to face him, her guard up and her body tensed as the fight or flight mechanism engaged.

Cole blinked, lifting his hands in a placating gesture. He backed up a step, then another, apparently understanding she needed space. Her reaction was alarming, and unbidden, just like in the studio, and despite her brave façade, it weighed on her mind.

He cocked his head to the side and stared at her with eyes that saw entirely too much. "What did they do to you?"

Drawing a shaky breath, she stepped around him, eyes downcast.

"I'll be in my room," she tossed over her shoulder, but his words stopped her in her tracks.

"Don't let your creativity suffer because you were burned. When faced with resistance, persist—don't quit. You owe it to yourself to let the music flow, fight

for it," he quoted, tossing the words she'd given to one of her readers back at her. "Who burned *you,* Alex?"

She stood in the middle of the room, brittle as fine spun glass, staring at the door—so very far away—and she couldn't move. His words sucked the air from of the room. Again, she fought to keep the dark memories from swamping her. Her shoulders slumped in defeat. Her hands were like ice, her heart even colder.

And then he was there, just behind her. Close enough that his warmth seeped into her, thawing her as nothing else could. How was it he made her feel safe when being near the others virtually paralyzed her with fear? Though he didn't touch her this time, his words forced her around until she looked up into his eyes.

"If you leave now...if you don't go back in that studio and finish what you started, you'll live with that regret for the rest of your life, Alex. And you'll regret it, I know you will. I've listened to the music you wrote back then—and the music you write in your head as you sit at that piano," he growled harshly, pointing at the Steinway beside them. Only Cole could blithely regard a Steinway as if it were any other piano. It was like saying a Stradivarius was just another violin, or U2 just another boy band, Elvis a passing fad. "Your music takes my breath away. How can you turn your back on such a large part of who you are?" He stepped closer, though he still didn't touch her. "How can you let your music die without putting up a fight?"

She closed her eyes and dropped her chin to her chest, defenseless and dejected. He reached out at last and drew her hands up, cradling them in his large, warm palms in the slim space between their bodies.

"Alex..." He smiled, squeezing her hands. "Trust

me, the guys—Zack and Danny—they're harmless. They're used to women falling at their feet, and it goes to their head sometimes. I promise you, they know what the word no means. Nothing will happen under this roof that *you* don't want to happen."

She tensed again, but he refused to allow her to pull her hands back, refused to let her run scared. The heat in his eyes intensified, fierce and protective. His eyes pleaded with her. "Let me fix this."

Cole waited in silence as she battled insidious demons that preyed on her very ability to trust. At last, she drew a deep breath and nodded, relaxing her stance the slightest bit.

Cole's gaze held triumphant sparks of hope. "Will you come back with me to the studio?"

She nodded, clearly reluctant, her mask of cold professionalism slipping back into place right before his eyes. He frowned, looking as if he wanted to say something, but in the end he remained silent.

Upon their return, he made proper introductions. Alex nodded to each man in turn. With every new face he identified, her spine stiffened a little more, an anxious reaction to being in the room with the band. She understood why that was so. She'd been expecting it. What she couldn't figure out was why she didn't react like this when she was alone with Cole.

Pointing first to the tall dark-haired Casanova, and then to the blond she'd forced to his knees, he offered with a wry twist of his lips, "I believe you've already met Danny and Zack."

Each nodded in turn. Danny's cheeks flushed an embarrassed red, while Zack eyed her with cautious reserve. "Danny's our bassist. He takes care of backup vocals too. Zack's forte is acoustic guitar, but he covers electric when the need arises. They're both harmless."

She noted that as Cole said the last, his eyes held a menacing warning as he stared the two men down, as if daring either of them to argue. Seemingly satisfied that neither would contradict him, he moved on down the room, pointing out one of the sports fanatics she'd seen in the gazebo.

"Devon's on keyboard," Cole remarked and then motioned to a man she'd never seen before. "This is Deacon, the newest member of the band. He's on electric guitar, though he dabbles on the keyboard and drums." Deacon gave her a barely perceptible nod, lounging in his chair, eyes the color of pale gold flickered with mild interest. Cole turned a shrewd eye to Styx and added in a mock threatening tone, "Which, it seems, is fortunate for us considering we *may* be in need of a new drummer soon."

Unaffected by Cole's thinly veiled threat, Styx rocked back in his seat, stacked his hands behind his head, and shot Alex a shameless grin.

"Guys, this is Alex Sinclair, our new lyricist." Cole placed a proprietary hand on the small of her back, unaware of how protective, how possessive the gesture appeared to the others...how possessive it *felt* to her. Broad, speculative grins spread across the room at large. She frowned at them. Had they all lost their minds?

Apparently oblivious, Cole turned to Alex. "How would you like to proceed?"

Putting a little space between them for her own piece of mind, she suggested, "Why don't you go on with the session like you normally would? Just pretend I'm not here. I'll just get the feel of things for today, if that works for you?"

Cole nodded, though his disgruntled expression left her confused. Giving a mental shrug, Alex moved to a chair in the corner and made herself as unobtrusive as possible while the band began warming up. By the end of the session several hours later, Alex was much more relaxed around the band as a whole, and overall, felt it reasonably safe to chalk the day up as a win for all involved.

Now, if she could just get a handle on this strange affinity she felt for their lead singer, she'd be sitting pretty damned good.

****

That night, as the shadows of sin stretched long over the city, a lone figure—more monster than man—slithered through the nightclub scene, his nostrils filled with the scent of Human females. They were such easy targets, after all. Like lambs to the slaughter, he chuckled. He danced with some, flirted with others. A caress of the eyes for this one, a brush of the hand for the next... He lured them right to the edge, delighting in their naïveté. They all saw what they wanted to see...muscles no gym could replicate, striking good looks, and bedroom eyes. Not one of them realized they flirted with death itself.

Too easy by half.

As with any predator, he was wholly aware of his surroundings, attuned to every stir of the air. One eye was always on the door, watching and waiting. At present, a curvy blonde writhed in his arms while a tortured soul crooned over a broken heart left to bleed. He smiled over the irony as his little lamb stepped in from the night. Her short cap of red curls the flame to his moth. He stalked across the dance floor, the pouty blonde forgotten like the face of the waitress who'd served him unconsumed drinks all night.

As the redhead approached the bar, he slipped up beside her. Propping an elbow on the polished teak, he consciously turned the burning gleam in his eyes down a few notches, closer to the *I could take you for one hell of a ride* range and a few steps farther away from *You'll whimper my name as you die in my arms* territory. When the redhead's friend gave her a sharp elbow and a definitive nudge in his direction, she turned limpid blue eyes his way. God, they were all so easy to read, it was pitiful. Cocky, arrogant, he smiled and slid closer, leaning down until his lips were little more than a fang's breadth from her jugular.

The Party Crasher's drawl was honey smooth and dark as sin itself as he whispered in her ear. "Hi there, angel."

"Hi yourself," she replied, batting her lashes.

His breath rippled against her neck, and he watched gooseflesh ripple over her skin. Though they'd never officially met face to face, he pouted, "I've been waiting for you."

She eyed him coyly, her head tilted to a flirtatious angle. Playing along, she cooed, "I'll just bet you have."

He brushed the back of his knuckles across her forearm, the lightest caress of butterfly wings. A predator toying with his food. "Let me buy you a drink, and you'll make my wait worthwhile."

Pursing her lips, the redhead played at considering his offer. Turning to her companion, she gave her the silent nod, the one that says *I'll see you later...with any luck, not until tomorrow morning.* Accepting his offer with a gracious smile, she followed him back to a corner table, away from the bar, away from the dance floor. Away from safety.

As the redhead followed where he led, the thrill of the chase began to grow. She had nothing to say that held any interest to him. He'd been watching her for weeks now, and though they'd never met, he knew all there was to know about Miss Madelyn Kinney, from the time she left for work in the morning from her two-bedroom, third floor apartment in Encino to the clubs she frequented with her friends. More important, he knew everything that mattered. She was the Studio Coordinator at Fast Trax Records. She was thirty-three Human years old.

And she was his next mark.

All that remained was a little lip service, and a small bit of...*convincing*...a little insurance, if you will. After all, he needed to make sure his little lamb was in the right place at the right time. Club Déjà Vu to be exact, three days hence.

Chapter 9

Alex settled into the band's routine as if she'd always been there. By the end of the first week, she'd earned the professional respect of the other band members, even the cynical Zack. She'd started to relax around the band, no longer tensing up whenever she entered a room where more than one of the group was present. The only thing Alex found unsettling about the whole situation was hearing Cole, with his sinful, arousing voice, singing the lyrics her heart had composed. His voice, unnerving and hypnotic, wove a spell of enchantment around her, pulling her deeper and deeper each time he sang her words.

Hell, it was just plain erotic.

She'd had less free time than she'd first assumed she would, but she didn't mind. Working with the band had proven quite enjoyable. Cole had been on his best behavior whenever he was around, which, oddly enough, wasn't often. He kept the most hideous hours. Then again, she reminded herself, his were common rocker hours. Up all night, sleep all day.

She'd begun to think he was deliberately going out of his way to avoid her. His behavior was a puzzle, a puzzle missing a few frustrating, crucial pieces. He'd gone from irresistible, charming, and intensely focused to rarely present and more than a little distracted in the space of one night. However, since she could avoid facing him in return—and therefore facing her attraction *for* him—his absence suited her just fine.

Late one evening, just after sunset, she let herself back into the house. She'd gone jogging through the grounds to clear out a temporary jag of writer's block from her head, down past a quiet stream shrouded in beautiful natural foliage that ran along the western perimeter of Cole's estate, and inspiration had struck.

Eagerly making her way to Cole's study, intent on the Steinway therein, Alex drew up short as soon as she opened the door without knocking first and her eyes immediately locked on the silhouette of a man cloaked in darkness. It took a second for her eyes to adjust to the shadows as she struggled to remember where the light switches were located. The silhouette stood motionless a few feet from Cole's desk, still as a statue. She couldn't see his face, but tension crackled sharply in the air. Alarm rang a sharp warning in her skull, and she hesitated.

Catching her lower lip between her teeth, she stepped just inside the door. "Cole?"

****

The sound of Alex's curious voice, pushing through the shadow-enshrouded room toward him startled an instinctive, furious hiss from his lips. He'd been so distracted by the unexpected package on his desk he hadn't heard her approach. Not good.

He recoiled at the muted sound of her approaching footsteps. His body, already tensed— already transformed by rage—stiffened as he turned farther away from her to conceal the harsh changes in his face. Cole had seen reflections of himself transformed, another myth debunked. It was a sight capable of striking terror straight to the heart of the most stalwart. Her vision wouldn't be as keen in the darkness as his was, so he risked a swift glance over his shoulder, only to curse himself for his primal reaction. His preternatural senses, all the more acute in the cover of darkness and in the height of fury, hadn't missed a single detail, right down to the nervous flutter of delectable pulse at the base of her throat. The alluring sight of Alex in a curve-hugging running suit was enough to push him straight onto treacherous, slippery territory.

"I'm sorry, I didn't mean to..." Then, as if sensing something was wrong, she stepped closer to him. "Cole? Are you all right?"

"Stay back." His voice was deeper than normal, gruff and hoarse. "Don't come any closer."

By the gods, run woman, he wanted to shout. *Find the nearest piece of pointy wood and hide.* But even that wasn't a safe bet, given his current condition. She'd be no match for his strength, and her flight might very well trigger his natural predatory responses. If she ran, he wasn't altogether certain he would be able to stop himself from chasing her down, wouldn't be able to stop from taking all he'd been dreaming about since the first scent of her filled his nostrils.

Alex froze. But she was still too close.

With a silent curse, Cole's gaze settled back on his desk, and the large, flat box as he tried to determine what to do next. Thinking with her this close, thinking in this state in general, was difficult...if not outright impossible.

The box itself was white, a stark anomaly against the inky bleakness of the room. The lid beside the box sported a garish red bow. Beside him, Alex lifted a hand and tucked a loose strand of hair behind her ear. Her scent, stronger for the internal heat of her recent exertions, raced through him like drugs hitting an addict's veins. His body convulsed, pushed to the point of exploding. She shouldn't be here, not while he was so close to the edge. And if she opened the album inside that box, she'd have more questions than he could answer.

Alex moved toward the lamp on an end table

"Leave it off." Cole's voice cracked like a whip in the room, and he cringed. Could she hear the layer of desperation?

She froze again, and then withdrew her hand. His tone, the very clarity of his speech sounded garbled, strained, even to his own ears. She crossed the room to his side, her steps cautious and slow, as those of someone forced to approach a dangerous, wounded animal. Maybe she was more observant than he'd given her credit.

Her heat called to him, her scent beckoned him, taunting him. Warm blood pulsed beneath that luscious, glowing skin, and his mouth watered. Cole hissed beneath his breath and moved away from the desk—away from her—his face fully averted. Balling his fists, he sucked in one deep breath after another in a desperate attempt to manage his baser inclination to seize her and drag her to the floor beneath him. The urge to bury his fangs deep in her neck was strong upon him. The urge to bury his painful, throbbing erection even deeper between her thighs was stronger still. The thought of doing both at the same time...

His body shook and tiny beads of perspiration broke over his forehead.

With every breath he dragged in, her scent wrapped itself around him, insinuated itself farther inside him, fueling that craving to hazardous levels. His already finely tuned senses sharpened, predatory instincts urging him to stalk her, to taste her, to ruthlessly claim everything she had for his own.

Behind him, Alex bent over the desk and peered into the box. He knew what she would see if she lifted the front cover, but he didn't trust his voice enough to caution her away. Didn't trust his hands to touch her. The cover of the photo album was white. The words "Let's Party" were scribbled across the face of the book in garish red lipstick. And inside...

"What is this, Cole?"

"He got in," Cole muttered. "By Loki, he came here and got inside...and I didn't know it."

Alex turned to him then, the book evidently forgotten as she approached him. Burning his arm with a calming, concerned hand, she craned her neck to peer into his face. "Cole, what's going on?"

Cole hissed and jerked violently away, reacting for all the world as if she'd just lit a pyre and requested he dance on top of it. Alex yanked her hand back, flinching away. Pain and confusion glistened in her luminous eyes.

He could feel the waves of turmoil rolling through her, and it tore at him. By Valhalla, he could *feel* her, with an awareness that went beyond the here and now, beyond the time and place. It was a fable, he told himself. A myth of mated pairs. They couldn't actually *feel* each other's emotions. That was impossible. It had to be. Besides, he and Alex had not mated. She was not his *Bride*.

The mere thought of it sent a wildfire of lust ripping through his body. He could still feel her touch, and his flesh burned for more.

Telling himself to get a grip, Cole swore beneath his breath.

He drew back two full steps, cautious to censor his explanation. "Someone's been trying to sneak past security. They've attempted to get in several times. I just came in a few minutes ago, and that," he ground out, pointing at the box, "was on my desk."

Her voice was soft, puzzled. "A photo album? Did you open it?"

"Yeah," he ground out. Anger boiled up inside him once more. "It's filled with pictures."

She stepped closer to him, her voice dropping to a near whisper. "What pictures?"

"Just...pictures."

Of course, she couldn't be content in just letting it go, not his Alex. "Have you called the police yet?"

He shook his head, sucking in another deep breath. Alex reached for her pocket. As she lifted her hand free, she flipped her phone open, her thumb depressing the number nine. In a move so swift she couldn't have see it until he was touching her, Cole grabbed her wrist, none to gently, and jerked the phone from her, snapping it closed.

"Cole..." She gasped, breathless with alarm.

"No." His tone left no room for argument. "No Hu...cops. No cops."

He let out a harsh breath, cursing himself for slipping, only narrowly having managed to bite off the word *Human*. If he'd worried the album would cause questions, imagine what kind of reaction *that* word would have sparked.

"But Cole..."

"No," he insisted, fisting his hands at his sides. "It won't do any good. Besides, I'll just end up with a crush of bad press, and right now, that's the last thing I need."

"Cole, whoever made this album, this person was *inside* the house," she pushed. "They could be dangerous..."

He stalked away from her, raking a hand through his already disheveled hair. Icy fury cut through his voice. "Believe me, they don't know what dangerous is. I'll deal with this. Just forget about it."

He tossed her phone back and reached for his own. Flipping it open, he impatiently waited for the call to connect, and barked, "Get up here—now."

Beside him, he could hear her teeth grinding. After a short moment of seething breaths, Alex marched to the door, calling over her shoulder.

"Since I presume your study will soon be full of people, do you mind if I use the studio for a while?"

"Go ahead." He turned away, his gaze absorbed once more with the box on his desk as he fought the inexplicable urge to call her back.

The door to his study closed with strategically applied force, and he flinched.

****

Cole's chilling gaze followed Styx's progress as he paced in front of Cole's desk, his eyes glowing pale amber, his fangs flashing with lethal fury at the nervous security detail. "How the hell did they get past you? I mean, last I checked, it was your friggin' job to keep the lunatics out, or was I wrong?"

Laying a restraining hand on the drummer's taut shoulder, Cole turned, addressing the two cowering Vamps before him in menacing, deadly tones. "I want new security cameras installed in all the locations I indicated by morning. I want an additional man patrolling the grounds during the day, two at night. And I want to be notified the instant anything suspicious happens."

"Yes, sir," the twin mountains rumbled in unison. As one, they turned on their heels and fled the room. They should be grateful to be escaping with their throats still intact.

Cole stalked across the room and stood immobile, fists clenched behind his stiff back, gaze locked on the Viking helmet in his display case. His voice was quiet, controlled as it had been with the guards. The underlying note of outrage reverberated, unmistakable. "You saw the pictures. Tell me it's not what I'm thinking. Tell me I'm wrong."

Styx paced around the room, his hands clenching and unclenching at his sides. "You want me to lie to you, Cole? Or do you want the truth?"

Cole shot him a withering look, thrust his hands

deep in his front pockets, and stalked back to the desk to scowl down at the open photo album.

"It's him, Cole." Styx stared at him from the opposite side of the desk. "It's him. Somehow he found out about us—about the fact we're working, hand in glove, with the TFRA—and this is his way of letting us know the hunters have become the prey."

Cole let out a long, drawn out sigh and scrubbed his palms over his face. The pictures before him were harsh, even to eyes that had seen centuries of war and destruction. The sadistic bastard had taken great pleasure in stalking his victims, his glee more than apparent in every candid snapshot. He'd paid attention to every painstaking detail of their life...as well as staging the scene of their demise, displaying the corpse for maximum shock value.

The shock value—in terms of Vampyre outrage—was the sheer waste. Blood pooled beneath the victim, congealing in the grime.

He'd known many of his breed who'd happily killed for the sake of killing. Many who'd blissfully ravaged and dismembered entire villages, wallowing in the bloodbath. Helheim, not so many centuries ago, he'd been one of them.

But these killings were different. They were irrational, useless, with nothing more than a killer's twisted sense of reason behind any of them. These killings hadn't been about revenge, or acquisition. These killings hadn't been about a feeding that had gotten out of hand. The killer hadn't fed from the victim at all. He'd bitten them, killed them, but he'd left the blood behind, as if it were tainted, too vile to ingest.

Why kill them at all? What was the Rogue gaining from all this? Except maybe the pleasure of watching the TFRA chasing their proverbial tails in growing panic. Even that illustrious, efficient agency wouldn't be able to keep these slayings under wraps much longer. They were too specific, too targeted to one industry for its people to not notice, to not start asking questions. Why?

*Because I c...*what?

Styx's voice broke into Cole's thoughts. "Have you called Crispin yet?"

"Yeah. Tommy too..." Cole turned away from the pictures. The lingering scent of Alex caught him. "Did you happen to see Alex when you came in?"

"Yeah," Styx admitted with a troubled frown, his fangs receding out of sight. "She looked pretty tense, told me to come in...that you probably needed to talk to me."

He'd been a jerk. He owed her another apology. By Thor, this was fast becoming a habit...apologizing to her. He couldn't say he cared for it much. The shrill ring of his phone interrupted his reply. He checked the ID and frowned when the word security pop up on the tiny screen. Flipping the cell open, he placed it to his ear with a terse, "Yeah?"

Cole snapped the phone closed after a few seconds with a furious snarl. Rage roiled through him again. "Son of a bitch!"

"What?" Styx stiffened, his hand dropped to his hip in a timeless, instinctive gesture Cole recognized with familiar sympathy. They'd both been born in a time of sword and shield.

"That was security. They chased someone across the grounds, but whoever it was got away...again. They said they caught the guy climbing out a window near the studio, moving too fast to be Human..."

Cole's eyes widened then, and Alex's parting words came back to him. The room swam before his eyes. "Alex..."

****

The Party Crasher fled into the night, flickering through the trees like a shade. Cole's hired thugs had been pitifully easy to elude, but it had been a close brush with the blonde. He hadn't anticipated her showing up like that. Ah, well, he'd handled it. Sucked that he had to take her down like that...it wasn't her turn, at least not yet. Oh, well. She'd be back up and around by the time he had use for her.

Now, to cover his ass...

Pulling the phone from his pocket, he thumbed in a speed dial number as he climbed into his vehicle. Turning the ignition over, cranking the stereo up, he leaned back against the seat as he waited for the call to connect.

"Yeah," Styx barked, panting into the phone.

"Hey, man, I—"

"Where the fuck are you?" A door slammed in the background, and he smiled.

"Ah...corner of...Thirty-second and Bla—"

"Fuck, man. He was here." Styx cut him off, his words punctuated by pounding footsteps.

"What's going on back there, Styx?"

Dead silence met his question. Then, music to his ears...

"Alex?" Cole's panic filled voice echoed in the background. His glee knew no end.

He bit back a chuckle when Styx's voice echoed through the phone line. "Alex! Shit!"

The line went dead. Laughing aloud, he shifted his vehicle into gear and cranked the wheel.

Chapter 10

He tore from the study at a dead sprint, Styx dogging his heels. Styx's phone rang then, and Styx answered, but Cole was too worried to pay the conversation any mind. He passed Danny and Zack in one of the halls without stopping to offer an explanation. Curious, the two followed in their wake. Cole froze the minute he opened the door, his heart lurched in his chest. His three companions crashed into his back, craning their necks to see what caused Cole's palpable distress.

The studio was in shambles. Sheet music littered the floor. Instruments, always carefully stored away, lay in twisted chaos all about the floor. On the far wall, dozens of enlarged, autographed glossy PR pictures of Cole smiled through a haze of blood red scribble.

Cole staggered into the room, his heart hammering in his chest now. Wild honey wafted to him on the gentle breeze, stirred by the air conditioner. Wild honey...and blood. His nostrils flared at the sweet tang. He'd know that scent anywhere.

His voice broke as panic consumed him. "Alex?"

Silence met his query, and then Styx's voice filled the void. "Alex! Shit!"

Cole's gaze swung away from the control booth, his eyes dropped to the floor, just around the corner from the door. She lay on the flat, gray, acoustical carpeting, face down and motionless. Danny's guitar sprawled on the floor beside her head, broken in two with nothing more than the strings to hold it together.

Cole leaped across the distance to kneel at her side, his heart lodged in his throat. His hands shook as he reached out to brush the hair from her brow. He swore, viciously, his vision turning red at the sight of the large, purplish bruise already forming on the side of her pale cheek.

A bright, crimson trickle of blood, the product of a small cut where the jagged edge of splintered wood scratched her delicate skin, traced a path over the pale smoothness of her injured cheek. Protective rage swelled to dangerous levels inside him. Before he stopped to think, before anyone could caution him against it, he scooped her up in his arms to cradle her in his lap, pressing her against his chest. Her heart still beat. Her lungs still pulled air in and pushed it out. She was still alive...but she'd been hurt.

The scent of her blood stroked his hunger, but he ignored it, concerned only with her safety. A woman like her was meant to be kept locked away in an ivory tower. One only he held the key to. This was his fault. If he hadn't allowed himself to become so distracted with that damned album... If he'd taken more care with security... If he'd just...

"Alex," he rumbled, hoarse with emotion. His hand feathered over her uninjured cheek and down to test the rise and fall of her chest. The faint, fluttering pulse at the base of her throat both tempted and reassured him. This could have been much, much worse, he told himself. Fear fisted in his gut, twisting like a splintered stake in his heart. His voice was raw. "Alex, come on. Sweetheart, wake up."

Behind him, all sound stopped as three males froze. Cole never allowed emotional attachment with any female. Ever. And most especially not a *Mortal* female. He was certain curious, shocked glances flew his way at the telling endearment, but he didn't give a damn. To the last man, all were smart enough to withhold comment.

"Cole." Styx nudged his shoulder after a long, silent moment, drawing his attention. "We should call an ambulance."

Cole was just about to agree, when she stirred in his arms, moaning.

"She's coming around." Cole urged anxiously, "That's it, Alexandra. Open your eyes."

"Don't call me that..." Her assertion was fierce, but her voice sounded kitten weak. "Only...Lily calls me...Alexandra...hate it."

Hoarse with worry and fear, Cole ordered, "Zack, get her some water."

"Cole?" Groggy, Alex peered up at him, blinked with confusion.

Her eyelids fluttered closed, and he tensed, alarmed. She blinked, working to refocus. Flinching, a trembling hand lifted to her cheek, and she groaned her pain aloud. The sound of it ripped through him. His worried gaze locked on her pale face. She blinked again, visibly pushing the pain back down.

"I think I'm okay," she murmured, her eyes unfocused, hazy as she moved about cautiously. Then her eyes refocused on his face, and she added, "But you look like hell."

His heart twisted.

"You're going to be all right, sweetheart. Everything's going to be all right." He squeezed her to him for a moment as relief lapped through him in staggering waves. "Can you tell me what happened?"

She struggled in his arms, intent on sitting up. Cole refused to release her. She gave up without a fight and sagged against him, cradling her head with her hand.

"I, I don't...I'm not sure. I opened the door,

walked in, and flipped on the light. It just happened so fast. Someone rushed me. I thought..." She shook her head, pressing the heel of her palm to her temple, cringing. "For a moment, I thought I saw the edge of a guitar, but then everything went black."

Even as she spoke, Danny scooped up the pieces of his Stu Hamm DTUNER from the ground, looking for all the world as if a close friend had just sustained a mortal injury. Zack handed a bottle of water to Styx, then began sifting through the chaos, picking the music and discarded instruments up off the floor, settling them back on their stands. Danny's guitar wasn't the only instrument to sustain damage. Devon's keyboard looked as if it had tangled with the underside of a Mack truck...and lost. The only thing missing were the tread marks.

Styx pressed the water into Alex's shaking hand. Worried amber eyes searched her face. "Here, Alex. Drink some of this."

Following his instructions without balking, Alex took a few tentative sips and handed the bottle back with a weak smile of thanks, snuggling against Cole's chest. His hands smoothed over her back and neck.

Styx pressed, "Did you get a look at his face?"

From the protective cradle of Cole's arms, Alex closed her eyes for a moment, pressing a hand to her temple again. "No, I don't think so. It was fast. A black hood, that's all I remember. A black hood...and the guitar."

"Ok," Cole cut in, seeing—*feeling*—how much pain she was struggling to fend off. By the looks of that bruise, she had to be fighting off waves of pain pounding through her skull like a drummer jacked up on speed. By Thor, his own stomach rolled with it. "We need to take you to the hospital, have you checked over."

"No," Alex blanched. "I'm fine, no hospital."

"But Alex," Styx reasoned. "You're hurt—"

"No," she insisted and began to shake her head, only to wince and fall back against Cole's shoulder with a soft moan.

Styx raised concerned eyes to Cole, wordlessly urging him to intervene. Cole gritted his teeth, nodding acknowledgement. "You need a doctor, sweetheart."

"Please, Cole," she whispered against the side of his neck, cringing as if the sound of her own voice ricocheted off the inside of her skull. "No hospitals. I can't...I can't stand hospitals."

It took several long moments, waged in silent tug of war, but he finally conceded, "All right...but only if you let me bring somebody in to look at you."

"Fine," she allowed. "I just want to go lie down now."

"No!" Both Cole and Styx barked the word, making her groan and clutch at her head with both hands. Then Cole continued in a much more reasonable tone, "You could have a concussion, Alex. You can't go to sleep."

He turned to Styx. "Find a doctor, call Tommy..."

The Spaniard nodded, and Cole rose, lifting Alex with him as if she weighed no more than a guitar pick. He cradled her against his chest, her head resting in the crook of his shoulder. Alex wrapped her arms around his neck without the slightest argument, burrowing closer to his warmth. Pivoting on his heel, Cole strode from the room, leaving Styx and the others to deal with the mess.

Alex's soft comment caressed the side of Cole's neck. "You know, I believe you're starting to make a habit of this."

"What's that?" Cole frowned, not liking how thready her voice sounded. He quickened his pace, more worried about her condition than he was about having to explain how he could move so quickly.

"This whole white knight charging to the rescue thing you've got going on, carrying the damsel in distress around and all that." A small smile flirted at the edges of her soft mouth.

Cole couldn't seem to help himself. Despite his worry, a chuckle over her assertion rumbled up in his chest. Imagine. Him...a white knight. Not even on his best day. He slowed some, figuring if she could joke like this, then she might not have been hurt as seriously as he'd first feared.

His chuckles died on a strangled groan when she pressed light, nibbling kisses to the side of his neck. "I must admit, Cole. I do find it rather irresistible, the way you keep sweeping me off my feet. Although, to be honest, the first time I saw you, I pictured you more as a ruthless Viking, out to conquer the world," she murmured, groggily. Cole missed a step, but she must have been too dazed to feel it, she didn't comment. Her hand smoothed over corded muscles that flexed and tensed beneath his tattoo, branding him.

Her sigh was dreamy. "I think I could get used to this."

His entire body came alive with memories of well over a millennia ago. A time when a man with enough strength and power could take what he wanted, anything he wanted, and no one could stand in his way. A time when men were conquerors...and women prizes.

The prize in his arms hadn't finished torturing him just yet. She nuzzled against the side of his neck, murmuring, "Have I told you how sexy I think your tattoo is, Cole? Who am I kidding? *Everything* about *you* is drop-dead, mouth-watering sexy."

He stopped in his tracks. His mouth fell open at her uncensored, uninhibited words. His body went rigid. The blood surged to his groin, painful and greedy. Unadulterated lust raked through him with greedy claws. Sucking in a sharp breath, worried anew by her odd behavior, he flew to the study and pushed his way inside.

It seemed both forever and yet seconds, before Cole lowered her to the sofa in his study. Her head sagged back against the cushions with a sigh. Cole knelt before her and stared into her dilated eyes. Alex leaned forward then, catching him off guard. She raised both hands, cupping his cheeks with aching gentleness. Without apology, without warning, she drew his face to hers and pressed her lips to his. He froze for half a second, his eyes widened in stunned shock before sinking closed in surrender.

Alex smiled against his lips and murmured, "Hell, why not. If I'm dreaming...I might as well go for the gold."

Her tongue slipped inside his mouth to tangle with his in an erotic game of love-play that sent tremor after tremor racing through his body. The feel of her tongue in his mouth, daring and enticing, stopped Cole's heartbeat dead in its tracks.

Her hands slid to the back of his head, her fingers tangled in his tawny locks, holding him still for her shameless assault. Cole's hands gripped her hips, tugging her to the edge of the sofa, and Alex moaned, angling her head to deepen the kiss. She skated her hands over his neck and shoulders to caress his chest with bold, questing fingers, purring feminine approval deep in her throat.

Her hands on his body shook him from the inside out. His control slipped through his fingers like running water. The ancient, primitive beast within growled lusty approval. His hands spanned her waist just below her tank. The silken texture of her skin taunted him to take more. Cole wrested control of the kiss from her, devouring her lips, lapping at her tongue. He nudged her legs farther apart, yanking her tight against him, wedging his hips between her parted thighs.

All too soon, reality came crashing down on Cole, even if it was lost on Alex. The brush of her fingers slipping into the low waistband of his jeans—tugging at the button and working the zipper—wrung a tortured gasp from him. She pulled him harder into the cradle of her thighs, and lust hit him hard, licking at his control like a flaming torch set to dry kindling.

Dreaming... Her words came back to haunt him. She thought she was dreaming...

Kicking himself for giving into the temptation of her kiss—cursing himself for his sudden attack of conscience—he captured her wrists in his long, nimble fingers, and held her wayward hands trapped between them. It almost took more will power than he possessed to tear his lips from hers.

Cole leaned back and sucked in one long breath after another, gasping for air, grasping for control, trying his best to ignore the seductive pout of her kiss-swollen lips. The wanton, come-hither look in her eyes was nearly more than he could deny. Forcing himself to turn away before he set them down a path she may never be able to accept...a path he may never recover from, he pushed her back against the seat, refusing to let her lie down.

"No, Alex, not like this." Keeping his face turned away lest she see the unholy glow in his icy blue eyes, he sat down beside her and tucked her against his side. Conscience warred with instinct.

Why couldn't he take what she so blatantly offered? She was hurt, and vulnerable. Any other woman, any other time, and he wouldn't have thought twice. A wicked voice hissed inside his head again, sending a shiver of something foreign slithering down his spine. *My woman.* Cole's heart pounded inside his chest, need surged through his veins. His fangs lengthened, slicing at the inside of his lower lip. Wrapping her in his strong arms, he pushed her head against his shoulder, tilting his own head back against the cushions.

Alex murmured a disappointed protest, but settled against him nonetheless. Cole's blood pounded in his ears, throbbed in his rigid erection. His nostrils flared. He could smell her arousal, could *feel* it, and he gritted his teeth, fighting through it, keeping his lips clamped tight to hide his huge fangs. He could do nothing to hide the burning, glowing need in his eyes...or the rigid bulge in his jeans.

Not soon enough, Styx pushed his way into the study, a cell phone pressed to his ear and a bag of frozen peas in his hand. "Yeah, ok... No, no I don't think so. I'll..."

His words trailed away as he caught sight of Cole's face...the sight of Cole's eyes and the trace of crimson on his lips. Styx's startled gaze flew to Alex's neck, then back to Cole's mouth. Snapping his attention back to the man on the other end of the line, Styx muttered, "Sure, sure... We'll see you in a few."

Styx snapped the phone closed, and sat down in the low table, facing the sofa. When he reached for Alex, a snarl, instinctual and possessive, rippled through Cole. The Spaniard's hand froze mid-stretch. He blinked, then withdrew his hand with extreme care. Leaning back, he tossed the bag of peas to Cole. "Put that on her cheek for the swelling. Tommy said he'd be here in less than half an hour. He's bringing the doctor with him. Has she lost consciousness again? Does she seem confused or disoriented?" Then his eyes lingered on Cole's bloodstained lips once more. "*Madre de Dios*, you didn't..."

"No!" Cole snapped, but heat rose to his cheeks. His voice was low, the look in his eyes one he knew Styx had never witnessed, at least not in him. "She hasn't passed out again. But, I don't think she's functioning at full capacity just yet."

Styx frowned. "What do you mean?"

To Cole's chagrin—and, he was certain, Styx's eternal amusement—Alex gave a soft little sex kitten purr. She snuggled against Cole's side, dropping her hand squarely on Cole's straining zipper, rubbing the bulge suggestively. She couldn't have stunned either male more had she just plopped a live grenade in the middle of the room. "Cole has the sexiest tattoo. Kiss me again, Cole. I *sooo* like it when you kiss me..."

"I see what you mean," Styx managed between loud guffaws.

Cole groaned aloud, shifted on the sofa with a pained grimace, and grabbed her wrist, pinning her questing hand against his chest. He shot a warning glare at the laughing Styx, and, with a warning flash of fangs, snapped, "Don't you have something else to do?"

"No, no," Styx cooed, smirking with poorly feigned innocence. "I wouldn't dream of leaving you in your time of need. She looks like she could be a real handful, *amigo*."

"Get. Out. *Now*," Cole barked, turning the full impact of his fury on the drummer.

"I'll bring the doctor in when he gets here." Chuckling, Styx stood up. "Oh, ah, by the way...you got a little, just there." He tapped the corner of his mouth.

As Styx closed the door behind him with a soft chuckle, Cole licked the blood from his lips. Tipping his head back against the cushion again, he closed his eyes, praying to every god he could think of for patience and control. Alex squirmed against his side, rubbing her breasts against his ribs. She nipped playfully at his neck. The sting of her teeth on his skin sent another ferocious wave of desire rolling through his system, cranking his blood back up to a hard boil.

Chapter 11

Fortunately, the doctor arrived sooner than expected. Unfortunately, he determined Alex did indeed have a concussion, recommending she not sleep for at least six to eight hours. Which, of course, required close monitoring.

Someone would have to spend the night with her.

The aging doctor reassured Cole her odd behavior was a temporary side effect of the concussion, and that she should be back to herself in no time at all. He left his personal number with Cole in case Alex suffered any further symptoms later on, checked her eyes once more, and then left.

Cole disentangled Alex from his arms and pushed to his feet. Wrapping his arms around her waist, he helped her up, guided her down the halls until they came to her door. Inside, she headed for the bedroom, but he took her by the shoulders, turned her and pushed her toward the bathroom instead.

"Why don't you go in and take a shower," he suggested, thinking he could use a few minutes to get his body back under control. He had a feeling he was going to need every precious moment he could steal if he was going to spend the rest of the night with her and not give in to her involuntary seduction.

Licking her lips, she raked hungry eyes over him, hot and greedy. "I like the sound of that. I can't wait to see you naked and covered in soap bubbles..."

He groaned, racked with the image of *her*—naked and covered in soap bubbles—and he broke out in a cold sweat. Loki take her, how much more could he endure this night before he caved? Cole propelled her into her bathroom and closed the door behind her with a definitive click, muttering to himself in the ancient language of his birth.

He waited for a few minutes just outside the door. As soon as the showerheads turned on, he prowled across the room, restless and edgy. Dropping onto a chair in the farthest corner, he stared, tormented and unmoving, at the bathroom door. She was in there. Beyond that thin slice of wood. Removing her shirt. Sliding those snug shorts down those delicious legs. The steaming spray of water would slide over her skin, glistening and...

Snarling a tight curse, he pushed to his feet and rushed from the room before he gave in to the temptation to join her.

Cole jogged to his room to grab his own shower—an icy cold one—and a quick shot of blood—also cold—before he returned to her. By the time he got back, less than fifteen minutes later, barefoot and clad in a muscle shirt and worn sweats, his body and his control were back online. For the most part.

He'd assumed she'd be done when he got back, and worry rushed through him when he entered her room after a light rap, only to find her still ensconced in the bathroom. Cole crossed to the door of the bathroom and knocked. When he received no answer, he twisted the knob and eased the door open a crack. Wild honey scented steam rolled through the opening. The sound of running water pattered like gentle rain on the tiles and his imagination ran away with him once more.

"Alex," he called. "You okay in there?"

A startled oath slipped from her lips and a plastic bottle collided with the floor. "I'm fine. I'll be out in a minute."

Easing the door shut, Cole let out a long, trembling breath, unsettled at how his worry had cranked back up to full throttle. He crossed the room and flopped onto the sofa, flipping the TV on. He did a little channel surfing while he waited, wondering what in the name of Valhalla he was going to do with her for the rest of the night.

Unfortunately, he wouldn't be spending the night with her in the way he'd envisioned...every day since he'd first laid eyes upon her. Not while she was hurting. There'd be time for those things...later. He glanced at the clock and groaned. Only seven hours of torture to go. Rolling his eyes, he clicked the remote.

The bathroom door opened behind him, and he turned to glance over his shoulder. His breath caught in the back of his throat. Alex stepped through the door, her hair hung in damp strands of gold down her back. A thick white terrycloth robe clung to her damp curves, hanging just past her knees. Her feet were bare, and her dainty toes winked candy-apple red nail polish. Her skin was a radiant, scrubbed pink, all except for her injured check, of course, which was fast approaching purple now. The doctor had cleansed the wound, but the scratch remained, vivid and enflamed. The sight of that mark upon her flesh filled Cole with a second wave of fury. The urge to lock her away and keep her safe at all cost was becoming harder to deny.

The minute their eyes connected, Alex's blush spread clear to the roots of her hair. Her mortified gaze slid to the floor. She stepped closer to the sofa and cleared her throat. Drawing a deep, bracing breath, she squeaked, "Cole, about earlier..."

He said nothing, blinking up at her as he waited patiently. The curl of his lips ruined his attempt at innocent serenity.

Her gaze slid away again, and she cleared her throat once more. "I owe you an apology," she began, toying with the robe's belt. "I was unprofessional and out of line. I don't know what came over me. I'll blame it on the blow to the head..."

His lips twitched, but he managed a straight face. The humor in his voice was beyond his control. "Don't worry about it."

Nodding, she turned away and began walking to her bedroom. She stopped just over the threshold, however, when Cole called her name, soft and low.

"Oh, Alex..." Cole waited until their eyes met to finish, his grin was wide, suggestive. "Just so you know—I *so* like it when you kiss me too."

****

Alex's mouth fell open and her eyes rounded, shame surged heat into her cheeks. Unable to respond, she stepped back and slammed the door between them, desperate to drown out the dark tumble of Cole's laughter. The door was no barrier at all.

She glared at the panel of wood for a moment, frustrated...mortified, then yanked the robe off and tossed it on the foot of the bed. Shaking her head, she dug in the chest of drawers, pulling out an old pair of boxers and a plain white v-necked tee with a shrug. If she was going to be up all night, she may as well be comfortable. Her one concession to propriety's sake was the white satin and lace bra.

She tugged the brush through her hair, over and over, then slathered moisturizer on her skin. Eyeing herself in the mirror, she heaved a resigned sigh, certain she couldn't put off facing Cole any longer. She stepped back into the living area, head held high. Her shoulders were squared, her chin elevated, prepared to face her humiliation. Instead, she received another surprise.

Cole sprawled on her sofa, a huge tray sat on the

table before him, filled to overflowing with an odd assortment of food.

"With all the excitement earlier, I wasn't sure if you'd had time to eat, so I figured I'd just have a little something sent up," he offered by way of explanation.

Some of the starch went out of her spine, and she cracked a small smile. "That was very...considerate. Thank you."

"I'm trying to butter you up." He grinned, offering her a can of Coke and half of a thick ham and cheese sandwich.

Her brow puckered and she hesitated. "Why?"

"I don't want this mess to scare you off," he admitted, shooting her a probing, entirely too serious look.

"We agreed to three weeks," she reminded him, dropping down to sit beside him on the sofa. Alex tucked her bare feet up underneath her, adding, "This wasn't your fault, Cole, and it didn't change anything."

His eyes narrowed and he tilted his head. "And then?"

"And then, we'll see." She gave him an ambiguous shrug, taking the sandwich and the Coke from him.

He drew an annoyed breath and leaned back, slinging a long, muscular arm over the back of the sofa behind her. His powerful legs stretched out in front of him. His tawny hair had begun to curl as it dried. He smelled of soap and shaving cream with a light trace of spicy cologne. Alex did her best to focus on the sandwich in her hand. She could have been eating cardboard, for all she could taste of it. Oh, dear God, was she about to suffer through a second wave of hallucinations?

"So," he drawled, toying with a damp tendril of her hair, winding it around his fingers as if savoring the texture between thumb and forefinger. "Got any suggestions for the rest of the night?"

The way he played with her hair was doing funny things to her insides. His words brought images to mind—very dark, very erotic images—that burned her cheeks. What was it about this man that made her walk around looking like she had a perpetual sunburn all the time? Her gaze flickered away from his face, unable to meet his eyes, and she tipped the soda can to her lips, buying time.

"You know, I'm sure I'll be just fine. You don't have to stay."

"No way," he argued, shaking his head. "You heard the doctor. You're stuck with me *all* night." Cole cleared his throat then, as if he too suffered unmanageable thoughts, and this time, he was the first to glance away.

"We can watch TV for a while, but I'm afraid I'll fall asleep on you before too long," he warned.

"Yeah," she agreed, wrinkling her nose. "I don't think I'd do so well there either. Don't suppose you play chess?"

"Actually I do." His eyes lit up at the unexpected boon. "If you promise not to fall asleep while I'm gone, I can run to my study and get the board."

Grinning, she crossed her heart and shooed him on his way. Alex finished off her sandwich and the Coke while she waited, and reached for a thick slice of chocolate cake. She *was* on a vacation of sorts, after all.

Alex was just taking her first guilty bite when Cole returned. She set the cake down, licking the rich icing from her lips. "I shouldn't be eating this."

"I won't tell a soul," he swore and grinned as he knelt beside the table.

"Here," she offered, holding a bit of the gooey confection on the end of the fork for him. "You didn't eat anything earlier, and I won't feel guilty if I don't eat the whole thing by myself."

Cole eyed the cake and grimaced. "No, thanks. That stuff would...mess with my system. You go on and eat it though. Everyone's entitled to a little guilty pleasure now and again." His smile grew, wide and loaded. "Your secrets are safe with me."

She shot him a questioning look, but she settled back against the cushions without an argument. Cole set the board up and arranged the pieces. Taking him at his word, she finished the cake off, savoring the last smear of frosting with lavish pleasure.

His hungry stare followed every move she made. "By the gods, what I wouldn't give to be that fork right now."

She gaped at him, astonished. Before she could comment, he turned away, centering his focus on the chessboard.

In the arena of chess, they were evenly matched. As the hours stretched on, they relaxed into each other's company. The conversation flowed easy between them, and Alex was surprised to find herself having a thoroughly enjoyable time. They talked of their careers and their ambitions, of their likes and dislikes. It was natural, ordinary—a connection neither of them had enjoyed in a very long time.

As Alex moved her queenside bishop into position and exclaimed checkmate, Cole leaned back against the sofa, grinning.

"You cheated," he accused good-naturedly.

Her eyes sparkled. "Prove it."

From there they moved on to discussing a few of the songs the band was working on, talking shop for the next several hours. Somewhere, over the course of the evening, Alex let her guard down, allowing him a rare glimpse of vulnerable trust.

As the night pushed on to morning, and the hour

approached dawn, they ended up side-by-side on the couch. Cole flipped on the television, and a blood-curdling scream filled the room. Alex leaned closer to the screen, peering with undisguised interest at the programming.

"Oooh, *Nightmare on Elm Street*," she exclaimed after a few seconds. She wrinkled a brow, assessing, and added, "Part two...Freddy's Revenge."

"Oh, no," Cole groaned, rolling his eyes for effect. "*Please* don't tell me you like those movies."

She narrowed her eyes in mock threat. "What do you mean by that...those movies?"

"Freddie movies..." He wrinkled his nose with transparent mock distaste, and pointed at the blood-splattered screen. His tone was sarcastic, clearly unimpressed. "Those things are so...unbelievable." He adopted a whiney, high-pitched tone, and blathered, "Oooh, I'm so scared. I'm going to try to outrun this freaky, deformed monster who has to manufacture his own claws. Oh no, silly me, I forgot I'm wearing ridiculous high heels and now I've fallen down. Now, I'm just gonna lay here and scream my head off, as if that's going to make him change his mind about killing me..."

Alex gave him a stern look of reproach and shoved at his shoulder. Then, giggling with wicked delight, she watched another gored victim fall beneath Freddie's tender mercies. "They're *classics*!"

"No way," he shot back, lifting a condescending brow. "If you want a classic, you need to think *Halloween*, or *Texas Chainsaw*. Of course, *The Howling* series is a big contender."

She blinked up at him, intrigued. "The what?"

"*The Howling*," he repeated, then gaped at her as if she'd crawled out from beneath a rock. "Don't tell me you watch horror films and you've *never* seen a *Howling* movie. Gods, where have you been, woman? There were what, six or seven of them...at least. It was this series of Werewolf movies from the eighties. Now, those were classic."

Settling back onto the couch, watching the movie with half an eye while discussing the finer points of horror films, Alex shivered. As though the maneuver were totally natural, he drew her unresisting form against his side, reaching behind them to retrieve the chenille throw. Turning on the couch, he reclined, propping his large feet on the table as Alex snuggled against his chest, curling up in his arms. He did his best to debunk her misguided theories on gore and dismemberment, while she scoffed at his far out theories of creatures of the night. Where did he get this stuff? They debated the scare power of Vampyre versus Werewolf, and, tucking her beneath his arm, he rested his cheek on the crown of her head.

She drifted to sleep with a smile on her lips, and hopeful possibilities filling her dreams.

****

A few hours later, Cole woke with a start. His neck burned all down one side from lying at such an odd angle. Stranger still was the very pleasant sensation of warm, female curves stretched out, full-length on top of him. He blinked down at the top of Alex's head, and recalled she wasn't—*absolutely was not*—supposed to be sleeping.

"Shit," he hissed, shifting her in his arms until he had a clear view of her face. He stroked her soft hair back from her cheek. "Alex... Sweetheart, wake up."

She didn't stir, didn't so much as flutter an eyelash. Alarm swam through his veins like acid.

"Alex!" Cole exclaimed, giving her shoulder a gentle shake. "Alex, open your eyes, baby, come on."

She began to show signs of life. She snuggled closer to him with a slight frown of displeasure puckering her brow. Groaning a little, she strained to hold the morning back, pressing her face to the side of Cole's throat.

"Alex, you have to wake up."

He glanced to the clock. Ten-thirty. Thank the gods she'd left her blinds closed, or she'd be lying in a pile of ash right now. There was no telling how long they'd been asleep. The last time he recalled looking at the clock, it had been just after five. She stretched, catlike, in his arms and lifted her head to peer down at him. Confusion wrinkled her brow. Her voice was husky with sleep, and it stirred him.

"Did I sleep *on* you?"

He let his gaze drop to where her breasts crushed against his chest, and lifted his bold stare to hers, as if that were sufficient answer. Then again, if that weren't enough of an answer, the rigid swell of his arousal pressing intimately at the juncture of her thighs should have been explanation all by itself. Blushing, Alex rolled to Cole's side, untangling their legs before she dropped to the floor. She pushed herself up and away from him.

"How are you feeling? Head hurt? Dizzy?"

"My head's a little sore, and my cheek throbs a bit. Other than that I'm fine."

Cole sat up and rubbed at the stiffness in his neck. Noticing his discomfort, she climbed to her knees on the couch at his side and pushed his hand away. Her hands replaced his, and she began kneading at the knot between his neck and shoulder. In a matter of minutes, she'd dissolved the knot and moved on to the rest of the soreness in his shoulders and upper back. He groaned deep in his throat and gave himself over to the pleasure of her hands on his body.

At length he drawled, "Screw the music, can I keep you just for this?"

Then the realization hit him right between the eyes, right through his hammering heart that the music and all the rest didn't matter. He just wanted to keep *her*. End of story.

Laughing, oblivious to his line of thought, she patted him on the shoulder and scooted back to sit beside him. "Sorry, big boy, I'm out of your price range." Then her look turned serious, and she remarked, "You took such good care of me last night, Cole. I don't know how to thank you."

He stared at her, lost in the aquamarine brilliance of her eyes for a moment. Gradually, he pulled himself free, but he let his gaze drop to her lips, and he sank again, suggesting, "Oh, I'm sure we could think of something."

Alex's eyes widened. She slid back a bit, pushing a little more space between them.

Disappointed, Cole yawned and pushed to his feet. "Take today off. You're overdue."

Stifling a yawn of her own, she stretched and blinked up at him. "You'll get no argument here."

As soon as she began to stretch, her breasts straining the fabric of her shirt, he clamped his teeth together, fangs stretching long, and spun on his heel, darting for the door. She trailed in his wake. "I think I just might take a quick swim, and then head back to the city for the day. I need to check in on my place. Maybe I'll do a little shopping. I'll be back this evening."

He nodded and, unable to stop himself from glancing over his shoulder at her, he hesitated. The craving hit him. Wave after wave of hunger. His hands gripped the doorframe so hard he left indentations in the wood.

Instead of sweeping her up into his arms, as he so desperately longed to do, he offered, "Drive carefully."

Then he forced himself to walk away. It was one of the hardest things he'd ever done.

Chapter 12

Alex broke the undisturbed surface of the pool in one long, smooth dive. She swam beneath the surface for nearly the length of the pool then came up for air before making the return trip to the other end. The water was cool and deliciously invigorating as the warm late-morning sun kissed her skin. It was pure bliss. Quiet. Serene.

As a rule, the band and their devoted hangers-on didn't stir until well after noon, at the earliest. Alex took advantage of the opportunity for a solitary swim every chance she got. She gave into the urge to take one last lap before climbing from the shimmering water. As she stood on the patio, toweling herself dry, Alex caught a flash of movement from the corner of her eye near shrubbery on the south lawns. Blinking, she paused and peered closer, but whoever was there had gone. Shrugging, she wrapped the towel around her as she headed for the French doors.

A little more than an hour later, Alex had showered, dressed, and buckled herself behind the wheel of her car. She eased the Shelby from Cole's garage, slowing for the security gate, then let the powerful machine roar on the drive back to the city. There was something therapeutic about throttling the motor wide open and letting the wild whip of wind rake through her hair. A wide, self-satisfied smile curved her lips as the ache in her muscles and the throb in her temple dissipated with each passing mile.

Her cell rang as she pulled up in front of a

modest gray townhouse with its cranberry trim, its tidy lawns stretching back toward the beach. Nearby, waves crashed against the shoreline, the rhythm of the ocean's heartbeat, fierce and relentless. Gulls cried their distinctive greetings, circling and diving from the crisp azure skies to snag a meal from the ocean's bounty. Myriad flora perfumed the salty air, sinking through her, relaxing her as no manufactured aromatherapy ever could.

Her gaze swept over the lush lawns with a distinctive note of pride. This was *her* domain. The first thing she'd purchased when she'd broken into music and begun to live on her own terms. This piece of real estate had been her stab at independence. A real home. It had been the best thing she'd done for herself to date, the only thing she'd done that hadn't resulted in one regret or another. Her brow wrinkled as her eyes skimmed over the hedges separating her yard from the neighbors. They were a little ragged around the edges, and weeds were making a debut appearance in the flowerbeds lining the walk. Alex made a mental note to speak to her gardener about that as she flipped her insistent cell open.

"Alex Sinclair."

"Good afternoon, boss lady," chimed a cheerful, feminine voice. "How goes the music biz?"

"Hello, Rita." Alex jingled her keys as she made for the front door. "What's up?"

"I just wanted to see what you thought of the column," her assistant hedged.

Alex zeroed in on the cagey note in her assistant's smooth and collected voice. "And?"

Rita paused for half a heartbeat and heaved a troubled sigh. "Someone called the office this morning. Claimed he was a reporter, though he refused to give his name or the name of the paper he worked for. He was asking a whole lot of questions about you...personal questions, Alex. Questions that didn't seem to have anything to do with Griffin."

A slight frown puckered Alex's brow as she let herself inside and nudged the door closed with the back of her foot. Distracted, she dropped her purse onto the small table just inside the door and murmured, "I see."

"I told him I'd be happy to make an appointment, and I refused to answer any questions." Alex could hear the faint click-clicking in the background as Rita toyed with her pen...a sure sign her assistant was anxious. Then Rita's voice skated into the arena of agitated, and the fine hairs on the back of Alex's neck came to attention. "Whoever he was, Alex, he got...freaky."

Alex paused as she set the keys down beside her purse. It wasn't like Rita to become flustered, and she wouldn't be calling Alex with this if she didn't think it was important. "How so?"

"He kept telling me I wanted to help him. Kept saying I wanted to tell him whatever he wanted. His voice was...weird, soft, like...I don't know...coaxing. He was just kinda creepy, you know?" She paused, as if expecting her next comments would earn her a reprimand, though Alex had always been more than accommodating as a boss. "When I refused to cooperate, his patience seemed to...snap. He started ranting and rambling about 'Cole' this, and 'Cole' that...making him see what a mistake he'd made sticking his nose where it didn't belong. It was just..." Rita trailed off. "Alex, I know I'm supposed to remain professional no matter the provocation, but he was just so...I hung up on him. I'm sorry."

"That's okay, Rita," Alex reassured her. "Don't worry about it. Just let me know if he calls back. Document the time and date of the call, take notes of whatever he says. And don't give out any information to anyone. You did just fine."

Sounding a bit more steadied, Rita replied,

"Sure thing."

"Oh, Rita," Alex added. "I read over the proofs, everything looks great. Terrific job! I knew I was leaving the column in good hands, but you blew me away."

"Thank you!" Rita's pleasure glowed through the line. Then, without so much as a momentary pause, she rushed on in her effervescent way. "So, spill the beans. Is he as gorgeous as all his pictures?"

With feigned innocence, Alex murmured, "He?"

"Cole Gunnarrson! Honestly, Alex," Rita exclaimed. "I swear! You're torturing me here."

If she only knew...

"I'll be in touch," Alex remarked with a small, self-deprecating smile, before flipping her phone closed.

She watered her plants, called the gardener, and putzed around the house for an hour or so. She'd come to fill her days—and her nights –with work. Now that she didn't have that to focus on, she was bored senseless.

She stared at the ornate clock on the wall and chewed her lip, sighing. She didn't want to return to Cole's just yet, but she didn't have much of anything to do here either, certainly nothing that would require more than ten or fifteen minutes of her attention. There was no question about it. She needed to get a life.

Flipping her cell open again, she thumbed in the number to her salon. Luck was smiling on her today. A slot to have her nails done had come available just moments ago, and, as luck would have it, that appointment flowed into an available opening with her stylist. By the time she hung up the phone, Alex had the rest of her afternoon booked full of nothing but personal pampering time at the salon. Something she hadn't done in too long to remember.

Late that evening, as Alex drove back to Cole's

she glanced in the rear view mirror to survey the small mountain of department store bags, smiling without the slightest hint of guilt. She'd topped off her day at the salon with a small shopping spree.

Okay, she allowed with a slight smirk, so it hadn't been so small. Her Visa was, most likely, traumatized—passed through so many hands it probably needed therapy—but she shrugged with glee, floating on a euphoric rush of shopping adrenaline. She consoled herself with the knowledge that she'd pay it all off tonight with a couple clicks of the mouse.

Already, her mind sorted through the clothes and the shoes filling her back seat, snagging on one ensemble in particular. It was a sleek little red number with matching stilettos. She couldn't wait to try it on again. She determined she'd save that one for a special occasion, but she hadn't been able to resist wearing the black belted sheath dress right out of the store. The designer original had just looked so damn good with her new haircut she couldn't fight the urge.

Glancing down at the svelte, black dress and matching mile-high heels, she couldn't help but wonder what it was about a new dress, a day at the salon, and a new pair of shoes that made a woman feel...well, like a new woman. If only she didn't have that hideous bruise on the side of her face, she'd be sitting on cloud nine. The facial and the expert make-up application hadn't gone very far towards concealing the nasty reminder of her run in with Cole's intruder.

She flipped the air conditioner on to fend off the stifling summer heat, unwilling to open the windows and end up ruining her new hairstyle. She loved the way it flipped away from her face. It made her feel...girly. Alex gave the security camera a small, cheerful wave as she drove through the already open gate, then glanced into the rear view as the wrought iron closed behind her. That sight didn't bother her as much as it once had. Curious.

Alex guided the car back into the stall Cole designated for her use, then slid from of the vehicle. As she reached up to lay her purse on the roof of the Shelby, her nails glinted against the car. Red on red, identical in shade. What a fluke. She giggled. Catching herself, she shook her head in wonder. After all, she was not the kind of girl to giggle. With a soft snort, Alex bent at the waist and scooped her shopping bags from the back seat.

Humming, Alex backed out of the car, her small fists full of shopping bags. She juggled until she could reach for her purse, dropping it into one of the bags. Elbowing the car door closed, she turned around and bobbled the bags, gasping in surprise to find Cole a few, short feet away. Where had he come from?

He stared at her with enough heat in his eyes to turn her golden skin bright, sunburned red. He was clad once again in worn, low-riding jeans and combat boots, but he wore no shirt at all, his smooth, muscled chest stripped bare for her admiring stare. A smear of oil adorned his brow and right shoulder. The allure of sexual bliss oozed from his every pore. He was scrumptious, sexy enough to devour in large greedy gulps. Her arms fell to her sides beneath the manageable weight of her purchases—beneath the unmanageable weight of his hungry stare—and her lips parted uncertainly.

Desire—raw lust—had been wreaking havoc on her common sense from the moment she'd first laid eyes on him. Now it reached inside her with a fist of searing hot iron and set down roots—deep, *deep* roots. The sight of him right now damned near brought her to his knees for a devout round of hallelujahs and amens.

His bold icy-blue eyes swept downward, over the curve-enhancing dress, lingering on the daring, plunging vee that reached to her sternum. His gaze was as intimate as a physical caress, tracing the dip of waist and flare of hip, and the muscle in his jaw ticked with a fury. His heated stare skated down her legs to the tips of her sexy, black heels. She felt...naked...beneath his intense perusal.

Unable to speak, Alex watched him watching her as he drew a long, labored breath, and then he lifted his burning stare back to her face...very slowly. Her pulse tripped double-time as he walked forward—stalked forward—without a word, trapping her in the hypnotic snare of his stare. He didn't stop until scant few inches separated them.

"I went shopping," she managed to squeak, frantic to break through the heady tension.

"I see that." He reached up to slip a finger beneath the thin strap of material at her shoulder. The back of his knuckles grazed her skin, gliding downward, feathering over the upper curve of her breast.

Her breath snagged in her throat as his finger lingered there, so close, yet not touching, her nipple. Then his fingers slid back up the length of the strap...up, up, until his thumb hovered deliciously at the erratic pulse at the base of her throat.

"New dress?"

She forced a swallow, cleared her throat, and tried twice before she managed to murmur, "Uh-huh."

He edged a little closer, his thighs brushed against hers, and he tilted his head, his eyes probing, entrancing. Compelling. His voice dropped to a deeper, sensual note. "New shoes?"

"Mm-hmm," she breathed, her eyelids sank to half-mast.

His other hand came up to feather through the

soft wisps of hair near her ear. "New haircut?"

"Hhhh..." Her head wobbled, as close to a nod as she could muster. What happened to all the air? Her lungs struggled for oxygen as a swarm of butterflies took flight in the pit of her stomach.

Cole's head dipped close to the side of her neck. His lips hovered, brushing over the raging pulse below her earlobe. Her head swam with the heady scent of him, with the velvety heat of his lips on her skin. She could *hear* him drawing her scent deep into his lungs, and the erotic sound did odd things inside her.

His voice dropped another octave, husky and hungry. His breath soothed her hot flesh. "Same perfume though."

By now she'd lost all ability of speech, was fast losing her tenuous hold on the ability to think, and so she wobbled her head again. His head dipped closer, shifted, his lips whispered over the skin at the crook of her neck, branding her flesh. He lifted his head, and their stares connected. His mouth drifted over hers, so close...so close...but just not quite there. The deep, husky rumble of his voice— the very essence of seduction in its purest form—a dark, possessive sound growled forcefully, "*Never* change that. I like it. *Very much.*"

She whimpered.

Their lips collided, and, at that first contact, desire arced between them like a hot, live electrical current. His tongue swept into her mouth, hot and questing, possessive and elemental, intimate. He leaned into her, pressing her back, pinning her between the car and his towering, hard body.

One long, dexterous hand claimed the curve of her hip, the other curved around her neck so that his thumb rested at the base of her throat, just over her throbbing pulse. The bags dropped from her hands, forgotten, and she jumped, euphoric, into the blazing heat of his kiss. Her hands rose to his waist, then skated upward over the long, sinuous muscles of his back. His skin was so incredibly hot beneath her hands—decadent velvet encasing tempered steel—and she reached for more, greedy now.

The thin, expensive silk of her dress rubbed between their bodies, erotic and taunting, heightening the sensations already overwhelming her. The rigid bulge of his arousal pressed against her, and her body responded, reacting like a chemistry set beneath the magical hands of a Nobel genius. The scent of him, spicy male heat with a hint of motor oil, slipped through her system like a heady aphrodisiac, potent and undeniable.

Cole angled his head, deepening the kiss to the point of devouring her. At her willing surrender, he growled low, exultant. His hands slid over her body, hard and possessive. His knee wedged between her thighs. He surrounded her, overwhelmed her, kissed her utterly senseless, and Alex reveled in his masterful seduction, satisfying her curiosity and whetting her appetite for more. His kiss was intoxicating...*he* was intoxication at its finest. She whimpered again, rubbing against him like a kitten begging for attention.

Alex couldn't think. She could only feel. And, oh dear Lord, did he feel good! Her knees had turned to water. Thank heaven, his solid body held her trapped against the car, or she'd be sprawled on the concrete. She burned with a fire she'd never known. For a fleeting second, a sharp sting on her lower lip—just where his teeth raked over her flesh—brought her near the surface of reality. But the sensation was gone in a heartbeat, leaving behind the salty, coppery taste of her own blood. In a flash, that, too, was gone, and all she could taste was Cole's raw hunger. A hunger that raged out of control.

His hips rocked against her, violent and demanding, grinding his rigid staff at that sensitive place between her thighs, and she purred deep in her throat, silky and inviting. Her control, what precious little there had been left of it, snapped. Her hands clutched at him, her breathing ragged. She had to have more of him.

With one hand cupping and kneading her breast, he slid the other down her thigh to grasp at the hem of her skirt, drawing it upward. Her knee slid up the outside of his leg, caressing him, inviting him closer, begging for his touch. His mouth turned voracious, the harsh rumble of pleasure erupting from the back of his throat animalistic, feral. Thrilling.

"They were running low on high performance, but I managed to snag the last case of..." Deacon's voice trailed away, and he halted just inside the doorway to stare. Styx stumbled into his back, bumping him off balance.

Deacon's voice cascaded over Alex like a bucket of ice water. She tore her lips from Cole's and began shoving at his shoulders. Drawing a ragged breath, he eased back only the slightest bit, and reached down between them, readjusting the exceptionally large bulge in his jeans. Alex stared, goggle-eyed with shocked fascination. Her mouth hung open. She lifted her stunned gaze to his, and Cole shot her a wicked grin that coursed itchy need straight into her veins. Once again, the odd glow of his eyes held her bemused and captivated. The way he stared at her, the way his eyes pierced her shot a primitive thrill through her core. Damn the interruption. Damn the return of reality.

Turning, he strutted toward the Corvette at the end of the row of vehicles, leaving her to stare at Deacon and Styx with shame burning her cheeks. Groping blindly at her sides, she retrieved her bags and set out for the house on shaking legs, her eyes affixed on the door Deacon and Styx had just stepped through. The two men moved aside as she passed. Blind as she was, she couldn't miss the wide, knowing smirks glowing on their faces.

Chapter 13

Alex stumbled through the house, dazed. Almost half an hour passed before she regained control of her scrambled wits. This afternoon clearly hadn't been enough time away from the devastating effect Cole had on her system. Not nearly enough time by half. That torrential kiss in the garage had proven that fact...with alarming clarity.

Holy hell, what had she been thinking? Answer...she hadn't been thinking, plain and simple. Long before he'd claimed her lips, she'd lost her mind. That was the problem. Whenever Cole was around, she had a tendency to feel, not think. She needed to get her hormones under control...she wasn't fifteen anymore. She was a woman full-grown, capable of controlling her baser needs. Capable of making smarter choices for herself. Hadn't the last time she'd had her fingers burned taught her anything? The last *two* times?

The timely call she'd received from her friend Gina a little while ago, inviting her for a girls' night out on the town, had been a godsend, the perfect excuse to put a little space between her and the enigmatic singer. She hadn't seen Gina in six months, not since she'd moved to Seattle to be with her current scoop of the month. With any luck, she'd have ample opportunity tonight to prove to herself Cole held no specific power over her. That her hormones—not some undeniable connection with Cole—were what prompted her to lose control.

She'd looked for him to tell him she was taking tonight off as well, but she hadn't been able to locate him anywhere. Styx had proven impossible to find as well. So—before she could talk herself out of it— she'd left a note on Cole's desk, broke out the sexy little red number she'd bought today, and headed for the city.

Club Déjà Vu, Gina had said. The name didn't ring any bells, but she wasn't worried about finding it. Gina gave infallible directions. If a blind man got lost in a snowstorm in the middle of some cornfield in Iowa, Gina could have him snuggled up beside a toasty fire in some cozy farmhouse, steaming cup of hot chocolate in hand, inside of ten minutes, all via cell phone half a country away.

Pulling into the parking lot adjacent to her destination, 11011 Cedar Avenue, Alex smiled, not one wrong turn anywhere. Gina hadn't lost her knack. Getting through the crush of people on the sidewalk took a bit of negotiating, but the security at the door proved pitifully easy. A swish of her slinky red dress, a flash of pearly whites, a coy batting of lashes, and she was in like flint.

Finding Gina proved daunting in the darkened dance club. Alex elbowed her way to the bar, slipping into a narrow wedge of space between a short, unattractive balding man and a leggy, eye-catching woman with a short, curling cap of flame red hair. As Alex lifted her hand to signal the bartender, someone jostled her from behind, and she stumbled against the redhead.

"Sorry about that." Alex grimaced.

"No problem, it's a real madhouse in here tonight, isn't it?" Red reached for her drink. "I'm Madelyn. Come here often?"

"Alex. No, first time. I'm supposed to meet a friend here, though I'll be lucky if I find her in this crush. You?"

"A couple times. Mostly with friends, though tonight I'm meeting someone in particular. Actually,

I met him here. Sexy bedroom eyes, if you get my meaning. The guys here are *sooo* hot," the redhead giggled, then she was the one jostled. A small bit of her drink sloshed over the side of her glass, splattering on her knuckles.

The two women exchanged commiserating smiles, then someone near the door must have caught the redhead's eye, because she excused herself and moved away, her drink held carefully away from her body. Alex flashed a couple bills, ensuring the rapt consideration of the bartender. While she waited for her order, a hand landed heavily on her shoulder.

Before Alex could turn, a husky female voice hissed close to her ear. "Hand over the dress, and no one gets hurt." A smile tugged at her lips. Turning, Alex found herself the recipient of a bone-crushing hug as Gina gushed in her ear. "Where did you find that sexy piece of come-and-get-me? My God, I'm so jealous. I may as well go home now, because not a single male eye will be able to turn away from the sight of you."

"Don't be ridiculous, Gina." Alex feigned a Shakespearian sigh of resignation. "Next to you I am but a sad, pitiful wallflower."

"You are forgiven, oh pitiful wallflower," Gina crooned. Then she claimed Alex's hand and tugged her away from the crush at the bar, over to a table near the dance floor. The two sat for a time, catching up on the last several months over colorful drinks. The music was loud, the air warm and close, the lights dim and pulsing.

As Gina began to ramble, Alex's eyes scanned the crowd, her finger tracing a line of condensation down the side of her tall, thin glass. For one heart stopping moment, wild, sun-kissed hair crossed her line of vision, and Cole's face swam in her mind. Where had he gone tonight?

"So I decided to take the job." Gina took a long sip of her vibrant, fuchsia beverage, winking at a strapping stud two tables over with eyes like charcoal and skin the color of her favorite latte.

"Wait..." Alex squeezed Gina's forearm to gain her undivided attention. "What job? I thought you decided Seattle was the only place under the sun where you could be happy. And what happened to what's-his-name?"

Gina raised a sculpted brow and shook her head. The disgusted roll of her beautiful eyes spoke volumes. "Hell*oooo*.... Where have you been for the last fifteen minutes? Cuz, sweetie, it sure as certain wasn't here with me."

"I'm sorry, Gina, I kind of got lost in the zone," Alex mumbled, dipping her head to her neon blue drink.

"Maybe *I* should be asking *you* what his name is."

"Nobody!" Alex blushed at her own furious outburst, even as visions of Cole danced in her head. Taking another sip, she continued in bland tones. "There's no one, Gina, absolutely no one."

"Oh, sweetie, puh-leaze don't tell me you're still hung up on that pitiful excuse for an ex-fiancé of yours. Girl, he is *so* not worth your time."

"Good heavens, no," Alex denied, shuddering. Then she vowed, "Tell me again, I promise I'll listen better this time."

Shooting Alex a discerning, narrow-eyed stare, Gina sniffed. "Why I even bother..."

Alex bumped her shoulder to Gina's, breaking out a sunny smile. "I know, I know. You have such an aversion to talking about yourself. I should be tied to the mast and flogged for asking you to do it again."

Gina stuck her tongue out in a childish gesture and drained her glass. She waved to a passing waiter before turning amused eyes to Alex. "Okay, condensed version. Shemar was just too full of himself to invest the appropriate amount of attention in me."

Alex interrupted with a sarcastic snort. "And we all know Gina is the *only* one allowed to be the center of attention..."

Gina scowled archly. "You want to hear this or not?"

Holding her hands up in a defensive motion, Alex leaned away, grumbling, "This is me, shutting up..."

Clearing her throat for dramatic effect, Gina lifted her nose in royal disdain. "As I was saying...we didn't see eye to eye on certain...aspects of our relationship. And, sweetie, this hair was meant to tolerate only so much rain." Alex snorted again, and Gina's eyes narrowed, forcing Alex to bite off the caustic remark before it left her mouth.

"I've been putting out feelers, and a friend dropped a good word for me over at Phoenix Records. Seems their receptionist up and quit—no warning, no notice—just...disappeared." Gina shrugged, snapping her fingers for effect. "I've already put down a deposit on a quaint little condo. Start work Monday."

Alex could only marvel at Gina's resiliency. "That's terrific, Gina. It'll be wonderful having you back."

Gina was too busy flirting with her potential new flame...or at the very least tonight's entertainment...to give Alex's envious congratulations more than a pompous nod. Gina's efforts had not gone unnoticed, as the object of her attentions gained his feet, and was, at present, strutting his way to their table.

His unremarkable friend, a tall, lean specimen with a thick curtain of black, silky hair and a dimple in his chin trailed close behind. Kohl lined his eyes, giving them a bruised and hollow, yet strangely sultry look. His skin was so pale she wondered that he'd seen the light of day in the last decade. Though he didn't dress Goth, he could pass in every other way. He wasn't her normal type, but, given how well her instincts had worked out in the past, she was willing to give him a fair chance, or a fair dance at the very least.

An odd prickling sensation fluttered at the nape of her neck when she placed her hand in his, accepting the offer to dance. In short order, the quartet headed for the shadows on the dance floor writhing fluidly beneath a vintage disco ball and strobe lights. Swiping her hand over the back of her neck to dislodge the pesky tickle, Alex stepped into the tall man's outstretched arms, wordlessly allowing him to draw her close...very close. That prickling turned to a full on, physical itch. As they moved with the rhythm, Alex waited for that breathless, intoxicated sensation to sweep down on her. Any second now, she told herself.

Maybe if she concentrated really hard...

But it wasn't working. She had no trouble breathing. Her head did not swim, and her heart did not pound. No sparks leaped between them. There was no sizzle. Only that strange, uncomfortable sensation at the nape of her neck. Disappointment weighed on her, though she kept a cheerful smile plastered on her lips. Heaven help her, what in the name of blue blazes was wrong with her? Where were her hormones when she needed them?

****

The Party Crasher eased close to his prey. His blood pulsed and churned in anticipation. Just then, the notes changed, the tempo picked up for a new song. The music shook the walls, vibrating the floor beneath their feet, dark and erotic, and the Crasher smiled, a sinister chuckle tickling the back of his throat. How ironic. Accompanied by the distinctive riffs and rhythms of Stolen Innocence, Cole's voice, deep as the shadows in the night, rich and smooth as fine cognac, belted out his band's latest chart-topper, *Moonlight and Blood*. The timing couldn't have been better had he planned it himself. He'd have to remember music the next time. It certainly added just the right touch.

His partner smiled up at him, and he eased her a little closer. His body brushed hers with practiced finesse, hinting at attraction, but not overwhelming enough to make her worry. She was relaxed, pliable and just the tiniest bit inebriated.

Moving with smooth deliberation, he leaned close, his lips hovering at her ear. So close to that precious little artery, he could almost taste the Bailey's she'd been tipping all night. "It's awfully warm in here, angel. Wanna go outside to grab some air?"

She hesitated. Could she sense his eagerness, his anticipation? Maybe he should have bought her one more drink. Stealing a glance at the illuminated face on his watch, just beyond her shoulder, he strangled back a vicious oath. Ten to eleven. Adrenaline surged. He was running out of time. It had to be just perfect. It all had to go exactly according to the plan. If she didn't die at exactly eleven…he'd have to start all over at the beginning. The message would be lost.

Drawing a deep breath, he steadied his body. There was still time. He still had a few minutes. He'd just have to move a little faster than he'd anticipated.

"Man," he mumbled, holding a hand to the side of his forehead, swaying on his feet. "I'm not feelin' so hot." He gave a tipsy chuckle. "Then again, maybe I'm too hot. I shouldn't have had that last drink."

"You hardly touched it," she protested. Her eyes narrowed with concern, her palm cupped his lean cheek. "You do look a little pale. Maybe we'd better go outside. Can you make it to the back door?" She motioned to a point just behind him. "It's right over here."

"No!"

Her eyes flared, and he shot her a fuzzy, disarming smile. Styx, the ever-reliable watchdog, lounged near the rear entrance. Where Styx was, Cole was sure to be close by. "No...those back alleys give me the creeps."

"Okay," she encouraged as she drew his arm around her slim shoulders. "Just lean on me if you need to...and warn me if you're going to get sick."

Nodding, he staggered beside her, allowing her to guide him from the club. However, the crowd outside the doors was hardly any better than inside. He commented as much, ducking and passing a hand over his face when another familiar profile floated in the crowd.

"Here, let's just step around the side of the building," she suggested, angling through the crowd. "There's no one over there, it'll be much easier for you to catch your breath. Are you all right?"

His eyes had begun to burn, his fangs to extend in anticipation of the kill, so he kept his face tilted away from hers. He pressed a fleeting kiss to her crown of short red curls and grinned, praising her, "This is perfect, Madelyn. Just what I was hoping for."

"I can go back inside, get you some ice water...or something."

"No," he murmured, edging between her and the street, slowly lifting his face to the dim streetlight. "I'm feeling much better now."

"Are you sure? You didn't..." Her words trailed off on a slight gasp as she stumbled backwards.

Her mouth fell open on a soundless scream. In a flash, he seized her by the shoulders and lifted her effortlessly, carrying her deeper into the night. She struggled in earnest now, crying for help. Her pleas went unanswered, drowned out by the life inside the club. He didn't stop until he had her right where he wanted her.

"Shhh, pet, it will all be over soon." He glanced down at his watch. "Very soon now."

"Let me go, please," she pleaded. "I swear I won't tell anyone."

He sent her a disgusted look.

"What are you? Why are you doing this?"

And here he'd thought she might be the one to die with a little dignity. He should have just kept his hand over her mouth. She wasn't any better than the others, with her twenty questions and her pathetic begging. Why couldn't these Humans understand death couldn't be reasoned with? It was their fate. The how and the why might vary, but in the end they all died.

"Because they haven't figured it out yet."

"Who...who hasn't figured out what?" Her whining was starting to grate on his nerves.

Narrowing his eyes, he glanced at his watch again. Was the damn thing slowing down? Maybe he'd better replace the battery, just in case. Heaving a sigh, he fixed his burning gaze on her throat.

"Others of my kind...and don't play dumb, pet. You know exactly what I am," he snarled, flashing fang at her. "Faking stupidity now isn't at all becoming."

"Why?" Her struggles were weak now, her voice a breathless whisper. Her terror coated the air. He dragged the flavor in through flared nostrils, savoring the acrid scent as these worthless Human females enjoyed the scent of fresh cut flowers.

"Why? Because sheep have no business ruling

the world while the rest of us hide, concealing what we are so the *food* doesn't panic. Now, be a good girl, and hold still. This shouldn't hurt...much." He smoothed a hand over her crisp curls, his grin wide and menacing. Then he fisted his hand in her hair as he wrapped an arm around her, quelling her renewed struggles. Jerking her head back, he tasted her fear with the tip of his tongue. Ambrosia. He graced her with one soft pass of his lips across her flesh.

And then he opened his mouth. Wide.

****

Cole scented her the moment she'd walked into the club. Every nerve ending in his body went on high alert. *His* female was here...in the very club he and the TFRA expected the Party Crasher to make his next move. *Tonight.* She was definitely here, and so were several others of his kind. The club was infested with Vampyre.

His eyes zeroed in on Alex like heat-seeking missiles, and his heart knocked against his ribs. By the gods, she was devastating tonight. She outshone every other female in the place. Then his eyes narrowed, nostrils flared. Another male, one of his own race, drew her out onto the dance floor. Primitive instinct flared up inside him, and he forgot all else but the fact that another male dared to touch what was his.

He didn't know the male holding Alex so close. He'd never talked to him, never laid eyes him. He didn't even know the male's name. It made not one bit of difference.

Cole wanted the Vampyre dead.

Styx leaped in front of Cole, and, at risk of a nasty bite, braced his hands against Cole's enraged, heaving chest. "Wow, Cole, power down, man."

He dropped his gaze to Styx's hand, although every muscle in his body strained to exact

150

retribution, to bleed the Vamp holding his female dry. As he became aware of curious eyes upon him, Cole lowered his head and closed his burning eyes, dragging in deep gulps of heavy air in vain effort to regain control of his temper.

He'd come here to hunt a killer. Statistically speaking, tonight was the night. And this could very well be the location. He'd been running all the angles, trying to get inside the mind of the Rogue.

What the hell was she doing here...*here*...tonight of all nights? On the eleventh... He'd thought he'd left her at home, secure behind lock and key.

He'd just gotten the surprise of his life. Surprise, *Helheim*. She'd ambushed him, goddamn it.

And, by the gods, that dress... He'd thought the little black number she'd had on earlier was tempting. This one was sin incarnate, leaving precious little to the imagination, hugging her lithe body in all the right places, exposing an indecent amount of her succulent flesh. Without a doubt, she'd handpicked this dress to torment every male inside a fifty-mile radius into a slavering state of mindless lust. As far as he was concerned, she'd succeeded. Stupendously. She couldn't have tempted him more had she strutted through the room, carrying a decanter full of fresh O negative...buck-naked.

Drawing another deep breath, he eased back, nodding to Styx.

Styx released him, and Cole shot forward, leaving a cursing Styx to trail in his wake. Cole pushed through the tangle on the dance floor. He didn't stop until he stood behind Alex, scowling ferocious warning at her dance partner.

The nameless Vampyre took one look at Cole and released her, backing up so fast she stumbled forward. He stammered an apology, though Cole wasn't certain if it had been for her benefit or his. Then the male spun on his heel and beat a hasty retreat. Cole hadn't even had to bare his gleaming fangs.

He was almost disappointed.

As Alex stood there, staring after her retreating partner, Cole slipped close, molding himself against her backside, his hands claiming her waist with possessive force. She stiffened, jerking away, her head whipping around so she could peer over her shoulder. He lowered his dark glasses with the tip of one finger, searing her with a scowl. The second her eyes connected with his, her breath seeped out in a loud whoosh, and her jaw dropped.

"Cole..."

Anger still simmered beneath the surface, giving Cole's expression, his movements a dangerous, edgy energy. Without a word, he jerked her back, until the firm globe of her bottom crushed against his loins. His chest pressed against her bare back. His arms caged her to him, steely strong and unforgiving. His nostrils flared, isolating her scent, dragging it in. By Odin, the smell of her alone was enough to reduce a Vamp to a pile of groveling, lusting ash.

Slowly, methodically, he began to move.

Hips first. Grinding his thick erection against her backside, rock-hard and unmistakable, surging and swaying until she caught the fever.

Then his mouth. His lips caressed the curve where her neck met her shoulder. Hot and wet. Open. His tongue tasted her skin. Licking and suckling at her flesh. Kissing and lapping, nipping up the side of her throat until her chest rose and fell in quick bursts, and she was putty in his hands. His name tumbled from her lips, breathy and tormented, confused and aroused. The low moan, tugged from deep in her throat, wrung a low growl from him.

Instinct...impulse...he wasn't sure which drove him, but he nicked her, just below her earlobe where her pulse thrummed hot and irresistible. The sudden, intoxicating flavor of her blood blossoming on his tongue shot need—more ferocious than any he'd ever known—straight to his core. But this was neither the time, nor the place to quench that hunger. With a reluctant groan, he licked the tiny wound, sealing it closed, resisting the urge to take more.

He moved his hands. Inch by slow, agonizing inch, they slipped over her body, until his palms pressed flat against her stomach, pinning her against the length of his body. Primal possession influenced every caress, every stroke and every taste. He would seduce her, tempt her as no one else ever would. By the time he was done, she'd never look at another male again.

Her head fell back against his shoulder, her eyes closed tight. Fireworks exploded between them, majestic and awesome. Incendiary. It was the first time he'd ever looked forward to burning.

The music changed, the tempo increased, and still Cole moved with deliberate, seductive purpose, their clothing no real barrier to the aching desire raging through him. Cole's own voice poured from the club's speakers, *Moonlight and Blood*. When he'd penned this song, put it to music, he'd no idea how sensual, how erotic the lyrics could be, given the right context.

Now he knew.

The crowded, pulsing dance club faded to nothing...until there was only the woman in his arms and the need she stirred deep inside him. With every throb of the music, his movements became slightly rougher, less restrained. His fingers splayed, his hands quested. Her thighs. Her hips. Her stomach. Her breasts. Her throat. He left no place untouched, no place unclaimed. Her skin was softer than the silk dress she wore, so delectable beneath his lips. His mouth watered.

As the music climbed again, growing to a faster bump and grind, Cole spun her in his arms. Her eyes flew open, registering surprise, locking on his. Glowing, icy-blue to dazed, desire-clouded aquamarine. All around them bodies writhed, brushing against them, jostling past them. Surging around them.

Her tongue skidded across her lower lip, and Cole growled again, deep and low, the hunger growing. The animalistic sound so rough, so threatening, several dancers near them suddenly exited the dance floor. Others...faceless individuals Cole paid no mind to, soon replaced them.

Without warning, he yanked her to him. His lips covered hers, hard and fast. His mouth slanted, tongue plunged, teeth banged, fangs scraped delicate skin, drawing blood. Cole sucked the heady droplets away, wrapping an arm around her waist crushing her to him. His knee thrust between her thighs, and his hand squeezed her bottom, grinding her along his thigh. His hips surged in time with the tempo, moving with the beat of the music. Tongues mated and tangled, breath fused.

The scent of her arousal, the pounding of desire-ladened blood coursing through her veins, robbed him of his better judgment. Cole's breath ripped in and out of his chest, harsh and ragged. His fangs ached. Blood rushed in his ears. His loins pounded with urgent need.

To the casual observer, they looked like nothing more than a man and a woman enjoying a provocative dance...a *very* provocative dance. His large body blocked the front of her from view of anyone who might glance their way. As the mass of dancers swayed and gyrated around them, Cole kept his arm anchored around her waist and slid his other hand down the front of her body, caressing her breast before slipping lower between them. The hem of her dress had ridden up in their exertions, and his hand found its way beneath the crimson silk.

His mouth angled over hers again, deepening the kiss to the point of enthralling surrender...*whose* surrender he wasn't quite sure. His fingers traced the edge of her panties, slipping beneath, smoothing through her slick folds. The feel of her, hot and wet...all for him...ripped another growl from deep in his throat. His thumb flicked and rubbed against her swollen nub as two fingers sank deep into her tight heat. Again and again. Stroking. Claiming.

Her body convulsed and shuddering, exploding in his arms. Her startled cry of release, muffled by his lips, drowned out by the burning pulse of the music, was sweeter to his ears than all the music he'd ever heard...ever written. She melted into him, drooped against him, limp and pliable, her breath coming in short little bursts against the side of his neck. She clung to him, her arms wrapped around his neck.

His fangs, already stretched long behind his lips, throbbed. His entire body vibrated with need. He cradled her against him until she managed to get her feet back under her. Once she did, he led her from the dance floor, and pushed her down onto the seat she'd vacated earlier. Cole pulled another chair close to hers and sank onto it, draping his arm around her shoulders, as a lover would. He didn't dare drag her from the club, as he longed to do. If he did, as strung out as he was right now on desire for her, he'd bite her. There was no doubt in his mind. He wouldn't be able to stop himself.

Vivid color began to surge into her already flushed cheeks. He shifted, gritting his teeth against the urge to toss her over his shoulder and drag her to the parking lot. By Thor, as hard as he was, he didn't even know if they'd make it home before he had her naked and writhing on his lab, impaled on his...

Her furious hiss broke into his thoughts. "How could you... Are you insane? You just can't... You can't..."

"I can...and I did." His smile was tight, knife sharp, his eyes blazing, choking off her indignant anger, daring her to refute him. "Or would you like me to prove it...again?"

As if sensing the dangerous ground on which she tread, Alex changed the subject. "What are you doing here?"

"I could ask the same of you," he reminded her, evading her question.

Before she could respond, the woman he'd seen her with earlier returned, alone. Her gaze passed over Alex's bemused expression, lingered on Cole's possessive posture for a moment, then she aimed a hundred watt smile at him. His eyes followed the dark-eyed beauty as she took her seat. He curved his lips, as close to a smile as he could get with a mouthful of sharply aroused fangs.

Alex's friend shot her a teasing, accusatory glance. "You've been holding out on me, I see. Where did you find this *gorgeous* creature, sweetie? And, more important, there wouldn't happen to be another one like him lurking around in here, would there?" Before Alex could find her voice, her friend thrust her hand out to Cole, quipping, "Gina Marcello, by the way, Alex's utterly-green-with-envy friend. And you are?"

Cole grinned, though insatiate lust still held a sharp blade to his throat. He shook her hand, charmed by her vivacious bluntness. "Cole Gunnarrson. It's a pleasure to meet any friend of Alex's."

Gina's eyes narrowed for a moment as she considered his features, but before she could make the connection, Styx loomed over the table. Gina leaned back in her chair, her smile faintly stunned.

"Oh, my *God*, another one... Bury me now, I've died and gone to heaven."

"Gina, this is Styx." Alex's eyes lit up, and, sharing a smile with the man in question, she added, "Like the river, not the wood. Styx, this is my friend, Gina Marcello."

Styx shot Gina an absentminded smile, then turned troubled eyes to Cole. His gaze, like Gina's lingered on the possessive drape of Cole's arm. His nostrils flared, picking up on the faint musk of sexual arousal. His eyes widened, darting from Cole's face to Alex and back again.

"Hey, Slim," Styx greeted Alex before he addressed Cole in terse tones. "Cole, can I talk to you for a minute?"

"Later..."

"*Now*," Styx countered forcefully.

The lines at the corners of Styx's mouth were deep. His body was rigid, and his fierce frown deadly earnest.

Cole sat up straighter, his brow puckering.

Styx nodded once, too fast for the Mortal eye to catch.

Curses, vivid and culturally diverse filled Cole's head. He turned to Alex, leaning close to her ear. "Alex, stay right here. Don't go anywhere. Don't dance with anyone. And for God's sake, don't leave, not until I come back. Promise me..."

She blinked at him, baffled. "Cole, I don't..."

His demand was forceful, his eyes fierce. "Promise me, Alex."

A confused frown wrinkled her brow, but she nodded. "All right, but you're going to have to explain when you—"

He cut her off with a swift, hard kiss, and he pushed to his feet, disappearing into the crowd before she could utter another word. Cole swore again, this time aloud, as he paced after Styx to the rear entrance. This was his fault. What lay beyond those doors was just as much his doing tonight as it was the killer's. If he hadn't gotten so lost in Alex, so wrapped up in jealousy and so consumed with need, he might have prevented another innocent death.

Then another thought occurred to him, and he paused mid-stride, shaken to the core. Alex was here. Inside the same club from which the Party Crasher had just chosen his latest victim. Because of him, she was now involved in the music industry. And she was thirty-three. She could very well have been the tenth victim.

His blood turned to ice in his veins.

Cole stepped out into the darkened alley, and the coppery scent of freshly spilled blood overwhelmed his senses. It didn't take long to understand why. The Rogue hadn't just pierced her jugular, leaving his victim to bleed out with a broken neck. This time, the Crasher ripped the victim's throat completely out. Hers had been a cruel and violent death. Crimson splattered the wall beside him, pooling beneath her lifeless, still-warm body. In lieu of her absent throat, her forehead bore the unmistakable number one. Translation…letter A.

Cole rocked back on his heels as Styx moved to his side. '*Because I ca…*' It didn't take a genius to figure out where this was going…or that there would be one more victim, at least. The sadistic son of a bitch.

"Don't touch anything," Cole muttered, grim, reaching for his phone. He thumbed the number in, only to frown, his eyes darting up the alley when a cell phone began ringing. A second later, Special Agent Derrick Crispin separated himself from the shadows.

Shooting Styx a quick, speaking glance, Cole turned a wary stare to the agent. "Crispin...you move fast."

"Guess you could say I had a...a hunch." Crispin's eyes drifted to the victim, his notepad already in hand.

Cole lifted an eyebrow, searching the empty shadows behind the agent with discerning eyes. "Where's your crew?"

Crispin paused in his writing for a split second, though he didn't lift his eyes from the page. His answer was terse, enigmatic. "They're...elsewhere tonight. Been here long?"

"Not long enough," Styx offered, bristling at the agent's tone, and the unspoken implication that went with it.

"He's escalating," the agent murmured, his hand moving with swift efficiency as he jotted his notes.

"Escalating?" Styx moved closer to the agent, peering over his shoulder, then moved away, frowning, frustrated.

"He's getting closer to the edge," Cole replied, remaining motionless beside the door. His eyes, all of his senses reached out, blanketing the crime scene, noting every detail. "He's becoming more violent, doesn't display the same control with this kill that he did with the others."

Crispin paused in his scribbling to glance over at Cole, his eyes unreadable. Then, with a slight shrug, he pulled a camera from the pocket of his dark trench coat and began snapping photos from various angles. "That's typical of a killer like this. The agency profiler said we should expect this aberration in his MO. They expected him to reach this stage much sooner."

"Thanks for warning us," Styx sniped.

The agent blinked once at Styx before burying

his nose in his notes once more.

Undeterred, Styx pressed, "What else did your profiler have to say?"

Without looking up, his voice dull and unimpressed, Crispin offered, "He thinks, given the wasted blood, the Party Crasher is making a statement with these murders."

"Ya think?"

Crispin shot Styx an irritated glance now, the first sign of emotion they'd seen from the unflappable agent yet. "He's killing these Human females to prove that he can. But the broken neck, the swiftness of death, suggests he doesn't want them to suffer."

"Much more humane...kill them quickly, before they can suffer."

The three males stared down for a moment at the wide-eyed, open-mouthed horror on the once beautiful face. It didn't take a coroner to tell Cole this one did not have a broken neck, and she most definitely *had* suffered.

"He's getting careless." Cole's comment had the agent's head snapping up and around. Cole pointed to the female's handbag, haphazardly tossed a few feet away. "He's never left one of those behind before, has he?"

"No," Crispin remarked, moving to snap a few shots of the discarded purse. "No, he hasn't...assuming it's hers. With the others, we've had to identify them using Human data banks."

When he was done with his camera, Crispin knelt beside the purse. He snapped on a set of rubber gloves and opened the bag, dumping the contents out. The agent shot another round of photos, then stowed the camera as he reached for the feminine wallet.

His eyes drifted from the victim's face to the ID and back. "It's hers, all right. Madelyn Abigail

Kinney, age thirty-three." He thumbed through the wallet and extracted a laminated badge. "Well, what do you know? Miss Kinney was an employee of KEZI."

Cole and Styx remained silent, absorbing the news, absorbing the crime scene. Crispin made a quick phone call, then examined the body more closely before walking the scene. When he finished, he joined them beside the door.

"Pretty routine," Crispin murmured, nose buried in his notepad. "Same MO though he's grown more violent. I'd say, from the amount of blood covering the crime scene, it doesn't appear he consumed much, if any. Body temp of the vic suggests we missed the killer by minutes." He lifted his puppy-dog eyes to Cole, adding, "If you'd have made it out here a few minutes earlier, you might have caught him in the act."

Cole's gaze lowered to the lifeless female lying in a pool of her own blood, only a few feet from a rusty, filthy dumpster. A twinge of guilt flickered just beneath his breastbone. A few minutes earlier, he'd been so consumed with emotions too volatile to name. He'd been giving Alex a dance neither of them was likely to forget in this or any other lifetime.

And once more, it bothered him to no small degree that the agent seemed more concerned with details than the actual victim. The Vampyre behind those soulful eyes was remarkably cold and unfeeling. While he supposed the male was attractive enough, with a face some would even call handsome, Cole could only feel pity for Crispin's lovers. He possessed the compassion and sensitivity of a computer, coldly analytical and detached. More concerned with facts than feelings. Then again, maybe that's how the TFRA had earned their titles as *Enforcers*.

At Crispin's cue, Cole shrugged off his

unsettling thoughts and did a quick sweep of the alley for himself. As with before, the Rogue had been meticulous, leaving not one shred of evidence to implicate himself or a clue to his identity. With a mounting sense of frustration, Cole gave up and, having agreed to call Crispin in a few hours, followed Styx back inside the club. His troubled gaze searched for and found Alex.

He was weary, more exhausted than he'd ever been in his long, long existence. His face was grim, his body tense as he approached her. He could already see the questions forming in her all-too-discerning, beautiful eyes. His shoulders sagged a little, weighed down by guilt and deceit, as he began concocting a story for his abrupt departure.

When had it become so difficult to lie to a female?

Chapter 14

All the way to the estate, she'd examined and re-examined her hormone-charged exchange with Cole in the garage, and the erotic dance they'd shared at the nightclub, and chalked it all up to impulse and treacherous curiosity. His odd departure after their dance had completely baffled her, his explanation no explanation at all. Then again, she hadn't been operating on all eight cylinders at that point either. She could have misunderstood something along the way. On the other hand, how was one to misinterpret a mind-blowing orgasm?

Heat climbed to her cheeks at the mere memory. At least she'd had the drive back to the estate tonight, alone, to try to reassemble some semblance of composure. The things he'd done to her body tonight...things no one else in their right mind would have ever dared...still left her reeling. She couldn't believe she, who'd always gone above and beyond to be circumspect in her actions, had allowed him to touch her like that. In public, of all places. Not only had she allowed it, she'd gotten punch-drunk on his boldness, savored every stroke, surrendering herself to his masterful touch.

She couldn't blame it on the alcohol she'd consumed. She'd barely had more than a drink and a half. She couldn't blame it on the music, or the atmosphere, or the damned full moon. She might be spiteful enough to blame a little of it on Cole. But the truth was, she had no one to blame but herself. Herself and her raging goddamned hormones.

Regardless of her resolve to put it all from her

163

mind, sleep proved elusive. She tried a long, lavish shower, and that too had been an exercise in futility. The slip of water over her skin reminding her too much of Cole's hands as they'd cruised over her body while they'd danced. She'd paced, edgy and frustrated for close to half an hour. Now she sat, staring blindly at the screen on her laptop. Nothing. The words wouldn't come. Reaching up, she wrapped the length of her damp hair into a knot at the back of her head, jamming a pencil into the thick mass to hold it in place. Thanks to her new do, a slight wisp dropped down across her brow, tickling her nose. Snagging the offending lock, she shoved it behind her ear.

Her stomach growled, and her neck ached. The song wasn't coming along as she'd imagined it would, the mood continuing to elude her. Everything she'd written tonight had been so trite, so—used up. Removing the ear buds, she set Cole's IPod aside. Heaving a sigh, Alex saved the file, useless as it was, and powered down her laptop.

She stood, stretched the stiff muscles in her back, and glanced at the clock. It was shortly after four in the morning, and she was starving. She glanced down at the over-sized, soft v-neck T-shirt she'd donned after her shower, nothing more than a pair of lacy, black panties beneath it, and gave a slight shrug, figuring the chance of running into anyone in the kitchen at this hour while she raided Cole's fridge was slim to none. Cole *had* told her to make herself at home, after all.

Even so, she cautiously stuck her head out her door and glanced first right and then left. When she found the hallway vacant, she eased the door open and slipped out into the dim corridor. The marble floor beneath her bare feet was chilly, but the growl in her stomach was much more uncomfortable, driving her onward. She padded down the hall, heading toward the back of the house, praying she wouldn't run into anyone.

She heaved a grateful sigh when she pushed her way inside the kitchen undetected. Not bothering to flip on the lights, relying instead on the pale green night light near the sink, she went to the refrigerator first. Standing in the pool of glaring light pouring from inside the fridge, she pursed her lips. Heaving a sigh, she wandered to the pantry and gazed at the shelves.

Nothing even looked remotely appealing. She was just about to close the door and settle for a piece of fruit from the bowl on the table, when her eyes came to rest on a box of cereal. A bowl full of empty calories sounded divine. She gave in with a guilty smile and reached for the box. Alex walked back to the counter, set the box down, and began opening drawers and doors in search of bowl and spoon.

****

Cole reclined on the sofa in his study, relaxing in the dark after a useless foray into the night shadows looking for nonexistent clues to the identity of the Rogue. The murder at Déjà Vu tonight had gotten to him. This time, Alex had been at the scene. She could so easily have been the victim. She fit the criteria. Right age, right occupation. Right place, right time.

A soft whisper of movement in the hall snared his attention. The illusive phantom preying on innocent females immediately came to mind. Although the intruder was moving in the wrong direction, Cole was all too aware Alex was alone in her room. He moved through the study and out into the hallway, silent as a wraith. The moment he opened the door, the soft, alluring scent of Alex hit him with the force of a category-five hurricane.

No Rogue tonight, only temptation incarnate.

He told himself to turn around and go back into

his study, to close the door and forget she was inside the house. He knew pursuing her was tantamount to playing with fire—something no self-respecting Vampyre would even consider—and yet he could no more turn away from her than he could stop his primal thirst for blood.

He silently pushed the door to the kitchen open, and couldn't believe his eyes. There, standing in the middle of the room, softly humming the refrain from the song they'd been working on earlier, was the most delicious picture he'd seen since Alex's first night in his home.

His system, already revved by the feel of his fingers *inside* her, damned near overheated right then and there. He tensed, using every ounce of his extraordinary control to keep himself from pouncing on her, from dragging her down onto the floor and burying his throbbing erection between her luscious thighs, and his aching fangs in her sweet throat.

Her back was to him as she riffled through a drawer, blissfully unaware of the dangerous predator that had entered the room behind her. His eyes followed her as she pulled something from the drawer. Was that a spoon? His hungry gaze dropped to her bare feet, and very slowly, very leisurely traveled upward. Her smooth, golden calves flexed as she stepped sideways. His hands itched to skim over her soft skin—skin he'd been aching to touch again since he'd laid hands on her that first time.

Then, miracle of miracles, she went up on tiptoe, stretching up to a shelf high above her head. The hem of her shirt, which only barely fell below her hips to begin with, was steadily working its way up, riding impossibly high. His gut clenched, the muscles on his abdomen rippled, as her black silk panties became visible, and then, as the shirt rose higher still, her tattoo peeked at him.

For a breathless moment, the complete image

was clearly visible…the *Odhroerir. His mark.* His body went rigid at the sight of it. The itch in his hands turned to a fiercely burning, shaking need. His eyes devoured her exposed flesh.

Before Cole even realized he'd moved, he found himself directly behind her, his long arm extended alongside hers, his luminous, dilated eyes glued to the back of her neck. His gums ached as his fangs stretched. His fingers snagged on the bowl she'd been reaching for, and he slowly lowered it as she whirled on a gasp of surprise to face him. Cole stood, rooted to the spot, unable to move back, spare inches from pressing full length against her. He couldn't breathe, couldn't think, spellbound.

Her eyes rounded, her mouth formed a tiny, silent gasp. Tentatively, as if she feared his reaction…as if she feared he wasn't real, she lifted a hand to his chest. His gaze dropped to her fingers where they trailed their way down the defined double ridge of muscles covering his abdomen, down the smooth skin that ran below his navel. Odin's teeth, how he wanted those fingers to trail lower, to caress the bulge of his erection through the soft material of his comfortable old sweatpants, or better still…to dip inside the waistband. Then again, he feared he just might burst into flames if she did.

She gasped again, louder then, as if she'd only just realized what she'd done, snatching her hand back. Cole held no such reservations about touching her. With mesmerizing, exquisitely languid movements, he reached a hand up and wordlessly drew the pencil from Alex's hair, greedily watching the silken mass tumble and cascade down around her shoulders in damp, honeyed waves.

The scent of her shampoo ripped through him, sinking the talons of lust into him even deeper. His left hand came up to rest lightly on the curve of her hip, slipping just beneath the hem of her shirt. The fingers of his right hand sank deep into her hair, savoring the warmth of her scalp. He edged closer, until the softness of her T-shirt clad breasts brushed at his lean stomach, teasing him.

"Don't," she croaked. "Don't do that." She swallowed, sucking in a sharp breath. "I can't think when you're so close."

Cole's eyes narrowed—need intensified—at the power she'd just unwittingly handed him. Tired of the distance between them, the proverbial arm's length she'd insisted on, his hand tightened on her hip. "You don't need to think, Alex, just feel. Feel *me*."

At last, she succumbed to his plea for contact, physical and otherwise. With a soft, muffled whimper, she lifted her hands and laid them against his chest, tentative, her elegant, slim fingers splayed. She didn't push him away; instead, she feathered her hands over his chest, as though learning the texture of his skin and savoring the tensile, steely strength of the muscles beneath. Her wide eyes lifted to his once more, and her breath snagged in her throat.

Cole's gaze was riveted on her lips, leaving no doubt as to his intentions. He slipped his hand from her hip around behind her, claiming the upper curve of her bottom. With deliberate, sensual intent, he hauled her against him, pressing his rigid erection against her flat stomach, surging against her, telling her without words exactly how much he craved her. She caught her lower lip in her teeth, then exhaled a tiny burst of air when he rocked his hips against her. Unadulterated longing lanced through his system, and tiny shock waves of need swelled deep in his very core.

Cole lowered his head until his breath fluttered soft against her lips. He waited the space of a heartbeat, two heartbeats...drawing out the anticipation…then he skated his lips across hers. Once, twice. He nipped at her lower lip, suckling it between his, lapping at it with his tongue.

His hand slid down her nape, and his fingers trailed over her spine sending shivers rippling through her system, like the shockwaves after an earthquake. The flat of his hand pressed against her back, directly between her shoulder blades. He could barely breathe for the delicious thrill coursing through him as her soft breasts crushed against his chest, nothing more than whisper-thin cotton between them.

A small moan of pleasure gurgled in the back of her throat, and her fingers tangled in his hair. She pressed against him, drawing his head down, tilting hers in invitation. That was all the encouragement Cole needed. He slanted his mouth over hers. His tongue thrust between her parted lips, plunging deeply, savoring the taste of her. Erotic. Suggestive. Rubbing against hers with unbridled need.

His hands, pressing firmly against her, cruised over the wrinkled shirt that had somehow bunched around her waist, and down the sleek curve of her hip. Then he grasped the tight globes of her bottom in fierce hands. He lifted her, pressed her against him, and ground his arousal aggressively against her silk-shielded curls. She wound her arms around his neck and gave herself over to his seductive embrace with a whimper of surrender.

On a loud groan, Cole lifted her higher and sat her on the counter. His lips never left hers. His splayed hands ran down the length of her thighs, from hip to knee as he swept her away with the passion in his kiss. Cole hooked his hands around her knees and spread them, wide. Tugging at her knees, he dragged Alex to teeter at the very edge of the counter. Stepping purposefully between her thighs, masterfully guiding her legs around his waist, he pushed himself against her heat. The soft fabric of his sweats sagged low on his waist, giving him the delicious sensation of skin on skin.

Alex obliged by wiggling closer and locking her ankles over his ass, trapping him between her thighs. Right where he wanted to be. She groaned when his hands slid back up her thighs to fasten on her hips once more. He pulled her tighter still. His throbbing member pressed hard against that hot, damp spot, rubbing intimately—grinding mercilessly, pulsating with need.

Cole broke the kiss and leaned back, staring deep into her eyes, desperate to make her cognizant of his actions. His hand slipped beneath her shirt, the hem snagging on his wrist. His palm, hot and questing, fingers rough and callused, moved over her hip and waist, up her ribs, cupping and kneading the luscious swell of her naked breast.

Alex stared up at him from beneath lowered lids, moaned, and arched her back, pressing her breast against his palm. His fingers curled reflexively. He alternately kneaded the soft globe and drew at her puckered nipple. She moaned and his lips seized hers again. Her hands fisted roughly in his hair, pulling him closer still.

His hand slid intently up her back, pulling the offending material up and over her head. She released him long enough to remove her shirt, but then her hands went back to his shoulders, gripping, touching, pulling at him. Her breathing was as erratic as his. When Cole's lips skated down the length of her neck, Alex drew in a ragged breath. His tongue lapped at the skidding pulse at the base of her throat, and the ache in his loins grew to painful proportions.

His mouth branded its way over her collarbone, and down the curve of her breast, closing over a pebbled nipple, drawing it into his mouth, suckling hard. The rough scrape of his teeth on the delicate skin of her breast sent gooseflesh racing across her skin, and she bucked against him. His lips worshiped her skin as he trailed reverent kisses back up the graceful column of her neck, but when his lips sealed over hers, there wasn't an ounce of gentleness left in him anymore.

His hands were hard and strong—rough and impatient—as he crushed her to him. Desire rode roughshod over him, raw and insatiable, pushing him to ravish, driving him to ravage. The deep, dark voice in the back of his mind urged him onward, urged him to take all she offered, and give her more in return then she'd bargained for.

That voice of midnight urged him to give her forever.

Cole wrestled with the very idea, torn for the first time in his long life by the one thing he'd never before considered doing to another living creature. He hadn't been given a choice when he'd been turned. He'd never sired another Vampyre, and always swore he never would.

Yet right now, the very thought of spending the rest of eternity in this woman's arms was enough to render his personal morals inconsequential...enough to render her own wishes on the matter—her very ability to make the choice for herself—insignificant.

Fated mate or Vampyre. Either way, he'd be able to keep her forever. *His Bride.*

His lips fastened on her throat. His fangs scraped her delicate skin. She moaned, the sound of his name on her lips drove all thought—what little of reason he'd managed to retain—from his mind. His fingers fisted in her hair, ruthlessly pulling her head back to expose the sweet flesh of her neck. His eyes glowed, dilated, focusing on the erratic throb of her pulse. His mouth opened wide in anticipation of the ambrosia he'd soon be savoring. His fangs stretched, long and lethal, demanding as they descended toward her flesh.

"*Madre de Dios!*"

The surprised hiss from the doorway broke through the haze of his need. His head reared back, whipped around to glare over his shoulder at the owner of the voice. His deadly fangs gleamed with dangerous menace and he snarled.

Styx blinked, clearly astonished, staring at them in shock for a startled moment, a gaping Zack peering over his shoulder. Then a wide, devilish grin spread over Styx's lips. He elbowed Zack back out of sight and pivoted on his heel, beating a hasty retreat himself.

Alex froze in Cole's arms, and Cole echoed Styx's sentiment, albeit silently. He couldn't believe what he'd been about to do. He snapped his mouth closed, concealing his fangs, and turned to face her, watching from beneath lowered lashes as her cheeks flamed. Disappointment stabbed at him when she unlocked her ankles and pushed against his chest, muffling a whimper.

Reluctant, his hand loosened and untangled from her hair, the other fell away from her breast and he let her go. Already he missed the weight and the texture of them both against his palms. She swore beneath her breath, her voice breaking as she leaped from the counter, her eyes glued to the floor in mortification. She snatched her shirt up and tugged it over her head, hiding her beautiful body from his hungry stare.

He'd never been more lost, more desperate, than he was at that moment. Cole took a step toward her, stretching out a hand, but she brushed past him and fled the room before he could say a word. Instead of chasing after her, as he longed to do, he leaned back against the counter, dropping his chin to his chest, heaving a sigh that sounded remarkably like regret.

Chapter 15

Cole sifted through the thick stack of mail covering his desk, his mind distracted by memories of last night at the club...and this morning, in the kitchen. Those vivid scenes haunted him with startling tenacity. He couldn't deny she had a strangle hold on him, couldn't try to justify her presence as a necessity for the band and his cover any longer.

The truth of the matter was simple. He needed her...had ever since the first moment he'd laid eyes on her. With each passing day, his need had grown into a ravaging hunger pain that wouldn't be denied for much longer. Hell, last night he'd been willing to *change* her, by the gods...and without her consent...just to keep her.

The burden of indecision weighed upon him. Did he go against his own principles, and make her as he was? A creature of the night. A predator haunting the shadows. A demon of hell, some less educated would say. Could he refuse to change her and willingly cross the line between Immortal and Mortal, thereby risking an attachment that guaranteed unavoidable, unbearable pain...for him? And, if by doing so, would she be able to accept him as *he* was? Could he risk his own heart, his own soul...his own immortality...and take her as his mate?

He cut that train of thought off before it could take root. The only sane alternative was to keep the playing field status quo and suffer his demons in silence. Unfortunately, he had trouble maintaining emotional...or physical...detachment where Alexandra Sinclair was concerned.

Dragging in a deep breath, he pushed the questions from his mind. With a curious frown, he drew a large, unmarked manila envelope from the pile of mail. Opening it, he pulled a stack of pictures out, only to drop the envelope and the pictures onto the desk in shock. As the pictures hit the desk, they fanned out, spreading, haphazard, across the surface, filling him first with confusion, then with dawning fury.

The picture on the top of the stack drew his eyes first. It was a shot of him standing in his drive, cradling Alex in his arms the first day she'd come to the estate. Bright red marker scribbled the words "tasty morsel" in bold, angry letters across the glossy photo. He picked the photo up and examined it closer.

Her shoes dangled by their straps from his fingers, her slim arms draped around his neck. A cold chill slithered down his spine. He reached for another picture. This was a candid shot of Alex poised to dive into the pool, the next was of her breaking the surface, and the next was of her coming up for air. Despite the creepiness of the why and how those pictures had been taken, the sight of Alex in her bathing suit, wet and sleek, sent a hot rush of feverish desire coursing though him.

There were several photos in the stack of Cole at odd endeavors...swimming, jogging, working under the hood of Danny's aging truck...all taken here on the estate, well inside the gates. His eyes passed over a picture of him conversing with the TFRA agent in a darkened alley, kneeling beside the body of one Madelyn Kinney, and he heaved a sigh of disgust.

So much for keeping that little arrangement on the down-low.

Then he came to more photos of Alex. Several had large, scribbled question marks over her face. She wore the same provocative outfit she'd worn back to the estate yesterday.

There were photos of her pulling up in front of and entering a comfortable looking gray townhouse with cranberry trim. Over all, there were close to three dozen shots, and every one of them turned the blood in his veins to an ice floe.

By Thor, the son of a bitch would pay. Cole seethed as he reached for the phone. He sank down onto the chair behind his desk, and waited for the call to connect. A bland male voice answered in distracted tones.

With fury poorly leashed, Cole snarled into the slim device, "Get up here. We've got a problem."

Without any further explanations, Cole snapped the phone closed, and then repeated the process, thumbing in a different number this time. He'd no more than disconnected the last call, when a slight rap at the door drew his feral gaze. Gathering the photos back into a stack, he shuffled them inside the unremarkable envelope.

"Come in," he roared, shoving the envelope inside a drawer in his desk.

Cole glanced up, careful to keep his demeanor calm when the entire band filed into the room. He was about to pull the pictures back out, when he noticed they weren't alone. Alex ducked into the room behind Deacon, her gaze carefully averted. Cole tilted his head curiously at the sight of Zack carrying his Gibson Signature Series Les Paul and Danny toting his Classic Fender and portable amps.

Styx sauntered to the sofa, informing him, "We think we're on to something."

A sense of excitement pervaded the room. "Oh?"

"Yeah," Danny jumped in. "We were messing around in the studio this morning, and Alex brought us something. We think we came across what we need for that mid-tempo ballad that's been giving us so much trouble. Check this out."

Without waiting for Cole's consent, Danny gave Alex a slight nudge toward the piano. Deacon shoved a sheaf of paper beneath Cole's nose and leaned a hip against his desk.

Devon slid onto the bench beside Alex, sidling close, and Cole experienced a quick, unexpected stab of jealousy at their proximity. He had to force himself to focus on the music in his hands, force himself to remain behind his desk, or run the risk of tearing Devon limb from limb with his bare hands.

In the blink of an eye, Cole's study transformed into a studio, and the room filled with music. The notes were, by turns, soaring and furiously angry, then plaintive and filled with despair. Zack filled an edgy riff with punchy anger, underscored by the desperate, roaring need from Danny's bass.

The song—the lyrics themselves—hit the gut first and then thrummed through the veins, wrenched at the heart. It wailed of one tempted against one's will, torn by desire so passionate and consuming, only to be burned and left in despair, yet still yearning for more of the fire. It was lust. It was addiction.

It was perfect.

Cole didn't need to look around the side of the piano to know that it was Alex's nimble, talented fingers coaxing the notes from his Steinway rather than Devon's. He sight-read the music as they played, the lyrics floating in his mind, pouring out of him in a husky, sensual voice steeped in sinful promise.

The song was good. Exceptional. The group stared expectantly at him, and he grinned slowly. "That's perfect! You sped the tempo up on the riff and slowed the bridge. It's perfect for the album."

Then he turned to Alex, who barely managed to meet his eyes, and offered her singular, heartfelt praise. "The lyrics are brilliant, Alex!"

Smiling, her cheeks a becoming shade of pink, she nodded, then her eyes slid back to the ivory keys. She hadn't uttered a single sound since the group had trouped into the room, and Cole gritted his teeth behind his smile. He needed to do some serious damage control there. He'd blurred the lines between work and play, and she was obviously uncomfortable with the results.

He'd brought her here for a specific reason, a reason that was more important than anything else. He'd brought her here for the band and for his cover. What had just happened here—the music they'd just created—was proof positive that she belonged here as one of them, as one of the band. Possibly indefinitely. He couldn't mess with that. But now he needed to protect her as well. Because of him, she was a target, and she had no clue. He had unwittingly put her in jeopardy. If and when she found out, she may never forgive him. There would not be a forever for them. He didn't need a Witch with a deck of tarot cards and a crystal ball to tell him that.

The trick would be remembering that brutal fact whenever he got within touching distance.

Unfortunately, the memory of her, dressed in that red slip of pure temptation she'd worn last night, writhing in his arms as he brought her a taste of ecstasy, had been seared onto his soul. There was no denying the truth, whether decked out in designer couture or sporting nothing more than Haines, Alex was irresistible—and hell on his self-control. Even the sight of her now, as she sat demurely at his piano clad in chinos and a vintage *Eagles* T-shirt, damned near cut him off at the knees. He shuddered to think what the sight of her clad in nothing but her own, satiny skin...his for the claiming...had the power to do to him.

The sound of Zack's amused chuckle broke through his self-imposed torment. "Cole?"

"What? Oh, yeah, let's put it on the track." He forced his focus back to business at hand, forced his eyes away from her. "We'll go down to the studio and see how it sounds later tonight. There's some stuff I need to deal with first. Styx, Danny, Deacon, you guys wanna hang back for a few."

It was on the tip of his tongue to include Alex as well, but he wasn't sure how she'd handle the information just yet. He knew she needed to be told—had every right to know the truth of the situation—especially now that it appeared she'd stumbled into the crosshairs, but Cole was seriously worried.

Would she call it quits if she found out there was some twisted psycho following her around—an Immortal killer with a taste for blood and a rapidly developing streak of brutality—taking snapshots of her...because of him? Following so closely on the heels of their latest series of intimate encounters, she'd likely decide this project was more trouble than it was worth. The last thing he wanted was his sexy little lyricist hopping into her sleek muscle car and never looking back. He just couldn't have that—wouldn't allow it.

A regretful, hungry gaze followed her as she trailed Devon and Zack from the room. The minute the door closed, he returned to his desk and reached purposefully for the packet of pictures that had shaken his calm. As the founding members of Stolen Innocence—aside from Deacon of course—the group had been together through thick and thin, obscurity and fame. He and Styx had been through a whole hell of a lot more. They'd had each other's backs in more sticky situations than he liked to consider, starting with a certain desert sheik, and not one or two, but every woman in his entire harem...all twenty-seven of them.

Danny had inadvertently stumbled on the truth of their nature, accepted them as they were, and proven himself trustworthy more than a few times. Deacon had been a fairly recent edition to the band, but he'd proven to be discreet in his own affairs, and the TFRA had cleared him to help with the case.

As such, the three of them deserved to know there could be a potential problem brewing. He waited until the door closed behind the others before he spoke. Danny and Styx perched on the edges of his desk, Deacon prowled restlessly around the den, as was his habit.

"I got this in the mail this morning." He drew the envelope out and tossed it on the desk between the drummer and the guitarist.

The three had obviously been expecting some grand announcement about the sexy new addition to their fold. They all stared at the envelope, varying shades of a frown darkening their collective brow. Styx glanced at Danny, and then to Deacon, and when it appeared neither had any intention of picking the package up, Styx reached for it himself.

Lifting the flap, he drew the stack of pictures out. His alarmed stare flew to Cole briefly, and then he shuffled through the deck, apparently too disturbed to pause long enough to appreciate the candid shots of Alex's svelte curves in her skimpy swimsuit.

Styx's pronounced accent thickened. *"Madre de Dios!* What the hell is this?"

Glowering, he held the stack out for Danny, his focus on Cole, obviously searching for some reaction. The bassist flicked a coolly inquiring look at the drummer and accepted the offering. Soon, he too, reflected Styx's sentiment. He handed the package to Deacon, and turned to regard Cole with a deep frown.

Cole leaned back in his chair and waited for the full impact of the situation to hit his companions. It didn't take long.

Chapter 16

Tension rippled in the room, like a live electrical wire flopping on the ground in a shower of sparks. Styx glanced to Danny and Deacon, finally to Cole.

"Has Slim seen them yet?"

Shifting uncomfortably in his seat, Cole hesitated to respond.

Danny accused, "She doesn't have a clue about *any* of it, does she?"

"I haven't said anything," Cole hedged, and then qualified, "yet."

"She needs to know," Styx pressed, his eyes going radioactive. "You need to tell her about this, sooner rather than later, Cole. About *all* of it. You know that, right?"

"I don't want to scare her," Cole growled. But he quickly conceded the point when Danny and Styx both aimed pointed, scrutinizing stares at him. The ever-quiet Deacon simply raised a brow. All three waited.

Cole grumbled, "I'll tell her."

Nodding, Styx stood up and paced the length of the room. Between Styx's pacing, and Deacon's nervous energy, the two were beginning to give Cole a blinding headache. The gods help them all if Danny joined in. Cole honestly didn't know if, at this point, he'd be able to stop from ripping one—if not all of them—apart.

Styx stopped in front of the display case in the corner. "You know it's just a matter of time, Cole, before he takes a picture of something we can't afford to have exposed. Then the *Enforcers* will come for us."

They stared at each other, silently acknowledging the danger this Rogue posed for them. The Vampyre world, while tolerating its members to live in the public eye, held very stringent rules about maintaining absolute secrecy in regards to their true nature. A Vampyre who was less than circumspect in his concealment was dealt with, swiftly and harshly. Few Humans knew the truth, and those that did either kept silent—or weren't long for this world.

Danny—the only Human in the room—was for all appearances completely unaffected by the seething Vampyre fury surrounding him. His voice remained level and cool. "So, how do we find him before he outs us, or gets to Alex?"

Cole took a moment to consider the males around him with shrewd eyes. "Danny, you and Deacon are good with people. Make a circuit of the clubs tonight, before business starts picking up...every one with some kind of connection to the number eleven, whether it's in the physical address or the name...whatever the connection. Talk with the bouncers and bartenders, see if they noticed anyone acting suspicious, anyone who's only shown up recently but just hangs around casing the place, probably alone." Then he angled his attention to Deacon. "Deacon, check the photo shops. The photo quality is too good for printing at home. My guess is he's using a sleazy, one hour joint, maybe passing a few bills under the counter, or using suggestion."

Styx opted for stepping up security, and minimizing access to the estate. By unspoken agreement, the Human police—and therefore the press—would remain out of the loop. Halfway into the discussion, the TFRA agent made an appearance. Tommy arrived close on his coattails.

Cole briefed Crispin and Tommy about the

pictures and, being Vampyre themselves, they were well aware of the ramifications of the situation. A council of war couldn't have been more grave. They were just wrapping up when a determined rap on the door broke into their discussion.

"Come in," Cole barked, tensing when Alex hesitantly stuck her head in the door.

"Oh," she murmured. "I didn't realize you were still busy. I can come back..."

"No, don't go, Alex," Cole called, motioning her forward. He shot Styx a pointed look, and then added aloud, "We're finished here."

Taking his cue, Styx ran herd, bustling the curious Vampyre toward the door. Crispin didn't get more than a passing glance and appreciative nod in Alex's direction. But, smooth charmer that he was, Tommy managed to elude Styx for a moment. He stepped close to Alex, drawing her hand to his lips.

"You must be the talented and very stubborn Ms. Sinclair." He smiled wolfishly over her hand. "It's a pleasure to finally meet you face to face."

Immediately recognizing the voice that had hounded her phone for weeks on end, Alex smiled with polite interest at the handsome face framed by hair black as a crow's wing. "And you must be Mr. St. James."

"Tommy, please. I'm a huge admirer of your work, Ms. Sinclair."

Cole cleared his throat, loudly.

Turning back to Cole, Tommy added, "I'll go over the list of cities you want added to the venue, see if they work out, and I'll get back to you."

Tommy's eyes slid back to Alex, slipping over her with polished finesse, nearly imperceptible but assessing nonetheless. Alex wasn't fooled, and Cole smiled when she extracted her hand from the agent's with patently practiced ease.

"I hope to see you again very soon, Ms. Sinclair."

She tilted her head in acknowledgement, but moved away without any further exchange with the talent agent. Her attention was already on Cole, her response to Tommy automatic, dismissive.

Smirking, Danny and Deacon followed a flustered Tommy from the room.

On the threshold, Danny paused long enough to shoot a considering look at Alex. A low growl erupted from across the room, deep in Cole's chest, and her gaze swung to his face. His stare warned Danny to walk away while he still could. She glanced between the two men, frowned. However, Danny only grinned with studied innocence, shrugged, and ambled from of the room. Leaving Alex alone with Cole.

Cole was all too aware the last time they'd been alone not a word had been spoken between them, but the entire dynamic of their relationship had changed. What's more, he didn't know how to feel about that.

"We need to talk." She approached his desk slowly, chewing the edge of her lip.

Color rode high in her cheeks, and she struggled to maintain eye contact. A swift shot of smug male satisfaction coursed through Cole's system. Apparently, he hadn't been the only one left hot and bothered.

Cole stood up, but thought twice about joining her on the other side of the desk, knowing he'd be putting her within arm's reach...within temptation's reach. "Alex, you can't—"

"No," she interrupted, holding her hand up to forestall whatever it was he'd been about to say. Drawing a determined breath, she plunged on, "I want to get this out before I change my mind, again."

Alex began pacing before his desk, her small hands twisting in front of her in a nervous tell.

"I agreed to come here—to work with you—with a lot of reservations." Cole's heart plummeted apprehensively inside his chest. "In the last three years, I've worked very hard to put this entire life well behind me. I've tried, and I've succeeded. My column, my life, my privacy have become very important to me. I was completely content with my life as it was."

Content, but not happy. He could read between the lines as well as the next guy.

But her hesitation shot alarm straight through his system all the same, and he completely forgot his resolve to keep her safely out of his reach. He charged around the desk and grasped her firmly by the shoulders.

Giving her a slight squeeze, he stared hard into her eyes. "You can't just come in here and tell me you're ready to walk away from this."

You can't walk away from me. He silently added. *Not yet. Not ever…*

"Cole—"

"Listen to me, Alex," he cut her off. "You can't let what happened between us yesterday… I should have…"

"Cole—"

"I can make this work," he argued, refusing to hear rejection. "Tell me what it will take. I can—"

"Cole!" She lifted her hand and pressed her fingertips to his lips. The action, the touch, startled him. The feel of her skin against his lips flipped his stomach over. "I've made up my mind. Let me speak!"

He nodded mutely, refusing to relinquish his hold on her. Not until he'd convinced her to stay. Seemingly of their own accord, her hands splayed over his tense muscles, feathered over him in a caress that sent his equilibrium—and his focus—careening madly.

"I don't know how to feel—what to feel—about what happened between us last night at the club…or in the kitchen, or yesterday in the garage, for that matter," she began, then hurried on when it appeared he was about to speak. "Regardless, that has nothing to do with our working relationship. I won't allow it to. I'm not here to discuss what happened between us, not yet anyway. I'm here to discuss this project...the band and the music."

She glared up at him. Pressing her hands against his chest, she forced a little room between them. Still he didn't let go completely. His hands slid down her arms, snagging at her wrists, holding her hands between them, holding them pressed to his chest. A lifeline he suddenly couldn't bear to sever.

"I've made a decision about your offer to continue working with the band." She finally allowed her eyes to meet his. The muscles beneath her trapped hands were rigid, his heart pounded anxiously against her palms.

The hint of a smile curved the corners of her lips. "I've decided to take my own advice. I'm not ready to walk away. The music is still in me, and I want to fight for it. I want the job if it's still on the table."

For a moment, Cole couldn't breathe. He'd convinced himself she was about to say no, and the world fell out from beneath his feet.

As soon as he understood she was *not* walking away, his grin grew, untamed and elated. Without warning, he dragged her into his arms and lifted her clear off the ground, crushing her to him. She had no choice but to hold on as he spun her around, laughter gurgled in her throat. Cole set her back on her feet, but before she had the chance to say anything else—before he stopped to consider his actions—his head swooped down, and his lips sealed over hers.

The kiss was fast and hard, demanding, and she responded. Her fingers slid into his hair, her body melted against him. Her responsiveness slipped through Cole like an intoxicating shot of ninety-proof, coursing through his veins, setting his insides on fire. He pressed Alex close and changed the angle of the kiss, deepening it, slowing it down. Spinning it out.

"Cole," she whispered against his lips, smoky desire clouded her voice. "Stop…"

Every cell in his body screamed to press on, urged him to overwhelm her with his passion. Take everything she could give and demand more. She wouldn't be able to deny him for long. But he held back, resolute that when they finally did come together, it would be of her own free will. Her choice. He wouldn't give her any reason to regret it, wouldn't give her any reason to be any angrier with him than she already would be when she found out what he was. He let his hands fall to his sides, silently waiting for her to go on.

"I agreed to stay on—to work." She crossed her arms defensively, protectively over her chest as she moved before the window, staring blankly out at the lush green landscape. "I'm sorry, but I can't let myself get involved—that way—with you."

Despite her words of denial, his gut burned with the knowledge that it was no longer a question of *if* he would have her, but a matter of *when*. No longer a question of *if* she would learn the truth, but a matter of *when*. And then she would have to decide…

His words were cold, brutally intuitive. "Can't, or *won't?*"

Drawing a deep breath, she turned to face him. Alex lifted her chin defiantly, clarifying, "Won't."

"Explain," Cole ground out tersely. Anger and lust thrummed through his overheated body, making her words distasteful and difficult to swallow.

"I don't need to explain, 'no' should be sufficient.

After all, it was you who told me that nothing would happen here that I didn't want," she snapped, turning his words back on him.

"You want *this*," he hissed, hurt for reasons he couldn't fathom. His fists clenched at his sides, but his fingers itched to tangle themselves in her hair and drag her into his arms. "I feel it when I touch you, when I kiss you. I know you do—"

"I don't!" She jabbed him in the chest with a sharp, perfectly manicured nail. "And if you want me to stick around you'd better get that through your head and stop pushing. This..." Alex waved her hand emphatically between them. "This thing between us stops now. We work together, we don't...we *can't* go there, not anymore. Not ever again."

Her tone had become brittle, her eyes wide, and she looked as if she might bolt at any moment.

"Okay," Cole ground out, wanting to hold on to what ground he'd gained, afraid of losing it all. Holding his hands up in a placating gesture of acquiescence, he nodded. If she wanted business, she'd get business. The rest... Well, the rest she'd just have to contend with later. He had not the slightest doubt that there *would* be a later. It was inevitable. Just a matter of time. Time he might very well be running out of. Nevertheless, he backed up a step. "Okay."

He thought of the pictures then, and mentally shoved them back in the drawer, buried them deep. No way was he pulling those out now and giving her yet another reason to second-guess her decision to stay.

Calmed some by his acceptance, she nodded and relaxed her stance. "All right."

"I'll call Tommy back and have him draw up the contract," Cole intoned, subdued, and crossed to his desk. He eyed her, took in her tense stance. "Why don't you go for a swim or something? You put in a long morning by the sounds of it."

"You're sure you don't mind if I knock off for a couple hours?" Alex came to stand on the opposite side of the desk. At Cole's nod, she replied, "Okay, I guess I should probably head into the office to talk to Sam and make the necessary arrangements. I'll make sure I'm back around six if that's all right, I know you wanted to have a session..."

Cole's hand froze as he reached for the phone, and the pictures raced through his mind again. His gaze shifted to the clock, and he only narrowly avoided openly grimacing when he considered the time. Thinking of the long hours of daylight left before sunset—of the long hours of discomfort ahead of him—he couldn't believe the words that came out of his mouth. "Why don't you let me tag along?"

"What?" Alex asked, eyeing him suspiciously. "Why?"

Cole scrambled to come up with a plausible excuse. The last thing he wanted to do was tell her about the Rogue, but having her running around out there—out where he couldn't have security watching over her without a reason...where he couldn't protect her—was simply out of the question.

If he was smart, he could survive the afternoon relatively unscathed. There wouldn't be any serious damage—and therefore any serious explaining—as long as he avoided prolonged exposure to direct sunlight. He'd gone out during the day before...when absolutely necessary. He'd just need a little extra blood and a little extra time to recoup.

"I wouldn't mind getting out of here for a while," he offered, letting the idea snowball as he spoke. "We could take in a movie, or find some nice quiet restaurant later if you want." Yeah, someplace dark was good. "I don't get out of here near often enough, and this would be the perfect excuse. We'll take care of your errands, and then we could hang out..."

"What about the session?"

Shrugging, he pushed it off. "It can wait till tomorrow."

She looked uncertain, and he pressed his advantage. "Come on, Alex. We're gonna be working together. We might as well get comfortable with each other—get to know each other better. This is the perfect opportunity."

She frowned, but before she could respond, he turned a charming, innocent smile at her. "Help me escape my gilded cage, Alex, just for a little while?"

Pursing her lips, she weighed his request.

"All right..." She narrowed her eyes in firm warning, adding, "If you promise to behave yourself."

Then, as only Cole could do, he sent her senses teetering on the edge of a nervous cliff by giving her a wicked glance and drawling, "Only as good as I have to be, honey."

Chapter 17

In short order, they were racing away from Cole's home and out onto open road. Alex laughed and leaned back against the soft leather seat. Closing her eyes, she savored the feel of the wind raking through her hair and slapping at her skin. Shooting a sly glance sideways beneath her lashes, she studied Cole as he expertly guided the Shelby through hairpin curves.

He grinned like a madman—like a kid hopped up on sugar and set loose in a toy store—and his delight was infectious. She couldn't believe she'd let him wheedle her into allowing him to drive. She'd never let anyone else drive her baby. Never. With a slight shake of her head, she had to allow that she'd been doing quite a bit of that lately—doing things she'd swore she'd never do. With a blissful, contented sigh, Alex settled back and let the wind, and Cole, sweep her away.

"Dressed like that, you look like a cat burglar driving a get-away car," she told him with a winsome smile, eyeing the dark shades and the dark, concealing clothing.

His only reply was to tip his sunglasses down and gave her an audacious, wicked wink above the rims, grinning shamelessly.

All too soon, they were idling into the parking ramp attached to the high rise containing the offices of the *Globe*. Cole reluctantly parked the car and turned the motor off. Drawing the key from the ignition, he glanced over to Alex. Handing her the keys, he pulled the glasses from his face. "If I'm extra good, do I get to drive back too?"

Laughing, falling into the moment, she replied primly, "I don't know. Two stints behind the wheel—that would take something pretty special."

Cole lowered his suddenly smoldering, *intense* stare to her lips, and remarked suggestively, "Baby, I could be so good you'd never let anyone else behind your wheel, ever again..."

She sucked in a sharp breath, and his heady gaze lifted to hers once more. That breath froze in her lungs. Her lips parted, and she blinked, twice. God, sometimes his eyes just seemed to...to glow. Their eyes locked, and she caught herself leaning toward him.

Rearing back as if he'd slapped her, her eyes went wide and accusatory. "Cole..."

He tossed his hands up between them as if to say, *backing off now*. Smiling roguishly, giving an unrepentant shrug, he murmured aloud, "Shall we?"

Drawing a frustrated, shaky breath, she reached blindly for the door handle and slipped from the car. Before she could close the door behind her, he was around the car and reaching for her elbow.

He prowled at her side through the dim parking garage, and together, companionably silently, they rode the elevator to the sixteenth floor. When the door slid open, the small cubicle was flooded with the muted, busy sounds of an office at the peak of business hours.

Stepping into the sunny lobby, Cole slipped his glasses back on and edged to the side to stand in the shadow of a slim section of wall that divided two windows, waiting while Alex walked up to a large horseshoe-shaped desk and spoke quietly to the receptionist. A few moments later, she led him down a long hallway, ignoring the astonished stares aimed their way.

They turned at the end of the hall and entered

the first office on the right. Just as Cole stepped through the doorway, Rita rose from behind the desk to greet Alex with warm surprise.

Whatever she'd been about to say remained locked in her throat, as she stared goggle-eyed at Cole.

"You're, ah..." Rita stammered. "He's, ah... Whaa... Holy shit!"

Shocked by her assistant's flustered state—let alone her inappropriate choice of words—Alex snapped sternly, "Rita!"

Turning a brilliant shade of scarlet, Rita gasped, "I'm so sorry..."

Smirking, Cole waved her apologies aside and extended his hand. "Cole Gunnarrson...and you are?"

Wide-eyed, Rita placed her hand in Cole's and allowed him to move hers up and down. "Hah..."

Alex couldn't remember if Rita had blinked since she'd clapped eyes on Cole. Trying her best not to laugh out loud, Alex finished the introductions. "Cole, this is my efficient and unfailingly professional assistant, Rita Gates. Rita, Cole Gunnarrson."

Rita nodded and sputtered, "Hhhh..."

"Rita," Alex called, snapping her fingers impatiently an inch from Rita's nose. Once her assistant's attention returned to Alex, she continued on, "I need to see Sam. We'll wait in my office. Don't patch any calls through, if anyone asks—I'm still on vacation."

Alex ushered Cole through the inner door, closing it softly behind him.

****

"Can I get you anything to drink?"

"Sure—got a beer?" Cole smiled flippantly at her, and then replied, "Whatever you got is fine."

He caught the icy cold can she tossed to him,

193

and popped the top on the soda. He took a tiny, obligatory sip, then set the can aside. *Gods, that stuff was disgusting.* Settling himself onto the small, stiff sofa by the window, careful to keep to the far edge and well away from the burn of the sun, Cole set the can down on the edge of the coffee table and waited as Alex took a seat behind her desk.

She shuffled through the inbox on the corner of her desk, and he marveled at the change that had come over her since they'd stepped off the elevator. Right before his eyes, she'd transformed back into the prim, aloof businesswoman. The same woman who'd coolly dismissed the mechanic in his study that first day.

He couldn't say as he liked the change, much preferring the Alex she'd come to be while working with the band—much preferring the Alex she was when she was in his arms. *His* Alex. All fire and desire. He let his gaze drift over the room, taking in the artwork, the furniture. It was feminine. It was efficient. It was tidy.

Impersonal, repressive and sterile, he thought with an inward snort of disgust. It wasn't her...not her at all. And it puzzled him. He was about to make comment, when the small box on her desk buzzed.

"Ms. Sinclair," Rita's efficient voice chirped. "Ms. Davies will see you now."

Alex rose and glanced to Cole. "Make yourself comfortable. I shouldn't be long."

He nodded and, after she'd left the room, stood and looked around. Heaving a sigh, he poured the contents of the soda can into the small potted plant perched on the top of a filing cabinet near the window and tossed the can in the receptacle at the end of her desk. He sat back down and riffled through the tidy stack of magazines on the spotless, glass coffee table, shaking out a recent issue of a glamour rag.

Restless, he settled back and leafed through the pages, all the while, his mind wandered. Nearly half an hour later, Alex stepped back into her office, silent, unnaturally subdued. She spent a few more minutes at her desk, dropping files and a few personal effects into a box, then smiled wanly at Cole.

"I'm all finished here," she informed him. "We can go now."

Her home was the next stop on her agenda. Cole immediately recognized the gray, cranberry trimmed house from the Rogue's pictures. His wary gaze scanned the surrounding area, but he could find no one out and about. Ducking his head, he shielded his face from the setting sun as much as he could while he waited for her to open the door. Even so, the UV rays beat harshly on his face and hands, making his exposed skin burn as though he'd leaped into boiling water.

Stepping inside the cool shade of her entry was like pouring a soothing balm over an open wound. He shifted the cardboard box in his arms, setting it down on a small table just inside the door as she indicated. Reaching up, he removed his sunglasses and glanced curiously around as he followed her farther into the house.

"I'll just be a few minutes," she called over her shoulder. "Make yourself at home."

Alex disappeared through a door at the back of the house, and Cole began wandering aimlessly around the room. He stopped in front of a wall of assorted-sized, framed photos. Each was a candid shot. Not a single professional photograph hung among the dozens that covered the wall. Alex was present in most every one of them, smiling and laughing. Living.

Surrounded by friends and family.

There were group photos of Alex with other men

and women. Some were obvious office shots, while others had clearly been taken during a night on the town with friends. Then there were the more intimate photos, those taken with family members—physical resemblances were obvious.

He paused in front of one such picture. The man was decades older than a teenaged Alex, yet she perched on his knee like a toddler. Their eyes were the same. There was another photo with a much younger Alex, learning to ride a bike. The man who ran along at her side was a younger version of the man on whose knee she sat in the previous photo. Cole knew a brief spark of jealousy, of loneliness, when he thought of his own family—his own brothers and sisters, his parents—all long gone centuries past.

Then his eyes lit on a photo that gave him pause. In this picture, Alex sat near an older woman. Near, but carefully not touching. The woman looked to be an older version of Alex, both women petite, both similarly colored. Both appeared to be smiling uncomfortably—painfully so—as if they could barely tolerate being close to each other.

The photo troubled him for reasons he couldn't name. Gritting his teeth, giving a mental shrug, he wandered across the room, taking in the eclectic tastes of the woman who so fascinated him. The priceless creation of a master hung beside the work of a street artist. An aged leather-bound edition of Shakespeare sat back to back on a shelf beside a Lindsey. A Tiffany lamp rested on an antique Duncan Phyfe end table. The end table sat beside an overstuffed Lazy-Boy recliner.

Smiling at her penchant for mixing classical and sophisticated with modern and comfortable, he moved on to peer inside a narrow, glass curio case, faintly surprised to see an odd assortment of relics. Among them, the remains of an iron knife and a spearhead rested beside an aged and cracked drinking horn. The centerpiece of the display was a small round brooch of bronze and ivory. The kind of brooch women of his time used to fasten tunics.

In a blink, he was lost, back in that otherworld, in that other lifetime.

Once trusting brown eyes stared up at him, lifeless yet filled with horror, from a face turned gray with the cold. Her sodden cloak twisted about her dead body, no use now for her frozen body. Strands of hair, limp with water and ice crystals, straggled over his soaked arm. Her sweet lips were blue, and so still now. Yet, her dying words echoed inside his head, damning and just. "You're a monster. I'll not let you turn me into what you are. Stay away from me."

Cole fisted his hands at his sides. His breath sawed in and out as the memory swept over him, fresh as if it had been only yesterday.

"Dagna," he had cried as he'd frantically edged closer, his eyes flying from her face to the edge of the cliff snapping so close at her heels. The frigid fjord below waited expectantly for her foot to slip, eager for her balance to shift just enough. "This doesn't have to change anything. I love you. We can still be together—"

"No!" She shook her head violently, her arms flailing to the sides as she tilted precariously closer to the edge. "This changes everything."

A pebble slid beneath her heel, skittering free, tumbling to the glacial waters below. He lunged forward, reaching out to pull her to safety. Frantic to escape him, she twisted away, tottering drunkenly closer to the abyss.

"You'll never change me, demon," she'd screamed at him, hysteria swam in her eyes.

Then she'd leaped.

With icy hands and pounding heart, he pulled himself free of the bitter memories. Turning away from the display, he glanced around the rest of the room. Regrets a millennia old dug a deep groove between his brows. Drawing a deep breath, he forced his attention back to the here and now.

The furniture was comfortable, inviting. A bit frilly for his taste, but definitely a step up from her office. The colors of the room were bold, yet he found the effect somehow calming. She emerged from her bedroom doorway, grinning as she hefted two large pieces of luggage. Gods, how long had he been staring at that brooch?

Eyeing the bags in her hands, he forced a grin. "I didn't realize you intended to pack everything, or I would have started out here."

Tilting her nose in the air, she quipped, "This is just the tip of the iceberg, bucko, just you wait."

He moved forward and took the luggage from her, setting it down by the front door. "Is there anything else you'd like to take?"

"No." She ran a critical eye over the room. "I think that should do it. I'll be back to check on things from time to time. If there's anything I need, I can just grab it then."

For some reason, her answer bothered him. The idea that she would maintain this bit of independence, this bit of self that had absolutely nothing to do with him, left him vaguely disturbed. He knew he was being unreasonable, but looking at those pictures on the wall made him realize how badly he wanted to touch her life...not just her body or her talent—but *her*.

He allowed that he'd grown attached to her in a very short amount of time, then he snorted with self-disgust. He'd never been one to lie to himself, and he wasn't about to start now. If he were being honest, he would admit he'd done a whole lot more than grown attached. He'd become obsessed. He now treaded a dangerous line, the line between fondness and falling in love...with a *Mortal*. He glanced uneasily at the brooch in her display case, and cringed inwardly. Until now, until *Alex*, he'd lived his life once burned twice shy. What was it about her that pulled him in? By all that was sacred, why couldn't he stay away?

He stared hard at her as she moved about her home, checking window locks, watering plants, puttering, oblivious of his perusal. Two little words, so full of hope...and dread...echoed in his heart. *What if...*

"Are you hungry?"

He blinked. "What?"

"Are you hungry?" Alex repeated. "I probably don't have much in the fridge, but—"

"No, I'm good," he interrupted. Then he thumbed at the intimate collection of photos. "You have an impressive display there."

She glanced over. Emotions skated over her face as she scanned the wall. Slowly, as if drawn by an invisible string, she moved to stand before the pictures and gazed fondly at the man teaching her to ride a bike.

"That's my grandpa," she told Cole as she fondly tapped the glass over the picture. A sad, faintly wistful note crept into her voice. Her words were soft when she added, "He passed away a few months back."

Cole moved to stand behind her, slightly to the side. The unmistakable sound of her sorrow tugged at him, and he placed his hands gently on her shoulders, pleased when she didn't pull away. But her body was rigid beneath his hands, her jaw clenched tight.

"I'm sorry." Cole squeezed her shoulders, urging her back until she leaned against him. Human suffering had never bothered him before, not on this level. He didn't like it, not one bit.

"He was sick for a long time," she murmured, blowing out a long breath as one more loathsome word slipped passed her lips, "cancer."

No wonder she'd had such an aversion to going to the hospital after the Rogue attack, he mused. Cole said nothing, but his arms crept around her waist. She relaxed against him, the tension draining from her body.

"He was always so supportive of me...of my music," she began quietly. "When my songs first charted, he took me out to celebrate." Her voice broke, but she pushed on. "It damned near killed me, watching him waste away, watching him fade."

He knew what it was to watch Humans he'd cared for wither and fade. Cole held her tenderly in his arms, surprised and honored that she would share this bit of her sorrow with him. He pressed his lips to her hair and silently willed her to go on.

As if sensing his encouragement, she drew a steadying breath. "My father died when I was very little. Grandpa stepped in, for a long time it was just he and I."

"What about your mother?"

She stiffened, and he immediately regretted asking the question that caused her to pull away.

She shifted, moving from the haven of his arms, muttering quietly, succinctly, "We aren't close."

"Alex..." Cole snagged her wrist when she made to walk away.

She lifted her chin and stared him straight in the eye, her expression carefully guarded. "She didn't approve of the music, of the band—or of me." She offered him a brittle smile. "When things...didn't work out last time, she had no compunction in rubbing the old 'I told you so' in my face. Any painful way she could. We generally speak once every couple of weeks or so, whenever I've done something else to displease her. Now, if you'll excuse me, I have a few more things to do before we go back."

Cole released her wrist, and she walked away, her back rigid with quiet dignity. His heart bled for her, unable to fathom how anyone—let alone her own mother—couldn't approve of her. How could *anyone* not be utterly proud of her and what she'd made of herself? He turned back to stare at the wall with new understanding.

Sensing she wanted to be alone, he waited for her to come back, fighting the urge to follow her—fighting to control furious indignation over her mother's callous treatment. When at last Alex returned, not a trace of her sorrow remained physically, her eyes were not red with tears...shed or unshed...and yet he could *feel* her quiet grief. But there was more. Resolve. He could feel that too, as sure as his heart beat in his chest.

Alex smiled at him, catching him off guard again. She held her hand out to him in invitation. "When was the last time you walked on the beach in the moonlight?"

Chapter 18

Returning her smile, a new understanding of the woman before him glowing in his heart, Cole enveloped her small hand in his large one. Once he had firm hold, he wasn't about to let go.

"It's been far too long."

Together they made their way across the gentle slope of the lawn, drawn to the soothing sounds of the ocean. The stretch of pale sand stood sentinel between her yard and the glistening, moon-dappled surf, beckoning them. For a time, they walked in silence along the water's edge, no sound between them but the gentle crash of uncounted waves.

When Alex spoke, the sound of her voice reverberated through Cole's system, sparking emotions he hadn't suffered for a long time. Emotions he hadn't experienced since a far off summer day, many, many centuries ago with a sweetly innocent girl on a clear night similar to this.

Alex finally turned her head to regard Cole with far more scrutiny than he'd ever garnered from anyone in his life, before or after he'd turned. He must have presented a formidable figure against the inky shadow of the night, bringing images of intrinsic mystery and dangerous menace to mind. Yet she didn't flinch away at his nearness. In fact, she walked close at his side, fearless and sure.

"I want you to understand why I was so resistant to working with you and Stolen Innocence," Alex began quietly.

Cole cocked his head to the side, his attention centered completely on her. Wordlessly, he waited for her to continue.

"I've never spoken of this with anyone—not even Grandpa. I honestly don't know why, but I feel as if...as if I *need* to talk to you about this. I can't explain it, I just do," she expounded.

The words began to flow then, tumbling out without restraint. "I was very young—very naïve— when I entered the music business the first time. When I started writing for Angel's Fury, it all happened so fast. The fame, the money, the band itself... It all overwhelmed me. Thanks to my grandfather, the money wasn't a problem. He taught me how to invest, made sure that my financial future was secure. The fame and...the band were a little more difficult to manage.

"In the beginning, I tried to fly below the radar for the most part. I just wanted to write. Then, by degrees, that became impossible. The band began to demand more and more of my time, until I'd completely alienated my friends. My grandpa and I even grew...distant. There's nothing I regret more than I regret that. I let myself get swept away until I lost sight of who I was..." Her voice trailed away, and he anticipated something more was coming, something he himself might have difficulty dealing with.

Alex drew a deep breath, shuddering. Cole pressed his warm palm against her icy one. Fingers, callused from years of strumming a guitar—callused from centuries of wielding a sword, smoothed over the backs of her knuckles with a gentleness that belied his extraordinary strength. Smiling up at him, she pushed on.

"I finally realized the toll it had taken...realized I couldn't continue to live that way. I went to the band one afternoon while they were in their studio to tell them I was finished..." Alex paused, then let it all pour out in a headlong rush. "They were...angry.

I guess they saw their sure thing walking out the door. They threatened to sue. They threatened to blacklist me. They..."

Alex's voice grew quiet, detached, as she stumbled through the explanation. "When none of that worked, a couple of the guys thought they could intimidate me. Maybe they thought if I wasn't any use to them as a writer anymore they could use me for—other things. Two of them held me down while the third... The third one..." Alex drew a breath, forced a swallow. "He would have raped me if their agent hadn't walked in at that moment and surprised them. I managed to get out somehow, and I never went back."

Cole's hand gripped hers too hard, she winced.

"Cole, you're hurting me," she gasped, tugged at her hand.

Cole immediately loosened his grip, though he refused to release her altogether. Instead, he tugged her around until she stood in the protective circle of his arms, her head resting on his chest.

He held her tenderly, his hands smoothing over her back and arms. He pressed gentle kisses to the crown of her head while she wept bitterly, brokenly, against his chest. All the while, rage seethed inside him, so black and so vicious it threatened to consume him. Images of his Alex—helpless and at the mercy of monsters far more evil than he—filled his mind.

He could only thank the gods she couldn't see his face at that moment in time, for the change was upon him, and he knew, beyond a doubt, that he'd never looked more fearsome, more monstrous. He wanted to track the bastards down, to show them what real terror was. He wanted to tear them limb from bloody limb. He wanted to drain them and leave their lifeless corpses to rot like the trash they were.

Instead, he comforted her, until the tears subsided and her breathing returned to normal. He held her longer still, until he managed to regain control of his physical appearance once more, until he wouldn't frighten her with his fury.

When at last she leaned back, not completely out of his arms, but far enough to face him in the moonlight, she smiled tremulously up at him and reached up to gently touch his cheek... tenderly, unwittingly touching the beast within. "I don't know what it is about you, but you make me feel safe...protected. Thank you for that."

Once again, Cole found himself wishing he held within his power the ability to control *her* thoughts. It frustrated him to no end he'd never been able to tap into her will. At that moment, he wanted nothing more than to wipe those brutal, hurtful memories from her mind. He wanted to take away her pain, wanted to give her only happiness in return. Frustrated by his own feelings of ineptitude and helplessness, he stared down into her trusting eyes and his heart shuddered, melting.

Slowly, lovingly, he took her chin between his thumb and forefinger, tilting her face up until silvery moonlight bathed the porcelain perfection of her features. His piercing, glowing stare searched her face, committing every detail to a memory that would last not only her lifetime...but his. Then, without a word, he lowered his lips to hers. Need swelled inside him. Desire swept through him. Yet he kissed her with restraint, offering her comfort and solace, putting her needs and her vulnerability before his own. The kiss was so tender, so filled with emotion his very soul trembled.

And he took the fall...heart first.

****

The Crasher sat back on his haunches and let the foliage fall back into place, concealing his dark shape. Tucking the camera back into his pocket, he eased into the shadows as only one born to the darkness can do.

His exceptional hearing had picked up every word of their intimate conversation. Poor little thing. That vicious old band she'd worked with had really done a number on her. Poor, poor terrified dear... No wonder she'd been so reluctant to work with Stolen Innocence.

A sinister smile curved the sensual lines of his mouth. The wicked gleam of fangs flashed in the night and bloodlust glowed in his eyes.

Just wait until she got a load of him...

He edged from Alex's yard and moved down the street, no more than an unidentifiable blur of motion to the Human eye, formulating the next phase in his plan. In a few short weeks, it would be time to send his last message. Cole had already figured it out, of course. He hadn't expected anything less. Cole and Styx had gotten so close at the last kill. They'd almost caught him. Like the music, that narrow escape had only added a certain...spice, a defining thrill to the sacrifice. Oh, he could stop now. His message had gotten through, quite clearly. But where would be the fun in that? Besides, he had a quota to fill.

And he'd already chosen the perfect messenger.

Sliding behind the wheel, he turned the radio up to drown out the sounds of the city around him, and pulled a cell phone from the pocket of his overcoat. As he eased onto the interstate, he flipped the phone open and pressed speed-dial. A few moments later, an accented voice replaced the ringing in his ear.

"Hey, Styx," he greeted the drummer with the ease of long-time familiarity. "I've been trying to get a hold of Cole. His phone keeps going straight to voice mail."

"Yeah..." Styx fumbled with something in the

background. A metallic clang echoed over the line, followed by a particularly nasty oath. "I think he went into town with Slim. What'dya need?"

"I've been going over this list Cole gave me, and a couple dates don't click with locations. It'd be a lot easier to go over this stuff face to face. He gonna be around later?"

"Dunno, might be," Styx mumbled. Another clang and a heated Spanish expletive followed. Irritation laced his voice, and he snapped, "Last I checked, I wasn't his mother or his friggin' agent. Didn't figure it was up to me to keep tabs."

"Yeah, well, he wants the information he ought to make sure he can be reached."

"If I see him, I'll let him know you're looking for him," Styx grumbled. "How soon before you head back out here?"

"Got one more stop to make, then I'll be out." He turned off the main strip, into the parking lot of the small, shady photo lab he used. The clerk inside was brainless, requiring next to nothing in the way of effort to control with suggestion. Fortunate that, as persuasion was an effect he hadn't quite mastered yet. "I thought I might stop off for a bite on the way."

He could hear the grinning interest in Styx's voice. "Hey, I could use a bite myself...something sweet, maybe. Pick up a blonde for me if you can find one."

He chuckled benevolently. Alex's long, golden locks floated through his mind, and his grin grew with evil intent. She'd be different from the others. Alexandra Sinclair was worthy. He wouldn't leave her to bleed out on the pavement. He wouldn't waste a single drop of her delectable blood. No, he had special plans for her...plans that would take a long, *long* time.

"Funny, I've been craving a blonde myself."

Chapter 19

Cole stood at his desk, a pervading sense of doom sent chills skittering down his spine. More pictures had arrived this morning, photos taken at intermittent intervals throughout his outing with Alex yesterday. Lots of them.

That aside, the very idea that someone out there posed a threat to Alex filled him with rage...and fear, never mind the risk of exposure to himself or any of the rest of the races. However, the photos that left him feeling cold as death itself were the ones taken last night on the beach while he held her, while he kissed her. Why hadn't he scented the bastard?

Every intimate picture had crimson scribbles over Alex's face. Then the last picture in the stack found its way to the top and Cole gasped in shock, forced to sit down before his knees buckled completely.

It was a candid, close-up of Alex's face, smiling as she climbed into the passenger seat last night in front of her house. The moonlight painted her in shades of silver and shadows. She was lovely, breathtaking.

Across her beautiful face, garish scarlet lettering boldly announced, 'Mortals Die.' And on the side of her neck, in small, scrupulous printing was the number fourteen.

With shaking hands, Cole flipped his cell phone open, his dilated, luminous eyes glued to the glossy photo. In short order, Danny, Deacon, and Styx were once again closeted in Cole's study, discussing the

Rogue. Only this time, the truth of the situation was far more treacherous. This time, the killer had made it personal.

"Crispin and Tommy are both on their way back," Cole informed them as the trio settled onto the sofa and chairs. His lips compressed with frustration. "Crispin's working up a list of Vamps known to be in the area. He's going to bring it up with him, see if there are any who might be pissed off at me for something or other...anything beyond the fact that I'm hand in pocket with the TFRA."

"That many, huh?"

Danny's cool attempt at humor fell shy of its mark, however, when Cole stared at him through flat, icy blue eyes and responded tightly, "You don't live over eleven hundred and fifty years without pissing a few people off now and again."

Clearing his throat, Danny shifted uncomfortably in his seat and reached for his beer. He'd known Cole for almost ten years, a long time for a human, barely half a drop in the bucket to an Immortal. It was too easy to see Cole the friend, and forget about Cole the Vampyre.

Deacon cocked his head to the side and stared hard at Cole. "You still ain't told her yet, have you?"

Cole shot him a quelling look, but his eyes closed and his head tipped back against the cushion as a heated string of Spanish expletives filled the air.

"*Madre de Cristo*," Styx snarled. "She has a right to know what she's up against. She's strong. She has a good head on her shoulders. Slim can handle it. If she's going to be staying on with us...if you're going to *be* with her...you're going to have to trust her with the truth."

Cole gritted his teeth against the foreign sensation of fear snaking through him. If she found out the truth like this—if she found out what he was and walked away—he didn't know how he would react. Could he let her go? Would he be able to? He owed her that much—the choice—even if it was the emotional equivalent of walking a tightrope with a flaming pyre on one side, and a flaming dawn on the other.

Grimacing, Cole drained the glass of repulsive cold blood, then set the empty Riedel tumbler down on the coffee table with a resounding thump. With a fierce scowl lining his face, he glared at the elegant *Odhroerir* etched on the side of the glass. Knowing he was making the right decision—that telling her the truth was the right thing to do—didn't make it any easier to stomach.

Styx shifted in his seat, eyeing Cole speculatively. "What about the premiere tonight?"

Cole gazed at the Steinway for a moment. "You go, take the rest of the guys with you. I'll tell her tonight—I have a feeling she might take it a little better without the risk of any interruptions."

Danny shrugged. "Sure, why the hell not."

As ever, Deacon nodded, offering little in the way of words.

As a unit, the men stood, three to leave and one to pace.

A short while later, Alex stuck her head inside the study and smiled at Cole. "Styx said you wanted to see me?"

"Come in, Alex." Cole shuffled the stack of photos into a pile, turning them upside down on the corner of his desk for the time being. Damn Styx...he could have given Cole a little more time to prepare.

"I figured you'd be getting ready. Doesn't that premiere start in an hour?"

"Styx and the others are going," he trailed off, watching as she wandered into the room and perched on the sofa—so relaxed, so damned sexy, he had a difficult time remembering what it was that had been on his mind when she'd walked in. Her confidence had noticeably grown over the last few weeks. Her comfort zone had broadened.

It killed him to know he might very well crush it beneath the weight of the truth and a couple dozen damning photos.

Alex tilted her head. A curious frown creased her brow. "But not you?"

"Not me. I...I have other matters to attend to."

"That doesn't sound good," she teased with a half smile. Then, seeing him frown, she sat up straighter, her tone turned serious. "Cole, if there's anything I can help with—anything I can do..."

"Actually, I..."

Whatever Cole had been about to say was cut short by the distinctive ring of a cell phone. Darth Vader? Odd choice that. Grimacing, Alex held up a finger and reached for her back pocket in an unswerving, conditioned response. Her face suddenly blanked, but Cole could literally feel the wave of anxiety washing through her.

She looked up at him, a half-hearted smile of apology on her lips. "I'm sorry, Cole. I should take this." Then her voice trailed away as she muttered beneath her breath, as if she wasn't aware she was speaking aloud. "If I don't she'll only keep calling back until I do."

"Go ahead, it's all right," he assured her, both frustrated and relieved by the interruption.

He retreated behind his desk, striving to make himself as unobtrusive as possible while she paced at the opposite end of the room with the phone pressed to her ear. Her voice, strained and edgy, drifted to him, and he tensed, angered by the resigned submission in her tone.

"Mother, I... Yes, that's right. I... No, I didn't stop to consider how my writing music again would make you look to your friends," she bit out, her voice held the sharp edge of anger fiercely suppressed.

"No, Mother... Yes, Mother... I'm well aware of that, I just don't see why..."

Then the silence stretched on. Alex stopped pacing, stood staring at the piano, standing so stiffly Cole feared she might shatter if she took too deep of a breath. Waves of emotion swirled through the room—anger and hurt, disappointment and regret.

With his extraordinary hearing, he caught snippets of her mother's portion of the conversation. He blindly balled up the paper in his hand in fury. The woman who should be supporting Alex's endeavors...encouraging her and praising her...was, instead, condemning Alex for her decisions, selfishly reminding Alex of her failure and embarrassment the last time she'd dragged the Sinclair name through the mud.

Fury seethed through him. He was at her side in a heartbeat. Reaching out, he took the phone from her white-knuckled grip, snapping it closed with a definitive click, just barely restraining himself from crushing the device in his fist. His eyes scanned her face, took in her pale countenance and her miserable eyes, and he could have howled his wrath. Cole cupped the back of her head, drawing her against his chest, absorbing her pain as his own, careful to keep his anger at her mother well contained.

When she withdrew from his embrace, she offered an apologetic smile. "I'm sorry—"

"Don't..." he cut her short. "She's a fool, and I'm here...whenever you need me."

She tilted her head and considered him with something akin to awe in her eyes. Emotions flickered over her face, emotions that sent his good intentions flying right out the window. Before he could draw her back into his arms, she stepped back, drew a deep breath, and reminded him of his reason for summoning her. "What did you want to see me about?"

Cole's guilty glance slid to his desk, to the stack of photos, and he cringed inside. How could he tell her about those now, so soon after her own mother had just raked her over the coals.

How could he not, a little voice in the back of his head countered viciously.

And yet, he hesitated.

In the end, he—the fearless Viking warrior—took the coward's way out, afraid of pushing her too far. "I only wanted to see how you were doing."

"Oh," Alex murmured, her brow wrinkling. She clearly didn't believe him. "I... Are you sure that's all?"

"Yeah, positive," he replied with a tight-lipped smile, but he turned away, unable to meet her eyes with the lie on his lips. "What else could there be?"

"I'm fine," she responded after a stilted moment. "Do you need anything else?"

Cole retreated to the safety of his desk and shook his head, his eyes lingering on the threatening stack of photos.

"Well, then... Good night, Cole."

"Night," he murmured, watching her walk from his study, her shoulders slumping dejectedly, kicking himself for letting her go without having told her the truth once again.

As Alex opened the door, her sharp gasp brought Cole immediate alert. He was around the desk and halfway across the room before he knew what was wrong.

Tommy stepped into the room, the smile he offered Alex an apologetic and charming smile. "I'm sorry, Ms. Sinclair. I didn't mean to startle you."

Cole relaxed, but then frowned. He hadn't sensed his agent's approach...in *any* way. Had he been so wrapped up in Alex that someone had actually managed to sneak up on him...so closely? Again? If so, how many times had it happened before? Then he tilted his head and regarded his agent with suspicion. Or was it Tommy in particular? When had he become so stealthy?

And why the hell was he looking at Alex like that? Like she was some goddamned midnight snack...

"Oh, excuse me, Mr. St. James. I didn't see you there." Alex mumbled, frowning as she edged around the talent agent.

"You don't have to leave on my account." Tommy invited, stepping closer. His eyes fixed on hers with mesmerizing intensity.

Cole growled warning at the poaching agent. Inexplicably unsettled, he couldn't resist the urge to get her far, far away from the cocky agent.

"Come in, Tommy. Alex was just leaving."

Chapter 20

Cole stepped through the French doors and prowled restlessly across the patio, drawn by the luminous, blue glow of accent lights beneath the surface of the pool. Laced with guilt over keeping the truth from Alex yet again, his body was tense with hungers of more than one variety. The glass of chilled blood he'd downed earlier hadn't gone far to ease his need, and so he thought to take the edge off with a quick swim. The thought of going into the city, hunting up some fresh blood was tempting, but he just couldn't bring himself to leave Alex alone. Especially not now that he knew how ineffective his security measures had proven against the Rogue.

With the band gone to the premiere, and the estate closed for the duration to groupies and hangers on, the place was a virtual tomb. He tried— very, *very* hard—not to think about the fact that he wasn't *completely* alone. Because, if he dwelled on that one little detail, he'd go to her like a moth to a flame, knowing there would be no one to interrupt should his hungers get the best of him again.

By Odin, he swore silently as he whipped his muscle shirt over his head, the scent that was so uniquely Alex haunted him, even out here, mingling with the scents of chlorine and night. Cole reached for the ties on the waistband of his sweats, and his hands froze—as did every other part of his body except for his blood, which surged violently with sheer, unadulterated lust.

The object of his obsession floated aimlessly in the pool of liquid moonlight, her slim arms sliding through the water beside her exercise-flushed body in languid, graceful strokes. The sight of her, all golden skin and temptation, clad in alluring scraps of seduction, utterly ravaged him. The instant, sharp bite of hunger...the swift, undeniable burn of desire hit him, and he shook with the effort not to seize and take complete possession.

Some inner sense must have detected she was no longer alone. Alex lifted her head from the water, her eyes probing the shadows. As soon as she spied Cole, she shifted, moving to an upright position. Her shoulders bobbed at the surface of the water, and the silvery liquid sluiced over her skin, streaming down the valley between her full breasts, kissing her with glistening dew. Relaxed, she smiled up at Cole in warm surprise, his name a softly murmured question on her lips.

The combination proved a more potent aphrodisiac than Cole could resist.

With fiercely measured movements, Cole stripped away his sweats, revealing a sleek swimsuit that left little to the imagination. Alex's eyes widened appreciatively as they swept over the chiseled length of his rock solid body. The tip of her tongue moistened her lower lip a second before she caught that lip between her small, perfect teeth. Wordlessly, purposefully, Cole strode toward the pool, a painfully sharp smile knifing his features, and he dove beneath the surface.

Cole swam beneath the water in ever tightening circles around her, like a shark scenting its next meal. Then suddenly he was there, standing before her. Well within reaching distance. His eyes held her trapped and immobile, unable—unwilling—to move away.

"I didn't realize you'd be swimming at this hour." His soft voice feathered over her in one long, sensual caress.

"I was restless," she murmured breathlessly.

"Me too," Cole rumbled, slipping through the water, edging a little closer. His gaze fell to her lips, and he knew his eyes glowed brighter.

Alex licked her lips again. Cole's hungry stare skated lower, drawn to the place where her pulse throbbed at the base of her throat. The blood in his own veins seethed and boiled.

"I usually swim in the morning, before the band or any of the others are up and about, but since everyone else was gone..." she rambled.

The only thing she succeeded in doing was remind them both that they were alone.

Completely alone.

Without a single soul to interrupt.

Alex's eyes called to him on a level he couldn't defend against. Jittery need swept through him like a firestorm. She whispered his name. The firestorm exploded with the force of a volcanic eruption, incinerating his restraint. In the flash of a heartbeat, Cole snaked an arm around Alex's waist, dragging her against him. His other hand cupped the back of her head, holding her immobile beneath his sensual onslaught.

He knew the time for waiting was over. He knew, too, that this first time with her would not be slow and easy. Not for them. The savoring would come later. No, this first time, it would be hard and fast. Explosive. Hot flesh meeting slick hot flesh. Souls fusing, melding.

As Cole wrapped himself around her, as his heat surrounded her and his tongue invaded her mouth, he left her no room but to give in. She closed her eyes, slid her hands over his wet flesh. Her tongue dueled with his for control of the kiss, and in the end there was no winner, no loser, only the taste of surrender.

Alex's bold caresses, her brazen kisses

unleashed the primal, untamed desires inside him. Her soft, supple body pressed against his in all the right places, turning his bones to liquid. Her mouth, hot and demanding, turned his blood into a raging inferno stoked by hungry desire, fueled by greedy need. His hands trembled as they stroked her flesh with fiercely controlled tenderness, so at odds with the ferocious demand of his kisses.

He ached, deep inside, and he couldn't get close enough, couldn't assuage the painful need tearing through him. Even wedged tightly between her thighs wasn't close enough. He wasn't close enough, not until he'd buried himself deep inside her. Maybe not even then. What had come over him? He'd never experienced this...this fierce *thirst* for any other woman, ever. Cole's hands slid down to grasp her hips, grinding his unyielding erection against her woman's heat, groaning against her mouth.

His lips skated over her cheek and down the underside of her jaw. He licked and laved at the racing pulse below the ridge of her jawbone, and she arched in his arms. Hunger of a different kind rose up inside him at the memory of her sweet blood on his tongue when he'd nicked her before, and Cole groaned deep in his throat. Squeezing his eyes shut, he fought against the urge to sink his fangs into her tender skin and sup on the ambrosia of her lifeblood.

He knew he could take her blood here and now—knew once his fangs penetrated her flesh she'd be lost in the thrall of a Vampyre's *Kiss* and would remember only sensual ecstasy afterward. Yet he fought against taking from her that which she didn't willingly—knowingly—give to him. If and when he took her blood, it would be because *she* chose for it to be so. He didn't know why it mattered so much to him. But it did.

Frustration made turning his lips away from her throat a punishing endeavor, but he forced himself to focus on what she willingly offered, forced himself to center his attentions on the hunger that she appeared all too willing to appease. His body quaked. His resolve shook when she nipped at the side of his neck with her small, blunt teeth. The slight sting swept through him in vicious waves of pleasure.

"By the gods, sweetheart," he moaned against her ear, his voice thick and dark as the night that surrounded them. "You're my addiction. The more I touch you, the more I want. The more I taste of you, the more I need. I crave the very scent of you." He fisted a hand in her hair and roughly pulled her head back so he could stare full on into her eyes. "I've been burning for you from the first moment I laid eyes on you."

The admission of her own desires smoldered in her eyes, and it was his undoing. Tenderness, gentleness was vanquished in the wake of vicious carnal lust. His hands became rougher, his kisses ravaging, savage. The thin straps of her bikini snapped beneath his ferocity, her suit disappearing in shredded pieces, and, somehow, his suit was gone as well.

He pressed Alex ruthlessly back against the hard wall of the pool. The searing, rock-solid heat of his rigid staff pressed between her thighs, rubbing against her, pulsing at the touch of her slick heat. The strained muscles of his chest crushed her breasts. Any thought of stopping—of slowing down at the very least—were gone as soon as they formed. He'd rather take a stake in the heart than stop now, rather face the dawn than slow down.

His arms caged her, locking tight. He broke the kiss abruptly. His breath was ragged against her skin. Cole pressed his forehead to hers, noses touching. His eyes bore into hers with unswerving intensity as his steely erection invaded her slick, hot flesh in one long, forceful thrust. As her womanhood clenched tightly on him, he tossed his head back and roared...the sound so loud and so primitively possessive that she shuddered in his arms, wringing still another groan from him. Then his mouth claimed hers once more, and he began to move.

As he buried himself to the hilt—ground himself deep inside her—he murmured between mind-boggling kisses, words in a language he knew she'd never heard spoken aloud, the language of the Norse gods, the language of his birth. The sound of those words sent rippling shivers through her, as if she sensed their significance, firing his blood even more.

As he withdrew, she cried his name. Then gasped it again, exultant, when he pounded back inside her. Over and over. Cole thrust deeply, mercilessly driving her up one shattering peak after another, until she hung limp in his arms. Only then did he allow himself release from the ecstasy that held his body a shuddering captive. With his face carefully averted—he could no longer conceal the change in his features—he growled his satisfaction against her shoulder and poured his heat into her.

Cole held her for measureless moments, long after the last quivers died away. Long enough for his face to smooth out once more, though the sharp sting of hunger was still upon him. Her sweet blood rushed through her veins, calling to him. Her hammering pulses pounded in his ears.

Even as he fought against his baser needs, his long, nimble fingers tenderly stroked her neck and back, his lips nibbled sweet kisses across her jaw and mouth. He'd never experienced this warmth, this sense of completion before, and he was suddenly certain, beyond all reason, that he'd found his Bride. The revelation left him stunned speechless.

Up until now, he hadn't really believed such a thing existed. He'd suspected, but carefully shied from facing the truth. He knew of only a few others of his kind who'd actually completed the Mating Rites. He'd certainly never imagined he'd be willing even to consider such a commitment. The very idea left him wrecked, completely devastated, and yet oddly giddy.

For Vampyre, there was no higher commitment—no vow held more dear—than that of the Mating, the commitment of a Vampyre pledging himself to his Bride, his fated mate, for infinity. It was a solemn commitment to cherish and love each other for all eternity, an unbreakable bond that not even death could sever. It was not one to be entered into without absolute certainty, for the commitment was very real. Absolute and unforgiving. Throughout time and space, the two would be drawn to each other, unable to stay away.

The actual Rites themselves were precise, requiring three specific elements to bind the mated pair. The two were required to drink from each other while making love, and the two were to recite the vow. Blood, sex, and spoken promises of the soul. From that moment on, the couple literally shared one heartbeat, one soul.

And, if one of the mates were Mortal, the Vampyre would no longer be able to draw sustenance from another.

Unbidden, the flash of Alex's tattoo blinked through Cole's mind. The same symbol he'd insisted be engraved on every one of his weapons and his armor as a reminder to himself that wisdom was the ultimate prize. Her tattoo was, in his mind, as good as a sign from the gods.

He wanted her to understand it all, wanted her to understand what she meant to him—the depth of his emotion where she was concerned—and what their future held. His love—a Vampyre's love—was something infinitely deeper than that of mortal emotion. A Vampyre's love was all consuming, greedy and elemental. It made no concessions, left no room for uncertainty. Once a Vampyre gave his heart, there was no turning back. It was forever.

Cole had given his heart to Alex.

"Alexandra," he began softly against her hair, his hands reverent as they swept over her body.

"Hmm," she mumbled against his collarbone, trembling, still adrift on the hazy aftershocks of their lovemaking.

"Honey, come with me," he urged, wanting her again already—still hard inside her—but determined to wait until he'd had a chance to explain everything. "Come with me back to my room. The guys will be back soon, and we need to—"

Without warning, she tensed in his arms, and began pushing at his shoulders, startling Cole into silence mid-sentence. Panic and fear filled her eyes. Not fear of him, but fear of herself and what she'd allowed to happen.

"Let me go," she insisted frantically, shoving harder, her voice held the honed edge of hysteria. "Oh, my *God*, Cole! What did we do? Cole, let go!"

Confused, stunned, he released her, sliding reluctantly from her body and backing up a step. His voice was sharp. "Alex..."

"No, Cole." She shook her head insistently, tears glittering in her eyes. "This should never have happened."

Then, without any further explanation, Alex turned away from him and pulled herself from the water, leaving him staring after her in mounting frustration. As she hurried across the patio, moonlight glistening on her lithe, naked body, his gaze fell to the *Odhroerir* tattooed on her back, and a primal rush of possession swept through him, filling him with resolve, leaving him dead certain he had not been mistaken.

Alex was meant to be his Bride.

Steely determination clenched his jaw, and he sucked in a deep breath, catching the scent of her that still lingered on his skin. With the same single-minded determination he'd used to control his fate over the course of his long, long existence, Cole made up his mind, then and there. Alex *would* belong to him—for all eternity.

He would accept *nothing* less.

Chapter 21

The next two weeks became a frustrating game of cat and mouse. Cole pursued her with undaunted, calculated determination. Alex's resolved evasion continued with a growing sense of panic. He used the excuse of a love ballad they were working on for the next album to force her into near constant, one-on-one contact, pressing her at every available opportunity with lusty stolen kisses and sexy, heart-stopping glances. He pilfered caresses, brushing against her at every opportune moment, dropping innuendo after pointed, seductive innuendo. She couldn't take anymore. Her resistance wasn't that strong.

Late one afternoon, after spending the better part of the day fending off Cole's persuasive advances, her poise—and her resolve—was in shreds. She snuck away while he was otherwise occupied, hoping to steal a few moments to reinforce her resistance. Like a bloodhound, he tracked her down and cornered her in the kitchen, in much the same spot as he had that shocking night not so very long ago.

Without a word, he stalked her back against the counter, trapping her with his body, pinning her with his sultry gaze. The spoon she'd been holding clattered to the floor as his lips closed determinedly over hers, robbing her of her breath, turning her knees to jelly, her resolve to mush.

Her resistance trembled and cracked, and he smiled knowing triumph against her lips. Panting, Alex wrenched her lips from his, pushing ineffectually at his chest. Undeterred, Cole's lips skated to her cheek, then lower to nibble at the tender flesh beneath her ear.

"Stop it, Cole!" She'd meant the words to be forceful, demanding. They were, instead, a pitiful, breathless, desperate plea.

"Why?" Cole murmured between nips. "You know that's not what you want. It's sure as hell not what *I* want."

"I don't want this," she insisted, but her voice wavered, unconvincing.

"Yes, you do. You want this, Alex, and you want me." He rubbed himself invitingly against her, trailing hot, wet kisses over her collarbone and up the other side of her neck. "I can *feel* it, sweetheart." When she didn't immediately agree, Cole's voice hinted at his baffled torment. "Odin's teeth, *why* do you fight this, woman? *How* do you fight it? It's all I can do not to take you right here."

His words shot liquid flames of desire through her veins as vivid images filled her mind. It took all of Alex's willpower to feign indifference.

"I don't know what you're talking about. There is nothing to fight, Cole, not anymore," Alex claimed, her throbbing pulse exposing her lie for what it was.

"Is that so?" His gaze glittered with blatant disbelief as he leaned back to probe deep into her eyes. His slow, smug smile accepted her challenge.

Cole's hungry eyes dropped once more to her lips, and he moaned aloud when the tip of her tongue slipped out to moisten her lower lip expectantly. Desire was etched in every line on his face, his body was rigid with his need—and yet he restrained himself. She couldn't decide whether to be relieved, or disappointed.

He shot her one last look of cold determination— the look of a triumphant conqueror assessing spoils of war—then he pivoted on his heel, stalking from the kitchen without sparing her the slightest backward glance. Alex stared after him, bemused. Some tiny voice in the back of her head urged her to run, to run and keep right on running until she'd put Cole and his overwhelming sensual assault on her senses far, far behind her. Yet, the very thought of running was ridiculous.

She was not a coward.

So she'd slipped once. She wouldn't be weak again. What happened between them had been nothing more than sex...mind-blowing sex, true...but it had been a serious mistake, nonetheless. From now on, she'd just have to make sure it was business only between them.

Business was unemotional.

Business was safe.

Alex wandered from the kitchen then, oblivious to the fact her spoon still lay on the floor where she'd dropped it, and the container of yogurt sat on the counter behind her, unopened.

She stepped inside the studio and blinked in surprise. The band was not alone. Several women had joined them, an anomaly she hadn't been expecting. The beauties lounged at various, strategic points around the room, indolently watching as the band eased into another session.

Gritting her teeth in vexation at this unwelcome change in routine, Alex took a chair in the corner, determined to ignore the unwanted distraction. She wasn't sure where they'd come from—the estate had been absent of excessive groupies of late, after all— but she sure as hell didn't appreciate their reappearance.

The band rehearsed for well over three hours, and at every pause, one or more of the women meandered unimpeded throughout the room of instruments, flirting with the musicians. Every time one of them drifted toward Cole—whenever one of them ran a manicured finger over his arm or trailed a greedy hand across his chest—Alex tensed, prepared to leap and dismember in an uncharacteristic, primitive surge of possessiveness.

When a leggy blonde slipped her arm around Cole's waist and pressed her garish red lips to the side of his throat, Alex's nails bit into her palms. Somehow, she managed to restrain herself with commendable control, not uttering a single sound, even though she longed so desperately to screech and tear the woman's hair out by her touched-up roots.

The woman stretched up on her toes and whispered into Cole's ear, letting her hand trail down his stomach and lower. He simply grinned with wicked interest instead of pushing her away. Alex had had enough. She stiffly stood up, chin proudly elevated, and silently stalked to the door.

"Yo, Slim! Where ya off to? We're not done yet."

"*I* am. You'll have to excuse me, but I just can't focus on the music with all the catty noise in here," she bit out, unable to hide the hostility brewing in her eyes. "When you're ready to have a real session, let me know." With that scathing remark, she shot a pointed look at Cole, then stomped from the room, letting the door slam in her wake.

She huffed down one hall after another, too upset to slow down. Somehow, she ended up in Cole's study. She shouldn't have been surprised. That seemed to have become a regular haunt of hers, though she tried to stick to hours when Cole wasn't likely to be around.

The sound of the lock sliding home hit Alex like a jolt of lightning, and she jumped in surprise. She spun around, only to find Cole standing in front of her. How had he moved so fast? Struggling to process how he'd managed to cover the distance in the blink of an eye, she sidled away, anxious to keep as much space between them as possible. But the look in his eyes hit her like a shockwave. There would be no interruptions this time, no reprieve. No escape. She could see it in his eyes. Her time for evasions had run out. Cole would not be denied. He stalked her step for step, his electric blue eyes drilling into hers. He was untamed and unleashed. A conqueror, eager to consume, dangerous and undeterred.

Molten desire surged through her system, but she fought it with everything in her.

"That's an interesting tattoo you have there, Alex," he murmured, his eyes roamed her body with a sultry familiarity that left her breathless. "I've been wondering. Why did you choose that particular symbol?"

His question threw her a little, as that very thing had been weighing on her mind since the moment she'd first walked into this room and had seen his collection. Bewildered, she sidestepped him again, wondering where her anger had gone.

A few moments ago, she'd stomped from the studio and down the hallways, fuming over the way he'd let that tramp crawl all over him, pawing at him like a cat in heat. Now, suddenly, he was here—giving her *that* look, using *that* tone—and instead of blasting him with her fury, all she could do was mumble and dodge, trying to get away before she melted in a quivering puddle of hunger at his feet.

"It's not so very special," she mumbled, slipping a few more paces to the left. But he dogged her every step, and she wanted to scream with frustration.

"Oh, I would beg to differ," he drawled, treating her to the full impact of his sensual smile. "I've never seen another woman with a tattoo quite like that. I'm certain of that. After all, I'm very familiar with that particular symbol. Every piece in my collection bears that same mark, Alex. But then, you've seen that for yourself, haven't you, sweetheart? Don't you think it a bit too—coincidental?"

Shrugging, muttering something noncommittal beneath her breath, Alex eyed the distance to the door, panic flashing through her. Could she make it before he caught her? As if reading her thoughts, Cole stepped between her and the door, his grin stretching, daring her.

Alex shifted course, but Cole was in front of her once more, and she could only blink. Astonished. Before she could react, he cornered her in the curve of the Steinway, hemming her in with a strong arm. A nimble hand landed on the piano on either side of her. He'd moved so fast, she'd had trouble tracking him. One moment he'd been several feet away, and the next, he was pressing against her, caging her in.

Alex struggled to mask her panicky surprise. She frowned up at him, but her voice wavered, betraying her. "What do you think you're doing?"

The smile came to Cole's lips, slow and sensual. That smile made her nervous, right down to the tips of her toes. What was it about him that was so different? Every time one of the others made a pass at her or a play for her attention, she could push them aside with cool humor now. They were no threat to her—held no interest for her. Yet with Cole, she couldn't remain detached, couldn't hide behind indulgent, sarcastic humor.

With him her defenses had cracked, and she was *flustered.*

His smug satisfaction took on a distinctive shade of wicked. At length, Cole reached up and drew the pencil from her hair, letting the mass tumble down her back. He glanced at the pencil in his hand with wry amusement, apparently remembering the last time he'd removed one of those from her hair. Then again, perhaps he was laughing at her penchant for using pencils rather than the traditional hair-clips.

Without warning, he tossed the pencil over his shoulder, and her unease grew. "I'm solving a puzzle."

Alex forced the lump of desire in her throat down with a hard swallow. Her wide-eyed gaze locked on his iceberg blue eyes. "What puzzle?"

Cole tilted his head, his eyes studying her face with infinite care. "You intrigue me, Alexandra Sinclair, with your prim, all-business attitude and your ruthlessly restrained hair. But there's fire in your eyes. I've felt it." His speculative gaze turned sultry, intense. "I've had a taste of it. It's burned me, and I find myself wanting more, and more still. And I can't help but wonder..." His voice trailed off as he traced the curve of her cheek with the back of his finger.

Although she told herself not to, she invited, breathless, "You wonder what?"

His eyes lock with hers and his head lowered, until his lips hovered just above hers. Their breath mingled. "I'm wondering how long it will be before you finally admit that you want me every bit as much as I want you?" His words race across her lips, sending sparks cascading through her, touching off a hunger neither of them could contain. "I *need* you, Alex."

Her eyes widened. Her lips parted, but before she could form a denial, his mouth sealed over hers, ravaging and ruthless. His hips pushed against her, and his tongue swept inside her mouth. The rigid heat of his arousal pressed against her in an unforgiving demand for surrender. Her knees shook, buckled.

She couldn't fight the moan gurgling up inside her throat, hardly aware she'd even emitted a sound. His mouth became greedy, voracious...driven.

Cole's long, agile fingers skimmed over her hip, up to cover her breast. The lace of her bra and the silk camisole were far more barrier than she could tolerate. In little time he stripped away her camisole, just as his lips stripped away her resistance. His questing fingers trailed across the scalloped edge of her bra, found the clasp between her breasts, releasing it with one deft flick. Baring her to his voracious hands.

Cole's lips left hers to trail hot, open-mouthed kisses down her throat and across the delicate skin of her chest, nuzzling the sensitive flesh in the valley between her naked breasts. A low rumble of pleasure escaped him, rapacious and primal.

The sound both startled and thrilled Alex, jolting her to awareness once more. Struggling to regain her senses, she began straining backwards, pushing at his shoulders, panicked at the thought that she'd been within a hair's breadth of diving headlong once again into waters best left uncharted. She'd already taken this swim, she reminded herself, and she'd lost her heart in the process. What more was she in danger of losing should she allow herself to fall prey to Cole's masterful seduction? Her sense of self? Her very soul?

He lifted incandescent eyes first, until their gazes locked, and then his tawny, tousled head. His lips pulled away from her nipple with palpable reluctance. Uncertainty and panic coursed in her veins. But there was desire as well. And something infinitely more precious. Her heart trembled inside her rib cage with the force of it.

Tenderness. Love. Reluctant and anxious, but a love all the same.

Oh hell.

She'd gone and fallen in love with him. The ferocious need in his eyes unleashed a similar need in her, a need beyond anything sane or safe. How had this happened? Self-preservation made one last feeble grab at sanity.

"Cole," Alex gasped. Her voice broke on a half-plea, half-sob. "We shouldn't..."

He pushed her words aside, sliding up her body, licking and nipping, suckling his way up the side of her neck. His hands were unyielding as they grasped her hips, tugging her closer, until they fitted together like pieces of a jigsaw puzzle once more. Snug. Faultless. He pushed his hips hard against her and nuzzled at her throat, his breath a ragged seduction, harsh and hot in her ear.

"Cole," she whimpered, drawing on the last dregs of her resistance. Her will power little more than vapor now, rapidly evaporating beneath Cole's masterful kisses and spellbinding hands. Her only hope was bringing one of them to their senses...bringing reason to a situation that was rapidly slipping toward catastrophic. His skillful lips didn't make it an easy task. "I refuse to be another conquest for you. I'm not some groupie you can just have your fun with and walk away from." A soft moan slipped from her as his lips fastened on the pulse at the base of her throat. "Cole...I'm not cut out to be a one night stand."

He tore his lips away from hers, glaring down at her with eerie, glowing eyes. His voice was rough, hoarse. "Does this *feel* like a one night stand to you?"

Oh, no. This felt like much, much more. This felt like fire, explosive and all consuming.

Cole seized her lips before she could utter another sigh. This kiss was different. No less forceful, no less fierce. But it held an added layer, one of wild tenderness and reverent abandon. By the time he lifted his head, there wasn't an ounce of resistance in her entire body, and, if his kiss hadn't been enough to melt her heart, his words were.

"You are nothing like the others. You aren't like

anyone I've ever met. I swear it. Now that I've had a taste of you, no one else will *ever* be enough for me. I need you...only you. Alex, you have my heart."

As the words passed his lips, they branded themselves on her soul. *He* wasn't like anyone else *she'd* ever known. He was thoughtful, vivacious and strong, poised, opinionated yet open-minded and sensible. Her confidence blossomed. She gazed up into his face, filled with wonder. He fascinated her. No one else had ever made her burn with want the way he did, no one else could make her as mindless with desire with nothing more than a kiss, a look...a smile.

On some level, that realization terrified the hell out of her. Yet she was powerless to resist, defenseless against the tenderness in his intense gaze.

He crushed her against him, kissing her with wild abandon. She clung to him. At that moment in time, the house could have burned down around her ears, and she wouldn't have cared less. As long as Cole kept kissing her as he was—kept touching her the way he was—the entire world could have burned.

His rough hands slid to her waist, lifting her up high against him. She wrapped her legs around his waist, her arms around his neck, and moaned delirious surrender. The room spun in a whirl of motion. Then Cole had her across the room and pinned beneath him on the sofa. His weight a delicious thrill as he stole a lingering, heartbreaking kiss. Her skirt was gone, as were his clothes. The only thing standing between them was the flimsy obstacle of her lacy panties. The scrap of silk and lace proved no hindrance for Cole, snapping beneath his urgent hands with stunning ease.

He covered her, hovered over her, and paused, the scorching tip of his granite erection poised at her entrance. His body was so hard, everywhere. She couldn't get her fill of touching him. He lifted his head, his startling, glowing eyes penetrated the passion-induced fog that shrouded her brain. His fingers flexed on her hips, possessive and bruising.

Cole's voice was deeper, far more powerful than she'd ever heard it before. "I want *you*, Alexandra Elizabeth Sinclair, you and no one else. Don't you realize yet? Haven't you figured it out? I love you, Alex. Be with *me*. Be *mine*."

Alex blinked up at him, amazed, overflowing with joy at his unexpected announcement, thrilled he needed her far more than she'd ever hoped. The knowledge kicked open the door of emotions she'd purposefully kept locked tight, letting warmth and pleasure flood her heart and leak out her eyes.

"Only you, Cole," she managed to reply, breathless but confident. She'd never been more certain of anything in her life. "I love you, too."

His reaction was swift, violent and elemental. He ravaged her mouth. His body invaded hers in one long insistent thrust after another. He drove into her, harder and harder, grinding to the hilt, and Alex wrapped her arms around him, reveling in his possession, glorying in his fundamental need for her. She locked her legs around him as he rolled his hips, straining deeper and deeper inside her. His breath pounded against her ear, his feverish lips seared her skin. Alex urged him on. Her hands clutched him tighter. Sensation welled and surged. Higher and higher.

As the crests began to break over her, her body shattering in his arms, he pressed his lips to her ear as he spilled himself deep in her womb, a rush of pulsing warmth. "There's no turning back now, Alex, *you are mine*. I'll never lose you."

Hours later—after they'd finally gotten around to the savoring—as she lay spent in Cole's arms, with his hands and lips stroking her tenderly, Alex scoffed at her fears of losing herself, of losing her soul. A small, contented smile pulled the edges of her lips up. She'd definitely lost her heart all right, and probably part of her soul as well. But she'd gained something immeasurably more valuable in return.

She'd won Cole's love.

Chapter 22

Alex floated in a dreamy haze for the better part of the following day. Perhaps, for that very reason, it was all the more difficult to accept the sight that met her eyes when she entered Cole's study late that afternoon. Styx reclined on the sofa with a brunette, gasping and panting with excitement, cuddled on his lap. His mouth pressed against her skin. A thin trickle of crimson trailed down the column of her slender throat.

The stack of papers Alex carried in her arms spilled to the floor. The faint shushing of paper against carpet snapped Styx's head up and around with an unearthly hiss. Huge fangs snarled at her, and his dilated eyes glowed wicked amber. Blood dripped from the lethal tips of his fangs, staining his lips a gaudy scarlet. A shrill, startled scream ripped from her chest, and then she fled, leaving behind ominous cursing in furious Spanish.

She ran down one long hallway after another, desperate to find a safe place to hide...some safe escape...until she collided with a broad, steely chest. Long, strong arms wrapped around her, locking tight. Hysterical, she began to struggle.

"Alex," Cole's voice snapped as the top of her head connected sharply with his chin.

As soon as his voice broke through the haze, Alex stilled, her gaze flying up to connect with concerned eyes the color of the cloudless midday sky. She collapsed against him, babbling.

He loosened his grip on her as soon as she stopped fighting to get away, but his hands tightened once more when she began sobbing against his chest. "Slow down. Take a breath, Alex. What's wrong, sweetheart?"

Alex sucked in a ragged breath, nowhere near calm. The hideous mask of fury that was Styx's face glared back at her every time she closed her eyes. She shook like a leaf in a hurricane. "Cole, we have to get out of here—right now! It's not safe here, I can't explain right now... He's... My God! We have to get out of here..."

"What happened?" He took hold of her shoulders and forced her back a step, staring into her panicked eyes. His brow creased. "Talk to me, baby. What happened?"

She tugged at his elbows, tearing at his shirt, frantic, but he wouldn't budge. "Cole, please..."

His tone was fierce, demanding. "Alex! Talk to me!"

Frustrated, terrified, Alex let the insensible words pour out. "I went into your study a few minutes ago. I thought you'd be there... I saw... My God! It doesn't make any sense..."

She pulled at him again, her body straining. Why wouldn't he move? They had to get out of there before it was too late...before that monster in Cole's study came for them.

****

Fearful apprehension snaked down Cole's spine, understanding burned in his chest. She fisted her hands in the front of his shirt, gritting her teeth as she strained to propel him away from the study.

"Cole, please... Styx was there. He had a girl on his lap, and he had... He had his mouth on her neck. When he heard me, he turned to me, and his face... God, Cole, please..." Alex trailed off, squeezing her eyes closed, shuddering. "His teeth were... And his eyes... He *hissed* at me. And the blood...there was so much *blood*."

Gods, it was worse than he'd feared. She was terrified, and it was all his fault. Why had he procrastinated?

Because he'd been searching for a gentle way to ease her into it, afraid of terrifying her and driving her away.

Brilliant idea, slick! Finding out this way was so much better!

"Alex." He measured his words with forced calm, praying he'd be able to get through to her, to help her see they weren't a danger to her. That she had nothing to fear from them. "Sweetheart, come with me."

He took her by the hand and tugged her the rest of the way down the hallway. With a confused frown, she followed for a few steps but then she began struggling. "Cole, you don't understand. We have to *leave!*"

Opening the door to his bedroom, he pulled her resistant form through the doorway behind him. With a resigned sigh, he pushed the door closed with the back of his boot, holding her firmly by the shoulders.

"Alex, listen," he began, willing her anxious eyes to meet his. "I know what you think you saw. I know what you must be thinking, but it's not—"

"I know what I saw Cole—"

"I don't doubt that. I don't doubt you one bit."

"You know about Styx?" She gaped at him, incredulous, and froze in his arms.

"Yes, I—"

"My God, Cole," she exploded, wringing her hands before her. "But he... This doesn't make any sense. There's no such thing as..." She trailed away, shaking her head, eyes wide and filled with denial.

Cole forced her to acknowledge the truth, speaking aloud the word she refused to face. "Styx is Vampyre, Alex."

Alex continued to shake her head, her eyes huge. All the color drained from her face, but Cole nodded. "Yes, Alex, he's Vampyre. You have to trust me. Styx wouldn't hurt you. He's my friend, baby. He has been for a...a very long time. He would never hurt you. Alex, believe me, Styx would only protect you...because you're mine."

"Styx is a...a Vampyre...oh my God. But Cole," she argued, her eyes darting to the door at his back. "I don't understand. He's your *friend*?"

"Yes, he's my friend," Cole insisted, relaxing now that she'd calmed down...somewhat...now that she didn't look as if she were ready to bolt at the slightest provocation. "You have nothing to fear, Alex. I promise you."

Alex drew a deep breath, emotions coursing over her face faster than he could track them.

"But the girl on his lap... And the blood... His teeth were..." She trailed off shaking her head again. Her eyes were wide, horrified. "Cole, he had *fangs*."

"He was feeding," Cole explained in calm, rational tones. His hands soothed up and down her arms. "He was careless, not locking the door. It was inexcusable scaring you like that, but I'm sure he didn't do it on purpose. He would never harm you, sweetheart."

"But..."

He could see the panic rising in her eyes again, her voice quivered, and so he rushed on. "The girl on his lap, she wasn't afraid, was she? She wasn't fighting him?"

"No..." Alex frowned. "No, she wasn't fighting him, but... Can't...can't a...can't one of *them* control their victim's mind or something?"

"Vampyre, Alex. Vampyre."

Cole paused; he was fast approaching dangerous territory here. He had to explain, just right, or he'd lose her for sure. "In a limited capacity, Vampyre can...offer suggestions a weak mind might be susceptible to. But, as with something like...say, hypnotism for example...in a strong mind, a strong will, the suggestion can be easily ignored. A Vampyre's bite can be quite erotic. The girl with Styx was a willing host, Alex. Fully cognizant and completely willing."

Alex was clearly overwhelmed, unable to process it all. Her eyes had gone strangely glassy, and her breathing was much too erratic. But he couldn't stop now. He needed to finish, he needed to tell her all of it. Now, before it was too late...

Look at her eyes, dumbass. It's already too late.

Letting go of her, he paced away, then paced back, dragging his hands down the sides of his face. Pausing a few steps away, he peered at her, hard.

"Do you believe me when I tell you Styx wouldn't hurt you?" Cole pressed, desperate to convince her. "Baby, I need you to trust me. I need you to believe me. You have to understand you have *nothing* to fear. You are safe, I swear it."

She nodded slowly, eyes wide and wary on his. Hers was the face of a woman on the edge, humoring a madman. Panic clawed at him. He wasn't getting through. He raked a hand through his hair, his mind racing. Then, without any indication of his intent, he closed the distance between them and swept her into his arms. His lips sealed over hers with a desperate mix of fear and needy tenderness. Severing the contact as quickly as he'd initiated it, he stepped back and peered into her eyes.

"Do you trust me?"

An odd look settled over her features. As if she couldn't quite believe she'd actually even consider accepting his explanations. Frowning, she nodded, slowly. She wasn't moving farther away from him, physically or emotionally, and he took that as a good sign. "Neither one of us would ever hurt you," Cole insisted, his eyes boring into hers with frantic desperation. His eyes began to glow, unnatural and bright, he could feel the change.

She gasped and staggered an uncertain step back. Her hand trembled as she clutched her throat, whispering, "Neither one of you..."

"Neither one of us would hurt you, Alex," Cole repeated, whisper soft and yet fiercely vehement, worried anew by the dawning horror in her eyes.

She narrowed her eyes and forced a swallow, her head jerking a defiant denial. "No, Cole..."

"Yes, Alex." He stepped forward, but stopped when she took a swift step back, holding her hands defensively up between them.

Alex abruptly spun away from him, closing her eyes. "No! Stop it! I won't hear this. This is insane..."

Knowing it was cruel to do it this way—knowing there was no other way to get her to face the truth—Cole set his hands on her shoulders and forced her around to face him. He let emotions swell and surge up inside him, deliberately triggering the change. Horrified, speechless, Alex gaped as he changed into a monster.

Cole opened his mouth to let her see the full truth. His fangs grew long and razor-sharp, right before her stunned eyes.

"This is me, Alex," Cole rumbled, the timbre of his voice dropped, dark and hoarse. His eyes pleaded with her to understand and accept. "This is a part of who I am."

Alex jerked away, drawing back in stunned fear. "Oh my God, you're...you're like him. You're a..."

"I am Vampyre," Cole finished for her, unable—unwilling—to apologize for who and what he was.

"I won't listen to this." She pressed a fist to her mouth. Tears welled and spilled over, crystal clear droplets of anguish. Her frantic gaze darted to the door, but her feet did not follow. "Oh, my God! The whole band..."

"No." Cole held up a placating hand. "Not the entire band, just me and Styx...and Deacon. Zack's a Werewolf, actually. The others are Human."

Her brows lifted at that, and for a split second, laughter, irrational and hysterical, burbled up in her chest. "Ah, hhh...a whaa...a Werewolf...of *course*..."

Not good. Concerned, Cole frowned and took a step forward, forgetting his fangs and glowing eyes as he reached for her.

She panicked. The laughter died on a fearful sob, and Alex scuttled away from him. His heart sagging beneath the weight of her torment. "Don't... Don't come any closer."

"Alex, please," Cole pleaded, an icy fist of panic clutched at his gut, twisting mercilessly. "This doesn't change anything. It doesn't change how I feel about you..."

"Stop it! Just *stop*..." Alex pressed her hands to her ears. She stumbled backwards, distraught tears streaming down her cheeks now.

"I love you, Alexandra Sinclair," Cole insisted, following her across the room, careful to maintain a tiny bit of space...for her sake. That space—the fear in her eyes—was driving tiny stakes into his heart. "You know me, better than anyone else ever has. You *know* me—and you love me, Alex."

"No, I... I can't..." But the truth was there in her eyes. Layered with fear, soaked in shock. But it was there.

She *was* in love with him.

He held on to that, fought for it.

Sobbing, she pressed her white-knuckled fists against her chest and turned away, sobbing. It was more than he could bear.

Her heart was on her sleeve, and he pressed his advantage. Turning her to face him, he captured one of her hands, pried her fingers open, and pressed her palm against his own chest. "Feel me, Alex. I *am* the same. Feel my flesh. It's warm, alive. Feel my heart beating in my chest, beating for you." His lips twisted in a wry grin. "Cut me and I'll bleed."

Confused, her eyes rounded. Her hand trembled beneath his but she didn't try to jerk it away. He tried to convince himself that, too, was a good sign.

"You can't deny it, Alex. Just like you can't deny your own heart. You can't because I know you, too. You *love* me. *Me*, sweetheart. You fell in love with *me*. And *I* won't let you deny it. I won't let you take it back. You know...deep down...you know I'd never harm you. You are my life."

The tears kept coming, and she turned away, sliding her hand from beneath his, covering her face with her palms. Great heaving sobs wracked her slight frame.

"Sweetheart..." Cole pleaded, his stomach dropping at the realization that his greatest fear was about to be realized. He was going to lose her. Desperation, despair filled him. How could he survive without her?

He couldn't.

Determined, he closed the distance between them in a blink and reached for her, steeling himself for her rejection. "*Feel* me, Alex. I am the same. *Please...*"

When his hands closed over her shoulders, Alex didn't jerk away in repulsion, didn't cry out in alarm. Cole took hope. He slowly turned her to face him, sweeping her long hair back over her shoulder, tipping her face up to his, cradling her cheeks in his palms. Her hands fell helplessly to her sides, and she gazed up into his eyes. Changed, stark and frightening. But still his.

His heart ached.

"Please, baby..." Emotion clogged his throat,

making it even more difficult to speak the words he feared she'd never believe. "I love you."

As if in a trance, Alex lifted a hand to trace the sharp angle of his cheekbone. Her fingers skimmed down his jaw. Her eyes probed his face, searching his eyes. He let all the love he felt for her glow in the depths of his gleaming, dilated eyes, willing her with every cell in his body to believe him. To accept him as he was.

And to love him anyway.

Tentatively, Alex trailed her fingertips over his lower lip, pressing with gentle reluctance. He parted his lips for her, exposing his fangs for her hesitant curiosity. Alex paused, sucking in a sharp breath when presented with the lethal length of them. She blinked, catching her lower lip between her small Human teeth. Cautiously, her finger traced the length of one fang, gum to tip, dawning wonder glistened in her eyes.

Cole shuddered at her touch. The stroke of her finger down his fang was akin to rubbing her hand boldly over his erection. Passion and hunger rose up inside him, making him ache, but he held them tightly in check. Determined to give her time to come to terms with all he'd told her. He stared at her, while she explored his face. Her confidence built, as did the fascination in her eyes. He fisted his hands at his sides, unwilling to risk frightening her. When she traced his fangs again, it took every shred of his control as he fought desperately not to yank her against him and give in to both of the hungers that rode him mercilessly.

Alex frowned then, chewing her lip. The fierce light of concentration darkened her brow. She reached for his fang once more. Cole wasn't fast enough to read her intention. He wasn't prepared for her actions. With studied, deliberate calm, Alex pressed the tip of her finger against the deadly point of Cole's fang. She let out a tiny gasp and jerked slightly when his fang pierced her flesh easily. Her eyes flew to lock with his, and she froze. Waiting for his reaction.

Cole couldn't stop the instinctual, predatory growl that erupted from deep in his chest. She flinched at the sound, but his hand shot out faster than she could track it, and he captured her wrist in a grip that was fiercely gentle. His eyes glowed brighter, his vision sharpened. His nostrils flared at the scent of blood—Alex's sweet, tempting blood— and he drew a ragged breath. Slowly, Cole drew her hand away from his mouth, lifting it between them. His eyes left hers long enough to glance once at the wound on her finger and the welling rivulet of crimson. When his eyes came back to hers, love welled in his chest for this brave, precious woman.

Just as slowly, just as deliberately, Cole guided her hand back to his parted lips. Before she could react, he drew her finger into his mouth and suckled, drawing the heady flavor of her blood into his mouth. The warm sweetness of it trickled down his throat, so innocent, so pure. He wanted more. He *needed* more. He sucked harder.

A new sensation raced through him, wildly erotic, completely provocative. Alex's blood, willingly offered. She gasped and stared at him through half closed eyes, unable to look away, and he knew she was getting her first, albeit tiny taste of a Vampyre *Kiss*. All too soon, Cole released her finger from the suction of his mouth. He held her finger up for her view once more. The blood was gone, but the wound remained. Before her astonished eyes, Cole licked her wound, and as his tongue withdrew, the wound was no more. Not a hint of the puncture showed.

Yet Cole's eyes still glowed, brighter than ever, and his fangs remained extended, seeming to have grown in size. The flavor of her blood lingered on his tongue. It surged through his system like an intoxicating elixir, rushing heat and life to every nerve, every cell in his body.

She tested her finger, lifting bemused eye to his, and nearly brought him to his knees with the passion and love...the acceptance...in her eyes.

Cole reached for her then, unable to stop himself. He pulled her against him, not roughly, but firmly enough to let her know he was the one in control this time. His lips descended, claiming hers in a kiss that drained away any lingering uncertainty. Her tongue slipped inside his mouth to duel with his for control. She traced the edges of his fangs. He groaned aloud.

Cole let the kiss stretch on, but when Alex pressed against him full length, he took her firmly by the shoulders and set her from him, determined to get everything out in the open. He wanted no more secrets between them. After all, it wasn't everyday a woman found out the man she'd been making love to—the man she'd fallen in love with—was Vampyre. He needed her to understand exactly what he wanted from her—exactly what he wanted to have *with* her. He wouldn't risk losing her again, later.

"Wait." He ground the word out through gritted teeth, his voice husky with forcibly suppressed desire. "We need to talk, and if you keep kissing me like that, it's going to be a long, long time before we get around to words. You need to hear all of it."

Alex allowed him to set her back on her heels, her eyes burned with desire, but she nodded. Satisfied she wasn't going to run from him, screaming in terror, Cole strode across the room to put a little distance between them, hoping to clear his mind a little. Turning to face her, Cole tilted his head, searching for the right words.

"Your tattoo—the *Odhroerir...* Why did you

choose that particular symbol?"

He'd asked much the same question before, but she'd been too afraid of her answer to respond. "I... I don't know. It just...called to me, I guess," she replied haltingly. Then a frown creased her brow. "Why do you have all those weapons in that case, Cole? Why are they all from the same period in history? And why do they all have the same markings? Where did you get them?"

Cole stared at her a long time. His answer would be a shock, but he refused to lie to her. "They are my history, Alex. They're mine."

"I know they're yours now, but..." Then his response took on a completely new possibility. She frowned, tilting her head to the side. "What do you mean, they're *your* history?" Before he could respond, her eyes suddenly widened. Her words rushed out on a hoarse whisper. "How old are you, Cole?"

"Old," he replied with a wry smile.

Barely a second passed before she pressed, "How old?"

His bark of laughter was short and blade sharp...fang sharp. His female was entirely too smart for her own good. His smile was grim. "I was born in the year 811 AD, Alexandra, in a small village on the western shores of Norway. I was a Viking warrior. The sword and shield...all the weapons in that curio cabinet...they're *mine*."

His heart lurched inside his chest as the color drained from her face and she swayed on her feet.

Chapter 23

Alex blinked, sliding down onto the side of his bed, trying to wrap her mind around the fact Cole was well over eleven hundred years old. Then, before she could draw breath, he was kneeling before her, grasping her hands in his, peering up into her face with a fierce frown.

"Stop doing that!" Alex snapped. One minute he'd been across the room, the next he was kneeling before her. It was…unsettling.

"I'm sorry," he offered, though he didn't seem certain why he'd apologized. "Are you all right? You just went white as a sheet."

"I'm not sure yet," she answered. Her hands trembled in his. She stared hard at him, recalling her first initial assessment of him—the brazen, sword-wielding Viking on the storm-tossed longship. Shaking her head at how close she'd hit the mark. "So, those weapons in the case, they really were…yours. You were a Viking?"

"Yes." He gripped her hands tight. "I've lived many lives, sweetheart, but that was the first."

So many questions raced through Alex's mind. She didn't know where to start. Dismayed, she asked, "How did you become Vampyre?"

Letting his breath out in a long sigh, Cole rose from his knees and sat beside her on the luxuriant king-sized bed. He slid back across the duvet, the black silk rustling against his jeans. He pulled her back with him until they lay side by side.

Alex cuddled full length against his side, in the protective circle of his arms, her head cradled on his shoulder. He did *feel* the same. Everything she'd learned about him so far had left her troubled and confused, but, oddly enough, the one thing that still held the power to give her comfort was the feel of his strong arms around her, and the thud of his steady heartbeat beneath her ear. His heartbeat...

There was another question. Vampyre weren't supposed to have beating hearts. They were supposed to be cold, the undead. More questions swirled forth.

The reassuring thud beneath her ear, the warmth of his skin contradicted what she knew of Vampyre lore. Then again, *he* was supposed to be nothing more than myth, yet here he was—*very* flesh and blood. Somebody really ought to notify Hollywood... They obviously had it all wrong.

Cole's voice was a husky rumble against her cheek when he spoke at last. He told her of his life before that fateful voyage, of being a favored son of a wealthy raider. And he told of the girl he was to have married upon his return, Dagna. Alex suffered a razor sharp pang of jealousy, hearing the note of fondness and regret in his voice as he spoke of his long lost intended. The realization the girl was over a millennia gone, didn't help much.

He glossed over the uncharacteristic winter raids of 840 and 841, how he'd amassed a small fortune on those endeavors. Then his voice grew distant as he recounted that final, fateful raid near the mouth of the Garonne, and the carnage that was his rebirth. She cringed as Cole told her of the monster they encountered on those far away shores.

"I'd been one of the first off the longship. The woods where we landed...where we were to meet the others...were empty, oddly silent. The...beast...greeted us with taunts as we walked into a small clearing in the forest, jeering at us as though we were...cattle. My boyhood friend, Errik and I approached it with arrogant confidence. We were the first to fall. I think Errik died instantly. My wounds were...severe. I fell as the others charged it...but I wasn't dead, not yet.

"The beast cut down every last one of these fearsome warriors I'd grown up with, raided with...loved as my own brothers...without remorse or hesitation. I lay on the cold ground, waiting for death to claim me. Praying for the halls of Valhalla before the monster returned to finish his work. I caught flashes of motion, glimpses of this beast...savaging those I knew and fought alongside." He shuddered in her arms, turning his face away and closing his eyes for a moment. Alex waited in silence as he mourned his fallen comrades one more time.

When he spoke again, his voice was harsh, roiling with turmoil. "The monster possessed phenomenal speed and unrivaled reflexes, was far more lethal than a berserker full gone with bloodlust. Its eyes glowed through the darkness with an unholy light as it gorged itself on their bodies where they'd fallen." His voice dipped, torn with emotion, as he whispered, "All around me, my brothers lay in mangled shreds, torn to bloody ribbons.

"I was horrified when I first realized it wasn't just...defiling their corpses, ripping them to pieces. The beast lifted their still steaming corpses and drank their blood right before my eyes. I would not lie there, waiting for it to get around to finishing me off. I don't know where the strength came from, but I managed to push myself to my feet. I knew not what the beast was, only that I stood alone against it." He paused, his fingers gliding through the length of her hair.

"As soon as I began to move, it crawled forward, dragging a limp body in its massive fist. It sat back down, putting the corpse—the body was too mangled to identify—to its lips while it watched me struggle to my feet." The hand not slipping through her hair covered her hand where it rested on his chest, giving it a gentle squeeze before pressing it tight to the steady bump of his pulse. "It seemed...curious. Maybe surprised, I couldn't tell. I lifted my sword—hadn't bothered with the shield as I knew it would be useless—and I screamed a war cry."

He chuckled then, startling her. "In retrospection, my fearsome war cry probably sounded a little...feeble at that point." His hand fell away from her hair to trail over the contours of her back. "Anyway, the beast finally stood, dropping the corpse on the ground at his feet, like an empty wineskin. It laughed. The sound of that evil laughter struck fear into my heart as nothing else I'd seen that night had. It came at me then, taunting me for my frail Human body...even as it commended me for my courage. In the shape I was in, the face-off should have lasted mere seconds. But it toyed with me...only the gods know how long."

He shifted in her arms, his troubled eyes met hers as shadows fell across the room. "Are you sure you want to hear this, sweetheart. It's not pretty."

His gaze remained steady on her. His memory of that beast, an ancient evil that chuckled and praised Cole for his courage even as he cut him down...an evil who'd been so impressed with Cole's valor, that he'd autocratically bestowed upon Cole a primordial curse of bloodthirsty immortality...wasn't something he'd ever shared with anyone else, she could see that. That he would share it with her touched something deep inside.

"I want to know what happened to you, Cole. All of it."

He searched her face for a long moment, his fangs gone now, but his eyes still glowed. At last, he went on. "I fell to my knees, too weak to stand any longer, cursing the monster with my dying breath. Searing pain stabbed my neck, and, at first, I assumed it had taken a sword to me at last. But I'd forgotten...the monster carried no sword. The only weapon it possessed was its fangs."

"Oh, Cole," she breathed, forgetting herself.

Patting her back, he pressed his lips to her forehead. Consoling her. He was silent for a long moment, and then he murmured, "Things sort of went...dark after that for a while. I recall feeling a warm trickle against my lips at one point somewhere in there. When next I woke, alone amidst the cold remains of my fallen comrades, I knew nothing but for the burning thirst."

She was positive he'd edited—liberally—that last bit for her benefit. But she got the picture, and it was horrific. The beast had brought Cole to the brink of death, only to pull him back with sip of tainted blood. He told her of crawling from the carnage, a monster in his own right, with hungers he could little comprehend, and of wishing to the gods that he'd died along with his fellow warriors. His newfound thirst had both disgusted him and left him with inexplicable powers. His strange existence on the shores of a foreign country and his struggle to survive had helped to shape the Vampyre he was today.

Where the telling of his transformation had been done in tones of detachment and varying shades of anger, his triumphant, yet ill-fated return to that small village of his birth and the woman he'd loved tore at her heart for the sadness lacing his voice. She cried for him as he told her of his intended's reaction to what he'd become. She'd been so terrified of him—of what he'd become—that she'd taken her own life, leaping into an ice-clogged fjord rather than letting him near her.

Cole's voice was raw when he spoke of plunging into the frigid waters to retrieve the girl's lifeless body, and how the other members of his village had driven him from their midst with glowing torches. His own younger brother's vengeful face had led that mob. That last, startling bit of his tale, told her far more than she'd ever thought possible, about the male at her side and the pain he'd suffered. Alex couldn't contain the tears that seeped from her eyes and soaked his chest, tears for the man who'd lost everything because of one cruel stroke of fate, because of something he'd neither asked for, nor wanted.

Yet that stroke of fate had led him to her. At length, Cole explained his abilities to her. He told her of his strengths and his weaknesses, helping her sort through the myths to find the truths of his race. He also explained that within his particular race, something called mated pairs—provided the female was still Human—actually possessed the ability to conceive and bear offspring. Mind-boggling. At her bemused stare, his mouth opened, but snapped closed, as if reconsidering. He fell silent.

His fingers traced idle circles around her knuckles, his body relaxed as Alex lay quietly in his arms. He waited in silence as she processed all she'd learned about him.

"And you've kept the weapons and armor all this time." Her voice held a quiet note of wonder.

"I guess they were reminders of...*me*," he stated in a pensive tone, and then he gave a cryptic shrug. "I had the *Odhroerir* carved on each piece as a reminder to myself to search for wisdom rather than rushing into the moment with blind arrogance."

Silence captivated the room for a long time then.

At length, she asked, "Do you ever wish you could be mortal again?"

"I did at first," Cole replied. "But then, after a

while I guess I adjusted. I came to realize that wishing to be anything other than what I am is pointless." He shifted her against his shoulder and stared down into her eyes, his brooding gaze unfathomable. "There is no miracle cure for what I am, Alex. There is no way to go back. I am what I am. Nothing's going to change that."

Somehow, Alex understood. Then she thought of the tattoo on her back.

As if reading her mind, eyes filling with conviction, Cole declared, "It was fate that brought us here, Alexandra. You bear my mark..."

Alex stiffened in his arms, modern woman that she was, balking at the implication of being someone else's possession. "I'm not a thing, like your sword or your helmet, Cole, and I won't be treated as such."

In a move so swift, it left her head spinning, Cole flipped her over, pinning her beneath him. The features of his face sharpened with his anger. His eyes flashed with offended insult, his tone harsh. "Don't you think I know that? Odin's teeth, female! Sometimes I swear, if alcohol could affect me, you'd drive me to take up the bottle."

He drew a deep breath then, visibly forcing himself to calm down. "I won't lie to you, there's still a large part of me that's very much the possessive, conquering raider. But, sweetheart, I would never view you as anything other than what you are—an intelligent, self-reliant, desirable woman. Gods, you're so much more than that..."

His voice trailed away, his words going a long way toward soothing her temper. Drawing another breath through flared nostrils, Cole stared down at her, as though his next comments would either complete him, or leave him devastated. His voice—already tugging seductively at her heartstrings—turned dark and smoky, sending shivers of want down coursing through her body.

"There's one more thing you need to know, something you need to understand."

Inexplicably nervous, Alex stared up at him, her eyes riveted to his, unable to do anything more than jerk a tiny nod and force a swallow.

"To Vampyre, there's nothing more revered—nothing more cherished—than the one he takes the Vows with, the one he shares his immortality…his very soul with. His Bride." Cole paused, frowning at her with a strange intensity. He traced the back of his fingers across her cheekbone, over her jaw, down the ivory column of her throat, as if unable to stop touching her. His voice dipped again, deeper, seducing her. "It's a very special, very extraordinary bond. Sensual…physical and emotional…all encompassing. It's a commitment a Vampyre can only make once in his Immortal lifetime."

Cole paused, and Alex's brow creased as she began to make the connections.

"A Vampyre can go his entire existence and never find his Bride. But when he does, Alex…" Cole stopped, dragged in a deep, fortifying breath. His burning gaze pierced her. "When he does, he will do *anything*—whatever it takes—to possess and protect, to honor his mate. The bond is unbreakable. They literally share one heartbeat, one soul. What one feels, so feels the other. Not even death can separate them, for the very moment one dies—so dies the other."

Alex's mouth went dry as she followed his speech. But his next words stole her very breath, made her heart thump against her ribs with panic and thrilled fascination.

"I never believed in the depth of the commitment…not until you. I meant what I said when I told you there would never be another for me. I've given you my heart. You were meant to be my Bride, Alex. I know it in my soul." Having said those fateful words aloud, his eyes glimmered with confident knowledge. That knowledge, evidently, gave him the courage to lay his heart at her feet, and again, she marveled at his bravery. "I have given you my heart, and all my love. I need you as I've never needed another. I would give you forever. I would give you my soul, Alex, if you will have me."

Alex stared up at him, astonished at the depth of his emotions, at the depth of his commitment. "But...how does it work, Cole? I mean, you're going to live forever. I'm just Human, a Mortal."

Cole gaped at her, as if hardly daring to believe. Hope soared in his eyes. "I know what I'm asking of you, Alex. Believe me. I swear to you, I would make you happy. I would love you as you've never been loved before."

"You'd..." Alex forced a swallow. "You'd have to change me...wouldn't you?"

Cole's smile sobered, but he shook his head quickly. "No. No, it's not like that for mated pairs...between a Vampyre and a Mortal. It *can* be done...it just hasn't been done that often."

"I don't understand..."

"I would give you my blood, as I would take yours." The very thought made him hard. "But I wouldn't drain you. You wouldn't die, so therefore you couldn't turn. Changing a mortal can sometimes be tricky...the change doesn't always...take. I don't think I could risk you like that... No, I couldn't do it. But the exchange of blood, the exchange of the Vows... There would be no changing your mind, Alex. By taking the Vows, you'd belong to me—truly belong to me. And I to you. *Forever*, Alex. You wouldn't have to become a Vampyre. But as my mate, you wouldn't be a normal Human anymore, either."

"What do you mean?" She frowned, biting her lower lip.

"You wouldn't gain any of the Vampyric traits—the thirst for blood, the extraordinary strength, the limitations with sunlight, or the preternatural senses. In essence, you would continue to be Human. Nevertheless, you'd live as long as I do. You'd never age. You'd never die. And you would always...*feel* me...as I would you. Wherever you go, I would be compelled to follow. I wouldn't be able to stay away."

Wide-eyed, Alex nodded understanding and swallowed.

Cole's heart sped beneath her palm, his pulse quickened at the base of his throat. His probing gaze held both warning and plea. "If we were mated...I would no longer be able to drink from another Human host."

He paused, and her brows drew together. She searched his glowing eyes. "Then how..."

"You would be my mate, Alex, my eternal Bride. I would only be able to draw my nourishment from you, love. Only your blood would sustain me." His eyes closed for a moment, his teeth clenched tight, the muscle on his jaw leaping to life. When his eyes opened, his gaze begged understanding...and acceptance. "There's more. You would have to drink from me on occasion, just a sip, to maintain your vitality, to keep you alive. For a Mortal, Vampyre blood—specifically the blood of their mate—is like the proverbial fountain of youth."

"But I would still be Human in every other way?" She stared at him, struggling to keep up. "Wouldn't that make you more vulnerable? I mean, you would die when I do, right? Even with your blood, I'd still be...susceptible to things like accidents and sickness, won't I? It would be much easier for me to die than an Immortal, wouldn't it?"

He nodded, letting her understand the full depth of his commitment. "You're right, Alex. At least about the accidents. My blood would prevent you from getting sick. In fact minor injuries would heal with extraordinary speed...unless the wounds were fatal. That's why most Vampyre rarely consider taking the Vows with a Human. Most simply choose to turn their mate, foregoing the Vows, then simply stay together, drawing sustenance from others. But for you, Alex... I would do it for you. As long as I have you, the rest doesn't matter. I want forever with you."

Her emotion swelled at his fervent vow. "Is it...difficult, being a Vampyre?"

He seemed to weigh his words for a moment. "At times, it can be. You have to watch the Humans you've come to care for die. The world changes around you, and sometimes you feel a little lost. But then there are new friends, and new lives to live, and that can be exhilarating too."

The side of her nose scrunched up in hesitant distaste. "What about the whole blood drinking thing?"

Cole dropped a kiss on the tip of her nose. "You get used to it, sweetheart."

"I don't know, Cole," she hedged. "I just don't know if I could... My God, this entire conversation is just surreal." She shook her head, but then pushed on. "I can't imagine myself drawing your blood, drinking it..."

"It gets easier with time." He leered down at her then, his grin beyond lecherous. "You can practice all you want to."

Batting at his shoulder, her lips twisted as she fought a smile. Then, as a new thought dawned, her smile dimmed. "Doesn't it hurt, being bitten?"

"It's like a sharp sting at first, like when you pricked your finger on my fang," his smile grew and his eyes flashed, "but the sting only lasts for a second. Then it's... It can be the most erotic thing you've ever experienced. I'm told a Vampyre's *Kiss* is very sensual."

Considering some of the things he'd already done to her, that was saying something.

"How often would you need to...you know..."

"Vampyre only need feed a few times a week, just a small amount...unless he's been severely injured, then he'd need to feed more often to recover."

He shifted his weight. His rigid arousal pulsed against her. The hard press of it at the juncture of her thighs both eased and escalated her anxiety. Distracting as his desire was, she refused to be sidetracked until she had all the information she needed. His next statement, however, shook her resolve to stay on track.

His burning eyes dropped to her lips, his hips rocked against her as his body sought to ease the ache in his loins. "To gain the full benefits of the blood bond, we'd have to be making love during the blood exchange."

Alex's breath caught in her throat as the full impact of his words sank into her, at the way his hungry gaze devoured her mouth. She forced another swallow, unable to disguise the quake of need in her voice.

"And this ritual..." Alex cleared her throat and chewed on her lip again, inviting Cole to enlighten her.

"It's *very* intimate." His stare gave her a hint of exactly how much. "While we make love..." He smiled down at her, his eyes darkening with undisguised interest as he shifted again, rubbing provocatively between her thighs. "While we make love, we have to drink from each other and then exchange the Vows aloud."

Overwhelmed, Alex considered all he'd told her. It all just seemed too fantastic, to bizarre. And yet, she believed him, unequivocally.

"And we'd be together..."

"For always," Cole swore. His reverent gaze spoke volumes about exactly how much he wanted exactly that.

Alex studied Cole's face, wanting to throw caution to the wind and leap into forever with him. But some sliver of her prudent personality held her silent. As her silence stretched on, Cole fidgeted with her hair, his frown anxious.

Finally, he demanded, "Say something, Alex, please."

"Cole, I... I just need time to process all this. It's so much to take in. I need time to think," Alex replied, pleading with him to understand.

Her heart twisted at the pained disappointment in his eyes, and she barely managed to bite back the need to say anything to make that look go away. Instead, she sought to reassure him the only way she could without giving in to a choice when she hadn't fully considered the ramifications. "I'm not saying no, Cole. I'm just saying that I need time. Please understand."

He forced a smile, but worry creased his brow. She lifted her hand to cradle his cheek, touched.

"I love you, Cole," Alex declared, urgent conviction rang in her tone. "I. Love. You. I can't give you the answer that you need...not right now. Not yet. But I can tell you that I need you. I can tell you that I want to be with you, right now."

Her words were meant to give him something to hold on to, something he'd apparently not had for many, many long centuries. Real happiness. Real hope. Real love. His lips swooped down to cover hers, and in a matter of a few, trembling heartbeats, he swept her into a realm of sensual abandon. The world, their differences, and the choice Alex was going to have to make held no sway here. Each caress was tender, each kiss intoxicating. In moments, their clothing disappeared, and skin met skin with greedy abandon. Hands explored, lips savored, bodies strained. Every time they came together, the connection between them grew stronger, harder and harder to deny.

This time, when Cole made love to her, she refused to allow him to turn away, to hide his face—or the change in him—from her. She stared, wide-eyed with fascination, at his face, fully changed and burning with desire for her...at his fangs as they lengthened, stark white and lethally sharp, in his mouth. Once again, she traced them with the tip of her finger, shivering with excitement in response to his shuddered groan.

Cole quivered atop her, his lips skimmed her neck over and over. But when her fingers strayed toward his fangs again, he snared her wrists and pinned them over her head. "Don't," he rasped. "If you prick your finger again...right now I don't know if I could...I don't think I could stop myself from taking your vein."

Alex blinked up at him through desire-misted eyes, filled with wonder. His words shot an amplified surge of desire through her. Without fangs, Cole was the stuff of erotic dreams. *With* fangs... God, *with* fangs he was beyond description...a dangerous, golden Adonis. Irresistible. Mouth-watering.

Divine.

"I'll be good," she agreed.

He released her hands. His muscles flexed and bunched as her palms skated over him. His body moved with predatory grace and strength, as he took her again and again, kissing her, stroking her, worshipping every inch of her. She moaned his name, crying out as he drove into her with unrestrained abandon, reckless and wild, higher and harder, seemingly unable to stop himself.

As he finally gave into his own body's demands,

and spilled himself deep inside her, he threw his
head back and gave a howl of satisfaction that would
have made his Werewolf friends envious. She
laughed at that. But her laugh turned tender, for all
he'd denied himself...for her.

Somehow, as much as he obviously wanted it,
he'd still managed to deny himself her blood.

Hours later, Alex's cell phone rang, echoing
throughout the bedroom with Vader-esque
resonance. Aggrieved, she squinched one eye open.
Cole's room was shrouded in darkness, but she
remembered—all too well—where she was and how
she'd come to be there. The feel of Cole's strong, hard
body pressed against her, wrapped around hers,
brought a delicious smile to her lips, even as the
phone wailed for attention once again.

Cole's dark rumble of displeasure competed with
the insistent, doomsday ring tone. His arms
tightened around her, preventing her from leaving
the bed. He nuzzled his lips against the side of her
neck and murmured thickly, "Ignore it."

Alex stretched and yawned, glancing at the clock
on the bedside table. She gave a small groan of
resignation. "I have to answer it."

"No...you don't, Alex," he grumbled. His hands
began an erotic quest over her body. His fingertips
trailed over the slight arch of her neck and lower,
gliding through the valley between her breasts,
down over the satin skin of her stomach, his target
explicitly clear.

His next command was oh-so-tempting, the very
definition of sinful pleasures. "What you *have* to do
is stay right here and let me love you again..." He
nipped at her ear. "And again." He nibbled the skin
below her ear. "And again." He licked his way down
the side of her throat. "You see, I just got started."
He turned her in his arms and suckled at the pulse
point at the base of her throat. "And I *don't ever*

intend to finish..."

As if wishful thinking had silenced the annoying device, Alex's phone went silent. Cole eased Alex onto her back and leaned over her with a sleepy, aroused smile. His lips closed over hers, and the phone began its insistent complaint once more.

Pulling back, Cole sulked, "Doesn't that damned thing have an off button?"

She grinned ruefully, exploring the defined ridges on his abdomen with her fingertips. "Yes, but I always forget to turn it off. You better let me answer...she'll keep calling until I do."

"The battery will give out sooner or later," he hinted with a smile.

"Cole..." Exasperated, she shook her head at him. As if on cue, Vader summoned yet again.

****

He frowned, but grudgingly moved off her. Reclining against his pillows, Cole stacked his hands beneath his head and blessed his Vampyre vision, thoroughly enjoying the view as Alex stumbled around his bedroom—wonderfully naked—rooting through their discarded clothing in search of the annoying gadget. She found her cell after a few muttered curses, and flipped it open, pressing it to her ear. Glowing in the dark with his rising passions, Cole's eyes raked over her, coming to rest with proprietary satisfaction on the tattoo at the small of her back.

Before she could utter a sound, a female voice rang out, loud enough for Cole to hear every word of the one-sided conversation sans any preternatural abilities. He bolted up in bed, protective instincts engaging in the space between one heartbeat and the next.

The voice cracked like livid lightning through the phone, "What do you think you're doing, Alexandra Elizabeth Sinclair?"

"Good morning, Mother," Alex replied, her voice flat and calm. But her body was rigid beneath Cole's discerning stare.

"Do not patronize me, young lady. How could you do something so—so utterly thoughtless?"

Evidently used to her mother's censure, Alex drew a slow, unperturbed breath. "What have I done now, Mother?"

"Your picture, yours and that...that *musician's*," an epithet if ever he'd heard one, "are splashed all over every trashy tabloid and social page in the country! Most likely Europe, as well." Her mother paused long enough to suck in a sharp breath, then she snarled into the phone again. "I told you this was a bad idea. Just like I told you it was a mistake the last time, getting involved with that Godforsaken band.

"Honestly, Alexandra! How could you be so careless? How could you be so indiscreet as to allow your sordid little affair to go public? When this blows up in your face, just like it did the last time, you won't be able to sweep this under the rug too easily. At least that darling Griffin tried to smooth the waters after his little slip up. Why you couldn't just let him make it up to you—"

"What pictures are you talking about," Alex interrupted.

"I'm talking about disgusting, careless pictures of you and that singer, kissing on the beach behind your house, and him carrying you around outside of some mausoleum. Every single one of these gossip rags has you dubbed as the latest in a long line of meaningless flings. For God's sake, Alexandra, they even know your name. They've trotted out every little piece of dirt on you that they could find. Everything! Do you hear me? *How* could you embarrass me like this?"

Alex swayed on her feet, but before she could

collapse, Cole was there. His strong arms wrapped around her, his strength holding her up, his lips pressing gently to the side of her forehead offering support.

"Are you listening to me, Alexandra?" Her mother berated her. "I don't know how, but you'd better find a way to make this go away. I don't know how I'll be able to hold my head up at the Yacht Club again. An actor was one thing, but a musician... After last time? It will be a small wonder if they don't ban us from the grounds after this. How could you bring such shame on the Sinclair name, *again*?"

Those last words brought the protective anger inside Cole to a boiling fury. Before Alex could respond, he snatched the phone from her numb hand and snarled into the piece, "Alex is a beautiful, independent, strong woman...no thanks to you...and she deserves your respect, not your abuse. The only shame she must bear is the utter embarrassment of a having a cold, heartless bitch for a mother, one who can't see past the self-indulgent nose on her own face."

Before he could say more, before he could give in to the black rage that poured through him, he turned the phone off and snapped it closed, tossing it into the pile of clothing. He pulled Alex against him, refusing to let her throw up the barriers she had the last time she'd spoken to that bitch of a mother.

At first she struggled against him. But when he refused to release her, Alex leaned into him and let her tears drench his bare chest. As soon as she stopped fighting him, he swept her up and carried her back to the bed, holding her close as she let the years of her mother's selfish, poisonous reproach spill out and drain away.

A long time later, when her sobs had quieted to an occasional snuffle and hiccup, Cole stroked her back and asked, "What can I do?"

Her response was immediate and wooden. "Nothing."

"Alex," Cole insisted, wrung out by her emotional collapse, and furious anew by her mother's callousness. "I can't make it go away, but I can work on damage control—"

"No, Cole," Alex insisted, shaking her head. Pushing up to stare down at him, she shoved the long tangle of her hair back over her shoulder. "I mean it. I don't want you to do anything. We will do nothing! I don't care anymore. I don't care what she thinks, or what the rest of the world thinks. I'm through trying to please her. The only person— besides you and me—whose opinion mattered is dead now. Besides, I have nothing to be ashamed of. I'm with the man I love."

He'd never known such pride as he did at that moment. His smoldering gaze dropped to her lips. He claimed them. Then he claimed her body, praying soon she'd let him claim even more.

Chapter 24

Alex stared at the sparkling surface of the pool, watching ripples move across the unbroken surface while she swished her feet in the cool water. She'd left Cole in his study a few hours ago, swamped in meetings and phone calls. She'd come here to think, attempting to sort the details he'd given her, trying to determine a logical path for her future. Unfortunately, she wasn't having much luck. Lily's call kept coming back to haunt her. She'd never had anyone, aside from her grandfather, who'd been brave enough to stand up to her mother on her behalf before. She almost wished she could have seen Lily's face while Cole told her off.

The man was amazing.

She'd only just turned her phone back on a few minutes ago, dreading what she might find. Thirteen missed calls. Twelve irate voicemails. She certainly had to give Lily points for persistence.

That last message, the calm one, had gotten to her. Lily had been oddly rational, completely in control. She'd informed Alex they needed to speak face to face, and requested they meet at Alex's home late that afternoon. That simple fact alone was cause for concern, as Lily had always made a special point of avoiding her place. In fact, since she'd bought the place three years ago, she could count on one hand the number of times Lily had been there—and still have eight fingers and two thumbs left over.

As Alex sat, warming herself in the late afternoon sunshine, she debated whether she should go or not. She knew Lily intended to do everything in her power to make her feel inadequate and guilty. Then she thought of Cole, of his angry, pointed defense of her before he hung up on Lily—something she'd been longing to do for years but had never had the nerve—and Alex finally understood that Lily only had as much power as she gave her.

Cole. He'd made her believe again, in herself and in love. He'd given her purpose and inspiration. He'd given her his trust. More than that...he'd given her his love. She wanted to be with him, more than anything in the world, regardless of what he was. No, she corrected, *because* of what he was. He made her feel safe, loved and needed. He made her feel strong.

Squaring her shoulders, Alex rose from the pool and snagged a towel off the chaise. She wrapped it around herself as she strode across the patio toward the French doors. Once inside the house, she went directly to her room to change.

She would meet Lily, on her own terms, on her own turf, so to speak. She would face her and tell her exactly what she thought of Lily's selfish, autocratic attitude. Then she'd tell Lily if she wanted to continue to remain a part of Alex's life, she'd have to accept Alex as she was, as well as her choices, namely Cole.

In all probability, Lily would rant and rail, threaten and guilt trip; and in the end, Alex would be forced to finally say good-bye. Lily was Lily after all, and she would never change. The bottom line was Alex couldn't continue as she had been. Submissive and insecure. Lily's emotional punching bag. Though she sincerely doubted she'd be able to come to any sort of truce with her mother, she owed it to herself to try at least for some kind of closure.

While she was there, she would make it a multi-purpose trip, and pack a few more of her things, she thought with a small, giddy smile. As Alex eased her

Shelby from the garage and motored down the long drive, her mind drifted back through the years. Always there had been her grandpa. School plays and dance recitals, sporting events and graduations. Lily had always been the dark cloud in the distance, never present, yet always on her mind, always hovering, always waiting to rain on the parade.

Well, no more, Alex determined. She was through being subservient, finished with accepting Lily's censure with docile obedience. It was over.

Smiling, a huge weight lifted from her shoulders, Alex flipped her cell open and thumbed the speed dial number for Cole's phone. It went directly to voicemail. As busy as his agenda was today, she hadn't expected anything else.

"Cole, I know you're really busy, and so I didn't want to bother you. I just wanted to let you know I need to take care of a few things in town. I'm on the way to my place to pick up a few things and to meet my mother. I have a few things to discuss with her that are long overdue."

She slowed for a traffic light, and then turned onto a scenic strip of highway. "I'll be back by sundown—ha, ha, bad joke, I know—and I was hoping maybe we could go for another midnight swim?" Alex paused for the barest space of a moment. A small smile lifted the edges of her mouth in anticipation of seeing his face tonight when she told him of her decision. "I love you, and I'll see you soon."

Alex snapped her phone closed and tossed it on the seat beside her with a giggle of anticipation, her mood buoyant. She cranked the radio up and hummed appreciatively as seductive, dark bass rocked through the speakers, vibrating the car. She settled back against her seat with a purring sigh. Her favorite band... She sang along, not feeling the slightest twinge of guilt about favoring this group over Stolen Innocence.

She shifted gears and tapped her thumbs against the steering wheel in time to the thundering beat. You just had to love these guys. What they could do with confident, suggestive words and certain, well-plucked notes...

Velvet Revolver's enticing, all-too-prophetic "Come On, Come In" poured from the speakers. Another deep riff punched straight to the gut, and she conceded the point that, in all fairness, maybe she just had a certain weakness for impossibly tall, gorgeously ripped blonds stroking a guitar with long, nimble fingers.

Alex chewed her lip on that thought and, just like that, her mind circled back to Cole. Her smile grew wide, filled with anticipation. She opened the throttle, letting the music and the wind carry her troubles away.

A short while later, Alex pulled up in front of her house and frowned at the Hummer blocking the driveway. She never knew what kind of vehicle Lily drove from one week to the next, but this certainly didn't seem Lily's style. Alex gave a slight shrug. The only thing predictable about Lily was her disapproval for her only child.

Alex slid the key from the ignition and stepped out of her car. As she walked up her sidewalk, she mentally girded herself for the battle to come. Reaching for the doorknob, she found it unlocked. Alex frowned slightly. Normally it wouldn't have bothered her. The point that irritated was the fact Lily had possessed a key for three years, and had never used it. Not until now.

She pushed the door open, only narrowly restraining herself from slamming it closed behind her in a fit of temper. She stepped into the living room and glanced around. Puzzled, she called out, "Mother?"

When no one replied, and a quick search of the house proved unproductive, Alex made her way to the back deck. Sliding the patio doors open, she stepped out into the slowly dying sunshine and let her eyes drift first to the unbelievable, serene view of the ocean before turning her gaze to the loungers at the end of the deck. A man reclined there, indolent and impossibly sexy, and she couldn't find her voice.

****

Cole sat down behind his desk and rubbed a tired hand over the back of his neck. He'd spent the better part of the day in meetings and phone conferences, ironing out all the fine details of Stolen Innocence's upcoming, six-country tour. It had been no small feat, but he'd managed to work his way through the list he and Tommy had been ironing out, in spite of the fact that every time he'd had an unguarded moment, he'd found Alex sneaking into his thoughts.

He was just reaching for his cell when Styx gave his door a perfunctory knock before strolling carelessly inside. "Hey, man... D'you get it all squared away?"

Cole grinned as he thumbed through his missed calls and voice mails. "Yeah, we're gonna push Japan back to the end of the month and move Sydney up to the first. We'll have a two week layover in Barcelona, just for you, *amigo.*"

Styx wandered aimlessly across the den. "Where are we off to tonight?"

"Deacon reported in on the photo labs. Dead end there. Crispin sent over a list of locations the Crasher may strike at tonight. It's a short list. He's running out of places with the number eleven in them, unless the Crasher starts reusing clubs."

"Sure wish I could figure out why eleven is so significant."

Cole leaned back in his chair, propping his boots up on the edge of his desk. "You and me both, man."

"You don't suppose he'll try for..."

"Don't even go there."

"Seriously, Cole, you saw the pictures as well as I did." Styx shot Cole an uneasy glance. "I got a bad feeling, man."

Cole tipped his head back, avoiding Styx's eyes. He'd been having the same bad feeling. "It's not the eleventh yet. Alex will be tucked securely behind lock and key tonight. I'll make sure of it. I've ordered extra security...they'll be here before we leave. She'll be safe here on the estate. We have a job to do. We'll find the killer tonight." And end any further threat to his female, he silently added. But the certainty about catching the killer didn't shake his unease about Alex. Maybe he should stay home, keep an eye on her himself.

Styx shot him a sly smile as he flopped onto the sofa, idly toying with the remote. "So... Will Slim be joining us on the road?"

"You better be careful, Styx. For being such a connoisseur of females, you're beginning to sound an awful lot like a nosy matchmaker." Although he joked with Styx, a worried groove remained firmly entrenched between his brows.

Styx gave a careless shrug, his smile indulgent. "I may be Vampyre, *amigo*, but I am still a Spaniard. I was born with romance flowing through my veins. How do you think it is that I am never without a *willing* female?"

Rolling his eyes, Cole gave a snort of patent disbelief. Then he reached the message she'd left on his voice mail earlier. It cut him off at the knees with a vicious slash of panic. He shot to his feet, his face drained of all color. Without warning, he ran to the door with a frightening string of curses pouring from his lips.

Styx was instantly on his feet, matching Cole step for wickedly fast step. "Cole?"

"It's Alex." Cole shot over his shoulder as he raced down the hall, madly dialing Alex's number, swearing and hitting the redial button, over and over. "Shit. Her phone's off. She's on her way into town, alone. She doesn't know..."

"*Madre de Dios*, Cole, you said you'd..."

"I told her about us. You didn't leave me any other option when you let her see you *feeding*, for Odin's sake."

"That was an accident," Styx snapped, guilty and letting it show. "I thought you—"

"Styx, she doesn't know about the Rogue yet."

Cole cut Styx's incredulous curses short with a fierce snarl. "Not now, Styx. There just wasn't a good time. Things just kept coming up..."

"Yeah," Styx growled. "I just bet I know exactly *what* kept coming up..."

"Fuck you, man," Cole hissed. "Just save it. She left a little while ago. Maybe we can catch her before she gets too far away."

The two men raced to the garage and slid inside Cole's Corvette. In a matter of minutes, they were tearing down the road fast enough to set even an Immortal's teeth on edge, cursing the warmth of the late afternoon UV rays through the heavily tinted windows.

****

Alex couldn't believe her eyes. Totally relaxed, as though he had not a care in the world, Griffin Myles basked in the last of the day's warm rays like a sun god renewing himself. His dark head had turned slowly in Alex's direction when she stepped out onto the deck. Idly sliding his designer sunglasses down to the end of his perfect nose, he stared up at her with moody, smoky gray eyes.

"Darling," Griffin drawled smoothly, positively

oozing sex appeal. Charm dripped from his very perfect, very British accent. "I'd begun to wonder if you were ever going to come home. I've grown ever so lonely without you, dove."

Alex was completely unaffected. Next to Cole, this sexy soap heartthrob was a pale, unappealing substitute. His poor choice of words—his very attitude—made Alex's eyes narrow and her claws curl. "What are you doing here, Griffin? How did you get in?"

"Come kiss me, Lexi," he commanded, pushing himself up straighter in his seat, holding his arms out to her indulgently. "Haven't you missed me at all?"

Unmoved, she coolly arched a disdainful eyebrow. "How did you get in?"

"Does it really matter, darling? I'm here now," he crooned, sending her the same smile she'd seen him successfully use to reduce many a lesser woman to complete, incoherent submissiveness. "Let's just put all this nonsense behind us, shall we? We've so many more interesting things to—discuss."

Alex glared at him, crossing her arms over her chest. Her stare was frosty, her voice cold enough to form icebergs. "I don't think so, Griffin. I'm going to ask one more time, and then I'm going to call the police... How did you get in?"

Griffin flicked a speck of imaginary lint from his slacks and pushed arrogantly to his feet, a displeased frown marred his perfect brow. "Come now, Alexandra, there's no need for things to be ugly between us. Your mother was kind enough to offer a key. She suggested perhaps I should come and see you. That, in light of current events, you might be a tad more reasonable about our future."

"We have no future, Griffin. I assumed you would have figured that out when I returned everything—including the engagement ring." Alex fiercely held her ground when Griffin took a deliberate step closer, refusing to let him or anyone else bully her ever again.

Griffin stopped in his tracks and took a hesitant, half step backwards.

"Lexi, sweetheart," Griffin cooed, stepping forward once more at risk of life and limb. "I made a mistake, a terrible mistake. We can easily get past this. We can look to the future and forget about all this unfortunate little slip-up. I'll even tell you I'm sorry if that's what you need to hear."

"You're sorry for what, Griffin?" Alex pinned him to the spot with furious eyes. "You're sorry for cheating on me—or you're sorry because you got caught? Don't worry about it, Griffin. I'm already over it. I'm over you. Or haven't you heard? I'd assumed mother already told you all about my shameful indiscretion. Then again..." Alex lifted a speculative eyebrow. "Did she pay you off? Is that why you're here?"

A spark of annoyance flickered through his eyes, but Griffin quickly blinked, masking his irritation. Oh, yes, she'd hit the mark there. "Be reasonable, Alexandra—"

"No." Alex held her hand up in warning, shaking her head. "Enough, Griffin, I want you to leave now. There is nothing more to say, we're finished. Hope you got your money out of Lily upfront. She won't give you a red cent if you don't come back with the prize."

"Why?" Griffin sneered, unable to hide the ugly side of his nature. He covered the space between them in two angry strides and glared down at her. "Because of that two-bit singer? What rot! Good God, Alex, didn't you learn your bloody lesson the last time you were involved with a band and ended up running away with your tail tucked between your legs?"

Alex's hand snaked out. The sharp crack of her palm connecting with Griffin's cheek shattered the air between them. She stared coldly up at him, unapologetic and furious. "I was a fool to ever believe I could love you. Cole is not some two-bit singer—he's a brilliant musician. He's everything you're not. He's honest and compassionate, and *faithful*. He'd never lie to me. He's twice the man you'll ever be."

The words had no more than left her mouth, when her patio erupted in chaos so quickly she could scarcely track it all. Infuriated by her slur, Griffin yanked her into his arms, his hands gripping her cruelly, fingers digging into her flesh. He sealed his lips over hers in a punishing kiss that drew blood, pinning her body between his and the unforgiving deck railing at her back.

A spare few seconds later—before Alex even had time to react to Griffin's vicious attack—Cole flew from the house, the fury of hell unleashed. Griffin went sailing through the air to crash in a limp heap against the side of the house with a whimper of surprise. Cole descended on him with lethal intent.

Only Styx's timely intervention prevented Cole from literally tearing Griffin's jugular out with his fangs. Even so, it took every ounce of Styx's own preternatural strength to hold Cole back and prevent him from doing any more harm to Griffin, to prevent Cole from ripping the man limb from bloody limb.

Alex sagged against the rail, the back of her shaking hand pressed to her bruised, bloodied lip. Griffin's unwanted kiss hadn't bothered her nearly as much as the sight of Cole's fury. He was fully transformed, a snapping, snarling, dark angel of the night filled with jealous fury.

Cole roared with untamed, animalistic vengeance. He strained against Styx, reaching for the fallen man, growling his desire to feel the hot rush of the bastard's blood gush down his throat, railing aloud his need to feel the man's dying pulse beneath his lips. Styx swore in a thick accent as he grappled with Cole, desperately restraining him. The muffled groan of the fallen man seemed to urge Cole on, as the scent of blood from a wounded animal drives a predator to complete the kill.

Alex couldn't believe her eyes. Cole was actually trying to *kill* Griffin. She cried out, and Cole faltered. At first, the sound was nothing more than a muffled sob. She called out to him again, hesitant at first, but then with more desperation.

"Cole," she sobbed. "Cole, stop! Stop it! You'll kill him, Cole!"

Her voice finally penetrated the fog, and he went deathly still in Styx's arms. As soon as Cole drew back, Griffin staggered to his feet and fled around the side of the house, screeching hysterically. When Styx was satisfied Cole wouldn't go after the distraught man, he released his hold, but, as if sensing Cole's fury had far from abated, he held himself alert to respond once more as Cole turned to face Alex.

Alex stumbled forward, her arms extended, sobbing her relief. But she drew up short, when Cole recoiled from her touch with a disgusted snarl, flashing lethal fangs at her in warning.

Chapter 25

Alex sobbed and lurched back, fear of him darkening her eyes for the first time. "Cole?"

"You're no different than the rest of *them*." Cole's words stopped her dead in her tracks, froze the lies on her treacherous lips.

He was a complete idiot, enraged that another man would dare touch *his* woman—enraged that Alex would come here to meet this bastard behind his back. How could he have allowed himself to be played this way, believing her when she'd claimed to love him. The sight of her in another man's arms—kissing another man—had driven him wild with jealousy, beyond all reason and control. But he was in control now.

Fully intending to inflict as much pain as he could in a fruitless bid to ease the hurt inside of himself, he sneered at her, his glowing eyes filled with loathing and disgust. "I guess it's true what they say. One man's treasure is just another man's whore. So that leaves only one question."

Her face was frozen in a mask of stunned disbelief.

Cole glared at her, too hurt and furious to feel the burn of the sun on his exposed skin. "I wonder, does that make you his whore...or mine?"

Her mouth dropped open, her eyes filled with tears. Then, slowly, right before Cole's icy regard, the light in Alex's eyes dimmed, then extinguished all together. She took one step back—away from him—then another, not stopping until the wooden railing surrounding the deck cut off her retreat. She pressed a fist to her stomach.

Alex whispered brokenly, "Get out."

Cole tensed, battling the urge to go to her, to sooth her pain any way he could. In self-defense, he shot her one last scathing look and turned, fleeing into the lengthening shadows.

****

Alex stumbled to the lounger Griffin had been sunning himself on and collapsed. She stared at the deck—at the approximate space in which Cole had been standing only moments before—her face carefully blank, her hands clenched together in her lap. Tears coursed unheeded down her pale cheeks.

Styx stood a few feet away, but Alex refused to look at him. She hadn't spoken to him since she'd seen him with his host in Cole's study yesterday. He approached her with hesitant steps, dropping down to his knee before her.

"Slim," he murmured, his voice filled with sympathy. She stared off into the distance, stared through him, so he tried again. "Alex."

She blinked and a sob escaped her as she finally looked *at* him. Styx reached out and laid a hand gently over hers. "I'm so sorry, Alex. He didn't see..."

His sympathetic words broke the tentative hold Alex had on her emotions. With a muffled sob, she tipped forward, dropping her forehead onto Styx's shoulder and let the tears flow. Styx froze, then he gathered her into his arms, offering comfort while she fell apart.

As the tears died, Alex became aware Styx was holding himself painfully rigid. She drew back, took one look at his pained frown and rapidly reddening complexion, and gasped. She was on her feet in a heartbeat, taking him by the hand, tugging him inside the house.

Alex cried, "Oh, Styx! Why didn't you say something?"

As soon as they were inside, she pushed him down onto the sofa and hurried to the kitchen. In a few moments, she was back at his side with burn salve.

"I'm so sorry," she began, smoothing the salve over his angry, red skin.

He took her wrists into his hands and forced them down so he could look her fully in the face. "It's all right, Slim," Styx insisted. "I'll be fine in a little while. Alex, he didn't mean any of that. He didn't see what happened before, he just saw you kissing that guy and assumed..."

"He assumed what, Styx?" She sat back against the cushions, defeated, dragging in a shaky breath. "No, don't say it—I know exactly what he assumed. And if he cared about me like he said he did then he would have given me the benefit of the doubt. He wouldn't have..."

Her voice broke on a sob as Cole's harsh words came back to haunt her. Dropping her chin to her chest, she pushed through the pain, trying to find that steely Sinclair courage that had gotten her through an embarrassing, broken engagement and a near rape at the hands of men she'd thought she'd known and trusted. She couldn't find it. Her courage, her nerve had vanished leaving only pain and fear in its wake. How would life ever be normal for her again?

When she raised her eyes to Styx's face, whatever she'd been about to say died in her throat. Right there, before her startled eyes, his skin—his burns—were healing. Astonished, she lifted a hand and grazed his flawless cheek, shaking her head in wonder.

Styx sat still beneath her exploration. His eyes searched her face, and he sighed.

"Alex, you have to trust me on this," Styx insisted. "He didn't mean any of it. You have to give him a chance..."

Shaking her head, Alex pushed to her feet. "No, Styx. I'm the one who made the mistake. I should never have allowed myself to trust—not again." Alex paced a few steps away, then turned back to him, her face devoid of all emotion, her voice flat. "I'm sorry, but I can't go back there. I'll send for my things later, and I'll fax the rest of the music as soon as it's finished. Please, let Cole know I'll have my attorney contact Mr. St. James about terminating the contract." Just saying his name sliced her heart to ribbons.

"Alex," Styx began, but she cut him off.

"My mind is made up. Please, don't try to change it." She smiled then, an odd, hollow smile, adding, "Thank you, Styx. And, please, don't worry. Your secret is safe."

Styx stared at her for several long minutes, then nodded and got to his feet. He glanced out the window at the sun as it dipped below the horizon. Nodding again, he let himself out of the house, closing the door quietly behind him.

****

The wait for a ride hadn't taken as long as Styx feared it would. Fortunately, Deacon had already been in town at a party and, as luck would have it, not far from Alex's place. The only problem was Deacon liked to drive as fast as Cole did.

All too soon, he stepped inside Cole's darkened study. His nocturnal vision assessed the damage, and he grimaced. The place was a wreck, completely demolished. Cole's glass display case lay on the floor, a twisted mass of wooden splinters and shattered glass, his weapons and armor scattered about the room. Half the priceless books previously residing on the shelves behind Cole's desk were now shredded and tossed carelessly in every direction.

Every piece of furniture in the room was

overturned, smashed, including Cole's massive desk. The plasma TV was now a useless pile of shattered components. But the true shame was the Steinway. It lay in a twisted heap, broken and splintered nearly beyond all recognition but for the mangled ivory keys resting among the shredded sheet music. Alex's sheet music, he'd wager.

"Cole?" Styx stepped cautiously onto the battlefield.

From somewhere in the far corner, Cole snarled, a ferocious, terrifying sound that skated chills straight through Styx. Stepping gingerly through the wreckage, Styx slowly approached his friend. He stopped a few paces away, however, caution and self-preservation warring with his concern.

He'd thought Cole was bad at Alex's house. That was nothing compared to this. He'd never imagined anyone, much less the ever confident, ever cool Cole in this shape, and frankly, he was a little nervous about getting too close. The look in Cole's eyes was deadly, and betrayed. The low growls pouring from deep in Cole's chest made the fine hairs on the back of Styx's neck rise up. Cole's shirt was torn, his hair was wild, and the change was upon him, untempered. He was a feral beast, wounded and backed into a corner.

Styx's nostrils flared at the scent of blood hanging heavy in the air, Human blood. Styx's heart stopped. Had Cole tracked Alex's ex down after all? Had he brought him back here and finished what he'd begun on Alex's deck? As his eyes searched the room, he found the broken shards of the crystal decanter Cole habitually kept his nourishment in, rather than the dead body Styx feared finding instead. He breathed again.

"Go away, Styx," Cole growled darkly, thickly, his voice barely recognizable.

"Not until you get a clue, man." Styx braced his

feet apart, preparing himself for the attack that was sure to come. "You fucked up, Cole."

With a destructive snarl, Cole flew across the distance, slamming into Styx with enough momentum to carry them both across the room, knocking plaster from the wall. Styx locked his arms around Cole and took the punishing blow, working to maintain control over the changes that were taking place inside his own body.

"You don't know what you saw out there, Cole," Styx insisted, dodging a blow that could have been fatal, even to an Immortal, had it connected. His fist shot out in an instinctual jab to Cole's side, and he hissed, "She wasn't cheating on—"

Styx's voice disappeared in grunt of pain as Cole slammed a fist into his midsection.

"You don't know what the fuck you're talking about." Cole howled, throwing another punch that went uncharacteristically wild, missing his mark by a good half a foot. "I saw her... I saw her with my own cursed eyes. I saw them kissing..."

Styx clipped Cole's jaw with a tight uppercut, making him snap his teeth together on the rest of his words.

"You didn't see jack shit, Cole." Styx ducked a wild swing, plowing his own fist into Cole's ribs. "I was there, man, in the shadows. I found them out on the deck while you were still searching the house. I saw the whole damned thing. I *heard* what you didn't hear." Styx feinted to the side, dodging Cole's blows like a champion prizefighter. "She wasn't expecting him to be there. Her mother set her up, man. Alex wasn't expecting that guy to be there...Dios, man, she was trying to kick him out. She's probably got bruises all over her arms from where that bastard grabbed her. He *forced* himself on her, man."

Cole staggered back, weaving on his feet as he

stared at his friend through gleaming, bloodshot, blood-thirsty eyes. Styx's fangs flashed. He wasn't done. He advanced on Cole, fisting his hands in the shredded T-shirt covering Cole's bleeding chest. Right up in Cole's face, he let the words lash at him until Cole finally backed down.

"She didn't know he was there at first. She didn't know how he'd gotten inside." Styx gave him a vicious shove. "She told him to leave, that they had no future together. She threatened to call the cops on him, dumbass. When he called you some two-bit singer, she defended you—told him you were twice the man he'd ever be." Styx's temper got the better of him, and he shoved Cole away. "*She told him you'd never lie to her, you stupid son of a bitch.*"

Cole swiped the back of his hand over his bleeding mouth. "I saw—"

Styx interrupted, shooting him an accusatory, disgusted look, "What you saw was that bastard ex-fiancé of hers trying to force himself on her."

"Ex..." Cole's voice trailed away in confusion. "She never told me she'd been engaged..."

Styx glanced to what remained of Cole's desk and the smashed pieces of plastic and electronic components...all that remained of Cole's laptop.

"Stay here. I'll be right back," he ordered.

In a flash he was back, his own laptop tucked beneath his arm. He flipped over the coffee table and pushed Cole, confused and bleeding, down to sit on the battered surface. Without ceremony, Styx thrust the laptop onto the gouged and battered surface beside Cole and began rapidly typing. After a few moments, he cranked the volume up and then spun the computer around so that Cole would have an unhindered view.

Then he stood back to wait.

Pictures flashed before Cole's eyes, pictures of Alex stepping out of a jewelry store on the arm of the man he'd thrown across her deck and nearly beaten to a pulp. There was a brief, snide comment by some glamour-glossed news broadcaster, then a sordid video clip of that same man pawing at some redhead. It took a moment for it all to sink in—Styx's words, and the video clip—but once it did, it was a good thing Cole was already sitting down or he probably would have fallen flat on his ass. He looked as if he'd been gutted.

His expression dumbfounded, Cole stared at the images on the screen as they looped, then led into a shot of Alex entering her office building as she struggled to dodge pushy reporters, shaking her head as she did her best to hide her face.

Styx slapped the laptop closed and glared at him. "She wasn't kissing him, man. The bastard attacked her."

Cole leaned over and raked shaking hands through his hair. He lifted anguished eyes to Styx, his voice echoed in the demolished room. "Odin's teeth, what have I done?"

From somewhere beneath the rubble, Cole's phone began ringing. Following the sound, praying it was Alex, Cole scrabbled through the room until he pulled his phone from the clutter near his desk.

"Fuck! Not now..." He threw the phone against the far wall and scrubbed his hands over his face. The phone rang once more, a slow, mutilated sound, the display flashing the name Crispin for a moment more. Then the phone went dead.

Chapter 26

Alex walked along the beach, her shoes dangling from her fingertips, forgotten. A stiff wind off the ocean swirled her white cotton gypsy skirt around her calves. The matching camisole was no barrier for the oncoming storm, and she shivered as the cool wind rushed against her bare arms, drying the tears on her cheeks as they fell. Her golden hair streamed out behind her, twisting and tangling as the current of air grew in intensity like a mournful ghost haunting the shoreline. She didn't feel much better.

Nothing made sense anymore. Nothing fit, and she'd never been so alone. As the first chilly drops of rain began to pelt her skin, she slowly dragged herself up the lawn toward the dark shadow of her home. For once, the structure held no welcome for her, offered no comfort. Alex crossed the deck and pushed the patio door open, stepping inside.

Unease tingled along her spine. Something wasn't right. She reached for the light, but the switch only clicked hollowly in the room. The darkness remained. Frowning, she moved across the living room, pale flashes of lightning in the distance giving her fleeting glimpses of shadow as she navigated around the furniture.

Goosebumps raced down her arms as she reached for the lamp beside the sofa. She stepped on something slippery and crinkly as she switched the light on and glanced down with a curious frown.

Ambient light poured over the sofa and the floor around her, and Alex's eyes grew wide with confusion and alarm. Everywhere she looked—the floor, the walls, covering the furniture—were photos. Alex bent slowly and picked one up, her eyes glued to the glossy surface with slowly mounting horror.

It was an image of Cole carrying her across his drive. Hesitantly, she reached out and snagged a snapshot off the sofa, lifting it to the light. Another picture of her, this time jogging by the stream on Cole's estate. She let it drift to the floor, mystified, as she reached for yet another.

The sharp black and white was of her and Cole kissing on the beach—on her beach—and bright red marker scribbled across their entwined bodies. The room began to spin as she reached for another photograph, and Alex let out a tiny, terrified gasp as the same scribbled words finally penetrated her overwhelmed brain.

Mortals die.

Over and over, the number *14*. Fourteen? Why fourteen? It made no sense.

Alex glanced to the patio doors, standing wide open, the sheer panels billowing in the stiff breeze, stark against the inky darkness outside. Terror clutched tightly inside her chest, and she struggled to draw breath, fiercely resisted the urge to panic.

The phone. Where's the phone?

Her frightened gaze flew around the room, to the hallway and the doors of the bedrooms, to the kitchen. The shadows shifted with every flash of heat lightning, striking fear into her very blood. The car... Her phone was in her car. And her car meant escape. She rushed to the table in the entry and froze. *God, where were the keys?*

The slight, metallic jingle by her ear made Alex jump, then freeze in horror. In that moment true fear raked its razor-sharp claws across her soul. The whisper of icy breath on the back of her neck sent gooseflesh racing over her skin. Her own breath sawed in and out of her lungs in short panicky bursts.

A smooth, deep voice whispered against her ear, "Looking for these, *Human?*"

Alex lunged for the door, a shrill scream ripped from her throat. But strong arms snaked around her, easily subduing her, and a white square of cotton dropped in front of her face. She sucked in a sharp breath and held it as long as she could, fighting madly against the extraordinary strength holding her firm, struggled desperately against inhaling any more of the cloying fumes soaking the cotton.

Darkness began to creep in around the edges of her vision, and still she fought. With one last desperate act, trapped as she was in the brutally tight arms of her attacker, Alex lifted both feet and kicked at the wall in front of her, slamming herself back against her assailant. They crashed into the wall, rebounding off the small table. She twisted and turned, fighting like a wildcat, and for one brief moment, she got a flashing glimpse of a pale, hauntingly attractive face in the ornate, entry mirror. Glowing, golden bedroom eyes and deadly, gleaming fangs leered back at her.

Then the darkness won.

****

Cole reached Alex's front steps at a dead sprint. He tried the doorknob, but it refused to budge. Fisting his hands, he pounded on the door and bellowed loud enough for his voice to echo several blocks away. "Alexandra, open this door! I'm not leaving until we talk."

No reply.

He paused, forcing himself to calm down, forcing himself to focus on the door and any sound on the other side. He couldn't hear anything, but he could smell the lingering scent of her there, just on the other side of the door. He was just about to start pounding again—or rip it from its hinges—when his super-tuned sense of smell picked up another scent.

The trace scent of Vampyre.

Fear ripped through him. Fear and disbelief. In one effortless motion, Cole thrust his shoulder against the door, shattering the lock and splintering wood. He rushed into the house, panic tearing through his chest. His wild-eyed gaze immediately came to rest on the table just inside her entry, toppled now with a splintered leg. Her meticulously sorted mail littered the floor. The silver gleam of keys lying among the clutter caught his eyes.

With a hoarse curse, Cole rushed into the living room. Any further sound died in his throat as he surveyed the pictures littering the floor, papering the walls.

Horror struck him anew, and Cole roared his rage.

He tipped his head back and dragged air into his lungs, air and scent. There was Alex's scent, fresh and innocently seductive, and filled with fear. The crisp bite of the oncoming rain blowing in through the open patio door came to him. Then he caught it, masked as it was by the cloying scent of chloroform...the scent he'd caught on her front step.

Vampyre.

It was too soon, his mind rebelled. It was only the ninth. Cole couldn't comfort himself with that fact. The Vamp might not kill her before the eleventh. But gods, there were other, equally terrifying things he could do to her in two, long days...

Cole's heart raced, pounding against his ribs in a warrior's cadence. He raced through the house, following the scent trail onto the back deck and across the lawn toward the beach, cursing the rain as it began washing the scent from the air. His feet kicked up sand as his legs pumped with superhuman speed along the waterline. He strained to catch the glimmer of scent hanging persistently in the air, focusing on it, forcing himself to greater speed than he'd ever attempted, pushed by the need to find her before he lost the trail completely.

Cole followed the fading beacon to a house overlooking a bluff less than a mile from her home. The lights were off. He could detect no movement on the grounds surrounding the isolated building. He slowed, approaching with caution, blending with the shadows, alert and prepared for a trap.

On feet silent as the wings of night, Cole slipped around the side of the house and edged up onto a patio. Peering through the glass, he reached for the handle. It wasn't locked...as if someone had been waiting for him. He clenched his teeth. The moment the door opened, the scent of blood—freshly spilled blood—hit him like a sucker-punch to the gut.

A *lot* of blood.

Panic and grief swelled, threatening to overwhelm him. But then rational thought...or rather the lack of the distinctive flavor of the blood...pushed through the fear. This blood was heavy and salty. Unlike the honeyed-sweetness he knew to be Alex.

She was here though...as was the Rogue. The Vampyre's scent was stronger here, distinctive. *Familiar.* Fury ripped through him. How could he have been so gullible, so completely stupid?

Cole followed Alex's scent trail to a door at the back of the house. He eased the door open, rage vibrating through his body, fear knotting in his stomach. Forcing himself to move with silent care, he descended the narrow stairs. The smell of damp concrete, and Alex's sluggish fear, swamped his senses. She should be terrified right now. Adrenaline should be coursing, thick and hot, through her veins. There were little more than light traces of adrenaline in the darkness below. What was wrong with her? A thought occurred to him—something so frightening that he pushed it aside, refusing to follow that idea to conclusion lest he lose all control. He waited at the top of the steps, searching the room with his senses, searching for his nemesis.

His keen vision found her then, and he barely stopped himself from flying down the stairs to her side. Alex lay in a heap on the damp floor, chained to the wall like an animal. She moaned softly, each tiny movement seemed to tax her. She lay silent for long moments. Only the feeble flutter of her heart reassured him she was still alive.

His vision went red, and he momentarily lost control of his senses as he turned his focus inward, forcing calm where rage and fury boiled, straining for release. Shadows and blurry shapes swam around her, slowly taking more solid forms, becoming wine bottles and wine racks. She shifted her wrists, and he cringed when the metallic clink of her restraints cracked through the room loud as a crash of thunder.

Cursing the bastard who'd done this to her, Cole struggled for rational thought. He waited for acknowledgement, waited for her captor to investigate the noise she'd made. No one approached her, no one spoke. After several moments, she pushed herself to a sitting position, the motion slow and wobbling. She winced, lifting her bound hands to cradle her temples. With a soft moan, she sagged against the damp wall, her hands falling, limp, into her lap. His gaze followed the aged, iron links to a point on the wall, a point high above her head. Those bonds would snap like thread in his hands, but for her meager Human strength, they would be inescapable.

Alex's breath was the only sound in the room, and it was too shallow, too fast. His heart twisted inside his chest. She sobbed then, a sob of fear, a sob of despair. He struggled to keep a level head. It was the hardest battle of his life.

Gods, why was she so listless?

The obvious answer to that question was the answer he'd pushed away earlier. He couldn't push it away so easily now, and his throat closed, an odd, unfamiliar knot formed in his belly.

The bastard had damned near drained her.

****

The air stirred somewhere nearby, and Alex froze, holding her breath. Her blurry gaze moved over the darkness. Her head swam making it difficult to register what her eyes were seeing. Her fingers dug into the chains that bound her. It was so hard to move now, so hard to think. Whatever hope she'd harbored, whatever thoughts of escape had crept into her mind, deserted her completely as the icy prickle of breath trickled over the side of her neck. The shallow rasp of razor sharp fangs against her skin sent terror clawing through her, clogging her throat.

Cole had been wrong. There was nothing erotic or sensual about a Vampyre bite. She would know. The one she'd sustained earlier had burned through her system like acid, leaving her weak and disoriented.

The voice that had surprised her back in her entry, deep and familiar, hissed close to her ear, making her jerk slightly. "That's far enough, Cole."

Alex's brows drew together, and she blinked into the darkness, groggy and confused. Cole was here? Hope blossomed in her chest. He'd come for her. The lethal press of fangs over her jugular warned her against the urge to shake the cobwebs from her brain. She couldn't move, not even fractionally, without risking impaling herself on those dangerous, painful points.

Though she couldn't see him, Cole's beautiful voice broke the silence. His fury was impossible to mistake. Every bit as lethal as the fangs hovering over her weakened pulse. "Let her go, Deacon."

Alex's mind reeled and she almost flinched...almost. *Deacon?* Yes, the voice...it was Deacon. Then the glowing golden eyes and the frightening fangs in her entryway mirror flashed back through her lethargic mind. Deacon!

But why was he doing this to her?

Pain lanced through her scalp as Deacon fisted a vicious hand in her hair, yanking her head back at an excruciating angle. A whimper clawed its way out of her throat, and Alex gritted her teeth, cutting the show of weakness off before it became an all-out scream of fright.

She could see Cole now, frozen mid-step halfway down the stairs. His hand clutched the wrought iron railing hard enough to bend the metal. Fury roiled in his burning stare, hot as a thousand torches, threatening to snap his slim hold on sanity. He looked like a gilded god of fury. A god of war. Like an agile cat, poised to spring. And not your average, garden-variety house cat, but a highly lethal, feral predator, the kind that slunk through the shadows of some sultry jungle, stalking its prey, poised to devour. He was breathtaking, and despite the press of Deacon's fangs, hope not only returned. It flared bright.

****

Cole's gaze flew from her colorless face to the marred side of her neck. Her eyes, even filled with obvious terror, were glassy and dazed. Her whimper sounded fragile, delayed.

And Cole recognized the signs for what they were.

She was weak from blood loss—severe blood loss—hovering on the edge of death. Fear and unconscionable rage washed through him. He wanted to fly down the last of the steps and *shred* Deacon, to swim in his blood. He wanted to sweep Alex to safety, to protect her with his own life.

She's mine, Cole silently railed. *Mine to cherish. Mine to protect. The bastard would die—slowly and painfully—for daring to touch her, for daring to drink from her.*

Then his mind faltered. *Mine to protect... Yeah...done a real bang up job there, haven't I?*

Deacon dragged her up, rubbing against her in a sickeningly intimate way. His hand twisted tighter in her hair. She flinched but remained silent. Cole snarled, taking a menacing step forward. As Deacon moved, maneuvering the dazed Alex like a rag doll before him, the *Odhroerir* on her back flirted with Cole's vision for just a moment. It was enough to push him back onto somewhat stable ground.

Wisdom.

Stop. Take a breath. Think before you rush in, Cole silently chanted.

Deacon yanked on her hair again, his arm slid around her waist as he bent her back...all the better to give Cole an unhindered view of the fangs pressing against her throat. Deacon's tongue skimmed across the delicate skin over her jugular, and the beast in Cole turned rabid. "Me and Alex here are gonna have a real good time when I'm through with you."

Wisdom and stopping to think fell by the wayside.

Kill the threat, the beast roared.

Protect my female, it snarled.

"Don't come any closer, Cole, or I'll drain her," Deacon hissed, flashing his fangs in warning. "I'll rip out her fucking throat. One more step and she's finished. That won't make me very happy, Cole. It's not time for her to die...not yet anyway."

Chapter 27

Fear almost paralyzed him. Fury drove him on. It took Deacon's fangs scoring her tender skin, and the unmistakable crimson trickle, to sink through the livid haze and stay Cole's movements.

The icy blue of Cole's eyes beamed like lasers through the darkness, eerie and unholy. He was sure he looked more like the monster who'd sired him right now than he ever had in his entire existence. His fangs were enormous in his mouth, throbbing for the kill. His skin stretched taut over sharpened cheekbones. His hands curled at his sides, claws aching to tear Deacon's flesh from his bones. Cole's blood raced, his heart hammered with the need to protect her.

"Your female bleeds, Gunnarrson." Deacon grinned, gloating as the taunt struck home. "She tastes so...*sweet*. No wonder you found her irresistible. Too bad these Humans have such pitifully *short* lives."

Kill.

Protect.

Kill. Protect. KillProtectKillProtect!

MINE!

And yet, Cole didn't move an inch, didn't so much as blink.

His voice was a harsh rasp, cutting through the darkness. "Why are you doing this, Deacon?"

"Because they're sheep!" Deacon exploded. "They're all useless, fucking sheep! They're *food*, Cole. Yet we tap dance around their tender sensibilities. We have the power. We should be masters, instead of timid shadows clinging to the night. You should try playing with your food once in a while, Cole. It's really rather...liberating." Deacon's maniacal bark of laughter ricocheted off the block walls hollowly.

His laughter cut out as quickly and unexpectedly as it had begun. His shrewd gaze snapped to Cole's, flashing golden fire in the darkness. Dead calm. "You shouldn't have gotten involved. I might have eventually...taken you under my wing." He chuckled then, hoarse and twisted, but the chuckle died a swift death, replaced with cold certainty. "We could have been unstoppable. There are so many others out there, others like us. We could have taken those fucking *Enforcers* out. Then there wouldn't have been anything to stand in the way. We could have ruled. We'd have lived like fucking kings. You should have told that prick Crispin to fuck off."

"You know it doesn't work that way, Deacon. Not with them." Cole did his best to keep the venom from his voice as he edged a little closer, down one more step...then another. He could do nothing about the glow of his eyes.

"Yeah, well, they're the fools now. They'll never catch me. I'll move on, start over...find others who believe as I do. They're out there, Cole. You know I'm right. They're out there, and they'll join me in a Human heartbeat. Those fuckheads, the TFRA won't even be looking for The Party Crasher anymore, not after tonight."

Cole eyed him, suddenly wary, the back of his neck starting to itch. Another step disappeared. "Why not?"

"Because they're gonna come here. They're gonna come here when *I* call 'em." Deacon's eyes flashed with smug pleasure. "And you know what they're gonna find?"

Apprehension fisted in Cole's gut.

"Those freakin' bastards are gonna find *her*." Deacon yanked Alex's hair again, straining her neck back until tendons and veins bulged. She whimpered, and Deacon's eyes locked on Cole, smiling at his reaction. "They're gonna find her down here with her throat ripped out. Oh, I'll bleed her dry first. She's mostly there anyway." His hoarse chuckle was short, then he pressed his taunts home. "I've found she's too tasty to waste. I might even sample a few other pleasures her body has to offer while I'm at it. But they're gonna blame you, of course." Deacon's grin was the embodiment of evil. "I'm gonna tell 'em I trailed you here. I'm gonna tell 'em that it was you all along, that I saw you kill her. And you know why those stupid fucks are gonna believe me?"

Cole slowly shook his head, a muscle ticked along his jaw. Another step slipped past.

"Because, when I'm through, even Styx will doubt you. He saw you earlier with her fleabag ex...yeah, I was there too. Didn't know that, did you? He saw the shape you were in when you left. Nice work on the study, by the way...that'll go a long way toward confirming my story. That...and because this is *your* house, Cole," Deacon informed him, giving a crazed chuckle. "Nice digs, by the way."

Cole's eyes narrowed. "This isn't my—"

"Oh, but it is. You have no idea how easy it was to buy this place in your name." Deacon's eyes narrowed, calculating and vicious. "And when they get here, I have a little added bonus upstairs. A little something...extra special."

The scent of blood when he'd first entered the house...

Cole dragged in a very slow, very deliberate breath and remained silent, waiting.

"They're gonna find that little...gift...I left, and

assume you're the one they've been after all along."

Cole's mind swirled. He had to keep Deacon talking, had to give himself time to do something. But what? "Why the number eleven, Deacon?"

Deacon's eyes glinted. His voice ripped through the room with barely leashed fury. "Because that's how long it takes for love to be sucked from a Vampyre's soul."

"What are you talking about?"

"I had a female of my own once. Didn't know that, did you, Cole?" Deacon's eyes flashed in the darkness. His fangs gleamed as his lips pulled back in a vicious snarl. "Eleven years...I had her for a measly fucking eleven years. That's like a goddamned tick of a second hand for a Vamp. I wanted to change her, tried to explain to her the dangers of her staying Human. But she wouldn't let me change her, wouldn't let me give her the gift of eternity." Some of the glow faded from his eyes, but his expression remained fierce, his voice edged with fury. "She wouldn't take my blood either. She swore she loved me, regardless of what I was, but she couldn't bring herself to drink from me.

"She was too weak to face eternity...and I was weak for loving her. Eleven years of my life, I spent denying what I was. Eleven years I wasted trying to be something I wasn't...for her, for a woman who died in my arms on a cold November night from a Human disease. She wasted away to nothing. Even after they diagnosed her with breast cancer, she wouldn't take my blood, Cole. My blood could have saved her, but she still wouldn't take it."

Cole thought perhaps Deacon might lose his focus for a second, just long enough for Cole to strike, but he didn't. Deacon didn't drop his guard for the tiniest moment, despite of the furious pain boiling in his burning gaze. "Hell, I'm doing you a favor, Cole. Lovin' a Human ain't worth the pain."

Alex hung helplessly in Deacon's arms, leaning limply against him. Her heart pulsed a little stronger now in Cole's ears. Adrenaline coursed thicker. Was she hearing this? Did she understand what was going on? She had to be terrified.

His woman was terrified.

Cole's breath sped, his muscles tensed. A snarl hovered in his throat, waiting to rip free. He pushed it down. *Wisdom,* he reminded himself, *logic and reason.* "You loved her Deacon. She was Human, but you loved her. How could you destroy all those women like that? Women like the one you loved? What was her name, Deacon?"

"Aw, man, don't go getting all psych 101 on me. Weren't you fucking listening?" Deacon's snarl slashed through the night. "She left me, Cole. She goddamned left me. She was weak, just like the rest of her kind. They're all weak." The glow of Deacon's eyes brightened, flashing through the darkness like lasers. "You know, on second thought...I can always pick another Human later for the final act. Our little Alex was supposed to be my number fourteen, you know. That was smart, by the way, figuring out my little message. The TFRA all looked like fuckin' monkeys chasing their asses. Ah well, I can always find another little lamb. I have plenty of time. They're so much better fresh. Say goodbye, Cole." Deacon's pupil's elongated. He lifted his head, bared his fangs, and smiled with sadistic cruelty.

So unwise...

With fangs stretched long and deadly, Cole launched himself off the last step, and flew through the air. An ancient warrior, a deadly predator...an enraged Vampyre protecting his Bride. A roar, dark and gruesome, erupted from Cole's chest, echoing in the cavernous darkness around them. He swooped down on Deacon, filled with the kind of fury only an angel of hell can deliver.

Alex jerked, listing to the side now that Deacon's malicious hands no longer held her trapped and his fangs no longer hovered, waiting to tear at her throat. She was free, but too weak to move. Then she was catapulting through the air as Deacon's body slammed against her. The unforgiving block wall met the side of her head and she crumpled to the floor. Unmoving.

Cole desperately wanted to go to her, to scoop her up and run with her. To carry her to safety. The searing burn of Deacon's fangs slashing through his shoulder brought his focus back where it needed to be...centered solely on the spitting, snarling Vampyre before him. But in the back of his mind, Alex's presence hovered like a flame in the night, her heartbeat weak, her breathing too slow now. Cole leaped between her fragile body and danger, becoming her shield and guard. As he grappled with Deacon, as the two of them clawed and punched, lunged and bit. Worry and fear danced through him.

Why wasn't she getting back up? Why wasn't she moving at all?

Rage swelled inside him anew, and he fought like a demon possessed. Wine bottles crashed and shattered, shelving rocked, splintered and cracked. Snarls and hisses rent the air, punctuated by the dull thud of fist connecting with flesh, and the sharp snap of deadly fangs. Vampyre blood splashed the walls and floor.

Deacon's fangs sank into his thigh, and Cole howled at the vicious pain. He fisted his hands in Deacon's hair, yanking, tearing it out by the roots, smashing his fist into the Rogue's nose with a satisfying crunch. Searing pain tore down Cole's side as Deacon's claws slashed at his ribs. Cole twisted away, darting swiftly back, determined to remain between Alex and Deacon. The bastard would never get close to her again.

Kicking out a leg, Deacon swiped Cole's feet out from beneath him. Cole's arm shot out, and he took Deacon down with a resounding grunt of pain. The two scrabbled and wrestled on the floor, both determined to get the advantage. Cole latched onto Deacon's wrist, wrenching his arm up and around behind his back. With his other arm, he grasped Deacon's jaw with hot resolve, twisting his head to the side, exposing his vulnerable neck.

Only one of them would walk from this cellar alive, only one of them would lay hands on his female again. And Cole was dead certain that it would *not* be Deacon. In a swift, violent move, Deacon wrested to the side, shoving away from the floor with superhuman strength, toppling Cole from his back. Cole came back in a flash, and the two rolled over and over across the small room, angling for the advantage.

A wild spray of blood arced across the wall.

In a matter of seconds, the wine cellar fell silent…nearly silent. Harsh, ragged breath echoed through the darkness as a massive form—a fallen titan—crawled slowly, painfully across the floor toward Alex's prone body, leaving carnage and death behind.

With gentle care, Cole turned Alex over and cradled her tenderly in his arms, wiping a forearm across his bloodied face. He closed his eyes and drew a steadying breath, dropping his forehead to hers. The sound of her struggling heartbeat, weak and uneven, echoed in his ears. A single tear slipped from the corner of his eye, trailing down his bruised and battered face, mingling with the blood covering his split lip, dripping from his chin onto her pale cheek.

Cole looked away for a moment and used his shoulder to wipe more of the blood from his face before he turned back to her.

His hand trembled as he cupped her cheek. "Alex, open your eyes. Gods, sweetheart, please open your eyes."

She didn't respond, and fear coiled in his stomach. Suddenly the walls were closing in on him. The scent of blood, Vampyre and Human, hung heavy in the air, revolting him. The shredded, lifeless body on the floor only a few short feet from them was more than Cole could stomach. He had to get her out of here. Now.

As he shifted her in his arms, the metallic clink of the chains drew his attention. Anger flared once more, and with an enraged tug, the metal snapped without a fight.

In the blink of an eye, he gathered her close, cradling her like a newborn babe. Cole lost his hold on reality, on all awareness, and didn't find it again until he lowered Alex to her own bed in her own house.

He stared down at her pale face and smoothed the hair back from her brow, drawing a shaky breath. Crimson trailed down the ivory, translucent column of her throat, and he cringed at the sight, cringed at the mark of Deacon's bite marring her neck.

He hurried into the master bath and quickly wet down several of the lacy hand towels hanging on the rack. Catching sight of himself in the mirror, Cole stopped long enough to quickly wash away the remaining evidence of his violent, fatal clash with Deacon. She couldn't see him like that. A monster like Deacon. She'd be terrified of him.

Lowering himself to the side of her bed, Cole gently cleaned the blood from Alex's neck and face. He leaned close and smoothed his tongue along the marks Deacon had left on her flesh. Then he turned his attention to her wrists. The iron manacles provided no resistance in his powerful hands. With exquisite tenderness belying the angry strength in him, Cole cleaned the blood from her chafed flesh and then dropped kisses softly upon her wrists. As his lips lingered over the frail pulse, grief sliced through him.

Why wasn't she waking up?

He knew the answer, knew the truth but fought with every ounce of his being against acknowledging it. He'd just found her. He couldn't lose her already. He'd rather greet the coming dawn, outside and exposed.

"Alex, don't do this!" Unable to control the raw grief surging through him, Cole slammed a fist into the wall beside the bed.

"Don't..." Her eyelids fluttered...finally. Opened. Closed. Her lips moved. Cole leaned closer, straining to hear her words. "Don't...wreck my...space."

"I'm so sorry, Alex. I'm so sorry." The words, anguished and filled with regret, tore from Cole's lips. "I shouldn't have left you... I shouldn't have even thought that you could ever... You never told me... If I'd have figured out who..."

Alex lifted a shaky hand and pressed her trembling fingers to Cole's lips. "Shhh...not your...fault." She shook her head, eyelids drifting closed, her arm falling limply onto the mattress at her side.

"Baby, don't leave me. Don't..." Cole's voice broke. He couldn't finish the words, couldn't fight them past the lump in his throat. Tears swam in his eyes, splashing down upon her cheeks.

"Cole." Barely a whisper. He pressed his ear closer. "Cole, I...love you. My answer...wanted to...tell you tonight...wanted forever, only with you..."

Her head lolled to the side and oblivion claimed her once more. Cole's heart seized inside his chest.

No, no. Please...

He pressed his tousled, tawny head tight to her chest and squeezed his eyes closed. Praying like he hadn't in a millennia. Prayed, bartered, threatened...

Odin. Freya. Forseti. Frigg... Anyone who would listen.

The tiny, fragile thud of her heartbeat finally reached his ears. Cole reared back, staring down at her, tears tracking down his cheeks. She was still alive. She hadn't died. Not yet. If Alex took Vampyre blood now, could it work without the words, without the rest?

Was she close enough to death that it would change her?

If he waited until the final thump and she died before he gave her his blood, he would turn her...or would it be too late. Would he change her into the same as him, Vampyre? *If he was lucky...* For the first time in his life, he cursed the fact that he'd never done this...never sired another. At least then he'd have some idea how to do this the right way.

She'd want to make that choice for herself, and he respected that. It was nothing less than she deserved. But right now, her very life hung in the balance. She was slipping away right before his eyes, slipping through his fingers. The change didn't always take. Sometimes the process was trickier with females, the success rate much, much slimmer, though no one knew why. But if he gave his blood to her *before* she died...

Would it be enough? What would it do to her if it did work?

As long as she lived, he didn't care what it did. Immortal, Mortal, Vampyre, Human... He loved her. He would *not* live without her, not for a single moment. If she was angry, if she turned? *She'd be alive, and that was all that mattered.*

If it didn't work, and she died...

If she died, he wouldn't be far behind...only as far as the next sunrise.

"Forgive me..." He whispered the words, even as he set his fangs to his wrist.

Tilting her head back so that her lips parted and her jaw fell open, Cole held his wrist to her mouth. And he waited.

Blood poured from his vein and ran in a steady rivulet over her lips and into her mouth. At first there was no movement, no indication that his desperate attempts were making any difference. His blood just pooled in her mouth, slipping into her throat.

She convulsed, swallowed, and sputtered. Swallowed again, and hope soared in his breast. How much would it take?

He held firm, even as her head lifted and her tongue snaked out to lick at the gash on his wrist. She swallowed again. And once more. Then she subsided back against the bed. Unnaturally still. Cole sealed his wound and sank back on the bed, his hip pressed to hers, leaning over her. The minutes ticked by. He swore an eternity passed as he waited for her to open her eyes. He listened, straining his ears for some sign she would recover.

Wake up, Alex. I can't do this anymore, not without you.

Chapter 28

Just as he was about to press his head to her chest once more, her body convulsed. Her back arched off the mattress and she went rigid from head to toe. She held there for a painful moment, before sagging back onto the mattress. Breathless. Motionless.

Cole's mouth fell open in horror. His hands clutched her shoulders. What had he done?

He'd killed her.

Oh, gods, he'd killed her.

Her body shuddered in his hands, hard. Her lips parted, and she dragged in a soul deep breath, her eyes flared open. Brilliant aquamarine. *Human* aquamarine. All the pent up anxiety in Cole's lungs released in a mad whoosh. Color slowly blossomed in her cheeks once more, and fire snapped in her beautiful eyes. Her heart beat strong in her chest, the sweetest sound he'd ever heard.

Those beautiful eyes locked on his for half a second, and then flew around the room, confused. She blinked, glanced down at herself, then up at him again as she pushed herself up to sit at his side.

"What happened? I was... Then I thought I saw... I couldn't move, but I could hear..." Her sentences were jumbled and disjointed, tumbling out one after another before she could finish the last. Then she froze, her hand flew to the side of her neck, and she gasped as her fingers encountered Deacon's marks, slack-jawed. "What did you *do* to me?"

Before Cole could reply, she scrambled away from him, eyes accusatory. "Did you change me?

God, tell me you didn't change me!"

He surveyed her with forced calm, though fierce emotion glimmered in his chest. His tone was utterly bland, his question throwing her off kilter. "Do you want blood?"

"What?"

"Do you crave blood?"

"Well, I..." She paused, as if considering his words, considering her own body's desires. "No, I... I don't think so..."

"Believe me, you'd know it if you did." Weak with relief, Cole pushed to his feet, dragging a shaking hand through his riotous, damp hair. "I gave you my blood, Alex. It was the only way I could think to heal you. You were dying. Deacon damned near drained you."

"But, I don't understand. I was so weak. Now I feel so...so strong. Are you sure you didn't change me?"

"It doesn't work that way. You would have had to die. Your heart would have had to stop. Yours didn't. My blood apparently restored you, brought you back from the brink. Though you better take it easy for a few days."

Her eyes widened in horror. Her hands began to shake. "He bit me. God...it hurt so much... I couldn't fight him off, I tried...but I couldn't..."

Cole flew to her side, the sight of her, shaken and fearful, was more than he could stand. The bastard had purposefully made the bite a trauma...he'd withheld the sensual influence of the *Kiss* and made her suffer. Cole wanted to tear out Deacon's throat, rip his head from his body with his bare hands all over again. "It's all right, *you're* all right. He can't hurt you anymore."

"But he's..."

"He's dead." Cole's voice was flat, emotionless, satisfied vengeance burned through his system.

Then she finally noticed the blood covering his clothes, speckles of it on his neck. Her fingers brushed where his skin was torn, and he sucked in a sharp breath, glancing down at himself. Odin's teeth, he needed blood...soon. Deep gashes covered his torso and arms. His wounds were severe. His limbs trembled from his weakened condition. And he'd given her his blood, weakening himself even more.

He'd do it all again, no matter the risk. Alex was worthy of any sacrifice.

"You killed him." Her words were little more than a whisper. "Why did he want me dead? Why did..."

"Alex, calm down. Take a deep breath. Let me explain..."

After a long, wary moment, Alex subsided back on the edge of the bed. Cole sat down beside her, drawing her hand into his. He searched her face, and sighed. *Where to start?*

"I love you." *Where had that come from?* "When I explain everything, when you get angry...please, remember that."

She nodded her head slowly, her eyes locked on his. "Just tell me, Cole. Tell me all of it, this time."

"First, please, let me tell you I'm sorry for losing it earlier, with your ex." The lines tightened around her mouth, and he squeezed her hand, urging her to be patient with him. "I should have trusted you. I was just so...jealous. I couldn't think straight. I reacted before I stopped to think. The sight of you in another man's arms..."

Her face softened, and Alex leaned toward him, silencing him with her lips. When she pulled back, her eyes were warm, forgiving. "That doesn't matter anymore. *He* doesn't matter. You do. And I love you, too." Then her gaze turned serious, warning. "But you better think twice before you fly off the handle like that again. Next time I might not be so understanding."

Cole swallowed, humbled by her words. He couldn't resist. His hand snaked out, cupping the back of her neck, gently drawing her forward for a deeper, more demanding kiss. Then, abruptly, before things got too far off course, he severed the contact, and pushed to his feet. His wounds were beginning to heal, but his limbs felt like rubber just now. He was going to have to get some blood in him soon, or he'd be in bad shape. Thrusting his hands deep in his pockets, Cole began pacing at the foot of the bed, shooting her worried, assessing glances now and again.

"Several months ago, a Rogue began stalking women, murdering them in the dark alleys behind popular nightclubs. Any woman involved in the music industry, in any way, was fair game. He followed a pattern, killing only on the eleventh of the month, and only at locations with the number eleven, or variations of eleven, in the physical address. All the victims were either twenty-two or thirty-three." Cole paused, dragging in a deep breath. He turned and faced her squarely. "A few months ago, the Task Force for Rogue Apprehension—kind of a Vampyre police force, if you will—contacted me. Enlisted me, is more like it, as they don't take no for an answer. Anyway, I was to be their eyes and ears inside the business."

Her hand cupped her throat. He could see the gears turning in her head. *She fit all the criteria.*

Cole stared grimly at her. "You heard what he said...about his female?"

Alex nodded, then held a hand up to stop him, palm out, her eyes filled with confusion and a hint of anger. "If there was a killer hunting women who got involved with the industry...and you knew about it...why did you pursue me? Why did you drag me into the middle of all this?"

Drawing another breath, Cole leveled a guilty gaze at her. "We needed you. The band did. In order to keep up appearances and guarantee I had access to circles I needed to monitor, I had to have a writer talented enough for us to stay at the top of the charts, popular. Then I met you, and I just needed...*you*. I thought, if I kept you close, I could protect you.

"Then I started getting pictures from the killer. Pictures of his handy work. Pictures of...you." Cole shifted, remembering his horror at opening those envelopes and seeing the female he'd come to admire and love, painted the target of a sadistic killer.

Understanding slowly dawned in her eyes. "That's why you didn't want me to go into town alone the day I resigned from the paper. That's why you tagged along." She waited a moment and then, blushing at the memory, added, "That night, when I went to the club with Gina...it was on the eleventh. You were there because you were expecting him."

Cole simply nodded. "No matter what we did, no matter where we hunted, Styx and I couldn't find him." Cole gazed at the flawless skin of her neck, puncture marks fully healed thanks to his kiss, and his eyes filled with remorse. "We never thought to look in our own house."

"Why, Cole? Why would Deacon go to such extremes?" She broke off, shuddering.

"He was crazed, sweetheart. Deacon was a Rogue, power-hungry and blinded by bloodlust and the loss of his female. I'm so sorry I didn't see it in time. I'm so sorry I left you alone and vulnerable." Cole dropped down to kneel at her feet. He gingerly cupped her hands in his, as if she were made of the most fragile glass. "I'm so sorry for not protecting you, Alex."

****

Alex considered him for long moments, torn deep in her soul. She wanted so badly to forgive him and forget about it all. She wanted to tell him that it was all okay. That she could put it all behind her.

But he'd shown her over and over that he didn't trust her. Not as he should if they were going to be together. He hadn't trusted her with the truth of what he was. She'd had to stumble upon Styx feeding to force the truth from him. He'd been so quick to jump to conclusions where Griffin had been concerned, and, despite what she may have claimed earlier, that still stung a bit.

Then there was the matter of Deacon. She'd been a target, for God's sake, and he hadn't trusted her enough to give her all the facts. He'd withheld vital information from her, and ended up putting her life in jeopardy. Every time he'd finally told her the truth, it had only been because his hand had been forced. His wounds had begun to heal, but blood still covered him, head to toe. Deacon's blood. Cole's blood. Hers...

Her eyes roamed over his face, over features she'd come to know and love. Hopelessness engulfed her, twisting her heart. He didn't trust her. Without trust, there could be no future, love or no love. That was the bottom line.

She closed her eyes against the look on his face as she carefully, ruthlessly, untangled their hands and pushed to her feet, walking away from him. Alex paced to the far corner of the room, before turning to face him, briskly rubbing her arms, chilled to the bone. Despite the fact that every mark of Deacon's cruel treatment had already begun to heal, she died inside, little by little. Her words were the knife plunged into her own heart, twisted by her own hand.

"There is no future for us, Cole. You don't trust me. You've lied to me, again and again, and I can't be with someone when there's no trust." She paused, aching inside, as he shot to his feet with shock and anger warring upon his beautiful face. With voice carefully controlled, meticulously modulated...emotionless...she quietly ordered him, "I need you to leave now."

His reaction was instantaneous. Explosive. "The hell I will!"

"Cole..."

"No! Don't you dare stand there and calmly ask me to leave as if you don't feel anything for me anymore!" He was across the room in a flash, stopping only when he towered over her, glaring down at her with poorly restrained temper. "I'm not leaving here, do you hear me? I'm not leaving until we get this all sorted out."

"It is sorted." She raised her tortured gaze to his, gritting her teeth against the pain in her heart, pain reflected in his eyes, begging him to go before she dissolved completely. "It's over, Cole. Please, just walk away."

When he didn't move, she made to skirt around him, biting back a sob, but he planted a very large, very angry palm hard against the wall in front of her. She stopped, backed up a step, and turned.

His other palm slapped against the wall, effectively caging her in. "Neither one of us is going to walk away. *Ever again.*"

How dare he make this any harder than it already was? Alex spun on her heel to face him. Bracing her hands against his chest, she shoved with all her might. He didn't budge. Tears coursed down her cheeks now, unimpeded, and angry words rolled off her tongue. "Damn you, you conceited, controlling, domineering...*Vampyre!* How *dare* you decide what I will and won't do? I don't have to—"

Her words died when Cole abruptly captured her lips beneath his. His hands slid to her waist, even as her small fist beat futilely at his chest. When she tried to turn her head away, he fisted his hand in her hair, holding her firm, immobile, completely at his mercy. Cole leaned into her, his lips playing over hers with fierce insistence. And he didn't stop there.

He didn't just use his lips to kiss her senseless. He used his entire body. His tongue thrust and tangled with hers, his hips rubbed against her with alluring suggestiveness. His knee pressed between hers until she rode the hard muscle of his thigh. The muscles of his chest bunched and rippled, massaging her aching breasts. Damn him.

And his hands—his glorious fingers—explored and claimed every inch of her between jaw and knee. By the time he pulled back, not a single thought of refusal resided in her brain. Not a single ounce of resistance existed in her entire body. Even her very blood betrayed her, heating and throbbing in her veins, rushing to her head making it impossible to think.

"Now tell me no, Alex." He brushed his lips over her ear, nibbled at the sensitive flesh just below it. "Tell me to leave and never come back. If I have to...if that's what it will take...I'll go down on my knees and beg..."

She couldn't make the words come out of her mouth, couldn't even form them in her mind. She shook her head in mute denial of his offer.

"I was a fool, Alex, a jealous, stupid fool crazy in love." Kisses rained down over her face. "I was wrong not to tell you the truth. I've gone it alone for a long, long time, Alex. Give me a chance...I can get this right. I know I can. I need you. More than I'll ever be able to explain. I want you. I want forever...with you. Not just today. Not just this lifetime, but always. For all eternity as my Bride, Alex." Hot, open-mouthed kisses seared her neck.

"You're not leaving me, and I can't walk away from you. I won't let you walk away from me. Not without a fight."

"You're fighting dirty," she accused, breathless, unable to keep her hands from splaying over his shoulders, rubbing down his delicious back.

"I don't care." The kisses, the rubbing intensified. "I'll do whatever it takes to keep you. I can't go on without you, Alex. Mated or not, I won't survive without you. I'll take you anyway I can get you."

His lips skated across her bare shoulder, and she wondered hazily where her shirt had gone. His fangs grazed the base of her throat, and she instinctively cringed.

"It's okay, sweetheart," he murmured. His tongue lapped hungrily at her skittering pulse. "It's not supposed to be like it was with him. It's not supposed to hurt. I won't hurt you, I swear!"

She paused a moment, desire battled learned knowledge. Drawing a deep breath, trusting in him, Alex tipped her head back, giving him better access to her throat. She groaned aloud when he growled in response and kissed her flesh, open-mouthed and reverent, feverishly suckling the sensitized flesh. His fangs grazed her skin, and she battled back the unease. She couldn't take it any longer, couldn't deny him—or her heart.

"Yes." The word floated to Cole, husky and alluring.

He froze as if he'd crashed headlong into a brick wall. Slowly, he straightened and stared at her. He whispered, "What?"

"Yes." The word came out strong and steady now. Absolutely certain.

"Yes? You would agree? The Mating..." His eyes were hungry, his frown hopeful.

She gave a tiny nod.

He seized her by the shoulders, demanding, "You're sure? Gods, what am I saying...I should just drag you to the floor and have my way with you before you change your mind." But his hands remained firm on her shoulders. "You're sure...really sure?"

She blinked up at him, and burst out laughing. Her heart filled to bursting with the love and the hope in his eyes. Slowly, definitively, she nodded. "Yes, Cole. I want to take you as my mate." Then she quickly clarified, "I don't want to be changed...but I do want to be your Bride."

Cole blinked, stunned. His hands flew, tugging and yanking, ripping and shredding, until they stood, naked in the pale moonlight streaming in through her windows. Spare moments before he gave in to instinct and dragged her to the floor, Alex managed to tear her lips from his, panting.

"Wait..."

"No!" His reaction was harsh, uncompromising. Obsessed. "I told you there would be no going back. It's too late..." His lips sizzled along her jaw.

"I'm not changing my mind. Cole..." She bit back a groan as his hand slid down over her backside, cupping and kneading the soft globes of her bottom, pressing his straining arousal insistently against her stomach. Pulsing against her.

He growled low in his throat and buried his lips against her neck, punctuating each word with a branding lick, a stinging nip. "Then why wait?"

"Because..." She gasped as he lowered his head to suckle at her breast, drawing her nipple hard into his mouth, grazing her with his fangs. "Cole!"

With a labored, resigned sigh, he lifted his head to frown down at her. His gaze was ravenous, glowing with impatient, relentless need as he slowly slid up her body, towering over her once more. She forced herself to draw breath, and pushed sound past her dry throat.

"It's just that I've...been wanting something for such a long, *long* time now..." She smiled up at him, licking her lips suggestively.

His fierce gaze locked on her lips, on her tongue. "What do you want?"

"You see..." She drew the last word out slowly, tracing the line of his neck with the tip of her fingernail. "I've been wanting to see you naked and covered in soap bubbles for ever so long now..."

Cole's eyes flared. He sucked in a sharp breath, shuddering. Faster than a beat of her heart, he swept her feet out from under her and carried her to the master bath. He made short work of running a tub full of water, bestowing generous kiss after generous caress while the water rose and the mountain of fragrant bubbles grew.

As Cole settled back in the deep tub, Alex straddled his lap, the smile spreading over his face was by turns wickedly sinful and blissfully elated. She'd never beheld such a vision, such a sexy, divine creation as the work of art in her arms...this ancient warrior wearing nothing but soap bubbles.

The look in his eyes sent shudder after shudder of pure need coursing through her veins. His shaft pulsed against her thigh, demanding attention. More than happy to oblige, she took his thick, engorged arousal firmly in hand, guiding it to her core.

He slipped inside her, hips rocking, thrusting deep, a low growl of satisfaction rumbled deep in his chest. His large hands found her waist, controlling her tempo. Once more, he stared deep in her eyes, and rasped, "You're absolutely certain?"

In answer, Alex leaned forward in his arms, lifting her hair away from the side of her neck, baring her throat in invitation.

Cole's entire body leaped expectantly. His *entire* body. He wrapped his arms around her and sat up straighter while her hips continued to undulate. His heat, deep inside her, burned, branding her. She slid up and down his swelling erection, gasping as it thickened, stretching her farther. Her whole body tingled, the sparks radiating from deep in her womb.

He surged his hips, thrusting deeper still.

Cole's deep, dark voice sank through her, swam in her head and shuddered through her veins. "Your blood and my blood. My soul and yours. We are mated. I am forever yours."

Alex tensed at the sharp sting of his fangs sinking into her flesh, then melted against him as he began suckling. The world exploded behind her eyelids in vibrant, life-altering color. Sensation, warm and gilded, rushed through her, overwhelmed her until tears streamed down her face from the sheer rapture of it.

****

He had to remind himself to go slowly, not to take too much. Despite the healthy color on her cheeks and the stamina with which she met each thrust, she was still weak from what Deacon had taken from her, and it would take time for her to recover. Still, he lapped hungrily, already addicted and aching for more.

Her warm, rich blood filled his mouth and slid down his throat like fine, aged whiskey, racing fire through him, pooling heat in his gut. His nerve endings began to vibrate, his hands to shake. Emotion swelled and surged inside his chest until he feared he might explode with it. He could *taste* her love for him. Dazed, humbled, he reluctantly let saliva surge into his mouth and licked one last time at the puncture marks, watching as they healed before his eyes.

Cole leaned back and gazed up into her face. Need surged anew at the look of utter ecstasy softening her features. She lowered her gaze to his, tilted her head down and sealed her lips over his, grinding herself down on him, hard and fierce. Stifling a groan, battling the urge to spill himself deep inside her then and there, he tore his lips from hers and set his fangs to his wrist for her once more.

The taste of her blood lingered on his lips. Sweet. Erotic. She was a ball of fire in his arms, sizzling, pulsing. Ready to burst. Watching her through lowered lids, he lifted his wound to her lips.

Hungry anticipation filled him. He burned for her. Insatiable desire. Eternal love. All for her.

"Your blood and my blood." Her voice was soft, yet filled with emotion. His blood stirred, boiling in his veins. "My soul and yours." His heart kicked up speed, fluttering so fast in his chest his head swam. "We are mated." His arm convulsed around her, his body spasmed. "I am forever yours."

She cupped his wrist in her gentle hand and pressed her parted lips against his skin. She drew his blood into her mouth slowly at first, tentative, and then faster, harder as power ripped through her, making her jerk in his arms. Cole's whole body tightened, then exploded. Spasm after delicious spasm of pleasure rolled through him. Everything he felt for her surged through his veins and into her, leaving him lightheaded and hovering on the edge of a second climax close on the heels of the first.

His head fell back against the side of the tub, and a soul deep, joyous howl erupted from his chest. His hips shot upward, driving his shaft hard into her. His fingers bit into her bottom as he drove her up and down his erection. She coiled around him, squeezing him tighter. Alex released his wrist, wrapping her arms around his shoulders, offering up her mouth as his sacrifice. He gripped her hips, thrusting vigorously into her.

Water and dissipating bubbles flowed over the side of the tub and splashed onto the tiles, and still he rocked inside her. Their shared blood, the Vows they'd given to each other, and the needs of their bodies coalesced and surged until he exploded inside her again in a cataclysmic, volcanic eruption.

He wasn't through with her. After licking closed the gash on his wrist, Cole swept her from the bath, carrying her dripping, limp body to the bed, where he showed her all the other things his Vampyre mouth was so good at. Time and again, as the moon crested and began its descent, he surrendered to the moonlight and passions of the night. Her body clung to his as their souls met and merged until only one remained between the two of them.

Solid. Whole.

Complete.

A long time later, as the moonlight poured over them, blanketing their joined bodies in the softest of silver, Cole pressed a tender kiss to the side of Alex's damp forehead. He fell back against the pillows then, his great Vampyre stamina weakened at last, his passions slaked as only could be done with his true mate. His Bride. His arms held her sleeping form cuddled close, and a slow, well-pleased smile curved his lips.

One word, reverent and proud, whispered past his lips, before he, too, gave himself up to satiated sleep.

"Mine."

A word about the author...

Always a voracious reader, Brenda Huber closed the cover on a book by one of her favorite authors, and said to herself...I can do this! Ever fascinated by all things mythical and mystical, Brenda decided to try her hand at Paranormal Romance and dove into her second great passion...writing. She lives in Iowa with her husband and two children.